MISTRESS OF LEGEND

BOOK THREE OF GUINEVERE'S TALE

NICOLE EVELINA

Lawson Gartner Publishing
PO Box 2021
Maryland Heights MO, 63043
www.lawsongartnerpublishing.com

Printed in the United States of America
First Printing 2018

ISBN
978-0-9967632-5-7 (print)
978-0-9967632-6-4 (e-book)

Library of Congress Control Number: 2018951438

Editor: Cassie Cox, Joy Editing
Cover Design: Jenny Quinlan, Historical Editorial
Layout: Qamber Designs and Media

Names: Evelina, Nicole.
Title: Mistress of legend / by Nicole Evelina.
Description: Maryland Heights, MO : Lawson Gartner Publishing, [2018] |
        Series: Guinevere's tale ; book 3
Identifiers: ISBN 9780996763257 (print) | ISBN 9780996763264 (ebook)
Subjects: LCSH: Guenevere, Queen (Legendary character)—Fiction. |
        Great Britain—History—To 1066—Fiction. | Queens—Great
        Britain—Fiction. | Lancelot (Legendary character)—Fiction. |
        Man-women relationships—Great Britain—Fiction. | LCGFT:
        Arthurian romances. | Historical fiction. | Fantasy fiction.
Classification: LCC PS3605.V424 M57 2018 (print) | LCC PS3605.V424
(ebook) DDC 813/.6—dc23

To Aunt Darlene and Uncle George,
I wish you could have lived to see the trilogy completed.
Rest in peace. I love you.

HIGHLAND PICTS
LOWLAND PICTS
DALRIADA
FIRTH OF FORTH
STIRLING
DIN EIDYN
(EDINBURGH)
ANTONINE WALL
VOTADINI
DAMNONII
LOTHIAN
FIRTH OF CLYDE
STRATHCLYDE
SELGOVAE
DÙN BREATANN
(DUMBARTON)
HADRIAN'S WALL
NOVANTE
DIN GUAYRDI
(BAMBURGH)
CARLISLE
BERNICIA
ISLE OF WINDS
SOLWAY FIRTH
CAMELOT
DIN GEFRON
(YEAVERING BELL)
RHEGED
YORK
ANGLO-SAXON TERRITORY
MIDLANDS
NORTHGALLIS
GWYNEDD
POWYS

Men went to Gododdin, laughter-inciting,
Bitter in battle, with blades set for war.
Brief the year they were at peace.
The son of Bodgad, by the deeds of his hand
        did slaughter.
Though they went to churches to do penance,
The young, the old, the lowly, the strong,
True is the tale, death oer'took them.

Men went to Gododdin, with eager laughter,
Attacking in an army, cruel in battle,
They slew with swords without much sound
Rheithfyw, pillar of battle, took pleasure in giving.

Men went to Catraeth, swift was their host.
Fresh mead was their feast, their poison too.
Three hundred waging war, under command,
And after joy, there was silence.
Though they went to churches to do penance,
True is the tale, death oer'took them.

Three hundred gold-torqued,
warlike, wonderful [~]
Three hundred proud ones,
Together, armed;
Three hundred fierce horses
Carried them forward,
Three hounds and three hundred,
Sad, they did not return.

He pierced three hundred, most bold,
He cut down the centre and wing.
He was worthy before the noblest host,
He gave from his herd horses in winter.
He fed black ravens on the wall
Of the fortress, although he was not Arthur.

—*Y Gododdin*, author unknown (stanzas 6-8, 91, 102)

PART ONE

The Broken Crown

Chapter One

Summer 518

Arthur's men caught up to us before we reached Lothian.

I thank the gods they did. Otherwise I would be dead.

Lancelot and I were camped in the woods less than a two-day ride from Camelot when they found us. No doubt they spotted our fire, but we could not be without one, for I lay on the ground, wrapped in Lancelot's cloak and shaking with fever. The burns on my left side that ran from above my hairline down to my foot stung with the fury of a whole nest of hornets and my skin glistened with sweat, yet nothing could warm me. We had had no choice but to stop, for I could no longer sit a horse.

Only days before, Arthur had tried to have me burned at the stake after Lancelot and I were accused of infidelity and treason as a result of our extramarital affair. Initially banished from Camelot, Lancelot returned just in time to rescue me from death, though I suffered severe burns in my escape. We had intended to flee to my mother's homeland in the Votadini territory, but my injuries proved too severe for so long a journey.

Now, a group of Arthur's most loyal knights—the Combrogi—approached on horseback, no doubt to drag us to back to face the justice we had fled. Lancelot was doubly condemned as both a traitor for his affair with me and for interrupting my death sentence, so he had even more to fear than I.

Lancelot drew his sword, ready to defend me. I stumbled to my feet, holding onto him for support. Each movement was fresh agony, pulling at my inflamed skin and taxing the damaged muscle underneath. But I was a warrior. No matter how ill I was, I would not cower on the ground while they dragged me away like the spoils of the hunt. Repositioning Lancelot's cloak to give me greater freedom of movement, I took up his dagger, prepared to use it if I had to.

As they approached, Aggrivane, Bedivere, and Kay held up their hands, still on the reins, to show they wielded no weapons against us.

"We come in peace," Bedivere called.

They would have to forgive us for not believing that.

My heart stuttered and squeezed at the site of Aggrivane, unsure whether to love or hate him. In our youth, he had been my lover. We'd planned to marry, but my father made a contract with Arthur before we could tell him, which trumped our plans. Then less than two months ago, Aggrivane was among those who betrayed Lancelot and me to Arthur, though Aggrivane later repented of his actions.

They dismounted, hands still raised.

"We are not here to arrest you," Kay said. "Arthur ordered us to bring you back to Camelot. He wishes to grant Guinevere a full pardon. He never intended to have her killed. That was the work of his bishop, who now awaits his trial in prison."

"How do we know you speak the truth and are not simply trying to get us to come along peacefully?" Lancelot retorted.

"If we had ill intent, would we warn you to flee, Lancelot?" Aggrivane asked. "Arthur may be merciful to his former wife, but he has not spoken of you. As far as we know, you are still exiled, still a subject to death upon your return."

Aggrivane was right. Arthur may once have been a king of justice and mercy, but with the events just passed, it was impossible to know if that still held. After all, if he could order his wife's death, what worse did he have in store for the man who'd cuckolded him? Even if they were telling the truth about him not wishing me dead, Arthur was still a wronged man who had a right to revenge.

I turned to Lancelot, his blue eyes frightened and conflicted. "You cannot return to Camelot, but I will not go without you. Let us carry on as we had planned."

Bedivere cautiously approached me. When I didn't lunge at him with the dagger, he put out a tentative hand, carefully examining my charred skin and weeping, red blisters. If he noticed how my teeth knocked together despite my clenched jaw, he didn't show it. "If you remain on the road, you will die. Only a priestess can heal these wounds, which I'm certain you know, seeing as you are one." He gently brushed a finger over the blue crescent moon tattoo on my brow—a mark that all priestesses of Avalon wore—as though to remind me.

Lancelot turned to me. "You must go with them, Guinevere. I will go on to Brittany. Send word when you are well, and I will make sure a boat awaits you in Camelot's harbor."

I made to grasp his tunic but stumbled as a wave of dizziness overtook me. Lancelot steadied me. "No. We will not be separated again. You are Arthur's best knight. Surely he will pardon you too."

Kay joined the two men at my side. "Arthur has reason to forgive you, Guinevere, especially in light of all you have suffered. But Lancelot defied him twice. He will not be inclined to be merciful, lest he set a precedent of weakness with the other Combrogi that could lead to his ouster. The people are not pleased with him after what he did to you." Kay turned to Lancelot. "You can take the risk if you'd like, but I do not advise it."

Lancelot growled in frustration, looking at the stars as though they could advise him. After a period of thought, his gaze returned to me, cataloging my injuries. To the Combrogi, he said, "She will get worse the longer she goes without aid. I will not sacrifice her life to save mine. Let me come with you as far as the edge of town. If I can see she is well received, then I can bear the guilt of knowing I abandoned her and that she suffers without me."

⁂

They carried me to Camelot on a stretcher. While it was not quite the indignity of being transported in a prisoner's cart or forced to walk behind the Combrogi in chains, it certainly was not the entrance any soon-to-be-redeemed queen wished to make. But I did not really care, for my wounds turned even breathing and blinking into torture. They throbbed and burned, rubbed even rawer against the fabric of the stretcher with every jolt. My fever came and went, plunging me into nightmarish visons where I relived my failed execution and created far worse fates for myself, only to be brought back to reality with startling clarity when the heat relaxed its grip.

I was between bouts of delirium when Camelot came into view. The castle loomed large on the hillside above as we trod the hidden track to a private entrance, rather than the wide thoroughfare used by noble guests, merchants, and all manner of visitors. The people need not know I had returned. There was no need to stir up a mob now, especially when I needed peace and quiet to heal. They would have plenty of time to voice their joy or displeasure later.

Seeing this place, this dream begun by Arthur's father and fulfilled in our reign, through fresh eyes was strange. When I'd first seen it as a new bride so many years ago, it was to me a place of wonder and majesty, a place of light and welcome. Now, its shadows held dominance, swallowing up the comfort I used to find within its walls, daring me to attempt to find solace here.

Kay and Aggrivane had just carried me into my old bedroom when Arthur met us. Grainne and Morgan—Arthur's second wife and my lifelong enemy—trailed in his wake, their blue robes of priestesshood covered by thick off-white aprons that signaled their readiness to see to my wounds as soon as I was released into their care. Arthur dashed to my side, his eyes widening as he took in my scarred face and neck, all that was currently visible from beneath my clothing.

"Guinevere! Sweet Mother of God, what have I done?" Arthur brought a hand to his blond beard, covering his mouth.

"You've nearly killed her, that's what you've done," Grainne shot back, already examining me.

Morgan moved in to help transfer me to the bed, but Arthur stepped in front of her. Her eyes widened in offense. If I was not in so much pain, I would have laughed.

Arthur leaned down to me, his blue eyes softened with tenderness and grief. "I did not intend to kill you, please know that. I gave no order, despite what you may have been told. You must believe me."

"Arthur, move away and let us work," Morgan snapped, elbowing past her husband. She dripped a few drops of a bitter liquid onto my lips, and I instinctively licked them away before recognizing my error.

"No. I will not let you poison me too," I yelled, flailing

my right arm at her and trying to sit up. A wave of nausea pushed me back to the pillows.

Grainne held me down with muscles honed from years of birthing babies and wrestling recalcitrant patients like me. "Stop fighting us. No one is trying to poison you. It is only a small dose of poppy juice, just enough to make you sleep. You do not want to be awake to experience what is to come."

"Why did she accuse you of poisoning her?" Arthur asked Morgan. When she ignored him, slicing into my dress with a dagger to expose the extent of my injuries, he turned to me. "What did you mean, Guinevere? You said 'too.' Who has she poisoned?"

I attempted to answer, but my lips felt swollen and my tongue wouldn't obey my commands. Snorting out a breath, I balled my fists and tried again, but the effort was too great. Blackness tugged at my eyelids, making them feel as though they were made of wet sand.

Finally, I managed to slur, "You," before I slipped into unconsciousness.

Chapter Two

Winter 519

The next month was a blur, lived in flashes that were more like visions than solid reality. First the world was black, then searing light pierced my eyes and the left side of my body was consumed by fire, burning, skin crackling and peeling back, leaving tender flesh and muscle exposed. Strong arms held me down when I tried to fight the sting of water and wine. By the time the sweet scent of honey and herbs reached my nose, I was worn out, numb, spent from the pain.

I slipped in and out of fever dreams that were no more pleasant for my mind and soul than the treatment my body was undergoing. In one, Arthur embraced me at Camelot's gates, only to sink a sharp blade into my side again and again. This blade did not kill me, but rather it gave him a place to begin peeling away my skin, which came off in searing strips until my flayed flesh was gone completely.

Sometimes this was intermingled with Morgan or Grainne's voice and the now-familiar scent of their healing salve.

Other times I dreamed that Bishop Marius had his boney arms around me, pressing his poisoned Communion chalice to my lips, only to wake and find one of the priestesses holding a mug of warm, earthy liquid to my lips and commanding me to drink.

Long stretches of blackness followed, interspersed with periods of agony. Had I an axe, I would have happily cleaved myself in two, if only to stop the sharp, burning pain. Many times in the past I had burned myself while cooking, on a candle flame, or practicing manipulating the element of fire in Avalon. Then, I'd thought I would die from a wound no bigger than my little finger. Now, with half of my body flayed, skin pulling and pinching as it tried to recover from the deadly kiss of the flames, I begged the Goddess for relief. *Deliver me, Mother, and I swear that from this moment forth, I will suffer small injuries in silence, without complaint. Deliver me, please.* But most of the time I could not form rational thought. All I could do was scream, and when my throat grew raw, my screams were silent.

In the cold gray days between the winter solstice and Imbolc, I woke to find the pain, while still present, was much more manageable. Grainne was sitting by my side, holding a cool, wet cloth to my forehead, her gray eyes as full of love and concern as a mother's for her child.

"Praise Brigid, you are with us once again." The relief in her voice was so great, I wondered how close I had come to dying. I tried to sit up, but Grainne placed a firm hand on me. "Do not move. Your wounds are exposed. I was just about to cover them when I felt you stirring."

My eyes were drawn to find the source of my pain. From my shoulder, down my left arm, to my hip, knee, and part of my left shin were pockets of angry red rivulets where blisters had once bubbled and burst. Around them, the skin was twisted, blackened, and tough. Slathered on top was a layer of the honey herb mixture I had smelled in my dreams. I had seen my share of battlefield burns and knew enough of healing to understand how badly I was injured.

I searched Grainne's gray eyes for some sign I was wrong. "These will scar, won't they?"

She pressed her lips together. "I'm afraid so. But at least you are past the risk of blood poisoning."

She relayed the events of the last few months as she wound me tightly in white cloth to keep my wounds clean. Arthur still held Marius in the jail. Morgan had brushed off my comment about her poisoning someone as a mistake of the fever, and rumor had it Lancelot was involved in a civil war with his brothers in Brittany, but Arthur still hadn't offered to pardon him.

I was only partially listening, having raised my healthy hand to my left cheek. The skin was leathery, pulled tight over my cheekbone. What was worse, I could not feel the touch of my fingertips. I moved my hand to my ear with the same result. Snapping my fingers, I was relieved to be able to hear the sharp sound with as much clarity as before. But when I brushed my hand through my hair, it came out in dry, straw-like black clumps.

I stared at it for a moment before the tears fell. "What have I become?"

She held me close and rocked me as I cried. "You are still you, a queen—regardless of what Arthur says—and a strong, courageous woman. You only need time to heal. By summer, you will be back to your old self. You'll see."

A knock on the door interrupted any further conversation. I wiped my eyes so that whoever it was couldn't see that I had been crying.

Grainne went to the door. From the bed, I could not see who was on the other side, but I heard her tell my guest I was awake.

She turned back to me. "It is Arthur. Do you feel well enough to see him?"

I scowled, tempted to say no, but reluctantly agreed. I couldn't avoid facing him forever.

Grainne slipped out as Arthur entered, leaving us alone.

Even nearing forty summers, Arthur's height and brawn were fearsome to behold. Where other men responded to the passage of years by curling in on themselves like the fronds of a fern, Arthur held his head high, shoulders squared, every inch the High King. Even his skin, which was crossed with deep wrinkles and battle scars, appeared chiseled rather than wizened. Had he not betrayed me so, I would have been proud to be married to such a handsome warrior.

Arthur made to embrace me, but seeing my bandages, he stopped himself. "Oh, praise God. I will offer a thousand Masses of thanksgiving that you are well."

I smiled, knowing it was expected of me, even though the gesture meant nothing since I did not share Arthur's faith. "I am alive," I corrected him. "But I have a long way to go before I can be called well."

I shifted in the bed, unsure of how to act but unable to flee. How does one interact with their former husband who might or might not be guilty of trying to have one killed? I supposed one could pretend everything was fine, but that was not in my nature. I desperately wanted to ask how Morgan had deflected his curiosity about the poison, but leading with that was likely not a good idea.

Arthur cleared his throat. "If you don't mind, I would like to explain what happened that night. I want you to know."

"Go on," I said cautiously.

He sat on the edge of the bed. "You may recall that at Bishop Marius's suggestion, I received Holy Communion and retired to bed after being unable to come to a verdict in your case. A night of prayer showed me how wrong Bishop Marius was in demanding your death. Upon reflection, I realized he was not in the least concerned with your affair with Lancelot, which was my reason for putting you on trial. He claimed to be concerned with your treasonous betrayal of me, but he was really acting out of his own selfish concerns—all because you do not share my Christian faith. You were unfaithful to me, yes, but as you said, I was equally disloyal to you. The whole trial became much more than anyone, Aggrivane and Mordred included, ever intended. They have told me how sorry they are."

I eyed him warily, pulling the blankets tighter to my breast like a shield. "They have shown me their regret by aiding in my rescue and healing. But what of you? I know you were unable to stop the burning. I saw it in a vision as I fought back the fire that raged around me."

Arthur's face lit up with hope. "If you had a vision, then you know I was ill, incapacitated." His words came faster now, as he sought to make me understand. "I have been over and over that night in my mind, trying to determine why I was so ill. It was no ordinary sickness, so I must suspect poison. The only thing I consumed that no one else did was Holy Communion, so I am holding Bishop Marius under suspicion."

In my mind's eye, I once again saw the bishop tip a tiny drop into the Communion chalice. He turned and handed the vial to a woman in a dark hood. Her face was obscured, but a strand of copper hair peeked out, betraying her identity. "He did not act alone. You likely will not believe me when I name his accomplice, but I must."

Arthur studied my eyes and squeezed his own shut. He pinched the bridge of his nose as though his thoughts pained him. "Please do not say it was Morgan."

"Why do you suspect her?"

"I don't, but the bishop has named her as an accomplice."

"He tells the truth, at least in that regard. That is why I refused to let her near me with those anesthetizing drops.

She heard me say she poisoned you. It is not so far a stretch to think she might not want someone who knows her secret to live."

Arthur scowled at me. "Morgan could never kill anyone, least of all you. You have known each other since you were girls in Avalon together."

"I would not be so sure." I told Arthur about my vision of him crying out that the burning should be stopped. He was alone, so no one heard, and he was so ill he could not stand to go to anyone and give them word that he did not condone what was happening in the courtyard below.

"Yes, that was exactly what happened." He bowed his head, hunching forward, elbows on his knees, encumbered by the burden of guilt he carried. "I don't know what exactly took place that day, but I aim to find out." He looked at me as though struck by a sudden inspiration. "Would you be willing to be the judge when Marius has his trial? I cannot act as judge in the case because I am its victim and certainly not impartial—"

"And you think *I* am?" I chuckled mirthlessly. "Do you realize you are giving me the chance to exact revenge on a person who has done nothing but antagonize me for years? Arthur, you are mad. If it is a judge you seek, ask any priestess. We are all trained in the same manner."

"No. It must to be you. And for now, leave Morgan out of this. I cannot bring charges against her until I know for certain—"

"What more proof could you need? Marius admits that she aided him, and I have told you of my vision. You have a claim and someone to corroborate it. That is enough for you to find them both guilty. I will testify if needs be, but I do not understand why you need me to act as judge."

Arthur rubbed the back of his neck. "I can try the bishop, but I cannot sentence him, not with the whole of the country watching. If I find him innocent, my soul will not rest easy, for justice will not be done. But if I find him guilty… well, he has powerful allies, so you know what that could mean. Open rebellion." Arthur's bloodshot eyes were pleading. "I am trying to save Camelot."

"So what you are saying is that if I don't act as judge in your place, you fear you will be viewed as unjust and someone may try to overthrow you." I made a disbelieving sound. "Who have you become, Arthur? You used to be a just man whom I respected. Now you are just as concerned with your reputation as every other noble I've ever known. Personally, I think that is exactly what you deserve. What you did to me, even putting Morgan and Marius's involvement aside, is unforgiveable. Yet you dare ask me for help."

"Is there nothing I can do to change your mind?" Arthur's voice was pleading.

I may not have been as conniving as Morgan, but this was an opportunity I could not let pass me by. This was my chance to set my life straight and I was going to take it. "Pardon Lancelot in open court and ensure his safe passage back to Britain. If you personally guarantee no harm will come to either of us, I will assent to your request."

A range of emotions flickered across Arthur's face—incredulity, pain, serious deliberation, and finally, acceptance. "It will be done. I swear it on both my God and yours. As soon as you are well, you will get your pardon, I will recall Lancelot, and we will have a trial for the bishop. I am more than ready to put this all behind us."

I squirmed, my wounds flaring up again. One day these events would be but a distant memory for him, but I would have to live with the consequences every day for the rest of my life. If he wanted me to act as judge, I would. But he should not expect the Mother's mercy. Too much had happened, too many trusts shattered, too many hearts broken. No, so much pain could only summon the wrath of the Crone.

CHAPTER THREE

The Combrogi leaked word that I had returned under Arthur's guard as though it was secret information intended only for a select few. They let it "slip" through tongues seemingly loosened by liquor in the taverns, traded it as currency in dim back alleyways, and passed it to servants during illicit relations. As expected, the news slithered from ear to ear faster than a flea-born disease.

When the proclamation went out that Arthur wished for all of his subjects to assemble in Camelot's courtyard, they eagerly complied. Some camped out overnight, wrapped in thick blankets and cloaks, leaning against buildings or sleeping on the cold stone pavers. Others straggled in near dawn, staking out their places with wooden crates or dirty quilts. Enterprising merchants set up booths and sold spiced wine, hot cider, roasted nuts, and fresh bread to the crowds as though this were a festival.

The pale winter sun had just crested the horizon when Sobian stepped into my chambers, stomping her feet from the chill. "They are riled up. Some are speculating this will be a hanging, while others hope you will be reinstalled as queen. They are taking bets as to whether by the end of the day, your head will sport a crown or end up in a basket."

I swallowed hard. "That's comforting."

"Don't worry. The Combrogi will guard you. Arthur will not let anything happen to you, not now."

By mid-morning, the courtyard was full to bursting with people sitting on every stall roof, leaning out of windows, and lining the walls. Those not as lucky were forced to wait in the frigid shadow of the gates or make do with a patch of open land on the road leading to the castle. By noon, they were packed in so tightly, no room remained for even a rat to scurry over the feet of the assembled people.

Arthur led me out onto a balcony overlooking the throng. As Sobian promised, the Combrogi lined the rail, shields at the ready to defect any rocks or arrows aimed at hastening the king's justice. Behind me, to my right, Morgan sat on a throne, her copper hair plated into a thick braid that wound around her head like the crown she was denied as only being named royal wife, rather than queen—a title I had held until Arthur stripped me of it during my trial. Her face was set into an impassive mask, despite the fact it must have been killing her to have me within Camelot's walls again. This was my first time laying eyes on her, outside of when she nursed me, so my heart was thrilled to see her misery.

After what she had done, she deserved so much more.

I was glad, however, that her four-year-old daughter, Helene, was not here to see her father and mother pitted against one another. As I had spent time in Lyonesse's household, so was Helene being fostered in the House of Rheged with the family of Morgan's first husband, Uriens. She would return here when she was older to assist Arthur and Morgan in running Camelot until she was betrothed.

Morgan's partner in their crimes against Arthur, Bishop Marius, stood to my left, wrists and ankles shackled, flanked on either side by Arthur's guards. His red tunic—which he claimed to wear as a symbol of the blood of Christ, but I'd long suspected he favored because it brought attention to him—hung off a thinner frame than I remembered, but he appeared otherwise well treated.

Mordred, Arthur's son by Morgan long before they married, rounded out our party, standing in his father's shadow. Surveying his people, he looked every inch the heir in his golden tunic and cloak, his thick necklaces glinting in the sunlight.

I leaned over to him. "I haven't had a chance to thank you yet for helping set me free."

He gave me a boyish smile. "It was the least I could do. I'm hoping now that you are here—"

The Combrogi ringing the balcony struck the butts of their spears on the floor to quiet the crowd. The resulting boom drowned out the rest of what Mordred said.

Arthur stepped forward, and two of the guard parted to let him through. "My people, I have long governed this land with the intention of being as just and as fair as possible. That means admitting when I have done wrong. I have committed a grievous error against a woman I should have honored above all.

"Hear me, people of Camelot. I was wrong to condemn Guinevere and even more in error when I considered ending her life as a fitting punishment to assuage my thirst for vengeance. I never intended her death; she never should have been sent to the stake. I was ill-guided but do not fall upon that as an excuse. I ask you here and now to witness my apology to the woman whom I wronged."

He fell to his knees before me, hands clasped as though in prayer, appearing more like a penitent at the feet of a priest than a High King addressing his former wife. "Guinevere, there are no words I can offer to make things right, but I can assure you of my deep repentance for the sin I have committed against you. I am truly sorry. Can you ever find it in your heart to forgive me?"

I let the silence settle like so much dust underfoot as I debated how to respond. For a king, much less the High King, to humble himself so publicly was rare indeed. On one hand, mere words meant little—were I not trained to manipulate the elements, I would have succumbed to the deadly flames. But on the other, his repentance was sincere. Around us, people shifted from foot to foot, hardly daring to breathe as they awaited my answer. Deep within, the nudge of the Goddess—as we collectively referred to all goddesses in Avalon—urged me to swallow my considerable pride and grant him clemency.

"I can, and I do," I said, allowing my voice to carry over the crowd, who cheered and applauded in response.

Arthur stood and embraced me. Then backing up a few steps, he removed his sword—one of the treasures of Avalon—from its scabbard and held it aloft. "In the sight of the citizens of Camelot, I hereby pardon you of all charges leveled against you, especially and including the charge of high treason and the accusation of heresy. You are allowed to practice whatever faith you see fit. Return to your life as a free and innocent woman in the sight of all."

Most of the crowd yelled encouragement and whistled, but their joy was countered by a not insignificant number of boos and hisses from those who had noticed Arthur had failed to directly address the charge of adultery.

"Heretic!" someone yelled.

"Whore!" called another.

I bristled at the insults but made no move to defend myself.

Arthur raised his hand for silence, and at his signal, guards elbowed through the crowd to remove those causing the most agitation before they could spark a riot.

Arthur said, "Bishop Marius stands accused of grievous wrongdoing in connection with these events. He will be tried at my convenience. While she no longer holds the title of queen, I have asked Guinevere to serve as judge."

Marius's eyes widened so far and so fast, they nearly popped out of his head. "I object most strenuously."

Arthur carried on speaking, either not hearing or ignoring his prisoner's protests. "You have seen her dispense justice and mercy in equal measure for more than twenty years, and I have every reason to believe she will render impartial judgment in this case as well."

Marius broke free of the steadying hold his guards had on him and rushed Arthur. "If I am to be subject to a farce of justice, then she should be charged as well." He gestured to Morgan with his bound hands. "Your beloved wife helped to incapacitate you. Arrest her for the traitor she is."

The rowdy crowd stilled, suddenly silent.

I looked over my shoulder at Morgan. She gripped the arms of the throne so hard her knuckles were white. Her face had paled like curdled milk, her blue eyes hard as flint and her jaw taut as though she was fighting to resist spewing forth rage.

She stood, graceful and silent, regarding the assembled people. Finally, she took three steps forward. "I am innocent, but if our king wishes to try me, so be it. I trust that justice shall prevail." She held out her arms to Arthur, offering them for binding like a prisoner.

Arthur faced her, still and solemn as a statue. To most, he likely appeared impassive, but I had spent enough time with him to be able to detect the warring emotions flickering across his features. He wanted to believe Morgan was innocent; that much was clear from his directive to not involve her in Marius's trial. But now that Marius had publicly accused her, Arthur could not ignore the charges. To do so would be proving the very point he was trying to invalidate—that he practiced favoritism with those close to him.

Arthur motioned to her. "Morgan, royal wife to the

king, you stand accused of conspiring with the bishop to interfere in my justice toward Guinevere and Lancelot. You will stand trial immediately following that of the bishop. In the meantime, I will not remit you to the prison, but know you are free only at my mercy."

It did not escape my notice, nor that of the grumbling people, that Arthur had reduced Morgan's crime from high treason in the form of attempted assassination to conspiracy to impede justice. While some cheered to see her publicly accused and humiliated, many others rallied to her defense, loudly reminding Arthur that she was his wife and deserving of his respect. Some even called for her to be named queen in my stead, while others demanded he divorce her on the spot as he had done with me.

In the back of my mind, a memory tingled, vying for my attention like an itch. More than thirty years prior, under a full moon in Avalon, the Goddess had predicted this moment. *"The day will come when sister shall oppose sister, both in this sacred place and without. Loyalties will be tested and betrayed, so heed my warning."*

The goddess of war would face the goddess of the moon, wife would turn against wife, two priestesses locked in a cosmic battle. We had come so close to this before, but always something had stopped us from engaging one another. It was still not our time. But the shadows were retreating, making room for us to stand in opposition. The culmination was not far off, and when it came, it would be to the death. The question was which of us would be left standing.

Chapter Four

"I know you asked that Lancelot be pardoned before we try Marius and Morgan," Arthur said to me one night several weeks later, "but I am beginning to wonder if I will be able to wrest him from his duties in Brittany."

I turned from watching out the window as the bitter wind drove leaden storm clouds pregnant with snow toward Camelot's spires to glance at Mordred, who was with us in Arthur's private study. He was pointedly ignoring our conversation, intent on his book. "Why is that?"

"Lancelot has pledged his service to the house of Dorngwenn. Their king is dead and the four heirs are engaged in civil war with each other and their sister. It is a terrible situation, one I fear becoming too involved in, lest they see my interest as an act of aggression against them. I have not forgotten my promise to you, but circumstances tie my hands."

I wrinkled my brow. "Did you say Dorngwenn, the family of the White Hands? Is that not Yseult's family? I thought Lancelot was fighting with his brothers? Why would he be at war with those responsible for Tristan and Isolde's deaths?"

"The war between the brothers ended shortly after you recovered, then he took up arms against Dorngwenn." Arthur shrugged. "As for why, that is for him to explain. Sometimes that man is too loyal and virtuous for his own good."

I glowered at Arthur, wishing he would at least hazard a guess. "Lancelot is nothing if not loyal." *If only he would be as loyal to me.* I was surprised by my own bitterness. I wanted Lancelot home, or at very least, to receive word from him. It was time for this farce in Camelot to end. But instead of saying that, I toyed with the open book on my lap. "How will you proceed?"

"I do not know yet. I've tried letters and emissaries, but the Bretons are determined to hold on to Lancelot until their war comes to an end."

"But that could be years!"

"I know. I may be his king in this country, but in Brittany, they are his lords."

Arthur might be content to bide his time, but I was not. Fortunately, a plan was already forming in my mind. "They do not know you intend to absolve him, correct?"

Arthur raised an eyebrow. "No. Why?"

"They have no doubt heard he deserted his duty to you and escaped imprisonment. You have every right to have him returned to you to face punishment, no matter what other duty he has promised. His first loyalty is to you. If you go to Brittany with a small contingent of the Combrogi, no one can accuse you of inciting a war because you won't have enough manpower. But you will have enough force to bring him home."

He hesitated. "Perhaps, but I would like to leave that as a last resort."

I turned on him, unable to stand his detached manner any longer. "Is this all a game to you? I will go over there myself and fetch him if you will not act. This is my life, my future you are gambling with, and I'll not have you make a sport of my happiness simply because you no longer have the power you once did."

Arthur stood, his chair scraping loudly across the stone floor. "Watch your tongue, woman. You may no longer be my wife, but I am still your king. I demand respect from you."

I rose, refusing to let his attempt at intimidation cow me. "You speak of respect, but the very reason we are here, together, is for me to adjudicate the result of your utter disregard for me. If anyone in this room should be demanding respect, it is I! Forget not that I am here as a favor to you."

"If that is the way you feel, then leave. I can handle the trial without you."

I gave a small, mirthless laugh. "Truly you are mad. Blind and mad. There is so much more at play here than your petty little trial, Arthur. If you wished, you could have sentenced Bishop Marius and Morgan without my aid. But no, you came to me because you are too weak to make a decision. People are beginning to sense that.

"Camelot is falling to ruin around you. Just this morning, Sobian returned from the quay with tales from the merchants that two of the Combrogi were injured in putting down a demonstration against you in Cornwall. It seems Constantine is actively speaking against you, seeking to leverage his claim as your heir." I placed both hands on the table and leaned forward, trying to make Arthur hear me. "Your people are turning against you, yet here you are, fixated on justice for your wife. Open your eyes, Arthur!"

Mordred shut the book he had been reading with great force, as though to remind us of his presence. "Those incidents are becoming more and more common. Yesterday, I heard Kay and Bedivere speaking of a similar event in Carlisle. They claimed the people there want to see you deposed in favor of me and demanded to have the charges against my mother dropped. It seems she has supporters even outside of Camelot."

"They don't trust you, Arthur." I rounded the small table so that I stood in front of him. "You ruined much more than our relationship when you let that priest lead me down the Bloody Lane in shame. You showed yourself to be an unfeeling despot who was willing to shed blood over petty jealousy instead of the wise, temperate ruler they thought they knew. You allowed them to see a future for which they will not stand."

"I didn't *allow* anyone to do anything! That is my whole point. That is what the outcome of this trial will establish. The bishop used me for his own ends."

"What will that do, Arthur? Yes, justice will be done,

but half the people will disagree no matter what ruling I give. It will not solve the bigger problem."

"I think you underestimate your influence," Mordred said. "As judge, you are acting in the Goddesses' stead since you are still sovereignty personified, regardless of whether or not my father wishes to acknowledge you as queen. It is an honor that cannot be reversed by mortal man. Those who follow the old ways know this. That is why some of the people are demanding you for their queen instead of submitting to my father."

My eyes grew wide and my mouth fell open as I struggled to voice my shock.

Mordred chuckled. "Sobian did not tell you?" He clucked his tongue. "The country is not only divided in allegiance between the High King and his two heirs, one of blood and the other of declaration. No, there are many who back you. You have been their mother-figure for more than two decades and they trust you. This is why the role my father has set for you is so important. It will not only show that the High King follows the same rules he enforces, but it will shore up the people's flagging faith in Camelot once again."

Arthur seized on his son's logic. "He is right, you know. You can turn the people's thoughts back to loyalty to our cause and end the brewing unrest before it blossoms into something worse."

I sat back down, stunned at the sharp turn this conversation had taken. I had come to Camelot to heal and do a favor for Arthur, and now the fate of the kingdom rested in my hands. I closed my eyes and inwardly groaned. Long ago, I swore as a priestess of Avalon to enforce the ways of might and right. Then on the day I was crowned queen, Arthur's subjects became my children, unruly and taciturn though they may be. I owed it to myself and to them to once again shoulder the twin weights of priestesshood and queenship, no matter how distasteful I found them.

But even more than that, Arthur and Mordred needed me. I may have had every right to be angry with Arthur, but he was still the man I'd once loved and my heart tugged me back in his direction. Mordred may have been Morgan's blood, but I'd acted as a second mother to him, watching him grow from a boy into the man who would be king. Mordred was as much son to me as the twins I had long ago given into the arms of the Goddess. I could not abandon father or son simply because doing so was easier. That was a coward's response, and I was not one to shirk my duty. The quick escape into a peaceful life with Lancelot I had envisioned would have to wait.

✦✦✦

After waiting another three weeks for word from Lancelot, but not enacting my suggested solution, Arthur chose to move forward with the trials. He gathered those concerned in his circular chamber, the one in which I had been tried and found wanting months before. Only this time, it was not I who was to plead for my life; Fortuna's wheel had turned, and rather than being crushed beneath its weight,

I rode it to its apex as judge.

I sat alone at the front of the room in the throne I'd always occupied when we met in council in this room. Unlike previously, Arthur did not sit beside me, choosing instead to stand off to the side where he could pace nervously. On my right and left, Morgan and Marius waited in the chairs previously occupied by Arthur's most trusted knights. Morgan's expression was serene, as attentive and composed as though she was going to lead a council session and nothing was amiss. Marius, on the other hand, fiddled with the chains binding his wrists. His uneven beard and wrinkled, dirty tunic indicated he had been plucked straight from Arthur's dungeon. He may have been gaunt from his travails, but that did nothing to extinguish the fiery loathing he threw my direction with every glance.

The remaining chairs were occupied by the top Combrogi. Others clustered behind them arranged based on allegiance—Accolon leading Gawain, Bors, and the others who supported Morgan and Arthur, while Aggrivane sat at the head of Bedivere, Sobian, and those who favored Mordred and myself. There was little difference from the groups that had formed at my own trial, showing loyalties only slightly shifted in my favor. Those eager to oppose me needed more than attempted murder to change their allegiances.

They shifted nervously, many refusing to meet my eyes. Now that I was the one in control, they knew I might exact revenge and so feared me. The temptation was strong. But my role as judge had its origin in the power of the Goddess herself, and so I tried to keep my pride and personal feelings in check. My role was to be as neutral as possible until the moment I was asked to render a verdict. Still, it would be easier if I could call the Goddess down into me as I had on the day I chose my champion. But this was not a ceremony or ritual; it was a judicial matter among mortals, and as such, I had only my instincts and conscience through which to hear the guidance of the gods.

Thankfully, Arthur had chosen the most secluded area of Camelot to hold this trial. Had we been in the great hall—or really anywhere else in the castle—the buzz and chant of the crowds likely would have been audible during the proceedings. Word had gotten out, and throngs of people waited outside, some of whom were shouting their support for Morgan or the bishop, while others made it clear they were already reserving their seats for an execution.

Arthur approached me and turned to face the assembly. Even though he was the victim as well as a witness, it was his duty as king to open the proceedings since the Archdruid was not here to do so. "As you all know, we are gathered here today to determine what really occurred last autumn when Queen Guinevere was erroneously sentenced to death by fire. She is serving as judge in my stead at my request, and she has intimate knowledge of the events from two perspectives, which she will share. But first, I invoke my right as the wronged party to tell my own tale."

He paced again, head bowed in concentration and hands clasped behind his back. "After listening to all assembled at Guinevere's trial, I retreated to the Grail Castle to be alone with my thoughts and pray. When night fell, Bishop Marius suggested I retire and ask God's guidance in my dreams. I was bone weary, so after taking Holy Communion, I did as he suggested. That night I slept fitfully, waking often to the sensation I had consumed far too much drink, even though I had not had any.

"By daybreak, I was retching and so dizzy I was unable to stand. I heard the crowds below and became concerned, but I was not yet alarmed. I'd given no order, so I never imagined what was taking place. However, when the wind shifted and blew the smoke to me, I knew something was very wrong. I tried to stand but fell to the floor. I needed to know what was happening, so I crawled to the casement and threw myself upon it. That was when I saw that the fire had been lit. Again, I tried to stand, but to no avail. All I could do was cry out my dissent, hoping someone would hear me and stop what was taking place below.

"Eventually, I must have lost consciousness because when I next opened my eyes, I was in Morgan's arms. She was rocking me and telling me I had become ill, but all would be well." He stopped and faced me. "It was only later that I heard about Lancelot's intervention and that you were alive." He looked over his shoulder at Mordred. "I wish to publicly thank my son for his part in setting you free. And when we finally locate Lancelot, he will have my gratitude and pardon as well. Please know that I would never have ordered you to be executed."

With that, Arthur ceded the floor to me and I was free to question him. His testimony matched up to what I had seen in my vision, but I still had a few questions. "Did you ever determine what made you ill?"

"No. There was no way to do so."

I didn't expect so. If only I could have gotten my hands on that communion chalice before the damn priest washed it. Even smelling the dregs or tasting the residue on my finger might have helped. I put that aside and turned to my next concern. "What was Morgan's reason for being in your chamber?"

Morgan answered instead. "Perhaps you would like to address that question to me rather than asking Arthur to guess?"

I fought the urge to roll my eyes. "Fine. But you have to wait your turn. I would like to hear from Bishop Marius first. And I suggest you remember that I hold your fate in my hands and address me with the respect I deserve." I eyed Marius. "That goes for both of you. Bishop, you may speak."

Marius cleared his throat and stood. "I stand here today an innocent in chains, much like our Lord and Savior before Pilate. But unlike him, I know my judge has already found me guilty and I have not the virtue to remain silent."

I took a deep breath, willing myself to remain calm. I should have expected a performance from this man. He never could resist an audience.

"I do not deny placing a drop of some liquid in the king's communion wine."

An astonished rumble went through the Combrogi. Marius raised a hand to silence them.

"But it was not poison, as everyone was so quick to

assume. I would never do such a thing to my king." He fell silent and did not seem inclined to continue.

"What was it then?" I prompted.

Victory glittered in his eyes. "I do not know. I was only following the orders of Arthur's wife"—he gestured toward Morgan—"whom I assumed had his best interests at heart. She is a healer and so could have given him any number of remedies for any number of conditions. I am but a humble priest who knows nothing of such things." He touched his breast and bowed his head slightly in a gesture of humility that made me want to gag.

"Now, as I have explained the only charge against me, I suggest you question her"—he nodded in Morgan's direction—"about the exact nature of the substance."

Arthur stood before Marius in three long strides, a finger poking the bishop's chest before I could even speak, his pent-up anger on full display. "That is not the only charge against you, you pompous traitor. How do you explain giving the order to kill Guinevere? I never offered my final judgment."

Marius looked at me as if to inquire whether I would allow Arthur to question him in my place.

I smiled coldly. "I was just about to ask the same question." I sat back, awaiting his response.

Marius's eyes shifted back to Arthur as a wolf-like grin spread across his face. "Oh, but you did. Perhaps you do not remember because you were so ill. You looked at me and clearly said 'guilty.'"

Arthur grabbed the priest by the collar of his tunic. "I said no such—"

Marius continued as though Arthur had done nothing. "The point is, I was still carrying out the king's will."

"No. You. Were. Not." Arthur ground out each word between clenched teeth.

"Morgan, you were there when Arthur was ill. Did he say anything of the sort?"

Morgan shook her head. "No. Marius told me before I saw Arthur that he had spoken to the king in private and he had passed his verdict. He said he was headed to help Guinevere meet her fate, but never elaborated."

"There you have it." I fought back a smile. "Two people say no and one, with a very strong motivation for self-preservation, disagrees. Plus, we have testimony stating you spoke of Arthur's will before anyone saw him that day." Given this evidence, there was no need for me to mention my vision. "It seems to me there is nothing left to be said. I am ready to render my verdict."

This was one sentence I did not have to deliberate upon. I had been waiting twenty-five years to avenge the wrongs this man had done to me—separating me from my first love and my family, turning Arthur away from Avalon, installing Morgan in my place, and trying to have me killed—and now I could do so in full knowledge it would be justice.

I finally allowed my grin free rein. "Bishop Marius, through the power granted to me by High King Arthur Pendragon, you are hereby found guilty of the crime of high treason for the attempted murder of a royal person, the punishment for which is death by the method of the king's choosing."

Marius's mouth hung open in shock.

"Take him back where he came from," Arthur ordered Gawain and Bedivere.

Each man took one of Bishop Marius's shoulders and dragged him toward the door.

"I protest! I am not guilty. I protest!" he yelled. "You cannot do this to me. The Bishop of Rome will hear about this! Arthur, think what having the blood of a priest on your soul will mean when you go before God."

Arthur shuddered involuntarily, which made me wonder if he had the stones to go through with the punishment demanded by law, especially since he was giving that damn priest time to frame himself as a martyr. I would have executed him on the spot.

Putting away such dark thoughts, I turned to Morgan, whose face had gone white, as though she only now realized this was not some silly play we were enacting; I truly held over her the power of life and death. "It is your turn to speak."

Slowly, she rose, regarding each person in the room before finding her voice. "I am guilty of no crime except caring for my husband. Each of you remembers what that day was like. By the time Arthur left this room, his nerves were frayed and he still had an enormous decision to make. I cannot imagine what he must have been feeling, but I knew he needed the clear mind that would come with rest. That is why I suggested the bishop add a drop of valerian to his cup. Arthur had already refused dinner and I knew he would argue with me if I suggested to him that he take it. I only meant to ease his nerves and help him sleep." Her eyes welled with tears.

Once again, I fought the urge to make a face. I had seen Morgan's false tears before and they did not move me. "You know as well as I that valerian doesn't make people violently ill."

"Not usually, no. But we also know that many things can change how an herb works. It may not have even been the valerian that made Arthur sick. It could have been anything."

For the first time all morning, Aggrivane spoke. "Is that the same excuse you offered Viviane when Rowena nearly died during the testing to determine the next Lady of the Lake?"

That Aggrivane remembered the incident was a surprise. But he had been close with us during our time in Avalon and understood what a puzzle that event had been to everyone who knew Morgan. She had always maintained her innocence, and no one had ever conclusively proven Rowena's poisoning was Morgan's fault. However, the rumor of her guilt dogged her, lending her a reputation for being talented with poisons, deserved or not.

Morgan's eyes narrowed and her cheeks flamed. "How dare you! Did Guinevere prompt you to say that? My life is on the line and the two of you are dredging up the past because it might help justify your hatred of me. Perhaps the bishop was right and we were both condemned in your eyes from the start." She was crying in earnest now, tears dripping onto her freckled cheeks.

"Oh, this is bullocks," Sobian muttered, just loud enough for those around her to hear.

"I have a question," Arthur interjected, perhaps to allay further argument. "Morgan, how did you come to find me that morning? I never had the chance to ask."

Morgan wiped the area beneath her eyes, giving Arthur a soft, sorrowful smile. "I couldn't stand to watch when the bishop went to get Guinevere. Something about his manner made me believe he was leading her to death, and despite all that has passed between us, that I could not bear. I went to your room when you were not outside with the crowds, nor in the great hall. I was worried something might have happened to you, especially in light of your uncharacteristic verdict."

"Something might have happened to me?" Arthur raised an eyebrow. "Like what?"

Morgan shrugged. "I don't know. I was scared you might have been taken by an ill humor and could be a danger to yourself. You were so upset the day before. Frankly, you hadn't been yourself since you removed our son from the Combrogi because of that woman's false accusation against him. Then there was poor Elaine's death, and then Guinevere betrayed you." She took Arthur's hands. "I couldn't leave you alone if you were still in pain."

Arthur looked at her with such tenderness, I thought I was going to vomit. I cleared my throat to break the spell between them. "Do you still have the bottle?"

Morgan blinked. "The what?"

"The bottle of valerian. I'd like you to take me to it so I might examine it myself." Morgan had no way of knowing I had seen the bottle in my vision and this was my way of testing her.

She blinked a few more times, as though considering my odd request. "If you wish."

She led Arthur, Gawain, Bedivere, and me through the halls to her chamber. A cheer went up when we passed the great hall. Through the cacophony, my ears discerned a few cheers of joy that Morgan was still with our party and two particularly loud shouts of protest over Marius's verdict from his acolytes Galahad and Peredur, who vowed the wrath of God upon our heads if we carried out his sentence.

When we reached Morgan's room, she knelt and unlocked a large chest sitting near the fireplace. She withdrew a small wooden box from within and lifted its lid. Inside stood a dozen small dark glass vials, each identical.

Morgan held two bottles up to the light before finding the one she desired and holding it out to me. "This is it."

It matched the vial in my vision, but so did all of the others in the box. "How do you know it is the right one? I don't see any markings on it." It was possible Morgan could have mixed up the vials and inadvertently given Arthur the wrong liquid.

She looked at me as if I was a child in Avalon once again. "I don't want untrained people pawing through my medicinal store and mistaking a poisonous herb for something innocent, so I use a special ink made from the milk of goat's lettuce that is only visible when you apply ash over it." She displayed a sooty thumb I hadn't even seen her dip into the cinders. "Once the milk is dry, it won't rub off, but the ashes will, so the bottles are unrecognizable to anyone else."

I took the bottle and examined it. Now that she pointed it out, tiny letters near the neck designated it as valerian. While I had hoped this test would clearly proclaim Morgan's guilt or innocence, all it had done was show that her case was not as cut-and-dried as that of Bishop Marius. I needed time to think. As much as I hated her, as much as I wanted to use this as an excuse for revenge, I could not do so out of hand, because everything Morgan said was plausible.

I handed the bottle back to her. "I was hoping that would provide us with a clear answer. But it has not." I rubbed my head. "Let us adjourn for today. I may speak with each of you tomorrow if more questions arise."

⁂

I left the council chambers and was on my way to the labyrinth at the center of Camelot, a courtyard garden made by Arthur for me as a wedding gift and meant as a place of refuge when I needed to clear my mind, when Arthur bellowed Aggrivane's name.

I raced toward the sound, only to find Arthur leaning over a letter in the great hall, a messenger at his side. The midday light revealed his anger, his eyes flashing as they skimmed over the ink, cheeks enflamed, golden hair standing at attention like stalks of barley.

"My lord?" Aggrivane stepped as close to Arthur as he dared, wisely well out of arm's reach.

Arthur looked up, seeming for a moment to have forgotten he'd called for Aggrivane. "I need as many fighting men as you can muster. Bring them to the barracks yard within the hour. I will survey them then." He turned to me. "Guinevere, I need you to find the Combrogi and call back as many as you can."

When Arthur made for the door, I grabbed his arm, stopping him before he could make it into the hall. "What is it? What is happening?"

"They—the house of Dorngwenn"—he stabbed the parchment—"have taken Kay hostage. I mean to get him back."

"Isn't there any other way? You said yourself you were loath to start a war."

Arthur glared at me. "It is this or receive my brother's body in pieces. They were very clear about that."

"Then let me come with you. You know what an asset I can be in battle. You can leave me there with Lancelot once everything is over."

Arthur studied me, considering my words. "No. I will not draw you into yet another war. Besides, your job here is not finished."

He turned away, but I stopped him, forcing him to face me. "Then I will tell you my judgment now and you can act upon it whenever you will. *Please*, Arthur. Let us call an end to this."

"No. I need someone here to ensure Morgan and Marius do not escape."

"So I am their jailor now?" I asked, aghast.

"Be reasonable," Arthur all but yelled. "Mordred will be concerned with affairs of state and I will be taking most of the Combrogi with me. I am entrusting them to your care because I know you will do what is right."

"And you aren't willing to be rid of me," I said under my breath, but Arthur did not hear over his own summons to Mordred.

Mordred trotted to Arthur's side before the echo of his name had faded. "Yes, Father?"

Arthur removed the torc from around his neck and placed it around his son's. "I turn control of Camelot over to you. I must go to Brittany as soon as possible and likely will not return for some time. Do not carry out the sentence against Bishop Marius or pass judgment on your mother until I return." He clasped his son's shoulder. "See that peace is maintained in my absence and watch over Guinevere."

Mordred beamed. "Of course, Father."

The exchange should have been innocent, but when Mordred looked at me, something in his smile chilled my bones. An ambitious and well-trained heir, he had been waiting for just such an opportunity. Only time would tell how much Arthur would come to regret this choice.

Chapter Five

Summer 519

As summer's heat slowly took hold, it became clear that Camelot was changing under Mordred's rule. With most of the Combrogi off fighting at Arthur's side, he enjoyed nearly absolute power, something to be feared in one so young and rash.

I was not the only one to take note, and that meant our people, already distrustful, became increasingly nervous. It began with rumblings in the countryside. The lowly men and women who came to Camelot on pleading day—a custom Mordred tolerated but delegated to me because it tried his patience—all told tales of the Picts massing as though for some great council. According to one woman, the northern tribes—the Damnonii, Novantae, Selgovae, and Votadini—were growing restless as well, no doubt spooked by the sudden activity of the Picts.

Next came whisperings in the marketplace, brought

back by Sobian's ever-observant ears. "Some of the women say the townsfolk are quietly taking sides. The whores at the Boar's Head say their patrons argue nightly. Some of the merchants' wives say their husbands have been discussing it too."

I stopped the spinning wheel in front of me, relaxed the arm holding the yarn, and looked at Sobian. "You cannot truly believe Mordred is planning an insurrection, can you?"

She leveled me with her most serious look. "I can, and I do. And I do not believe he will do it alone. He aims to unite the Picts and the Saxons against Arthur. The northern tribes too, if they'll take him. I think that's the real reason why he's keeping you here."

"Keeping me here?"

"Yes. Mordred easily could have sent you to Brittany with Arthur or put you on a ship following in his wake, but he needs you. You are Mordred's greatest asset, and also a threat. Regardless of what Arthur said that day in front of the Combrogi, you are still our consecrated queen. Arthur cannot undo that. He can renounce you all he wants, but only death can unmake a queen. We all know how the ancient law works. For another to become king, the power of sovereignty must pass through you. He needs your cooperation, if not your blessing, to fulfill his plans."

I considered her words. "I have already told Mordred I will not seek the throne, so I am no threat to him. How else could I be of help to him?"

Sobian fixed me with a hard stare. "Are you daft or in denial? He could marry you, for one. Do not tell me it never crossed your mind. He needs a strong wife to cement his power, and you have more than proven your skill. It is either you or one of the Saxons or Picts. He already knows and loves you. It is not so big a leap."

"But I am like a mother to him!" I swallowed hard to contain the bile that soured the back of my throat.

"Still, you are not his kin, so nothing is stopping him if he is of a mind to do it. All I am saying is to be wary."

Thanks to this exchange, that night at dinner, we both had our hackles up, especially given the extravagant meal. The largess was unusual and could not be without meaning. Who was Mordred trying to impress and why? I couldn't help but watch every move he and Morgan made, my eyes narrowing as I calculated the nuances behind the idle conversation as we slowly demolished the fully dressed swan and several additional courses.

The pageantry had to be for his mother's new champion, Accolon, the second son of the house of Rheged. I had never trusted that man, not since the day he'd tried so hard to catch his cousin Aggrivane and I in the act of a dalliance under Pellinor's roof. He certainly shouldn't be privy to the intimate conversations of our private meals.

For such dynamics to be at play, more had to be going on in Mordred's court than simply holding power in Arthur's stead. Waiting any longer to find out if the rumors were true, if Mordred was angling to make his temporary power into something more, would be dangerous. However, I couldn't simply ask him outright; I needed to use a question that would appear innocent to outsiders, yet test the limits of Mordred's willingness to confide in me.

Picking at my pudding with feigned disinterest, I asked, "The barracks and smithy were quite busy when Sobian and I passed them earlier today. You have given them some special assignment?"

"Only ensuring our standing army stays in practice and our weapons are at the ready in our king's absence," he answered.

"That does not explain the Saxon spears and Pictish swords I saw cooling on the racks," Sobian said, one eyebrow raised in subtle challenge.

Mordred shrugged. "Just because Arthur refuses to adopt the weapons of our enemies does not mean I will be as narrow-minded." He turned to me. "You were a battle queen. Do you not agree that we should have every useful weapon at our disposal?"

I ran a finger around the rim of my cup, considering his words. He did have a point. If his words were true, then my suspicions were nothing more than a case of mistaken purpose. Maybe the rest of the rumors were the same. The Pictish gathering everyone was so concerned about could have been planned long before Arthur left for Brittany. As for the villagers taking sides, wasn't it natural to compare the son to his father? It could all come down to a matter of interpretation. Having known Mordred for so long, I desperately wanted to believe it, to trust him.

"I do. In fact, I wonder that we did not think of it before."

Mordred smiled. "It is understandable. You had more pressing matters to attend to, such as securing the peace we now enjoy. But I wish to be prepared, for our enemies will only stay quiet for so long. We will be ready when they decide to move."

Satisfied with his answer, at least about the smithy, I settled back into my chair, casting a glance at Sobian to gauge her reaction. She was observing Mordred through lowered lashes, pretending—for I had learned many of her schemes in the last nineteen years—to be overcome by the generous food and drink. That she was employing such an act meant only one thing—she didn't believe him.

Though I accepted his answer about the weapons, I still harbored misgivings about his overall plan. Did Mordred know a strong contingent of his people were suspicious of his motives? He deserved to know what was being whispered behind his back. "I fear your good intentions may have been misunderstood."

Mordred wrinkled his brow and fixed me with a questioning look.

"Surely you have heard what the people are saying about you?"

"I have not," he said slowly, leaning forward over his plate, elbows on the table, intensely interested now.

I cleared my throat, unsettled by how much he looked like Arthur in that pose. "They say you are planning rebellion. They tell tales that you are allying with the Picts and trying to convince the four northern tribes to overthrow Arthur while he is in Brittany."

As quickly as they'd materialized, the similarities between father and son melted away. Whereas Arthur would have gone quiet at that news, blue eyes pensive with concern, Mordred merely nodded, a slight smile tugging at the corners of his lips.

"This news cannot possibly please you," I said, aghast.

"Of course it can," Mordred answered over the rim of his cup. "What did the old philosopher say? 'The enemy of my enemy is my friend'?"

Mordred's calm unnerved me more than if he had screamed his outrage. I narrowed my eyes at him as I ripped off a hunk of bread, needing something to do with my hands. "But the northern tribes are our allies. Whose enemy does that make them? The Saxons?"

"For one," Mordred replied around a mouthful of spiced plums.

I narrowed my eyes at him. "What exactly are you planning?"

It was Morgan who answered. "That is for us to know." She gave me an indulgent smile that reeked of triumph and stroked Accolon's hand as though he were a prized pet. "While we're talking about enemies, I have it on good authority that Mark's nephew, Constantine, may be our next threat."

"Is he still waving his sword around?" Accolon asked, more amused than concerned. "He is fairly impotent as long as Arthur and Mordred live."

"What about Helene? Does she not factor into the line of succession?" I asked, glancing at Morgan.

"No one would accept a woman as High Queen alone, much less a mere girl who has not yet lost her milk teeth,"

Accolon scoffed. "But as Arthur's daughter she will be quite a prize as she grows." He turned to Morgan. "You would do well to guard her against men like me."

She glared back at him, but said nothing.

Returning to his original point, Accolon added, "No, Constantine is not a real threat. His claim to Camelot rests only in that Arthur favored him before he knew about his son, so he can do nothing until the throne is vacant."

"Tell that to the people of the Summer Country," Morgan retorted. "I hear that he is working his way north and has his sights set next on Venta Belgarum. The people there are either fleeing into the hillfort or trying to outrun his army to safety."

Mordred's expression clouded. "Why did I not know of this?" His tone was sharp, a mixture of anger and accusation aimed at his mother.

"I only received word yesterday." Morgan placed her hand over her son's as though to placate him. "I have friends in the south who report he is showing signs of having taken after his uncle in ambition. They say he now demands his household function like a Roman villa. His confidants say he wishes to restore Britain to its former Imperial glory."

Mordred adopted Arthur's pensive look, staring across the room into nothingness.

"That is troubling." It was the only thing I could think to say.

"Indeed," Mordred mumbled, still deep in thought.

Morgan looked at us as though we were daft and threw up her hands. "Am I the only one who sees the opportunity here? Son, you need to act decisively against Constantine without delay. The people need a reason to trust you—perhaps even fear you. If you can secure Venta Belgarum, you will be a hero to the largest kingdom in Britain and you will demonstrate your might to the kingdom of Bernicia and anyone else who might oppose you."

Sobian leaned over and whispered in my ear, shielding her mouth from view with one hand, "She is acting like Mordred is king in fact as well as name, as though Arthur is dead."

I shivered involuntarily. "Perhaps to her, he is. He abandoned her without a ruling, and no one knows what will happen when he returns. If she doesn't act now, she may miss her only chance."

"Meaning?"

I shook my head, glancing at Mordred. "Not here. I'll tell you tonight." I sighed, watching Morgan quietly explained her idea to Mordred. Accolon nodded along like a devoted hound. "I don't like that she can so easily manipulate Accolon. He and Owain are a formidable force, and popular as well. If she can control them, Arthur may not have a throne to return to."

"Guinevere," Mordred called, breaking up our side conversation, "do you still have your set of Holy Stones? Bring them out."

"What? Why?" Despite my confusion, I rose, already obeying his command.

Why would he make such a request? Holy Stones, considered by some to be merely a game but taught to all priestesses as part of our training, was a method of divination long used by the Druids to advise chieftains in battle. Each stone represented a different type of solider, each triangle an opposing army led by a red queen. When combined with the sight and proper training, a Druid or priestess could use them to divine the outcome of a battle, thus ensuring the safest course of action for their ruler. It was normally only used in times of war or uncertainty.

Ah, that was it. Mordred was weighing the wisdom of his mother's plan and wanted to know what the gods predicted. Since Morgan's conversion to Christianity, she had forsworn such acts of divination. But lucky for Mordred, I had not and I had a different gift. Whereas she could see the future, I could see what was presently happening at a distance, which would give Mordred the chance to head off any future that his mother had already foreseen.

My stomach churned as I traced the halls to my chambers and back, a small round board under my arm and a bag of stones in hand. My feet moved by long habit, mind absorbed in the ramifications of what I was about to do. I had little choice but to read the stones for Mordred; while he did not hold me there against my will, I had nowhere to go if he tired of me or turned me out. Plus, angering him was dangerous; there were sufficient people who wished to finish what the bishop had started that I was best under Mordred's protection until Arthur could pardon Lancelot and see me safely to Brittany.

When I returned, they had all arranged themselves in front of the fire, leaving an empty place to Mordred's right for me. I set up the board with two sets of opposing stones, the clear quartz representing Mordred's army, the red jasper Constantine's, just as we had been taught in Avalon. But something was not right. Every time I looked at the board, I saw shadows to my left and right. There were more parties involved.

"Morgan, do you still have your set? I need more stones. They are telling me there is more at play."

She scowled at me but silently got to her feet and left the room.

While she was away, Mordred drew me off to one side, out of Accolon's hearing.

"I heard you and Sobian speaking earlier."

"And?" I tried to keep my voice light, but my embarrassment at being caught burned in my cheeks. How much had he heard?

He leaned in so that our noses almost touched, an oddly intimate gesture. "What is your ruling? Would you kill my mother along with the priest?"

I swallowed, not wishing to divulge my thoughts to him, especially without Arthur as witness. Although, since Mordred was acting king, he had just as much right to that information as his father. I took a deep breath.

"No," I answered slowly, forcing myself to look Mordred in the eye. "Just as when you were accused of raping that girl, I cannot determine her guilt or innocence with any certainty. She could be lying or she could be speaking the truth. As much as I want to punish her for what she has done to me and to Arthur, I cannot condemn a fellow priestess without irrefutable proof."

"So you would allow her to go free?" His warm breath brushed my cheek.

"Not exactly. I will recommend to Arthur that he set Morgan up in comfort in a remote estate of her choosing so she will be less prone to trouble. I wouldn't advise keeping her at court, lest she interfere again. And I don't recommend you condone whatever plan she and Accolon have concocted. Chances are good it benefits them more than you."

Morgan returned then, and we jumped apart like two children caught in the act of stealing a cooling bread roll from the windowsill. Morgan didn't seem to notice, holding out a bag to me. Her icy glare conveyed that if anyone outside this room ever heard that she still possessed a set of Holy Stones, she would make me regret it.

I tipped the bag into my palm and picked out the lapis, placing it on my left, before setting the malachite on my right. I breathed deeply, allowing the quiet rhythm of four people breathing and the soft crackle of the fire to lull me into that place between worlds where the voices of the gods could be heard.

The sight took over and I was no longer in the room with them. Flying above the field of battle and seeing through the eyes of the Morrigan's crows, I learned this skirmish was meaningless. Yes, it would stop Constantine from advancing—for now—but it was but a small thread in the tapestry the gods were weaving with our lives.

My fingers manipulated the pieces on and off the board until no more quartz or jasper remained. This war was not about the red and clear stones—Constantine and Mordred—at all. It was about those who were left, the blue—Morgan, the child raised in Avalon—and the green—me, the daughter of the Votadini. In the center, all alone, save for our two queens at the head of our armies, was the quartz king. But it wasn't Mordred or Arthur; it was both. The stones were saying that in the end, the fate of Camelot would not rest in the hands of other lords or even foreigners; it depended on those of us in this room and our absent king.

I came back to myself with a start. Mordred and Accolon were staring at me, but my attention was drawn to Morgan, who was gripping the edges of her chair, her eyes glassy and far away. She may no longer court the sight, but it clearly had a hold of her now. Her visions may well augment or explain what I had just experienced.

I rushed to her side. "What do you see?"

She did not respond immediately. Her eyes whipped back and forth, like those of a dreamer, watching something only she could perceive. "Arthur. He will never again set foot in Camelot."

Blood drained from my face and I grabbed her hand, seeking to steady myself on the arm of her chair. "He will die in Brittany?"

"No. Not death, not yet." Her eyes darted again as another vision overtook her. She paled and her eyes grew wide with horror, her mouth gaping, chin trembling as though she would cry.

"What is it? Please tell me."

She was back to herself in the space of a breath, but her

face still bore the etchings of worry and fear caused by her vision. She refused to meet my gaze, caught somewhere between this world and the next.

"Morgan?"

She did not answer, only shook her head slowly, gazing past me at her son.

I squatted in front of her so that I was at her eye level, breaking her line of sight to Mordred. "I know you bear no love for me, but you need to unburden yourself. We both know the pain will only grow if you do not confide your fear. What did you see?"

Her attention whipped back to me and her blue eyes fastened on mine. "I do not fear that which I can yet control." She rose, back perfectly straight and shoulders set. "We can yet avoid calamity." She took in Mordred and Accolon, who regarded her with a combination of curiosity and fear. "Arm yourselves, my loves. You have a battle to prepare for, one that will do much to cement your futures as leaders of Camelot. Guinevere can tell you more based on what she has seen. I have other matters to attend to if we are going to avoid the fate the gods have shown." With no more explanation, she stalked toward the door, muttering, "Goddess help me, I will not allow them to make fools of us all."

Who exactly were *they* and how did her visions fit with mine? What role did she and I play in the coming war and how—and why—did Arthur and Mordred stand between us? The stones had told us that the gods knew the answer, but they were not yet ready to make us party to their plans.

Chapter Six

he next morning, I woke from a dreamless sleep before dawn, certainty like a block of ice in my stomach. Morgan had gone to see Marius after we read the stones. Why hadn't I seen that before? Or at least understood it last night? I had been so caught up in my own visions and interpretations of them that it had taken the blackness of sleep to wash away the distractions.

Marius, Morgan's only ally in Camelot—outside of her son—was currently locked in Camelot's cellar, awaiting Arthur's return and his final punishment. In truth, it shocked me that Mordred had kept him imprisoned after freeing Morgan, but then again, Mordred bore no love for the bishop and at least this way he could keep him under close watch.

The opportunity for duplicity had been there all along, and now Morgan would see him as a willing pawn in whatever game she was concocting to stave off the darkness of her mysterious vision. As mother to the acting king, anything the prisoner desired was in her power, so striking an accord with Marius would not be too difficult for her. Knowing Morgan, she would do anything Marius wanted if it ensured the future she feared would not come to pass.

As I neared the cells, my skin prickled with panic and cold sweat dampened my neck. I would never again be able to go near this place without being taken back to my time here, when this very prisoner was plotting my death.

Taking a fortifying breath, I motioned for the guard to unlock the stout cell door. For a moment, darkness overwhelmed me, but soon my eyes adjusted. In front of me was an empty cell devoid of anything save a fresh coat of rushes under a small pallet. Marius was not kneeling in prayer or huddled against a wall or even mocking me for taking so long to visit him. He was gone.

I cursed. Depending on how long he had been missing, Marius could be halfway to Rome by now. Seething, I turned on the guard, drawing a long, thin dagger from my belt. "Where is he?"

The guard stood frozen and unresponsive, fear etched into his features.

Gritting my teeth, I tried again. "Where is the prisoner? Tell me, man, or it will be your blood upon these stones." I prodded him with the tip of the blade.

The guard swallowed hard, the motion making him wince as his Adam's apple grazed the steel. "He was released a few hours ago. The Lady Morgan—"

"Where did they go?"

His eyes bulged in fear. "I do not know. I only did as she commanded."

I sheathed my dagger. I didn't need to hear any more. Once Morgan had someone's allegiance, she didn't easily let it go, which was why many of the guards and servants still took orders from her. Damn Mordred for releasing her. Whether he knew it or not, he was slowly undoing all the justice Arthur had managed to impart before he left for Brittany.

Emerging into the dawn, I shielded my eyes, trying to uncover where they would have gone. Slowly, I turned in a circle, taking in the familiar landscape as if I could reveal their footprints by sheer force of will. Camelot's great fortress surrounded me on three sides, while the Bloody Lane branched off of the other. The castle's exterior doors were barred to intruders, so unless Morgan had made a deal with the guards inside, there was no shelter for them within. That meant they had to have taken the Bloody Lane into the village.

I had no choice but to set foot on the road that had once nearly led to my death. My stomach was in my throat by the time I reached the midpoint of the path. Homes, shops, and inns lined both sides, but few people were about at this early hour. I considered asking a woman loaded with sodden washing if she had seen a red-haired woman and a priest on her walk back from the river, but before I could approach her, I spied a small path leading between two buildings.

Narrow and nearly hidden by vines, it could be easily missed. Walls taller than a man cast deep shadows, plunging the path into perpetual gloom. This must be the Smugglers' Path where Sobian heard so much of her information.

I palmed my dagger, following the prodding of my instincts, which warned me this was not a safe place for a lone woman. But I was here and I had to see this through.

Stepping into the shadows, I recoiled at the sour stench of urine. At my feet, a beggar lay sleeping, covered in filthy rags. I gingerly stepped around him. The alleyway was not long; already, sunlight beckoned from the far end. For an area no wider than my outstretched arms, it saw a fair amount of activity. Against one wall, a prostitute plied her trade, the girth of joined bodies nearly blocking my passage. As I squeezed past, back toward them to show I took no interest in their activities, two thieves bartered with a third over the value of a purloined bracelet and a little boy begged for coins and scraps. *Thank you, Lady, for calling me to a station above this.* Though my role as a disgraced queen was not the life I'd chosen, at least I need not make my living here.

"Going somewhere, love?" The whore's patron gripped my bottom with a grimy hand, his other arm coming around my neck.

I ducked and tried to pull away from his grasp, but he was too strong. Abandoning his conquest for the moment, he pulled me against him, his naked prick rubbing against my back. My heart pounded. Memories of being raped and tortured by Malegant, one of the Combrogi, came rushing back as though they had happened just yesterday. They would not, could not happen again. I would not let it.

"Why not join us?" the woman called, revealing several missing teeth. "Tis always more fun with two." She laughed salaciously.

"I prefer to leave you to it," I answered, slamming my elbow into my captor's gut.

The air whooshed out of him in a grunt and he stumbled back, pinning the woman to the wall. I started to run, but he grabbed a fistful of my hair, pulling me back.

Despite my prickling scalp, I whirled on him. "I was trying to be nice, but you are making that impossible." I slashed out with my dagger, pinning his free hand to the wattle-and-daub wall.

Instinctively, he released my hair. His howl of pain followed me down the alleyway as I fled. Men with contraband items scattered before me like rats, the beggar boy clearing the way by raising the cry of "intruder."

I stumbled into the adjoining street and my foot found a rut made by a wagon wheel, ankle twisting. I sucked in a sharp breath at the burning wrench, but I did not stop. A safe distance away, I stopped, bending double, hands on my thighs as I fought to catch my breath and ease the stitch in my side.

Where was I? I had been so intent on escaping danger that I hadn't paid attention to where I was going. Before me, a low stone wall protected travelers from plunging into the churning ocean as they made their way to and from the port below to the village. In the sea beyond lay the Grail Castle, its red-gold copula gleaming in the rising sun. The tide was just beginning to ebb, uncovering the narrow causeway connecting it to the mainland.

I shielded my eyes from the brightness of the rising sun. On the near side of the island, a small boat bobbed in the current. Someone had journeyed there while the land passage was underwater—a risky maneuver in the best of times, but even more so in the twilight before dawn. Rocks and sandbars could easily wreck a vessel if one did not know where to steer, and though the castle was not far from shore, the water was deep and rough enough to drown even an experienced swimmer. Few people knew the area well enough to have navigated it safely. As bishop and one of the guardians of the Grail, Marius was one of them.

◦◦◦

The massive stones linking island to land were still slick as I raced across them, praying to catch up to Marius. If I did not, I likely would never find him again.

I rushed through the exterior gate, past the small cells lining the outer ring of rooms, only to be stopped by a knot of pilgrims waiting to be admitted to the inner sanctuary where the Grail was housed.

"What is this? Why are the doors closed?" They were never supposed to be closed. The Grail was always available to all, night or day.

"The bishop asked for some time to pray alone," answered a small woman who held a sleeping babe in one arm.

"Did he?" No doubt for some nefarious purpose.

I hurried down the circular corridor. What the pilgrims did not know was there was more than one entrance into the main chamber. Arthur had designed this building and could not talk about it enough during its long construction. As a result, I had its plans forever seared into my mind.

The maze of corridors led me to a small antechamber where the priests and deacons of the Grail prepared themselves to celebrate its sacred rites. As I'd suspected, the cabinets were thrown open, their contents askew, sacred linens rumpled in half-open drawers. Marius had likely pilfered the finest, intent on either selling them to finance his flight or at least provide a basis of riches to establish his life outside of Camelot.

"Going somewhere?" I demanded, bursting into the silent main chamber.

Bishop Marius blinked at me like a mole newly emerged from underground. He was on his knees in front of the Grail, a large pack belching gold patens and a small book with jewel-encrusted binding at his feet.

"How dare you disturb my prayer?" he exclaimed, his voice as sharp and cold as a newly honed knife blade. "I could have you arrested for disobeying my direct order of privacy."

"Why should I start listening to your commands now?" I countered, moving closer to him with each word. "You have no power over me. You never have. That is why you fear me."

Bishop Marius snorted. "If I feared you, I would not be

here. I would still be locked away." The bravado in his voice did not reach his eyes.

"It *is* convenient to have friends who are willing to do you favors when it suits them, is it not? Morgan would not have released you if it did not suit her. What deal did you strike with her?"

Marius glanced at the Grail. "That is none of your concern."

"Then call your guards. Have me arrested as you say."

Marius's gaze flicked back to the cup raised high on a pillar for all to see.

"No? Then you must not wish to draw attention to yourself either. What is your plan? Steal the Grail, then support Mordred's rebellion from afar?"

"I would never condone that pagan whelp as king," he said, his voice dripping with disdain. "My aims lie across the sea."

His destination had to be Gaul or Brittany. Morgan did say Arthur and Lancelot were in trouble. Surely she would not move against her beloved Arthur, no matter what her son may or may not be planning. So he had to be supporting Arthur in his current battle. Marius had mentioned once that he had friends among the Bretons and Gauls.

"How does this plan benefit you?" I narrowed my eyes, trying to position myself between him and the Grail.

"Let us just say I will have the gratitude of the king if I can bring this war to an end." Marius picked up his sack, its rich contents clanking loudly. "Now, if you will excuse me. It is time for me to depart." He moved toward the Grail.

"So that's it then. You pay off the Breton nobles and move the Grail where it will bring them unending revenue. How do you expect to spirit it away without everyone chasing you?"

Marius's smile was wicked. "Haven't you heard? Galahad dreamed that God wished it to be moved to Brittany, for they have held the faith much stronger than here. Or at least that is what we will tell everyone. Morgan has the ability to convince even Galahad it is true—and in many ways, it is. Arthur proved unworthy by placing power in his pagan son's hands instead of trusting in his closest advisor." He touched his own heart.

"You tried to have him killed with that drugged wine, remember? Why would he ever trust you?"

"Once he sees my role in ending the war and assuring his continuance as king, I will have his unending gratitude, even if I had to use the Grail to bring it about. It will wipe away all of my past sins and secure my position in his esteem."

"You were counting on his devotion to his faith to save you all along, weren't you? Arthur could never bring himself to kill a priest, no matter what he's done."

Marius gloated. "I know." He reached for the Grail. "And neither could you or you'd have done it by now."

A low chuckle made us both turn.

Mordred was standing in the entry, his arms crossed, with Mona, the Grail Maiden, at his side. "Then it's a shame for you his son does not share his faith. I have no such compunction."

Marius's face filled with dread.

"If you touch the Grail, I will kill you myself." Mona held up a large silver sickle, the weapon all Grail guardians wore at their sides. "You have proven yourself unworthy."

"You. How did you know?" Marius stuttered.

Mona lightly touched the crescent moon at her brow. "We guardians always know when our sacred charge is in peril. We are bound to it. Now I must demand justice on its behalf." Mordred grabbed Bishop Marius by the cowl and dragged him toward the Grail Maiden. "By your leave, Lady, I fear your punishment too swift for the likes of him. I have something else in mind that I assure you will satisfy both spiritual and temporal law."

⁂

"Is he dead?" I asked Mordred when more than a week had passed with no sign of Bishop Marius.

Mordred squinted at me, wrinkling his nose. "I'm not sure. We could go together to find out." He held out an arm, as though offering to escort me to the fair.

I looked at him sharply. "What have you done to him?"

"Come with me and see." He motioned for me to rise.

Pulling my shawl close around me against a chill that could have no natural origin, I followed Mordred. Past the cellar where Marius had been kept, past the place of public execution, through Camelot's gates, and into the forest, we trod. At the crossroads where two smaller Roman roads met to join the main road to Camelot, we stopped.

I peered around, searching the empty dirt road and the thick underbrush on either side. The only thing I found was a pile of offal, the reeking, viscous remains of some animal's recent kill. Other than that, we were utterly alone. I turned to Mordred, seeking an explanation.

"Look up," he said, pointing into the trees.

I did as he instructed. Suspended high above me was a pen made of saplings, its crisscrossing bars and domed roof resembling a bird cage. But inside it was no bird; it could barely be called human. Marius lay naked on his belly, arms and ankles bound behind him at unnatural angles like a freshly trussed boar. Blood was slowly dripping from his wounds onto the leaves at my feet. A low moaning scream escaped my lips.

As we watched, a carrion crow hopped from a nearby branch and landed on one of the bars. It cocked its head to one side, as though considering a thought, then craned its neck to peck something. Marius cried out in pain and the bird jerked away, launching itself into the air and taking with it a bit of Marius's flesh.

Marius moaned, his head on the bottom of the cage. He saw me, and his moans shaped into something resembling my name. Drawn as if by a spell, I moved closer until I was directly beneath him. I looked up, meeting his gaze. One of his eyes was obscured in shadow. No, it was missing altogether. One clear blue eye and one scabbed socket stared at me as he whimpered. I didn't dare look down or move in case his eye was decaying at my feet.

I twisted so I was facing Mordred, catching a glimpse of

what I had taken for carrion earlier. No, not carrion. It was bits of Marius's blood and skin and muscle torn away by animals. I took a few unsteady steps toward the hedge and vomited. When I turned back to Mordred, he was standing tall and proud, hands on his hips like some triumphant king returned from battle.

"What is this?" was all I could think to say.

"A gibbet," he answered as though I'd asked what manner of animal we'd treed. "Our ancestors used them often. They provide the guilty with plenty of time to think about their crimes, while sending a strong message to anyone else who might be fool enough to cross the local leader. They say even Boudicca used them when she terrorized the Romans." His voice reflected pride in being in such esteemed company.

"This is not the way of Camelot. This is not our justice. This is"—I searched for the right word—"barbarous." I scrutinized him, looking for any sign of the sweet boy I once knew. "I suppose you are the local leader with the message. Exactly what message would you send with this display of cruelty?" I gestured toward the dying priest.

"Camelot has a new leader now. One who will not stand idly by while guilty men get away with attempted murder and treachery. The gods demand justice for his actions, and that he shall get."

"You," I said slowly, "are a monster." I wheeled around and pulled out the dagger I always wore at my side. Trying to avoid looking at Marius, who was now opening and closing his mouth like a fish out of water, I followed the line of rope securing the cage in place to the base of a nearby tree and sawed at the knot.

"What are you doing?" Mordred demanded.

"No one should end their life this way," I answered as the first cord snapped and the cage swayed. "No matter what they have done."

"You cannot free him. He will die anyway."

"Perhaps." I grabbed the rope as the second cord snapped and sent the cage tilting wildly, then I fought for control as I lowered it to the ground. It hit the earth with a thud and Marius groaned. "I may not be able to save his life, nor in truth do I wish to, but I can offer him the quality that has always united Camelot and Avalon—mercy."

Mordred did not move to stop me as I pried open the door of the cage. Marius's wounds were far worse than I'd anticipated. Infected lash marks covered his back, indicating Mordred had had him tortured before throwing him in the gibbet. His skin was pocked where the birds had plucked out divots of flesh. I untied his bindings and slowly turned him over. Entrails protruded through gaps where the birds had had prolonged exposure to his body.

Marius was beyond sense now, trying to form words that would not come.

I placed a gentle hand on his forehead, willing him to focus on me. "Be still. Be calm. Your suffering is at an end." Despite all of my years of hating him, my eyes welled with tears and my heart bled pity for the broken man. "I may not know your god, but I know he would not condone this. The only thing I can do for you is assure you are quickly united with him. Do you understand?"

Marius's eye locked on mine and he whimpered. As I had on more battlefields than I could count, I took that for agreement.

"May your god be merciful to you. Leave this world in peace." I drew my blade swiftly across his throat, a trickle of red following in its wake.

He was so weakened, it took but a moment for Marius to breathe his last.

I wiped the blade on the grass, finding no vindication in his death, only a growing hatred of Arthur's son. "Do what you will with his body, but know this. If you string him up again, you honor his soul by allowing his bones to be picked clean and bleached by the sun, rather than rotting in a grave. *That* is the tradition of our ancestors."

⚬⚬⚬

The bishop's death only added to the rising anxiety of Camelot's people. Christian and pagan alike condemned the brutality with which he was treated, while fearing succumbing to the same fate under Mordred's increasingly brutal reign. Mordred was denounced from the pulpits of the Christian churches, and his name became anathema to those of the new faith. In Camelot and across Britain, priests urged Christian citizens to rise up against the usurper who'd martyred a man of the cloth.

I paid little heed to the clamor at first, believing it to be merely the rhetoric of rage that flares bright and hot but burns out just as quickly. We had seen such demonstrations of moral outrage before—such as when Arthur refused to either divorce me or denounce his marriage to Morgan, choosing instead to live with both of us—but they were usually words without much follow-through.

The first sign that this time was different came on a day in early autumn, a few weeks after Lughnasa. Earlier in the day, the Combrogi had arrested a handful of men for speaking out against Mordred in the market square, and six others had been detained for blocking the path of a party of Saxons come to meet with Mordred. But now as that meeting took place, all was calm.

I swatted a fly buzzing around my right ear, trying to pay attention to what Ida, King of the Saxons, was debating with Bors and Mordred, when a commotion in the courtyard caught my attention.

A man pointed to the west and gave the cry we all dreaded, "Fire!"

His voice carried clearly into the room, which erupted into chaos after a moment of stunned silence. Men and women jostled one another, some seeking immediate escape, while others crowded around the windows to try to ascertain the location of the fire.

I ran outside, dismayed to find smoke billowing from the western tower. By the time I'd crossed the massive courtyard and made my way to the foot of the tower, fire had consumed the upper floors. A bucket brigade tried in vain to douse the blaze, but it was slow, no match for the inferno raging above.

The hiss of flames set my palms sweating and my heart pounding. It was too soon since my own encounter with deadly flame. I fought the urge to cover my ears and cower as memories rushed at me from every side. My wrists raw from fighting the rope that bound them. The soles of my feet burning as the wood beneath them began to catch. The sulfurous odor of my hair catching fire as I leapt onto Lancelot's horse. I shook my head to clear it. This was not the time to give into fear. Someone could be hurt or dying and as a priestess I had a better chance of reaching them unharmed than anyone else.

"Is anyone inside?" I yelled to the people racing around me.

Either they did not hear or chose to ignore me.

I tried again, asking the same question of the man directing the line of volunteers snaking inside and up into the tower. "We don't believe so."

But they don't know for sure and I can't take the chance. Dropping my cape to the ground, I raced inside the tower, shoving aside well-meaning men who tried to stop me. They had forgotten I could control the elements and so could shield myself from the flames. I called upon Brigid as I raced up the stairs, seeking the source.

When the heat and smoke became too much, I mentally pushed outward, creating a pocket of clean air around me in every direction. I checked each room until I reached the end of the top floor. Only my chambers and Arthur's lay ahead, with his library above, connected by a short staircase only accessible from this room. I started to open

Arthur's door but stopped, sensing the pulsing heart of the fire within. Even with my training, entering while the fire raged unchecked would be dangerous.

I took a deep breath and sent my senses outward, searching for the nearest clouds. They were some distance out to sea, so I had to use the breeze to coax them in this direction, but that was easily accomplished. When they appeared on the horizon, I brought them together and drew them toward me. The sky darkened rapidly, wind whipping the flames into a frenzy. I raised my arms and brought them down swiftly, unleashing a torrent of rain. The fire hissed and sputtered as it fought the water, but it eventually gave in, curling in on itself only to expire in tendrils of steam.

Once the walls around me were no longer alight, I kicked in the charred remains of Arthur's door. Mordred had changed the room little since moving in when he ascended power. Here and there he had made it his own—the tusk of the boar he'd killed on the day he became a man hung on one wall, and the remains of his tunics dripped from their place inside a ruined wardrobe—but for the most part, it was as I remembered.

I ventured farther in, turning, seeking anything out of place. My gaze swept over the far side of the room, and I started. A large, black, man-shaped figure loomed from the shadows, and I swallowed down a rush of bile. If the perpetrator had been caught in here, he wouldn't have made it out alive. I took a few cautious steps closer and breathed a sigh of relief. The bulbous shape I had taken for a head was only the charred remains of a sheep's bladder attached to a wooden sparring dummy. I squinted. Around its neck was Arthur's torc, now melted into the wood, and the fabric draped over the form was the tattered remains of the ceremonial cape Morgan had gifted to Mordred when Arthur acknowledged him as his son.

My hand flew to my mouth. This thing had been dressed as Mordred and set ablaze. The fire was no accident then. This was a deliberate move against the acting king. Mordred's life was in danger. He had to be notified.

I stumbled down the stairs, drained from the shock and the effort of calling the rain. My shield from the fire had slowly slipped away, but I was out of danger.

When I emerged, a furious Mordred greeted me, water pouring from his cloak. "Are you mad? Who runs into a raging fire? What were you thinking?"

I smiled at him tiredly, leaning against one wall of the archway. "I am a priestess. I was in no danger."

"Are you sure?" Mordred brushed soot off of one of my cheeks and held up a burned strand of my hair. "Gods, Guinevere, I've already saved you from one fire."

I gestured to the scars on my face, arm, and leg. "Which is why I was unafraid of this one."

Mordred sighed heavily. "Sometimes I question the logic of Avalon in teaching you those tricks." He shook his head. "But I guess I should be grateful. It appears the worst is over." He gestured around us at the rain. "Will you please make this stop?"

I closed my eyes and thanked the gods and the elements for their aid. Then I commanded the rain to cease and swept my arms out in front of me, willing the clouds to disperse. The sky cleared.

"Mordred, you need to know something about the fire." He looked at me expectantly, so I hurried on. "It was not an accident. I found—I found an effigy of you in your quarters. It appears to be the source of the blaze."

Mordred stared at me, dumbfounded. "You're saying someone went through the trouble of building my likeness and setting it on fire in the very room where I sleep?" His voice rose in volume and tightness with each word.

I hadn't had time to consider the intimacy of the location. It meant that the person who did this was no stranger, but rather someone who had access to our innermost circle. Memories coursed through me of another time at Camelot, when someone had left a series of increasingly threatening notes addressed to me in private places, forcing me to live in fear. I fought back a wave of dizziness and nausea. This was different, but the feeling of violation was the same.

"Yes," I answered, putting a hand on his shoulder. "I am so sorry. But I thought you should be warned to be on your guard."

We left the volunteers to keep watch for any smoldering areas, and Mordred returned to the hall where nobles and other dignitaries were once again assembled. I slipped past, taking one of the side halls into the garden. When the door shut behind me, I breathed a sigh of relief before dashing to the stone bench beneath the apple tree at the center of the labyrinth. I collapsed upon it, finally letting go of the fear, tension, and anger that had fueled my fight against the flames.

Though my body gave in to exhaustion within the silent lullaby of this sacred place, my mind whirled, thoughts tripping over one another like water rushing over rapids. That had been far too close a call. Someone could have been hurt or even killed. Was that the point? Was this an assassination attempt gone awry? It certainly wouldn't be the first I had experienced, though I prayed it was the last. We were lucky that no one had been in that part of the tower when the fire began. Or had it been planned that way? It was no secret we were meeting with the Saxon leaders today. Perhaps this was more of a warning. Otherwise wouldn't they have attacked the hall?

Soon my spiraling thoughts eased, melted into oblivion by the morning light that filtered through the leaves of the apple tree, warming my face and slowly replenishing the well of strength within me. I dozed beneath its strong branches, grateful once again for Arthur's thoughtful gift of a protected place where I could gather myself in times such as these.

As I slipped in and out of sleep, I was vaguely aware of the birdsong around me. Perhaps that was why I dreamed a crow and a dove were fighting on the windowsill outside my room. But it was not the larger crow who was the aggressor. The cooing mourning dove aggressively raced at the crow, pecking at its chest, feet, anywhere it could reach. The crow cried out and I woke with a start.

I sat up from my slumped position and looked around. Something wasn't right. At first I thought I must still be dreaming, because the air around me was silent. Far too silent. Even the birds, whose coos and caws I had been enjoying only moments before, now refused to sing. I rubbed my arms as the tiny hairs stood at attention. Slowly, I scanned the space in front of me, ears attuned to even the slightest sound. I peered through branches and into shadows, but as far as I could tell, I was alone.

A shiver ran through me from neck to feet. It was time to return to the hall.

I had just emerged from beneath the canopy of the tree when a shadow moved on the outer wall. Someone was there. I could make out the silhouette of a man but did not dare move closer for a better look. A brief spark of light illuminated his face. It was one of the deacons from the Grail Castle. Before I could call out to him, he threw something toward me. It landed with the crash of shattering clay within the boughs of the apple tree. The upper branches burst into flames. Stifling a scream, I raced for the door leading into the castle.

"Run! There is another fire in the garden," I called to those inside. Following them toward the main entrance, I met up with Sobian. "Find Grainne and Morgan. I am too weak yet to douse this fire myself. They will be able to help."

She nodded and scurried off, but help never came. Eventually, word reached me that Grainne was still in Carlisle and no one could locate Morgan. By the time they did, it was too late. We had prevented the fire from spreading, but the labyrinth and gardens were destroyed.

As dusk fell, Mordred took me out on the walls to watch as a group of people in chains were herded into the courtyard below.

"Who are they?" I asked.

"Those responsible for today's fires."

"How do you know?"

"They admitted as much when my men found them. Christians to a one, they rejoiced, shouting that Camelot's last bastion of hell—your pagan labyrinth—was destroyed." He reached into a pouch at his waist and produced a broken piece of clay that looked like the neck of a bottle. "We found this among the ashes. It appears to be part of a bottle that was filled with oil. They stoppered it with an alcohol-soaked rag, which was lit on fire. When it broke against the trunk of the tree, it spread flaming oil everywhere."

From below, voices raised in protest as the guards led the perpetrators into the cells.

"You cannot arrest us for doing the Lord's work," yelled a bearded man I assumed was the rabble's leader. "We act in the name of King Arthur!"

"How can they claim to be working for Arthur when they have destroyed part of his capital and his home?" I asked.

Mordred rubbed the back of his neck. "They are also, apparently, organized against me. They don't like that I am a pagan. If they are the same group that burned that dummy, they don't like that I live either."

As if on cue, a woman yelled, "For Saint Marius!"

"Pray for us, patron saint of Britain," answered a man behind her.

So that was what Camelot had come to—arson,

incendiary weapons, and canonizing a monster. *Please, Goddess, let Arthur return to us soon.*

◦◦◦

We had little time to grieve our losses or even to rescue the remnants from the ashes before the fighting escalated. The following night, Mordred's supporters struck back, burning homes and buildings owned by known supporters of the absent king. But they didn't stop there. Fanning out into the countryside, they torched farms, slaughtered livestock, and destroyed crops, heedless of the consequences their depravity would have on all of Camelot's citizens. Come winter, we would all pay for their madness with shriveled bellies.

By dawn, the survivors were on our doorstep, their need turning the partially burned castle into a makeshift hostel. We set up beds in the great hall and sent the kitchens into festival-level day and night shifts of cooking. I split my time between helping Mordred and Morgan manage the chaos and providing healing to those injured in the attacks, as well as to others who normally did not have access to a healer. They were eager to tell their stories, to unburden their minds and hearts of the horrors of that night, telling detailed tales of cruelty and hatred directed against Arthur and his supporters.

"They will go any lengths to prevent him from ever sitting on his throne again," one man told me.

Outside, the whole town was buzzing, mobs forming

in the sodden, blackened streets. The fortress guards had their hands full trying to contain the crowds and keep violence from breaking out among rival factions. Their chants and demands reached us in Camelot's council chambers, where we were trying to sort through the mess Arthur's capital had become.

"This is not the way of Camelot," I said to the assembly. "Arthur and I founded this town on the ideas of peace and mercy, uniting our tribes, not fighting amongst ourselves." Though I was no longer officially part of the council, Mordred had asked me to join him in this meeting.

"Pretty words. But what do you propose we do to stop them?" Bors asked.

I glared at him but directed my words to Mordred. "Arthur left you king in his stead. You must make a public statement. The people riot because they are wondering whether the rumors are true. You must tell them once and for all whether or not you seek the throne."

"It is not a wise move, my lord, to turn against Arthur," Owain said. "I am told whatever message or bribery the bishop sent to Brittany before his death did its job. The war there is ending. Your father, the king, will return soon."

"Then we make our announcement now, gather what strength we can while Arthur is across the sea. That way we will be ready for him when he comes," Accolon said with conviction.

"*Are* you seeking the throne?" I asked Mordred. He had never been clear on that, preferring to let speculation play out.

Mordred was seated in Arthur's place of honor. Morgan sat in the throne of High Queen, a title which she had not been awarded, but she wore the mantle of power all the same.

"I have made certain alliances my father would deem foolish," Mordred said, choosing his words carefully. "We have at our disposal the armies of two powerful factions, should we choose to use them."

So he had allied with the Saxons and Picts. Mordred had previously admitted to learning from them, but he had given no sign how deep his diplomacy with them ran. Exactly what had he and Ida discussed in private when he was here? What negotiations had we not been privy to? Anything he would keep from the council had to be either illegal or unethical.

Bors must have been thinking along the same lines. "Tread carefully, my lord. Let us not forget what trusting the Saxons meant for the old tyrant Vortigern." He made a slicing motion across his neck. "Besides, I'll not fight along-side their filthy armies with their brutish women. Women are meant for the home, not the battlefield." He threw a poignant look at Sobian.

"Is that so? Well then, the next time I have the opportunity to rescue you, I'll pass you by. I've already saved you twice. That is enough," Sobian spat. "But Bors is right. The Saxons have been our enemies for sixty years. There is no reason to believe that if we ally with them now, they won't simply betray us like they did Vortigern."

"Ah, but we do have a reason to trust them," Mordred countered.

"And what is that?" I asked.

Mordred signaled to Accolon to open the doors. Elga stood on the threshold, her dark eyes shining with a powerful secret. A collective gasp went up from the crowd as warriors recognized their enemy from the battle of Mount Badon.

"What is *she* doing here?" Owain asked.

"She should have been killed on sight. An oversight that can be quickly remedied," Aggrivane said. He hand went to his side where his sword usually hung, as though he had forgotten all weapons were surrendered before each council meeting.

Mordred placed himself between them, but it was Elga who spoke, slithering past Mordred's shielding shoulder with a cruel grace Morgan would have envied. "You are still upset I evaded your pursuit after the war, I see. No matter. I would have killed you had we engaged, so it is better this way for us both." Her accent was still thick, but her mastery of our tongue was much improved.

Mordred turned to me, continuing our interrupted conversation. "I suppose it is time all of you knew the extent of my plans. My accord with the Saxons goes deeper than mere words. You see, Elga is my wife. We were handfast according to the traditions of both our peoples. The gods willing, we will soon be bound by blood." He patted her belly softly.

The silence that followed was so absolute that had it not been for the chanting of the protestors below, I would have thought myself back in that limbo between life and death. I stared at Elga, whose whole being radiated power. She was likely twice Mordred's age, but for all those years, she was still beautiful and could reasonably produce a few more heirs before her breeding time ended.

Aggrivane was the first to find his voice. "Is she to be High Queen then? We have never had a foreigner hold that title. You must know how upsetting it will be to the people."

"I am no foreigner," Elga countered. "I may have Saxon blood, but I was born on British soil. I would see my people rise to power, yes, but alongside yours. Badon taught me much, as I am sure it did you. The biggest lesson was that my first husband was wrong to try to annihilate you. My people are not ever returning to our ancestral lands and I know the fierceness with which you defend your homes, so we are at an impasse. We must learn to live side by side if we are to survive."

More pretty words. Elga couldn't be trusted any more now than the day I met her, the day she took the life of her newborn nephew. "How can we be sure the words you speak are not just lies aimed at softening our underbellies?"

Elga regarded me appraisingly. "You are wise to ask this, Queen Guinevere. I call you by your title for you still hold it according to our old ways. I will not ask you to pass it to me until after we have ascended to power. Only by my actions will you know my words are true."

Her actions? Which ones? Aiding in Mordred's rebellion? Engaging Arthur in another battle? "You are saying that by killing the king, you will prove to me you are not a traitor to Britain?"

Elga looked down, unconsciously fingering the blades hanging at her waist. "I hope it does not come to that. I would much rather live in peace with my husband's father."

"He will never accept you," Aggrivane sneered. "And neither do I." He rose, confronting Mordred. "No matter Arthur's trust in you, I cannot continue to serve a man who allies with Saxons. I will rejoin Arthur's army when he returns."

"Watch your back until then," Bors warned Aggrivane. "For you have just declared yourself an enemy of Mordred's crown."

"Indeed I have. But if you wanted to kill me, you would have done so years ago. You've had ample opportunity." He was in Bors's face now, pointing a threatening finger at his former brother-in-arms. "But if you wish, I will face you in single combat. I do not brook cowards, so don't even consider a sneak attack. We are all witnesses to your declaration, and I swear to you, if anything happens to me, there are men here who will hunt you down."

As if in agreement, Gawain and two of his friends drew their eating daggers, making a show of cleaning them on their tunics.

Owain bolted to his feet. "Stand down, all of you! We have enough factions at war outside. We do not need to create dissension among our ranks as well. I am not happy about Mordred's choice of wife, but I wish to hear him out. There is one question he has yet to answer. What about the Picts? How will you secure their loyalty?"

"Thank you, Owain. I have nothing so solid as a

marriage to offer you with the Picts, only a traditional alliance. We have been discussing how the borders of the ancient imperial walls hold no value in a world without Rome. Our agreement is based on the mutual understanding that when I become king, all the people of this island—Britons, Picts, and the tribes in between—will be one. I seek to expand north what my father started."

It was Sobian's turn to stand. "But first there must be a mighty battle to determine who is indeed king." She scoffed, disgust writ large in her features. "Neither you nor Arthur will have my sword. My girls and I will go seek our fortunes in Eire, where at least some bit of reason remains."

She signaled to her women scattered about the room, who detached themselves from the rest of the crowd. Without a word, they all headed for the door.

Sobian paused before me. "You are welcome to join us, but I know your heart lies across another sea. Call if you ever need me and I will return." She kissed my cheek and was gone.

My stomach lurched. As bleak as life in Camelot now was, if Mordred followed through on his plans, the future would be even darker. For all his playing at power, he was still relatively untested and idealistic, and so failed to grasp the repercussions of his bid for power.

"Mordred, have you fully considered the impact of your actions? Your intent is noble and it sounds reasonable in theory, but as soon as you let the Picts south of Antontine Wall, they will invade the Selgovae, Damnonii, and Votadini, who will then flee into Lothian, Bernicia, and on to Strathclyde. Do you really want them overrunning Camelot? Because it will happen. Look at the people who now call Camelot home after one night of insurrection. Can you imagine how much worse it will be when they are pursued by the Picts? Before you know it, you will be overrun with refugees and will have civil war on your hands, thanks to the prejudices against those living north of Hadrian's Wall."

Mordred sighed. "You are correct, but you are also thinking within old tribal rivalries. All of that will be gone under my reign."

I shook my head. "You are young and naïve. Do you really believe people will drop tribal allegiances they've held for thousands of years simply because you tell them to? You are merely giving them an excuse to harass each other in ways they've only dreamed of until now. Please, at least consider my words. I was High Queen for twenty years. I understand how our people think."

Mordred's expression softened. "I know that, and I respect your experience. It is one of the reasons why I keep you in close council. We have time yet before such things will take place. We can discuss them more later. But now"—he took Elga's hand and rose to stand beside her—"I have a populous to address."

As he strode onto the balcony, I slipped from the room with Aggrivane at my heels. I could not stay and listen to Mordred and Elga speak. The reaction of the crowd would be too painful, and it would be a betrayal of all I stood for to silently witness the shattering of the dream Arthur and I had created. But even the thick walls of Camelot could not shield my ears from the competing cheers and jeers that rose like an angry sea in the aftermath of Mordred's words.

Like it or not, we were in full-on rebellion.

Chapter Seven

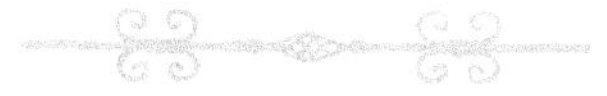

Spring 520

ime was running out.

The inevitable clash between father and son was drawing near. According to my latest communication with Pelles, Arthur and his troops were even now at sea, heading toward home. By the next full moon, they would no doubt be matched in pitched battle.

I set aside Pelles's letter with a sigh and looked out the window across the burned-out shell of the western tower, down to the village below, wondering if Arthur would even recognize his home when he returned. Though this day appeared no different from any other, with tradesmen, fishermen, servants, and soldiers all going about their daily lives, there was an undercurrent of tension in the air, as though we were under constant threat of a storm about to break. If we could feel it even here in the castle, how much more keenly must the villagers perceive it?

In the streets, clashes between warring factions were now the norm, even as Mordred's men struggled to keep order. Their exhaustion fed short tempers, causing Camelot's men to seek any release they could find. The barkeeps welcomed them with flowing ale and whores loved the uptick in business, but when the barrels ran dry and the women were all occupied, even the noblest of men resorted to beating his neighbor to a bloody pulp.

In the castle, things were little better. Aggrivane had already left to meet Arthur's party when they docked on the Lothian coast. If Owain could not make Mordred see sense, he was likely to follow. Bors spent his time whipping Mordred's followers into a froth by harping on the injustices done by Arthur and his men—some real, some spun out of whole cloth. Amid this tension, Morgan was strangely quiet, deeply withdrawn into herself, refusing to take sides between her husband and her son.

I was all but forgotten, which suited me fine. I had my own decision to make regarding the coming war. On one hand, Arthur was king and I his queen. But on the other, he had divorced me and declared my power void before seriously considering ending my life over my affair with Lancelot. Part of me still hated him. The other part could not bear to see our shared dream laid to waste.

I understood Mordred's ambition. After Arthur's role in my near-burning, many thought him unfit to rule, even if he was the victim of Morgan and Marius's machinations. Why should Mordred not step in? He could wait for Arthur to die, but Arthur's weakness and absence gave him the perfect opportunity to ascend while his father still lived. As he'd pointed out last time we spoke, he had been born for the throne, even before he knew he was Arthur's son. He had been raised by Uriens, King of Rheged, blessed with Morgan's cunning, learned statecraft from Owen, skills of the blade from Accolon, and was fostered by Lot, the realm's greatest strategist. Those things, combined with more than a decade at Arthur's side, made him a capable ruler.

Yet I could not offer my support to him either. For all his diplomacy and strategy, he was still a rash young man whose ambition could quickly get the better of him. He was so focused on becoming king, I doubted he ever gave a thought to what would happen once he was officially king and the ruler upon whom all of our lives depended.

A knock brought me back to the present. Mordred stepped into the room, a round board under one arm. "I hope I am not disturbing you."

"No, not at all. I was just thinking."

Mordred took a seat near me. "About the future, I am certain. It is on all minds these days."

I nodded.

When I did not elaborate, Mordred let the silence stretch between us. Finally, he pulled over a small table and set his circular board on it before arranging stones from a pouch at his waist into two triangles facing off across a field of wood. He sat forward, taking my hand. "I know it cannot be easy for you, being trapped between Arthur and me. You know I need your support for the people to accept me. You are Sovereignty herself. Those of the old faith will only back me with your blessing. But I know you also feel some measure of devotion to my father, in spite of all you've been through. It is my hope that these stones will show us where your loyalty should lie."

The same thought had crossed my mind, but I didn't want him to know that. "Then why not let me do it in private? What do you hope to gain from asking me to read these with you?"

"I simply wish to run the battle twice, once with your support and once without it. That will tell us if you are as important a factor as I believe you are." Mordred's attempts to sway me without being cruel or unjust were admirable. In that way, as in so many others, he really was his father's son.

"But you will also get a glimpse of how prepared Arthur is," I added.

"I did not say there would not be other benefits," he teased.

I exhaled a deep breath through my nose, looking at him, reluctant to succumb to his charm. "Only this once, and only because I see benefit in it as well. When I make my decision, you will stand by it, no matter what."

Mordred placed a hand over his heart. "On my honor, I do so swear."

I took a deep breath and closed my eyes, willing my whirling thoughts to still. Sending my being down deep, I sought the heartbeat of the earth. Focusing on my breathing, which settled to an even rhythm under such close scrutiny, I let all things go. Soon, there were no crying gulls circling outside, and even Mordred's presence became a memory.

I opened my eyes, focusing on the pieces, seeing in their place troops of men. Arthur and Mordred faced off in a grassy field bisected by a shallow river of quick-flowing, dark water. In the space of a heartbeat, the battle began, father against son, Saxon against Briton, Pict cutting down Combrogi. My hands directed the stones without my knowledge. The battle was fierce and bloody. In the end, not a single stone remained on the board.

Blinking away the trance that had overtaken me, I found Mordred staring at my cupped palms.

"Guinevere," he said slowly, reverently, "look at your hands."

I opened my palms to find the two red queens joined as though glued together. I forced them apart, examining the stones closer. They were red lodestone. That was why they were connected. They were naturally drawn together by their magnetic cores.

"This is not our battle," I said quietly to myself. "No matter who Morgan and I choose, the queens are set apart. Even should all fall in battle, we will survive." I set the two stones on the board, trembling in anticipation as they wavered, seeking to find one another again. Part of me knew what I was uttering was more than my human senses could perceive, but I was as powerless to stop it as the tides are to resist the moon. The two pieces snapped together again. "We are joined, in life, in death, in infamy."

"Is this my wife?" Mordred asked, indicating the queen

stone that belonged with his army.

"Or your mother. Both. We three have a fate beyond your own, one only we can fulfill."

We were silent for a time, both wrapped in private contemplation. Finally, whatever prophetic spirit had filled me fled, leaving me to piece together its meaning with a throbbing head and shaking body.

"So what is your answer?" Mordred asked, his voice clipped.

"I—I—what?" My thick tongue would not form words.

"Given what you have seen, do you support me or him?" Mordred's face was red, a vein in his forehead pulsing, just like Arthur's did when he was upset.

"How can you ask me that? You saw the outcome. It does not matter."

He brought his fist down on the board, making the pieces jump. "But it does. It means everything." He upended the board, bellowing, "Choose!"

I shrank back, more afraid of him in that moment than I had ever been, even when his cruelty toward Marius was revealed. *Be calm. This is nothing more than a display of temper. It will pass.* I breathed deeply. *He is a spoiled child who fears he may be denied his favorite toy, nothing more.*

I inhaled again then stood, looking him straight in the eye. "Long ago, before you were more than a seed in your mother's belly, I made a promise. I swore to watch over my people and guard them from all harm. That was my first vow. Those I made to Arthur, and any loyalty I may feel toward you as his son, are secondary. As you remind me,

I am queen, a woman above and apart. I cannot choose between the two of you any more than your own mother could. Fight your battles as you will, but with the gods as my witness, I wish no part in them." I turned on my heel, focused on the door.

"Where will you go?" he called after me, and I looked over my shoulder. "You have no one to take you in if I denounce you." He crossed to me in long, quick steps. "My father was merciful to you, and following his example, so was I. But once I become king, all of that can change. I will have the power to do with you as I will. I could sell you to the Picts as a slave, end your life with the snap of my fingers." His eyes brightened and he moved closer, his breath warm on my cheek. "Better yet, I know a certain Saxon woman who would take great pleasure in torturing you for the rest of your days." His words were directly in my ear now. "Think on that, my queen. I will give you one more chance. I want your answer by midnight."

⊚⊚⊚

Mordred's threats still rang in my ears hours later when I looked up from staring into the fire and found myself facing Elga. How long had she been standing there watching me? A shiver ran down my spine and I forced myself not to flinch. I would never show fear in her presence.

"I heard what my husband said to you earlier," she said by way of greeting. "He knows nothing. You were right. This is not your battle."

I stood, not wishing to give her the satisfaction of towering over me. Little good it did, for she was still two heads taller, but at least we were both on even ground. "You were spying on us?"

She shrugged, completely unapologetic. "I do what I must to know my husband's heart."

"You said this is not my battle. You wish me to side with Arthur then? Is that what you are saying?"

"Matters not."

A wave of nausea rolled through my stomach and I swallowed hard. Those were the exact same words she'd used years ago when we first met, just before she killed an innocent child. Despite my best efforts to hold it back, I shivered.

Elga perked up, as if sensing my discomfort, and sauntered over to the window, her movement making the silver tubes holding her blond curls rattle like wind chimes. "You are a powerful woman, but your time has passed, so who you back in the coming storm matters little. My husband says no one will accept us without your blessing, but he knows better. He would not have married me if he didn't." She turned to face me. "You see, I already have the loyalty of my people, and in the coming days, many of our enemies will fall by our swords. Those who remain can be controlled with or without you." She toyed with the line of daggers hanging from her belt, as if trying to decide which to select. "So we have no need of you."

"What then do you plan to do with me?" I asked. She could kill me on the spot if she so intended.

Elga's answering grin chilled my heart. "My husband was right that I would enjoy torturing you"—she removed a thin knife from her belt and inspected it, holding it up so it caught the slanting rays of late afternoon light—"but I am in no mood today." She pointed the blade at me. "You and I will do battle, mark my words, but this is not the time. You do not belong in Camelot anymore. You knew that when you ran to Lothian. So today I offer you a gift."

"And what is that?" I asked slowly, never taking my eyes from her knife in case I needed to evade its bite.

"Safe haven. Somewhere you will be protected until this battle is over."

"Why would you do that?"

"Have you not been listening? You are a liability to me. As long as you are here, some part of my husband will rely on you as queen. His devotion should be completely *mine*." She shoved the weapon back into its leather sheath with greater force than necessary to punctuate her point. "I will allow you to escape if you promise me one thing."

"What is that?"

"No matter the outcome, you will not seek to alter its course. You will let me rule in whatever way I see fit."

"If I refuse?"

"I kill you." Her voice was cold but even. This was a matter of political gain to Elga, not a personal one.

I stared at her a long time, weighing my options. If I stayed in Camelot and Arthur was victorious, would he believe I was innocent or that I'd backed Mordred? If he thought me guilty, I would be once again branded a traitor and he would seek my death. On the other hand, if Mordred won the war, he might keep me around until Elga was crowned. But after that, I was of no value, only a figurehead of a regime that no longer existed. Worse yet, I could be seen as an excuse for rebellion against him. Either way, my life was in danger. If he didn't end it, Elga certainly would. How had I gotten myself into this mess? Seeing no other alternative, I nodded.

Elga smiled. "Good. You may seek refuge at the convent of St. Peter. The abbess owes me a favor."

My eyes widened, cold sweat springing to my neck and back. Had I been duped? "But the abbess is—"

Elga's grin widened until it was more of a snarl. "My sister. You thought you were so clever, hiding her away like a precious jewel. It did not take me long to find her. But when I did, I realized she was of more use to me alive. And so she remains."

"Of use to you how?"

Elga shrugged. "All you need know is you both will be safe. You have my word."

What was that worth, the word of a Saxon who wanted to kill me? I could well be walking into a trap. But as she said, I had little choice. From holding all the power in the realm to being at her mercy, my descent had been swift.

"I am to journey alone, then? Is that not dangerous? Why not simply kill me now?"

Elga regarded me as though I was a simpleton. "My men will keep an eye on you from afar, but they cannot be seen escorting you from town. Too many questions. I have sworn my protection and that you will have. Now go. You leave tonight."

My jaw dropped. "Now? It is nearly sundown."

Elga flexed her hands at her sides, clearly growing agitated. "Have you forgotten you promised to share your allegiance with my husband by midnight? There is a place not far outside the city where you will spend the night. There you will at least be safely out of his grasp."

I had forgotten. "What will you tell him?"

"Leave my husband to me. Now, pack your things and be gone."

My feet automatically carried me out into the hall while my mind reeled with this sudden change of events.

"Oh, Guinevere," Elga called after me. "Do not forget. This is not farewell. We will meet again."

When I glanced at her over my shoulder, she was fingering one of her knives again. I swallowed. That was a promise—a threat—she fully intended to keep.

Chapter Eight

Sleet stung my skin as I approached the convent grounds, a small tract of land on the banks of the river Ouse. From behind a wooden fence, a small chapel rose with a forlorn frozen garden on one side, its long-dormant plants unresponsive to the gray light of dawn. Opposite, a long building attached itself to the church like a barnacle. Some distance behind, smoke rose from the open chimney of a kitchen.

The haunting melody of chanted prayer greeted me as the porter opened the gate in response to my ringing the guest bell. Without a word, the bent old woman motioned me inside and I followed her to the church door, the nuns' song growing louder with each step. Shielding my face from the biting wind, I gratefully stepped inside the nave.

Where I had expected darkness to rival the dreary day outside, I was greeted by light. Though the church wasn't large—five pairs of small pews each held three gray-clad sisters—and had only two small windows, one set high in each long wall, iron pillars filled with slender beeswax candles illumined each corner, filling the room with the subtle, sweet scent of honey. All attention was focused on the altar, which held a length of switch, its ruby thorns glowing bloody in the soft light, and a small equal-armed stone cross. Two fat candles held vigil on either side.

It was Lent, the Christian season for repentance. This austerity likely was symbolic of the shriving of sins and the penance each sister undertook this time of year. I had seen Arthur undertake the privations of Lent many times.

Though I did not share their faith, the beauty of their ritual stirred my heart. It had been a long time since my prayers were made out of anything other than desperation and fear. But here, with my body safe and warm, my spirit cried out for nourishment. As the sisters sang, I sank to my knees on the cold, hard floor, adopting the posture of submissive prayer used on Avalon, arms crossed over my heart, head bowed to the ground. Abandoning my bag of provisions at my side, I touched my right thumb to my forehead, lips, and heart, and prayed.

My thoughts were no better than a jumble of yarn, tying itself ever tighter with each passing thought. I had to start over several times before my mind produced anything intelligible. But I was able to offer a quick word of thanks to the goddess Ellen for a safe journey and a supplication that Morrigan would keep Arthur and Lancelot safe before my mind went galloping off again.

Nevertheless, the Goddess seemed to understand my heart, and as if in response to my prayers, a vision flashed before my eyes. Arthur and Lancelot were safely back in Britain. But Arthur was not in Lothian, nor was he heading for Camelot. He stood in the courtyard of Cadbury, watching Lancelot train a group of men on how to use the saddle with the stirrup in the nearby stables. That could only mean Arthur intended to mass his supporters at Cadbury and lead a march on Mordred.

Gods, preserve us from an attack on Camelot. Do not allow this foolish quarrel over power to further destroy what we worked so hard to build.

I raised my head only when the chanting came to an end. The sisters, their faces obscured by heavy black veils, filed solemnly out a side door and soon, only one woman remained. Even before she turned, her plump shape and the strands of curly blond hair peeking out from the bottom of her veil gave away her identity.

The years had been kind to Mayda, revealing her to be a beautiful woman who would always retain a hint of her childhood innocence. Her face, covered in Lenten ashes, was still round, but it had gained sleek angles from simple living, along with the ghost of lines at the corners of her eyes and mouth. Away from the cares of her tribe and dedicated to God in a place of safety, she now appeared far younger and healthier than her battle-worn sister. Clad in the black robes of the abbess, she radiated gentle power and confidence, much like the Lady of the Lake.

I rushed to embrace her. "Mayda! The gods be praised

you are well."

Forewarned I would be arriving, she was not surprised but radiated joy at our reunion. She clasped me with great affection. "Thanks to you and your husband. You gave me a great gift the day you assigned me here. I only wish I could have seen it at the time."

I pulled back, regarding her from head to toe but not letting go of her shoulders. "How are you? I see you have done much with your time here." I gestured to her robes.

Her smile was as radiant as I remembered. "I took your advice to heart. When I was young, my family tirelessly reminded Elga and me that we were meant to lead. They thought we would oversee our husbands' tribes, but here I have found a different kind of family to lead. It can be difficult, but it is all worth it when done in His service." She flicked her gaze meaningfully to the cross on the altar. "Truly, you and Arthur gave me the most loving, loyal spouse I could ever ask for. He may be invisible, but He treats me much better than any earthly man ever would."

Having seen the brutality of the Saxons, especially those who clawed their way into power, it wasn't difficult to believe she was right.

Mayda put an arm around my shoulders, directing me toward the altar. "Come, let me show you our dearest treasure." When we stood directly in front of the altar, she lifted the stone cross off its base. Only then did I see the center was adorned with a shield of glass. Behind it, small yellowed bits of what appeared to be bone and hair rattled with her movements. "These are the bones of the blessed

St. Peter and the hair of the missionaries who died protecting them. We hold them in our prayers every day, asking that their blood make us stronger in our faith." Her eyes gleamed with pride.

Bishop Marius had told us of the veneration which Christians paid to the bodily remains and sometimes possessions of their saints, especially those who'd given their lives for their faith. It was a popular practice on the Continent, but I had no idea it had spread here.

"How did you come upon these? Did not your St. Peter die in Rome? If so, they are far from their home."

Mayda's cheeks colored under the soot. "You are correct. They were a gift." She studied the rushes at her feet. "From my sister." Then looking at me, she continued. "The missionaries who brought these here from Rome had the misfortune of setting foot in our kingdom. This was only a short time after Badon. Our people were hungry to exact revenge, so they took it out on those who sought to change their ways. Relics such as these mean nothing to my people. But Elga was well aware of why the Christians so vigorously defended them. She saw an opportunity to gain sway over the convent and took it. After stripping the relics from their gold container, Elga sent these to us as a sign so I would know she was aware of my fate. She is now considered a great patroness, a protector, because they are a source of income from pilgrims, in addition to providing spiritual grace."

I wrinkled my brow, trying to piece together her story. "How did Elga know you were here? We were so very careful." Apology lay heavy in my voice, making it unsteady.

Mayda shook her head. "It was nothing you did. Elga is far more intelligent than anyone would think. A convent known to take in Saxon women was certainly not the first place she looked for me, but it was not low on her list either. How she figured it out matters little. When I was elected abbess, I think she believed she could control the convent, and with us, the whole of York. I told her I would rather meet the same fate as the martyrs she'd created than help her gain control of the country, even just this small part. We pose no threat to her, so for now, she does nothing, lest she appear as a tyrant." Mayda took a deep breath. "I have no doubt the day will come when she is queen and I will fall to her blade, just as she always intended, but at least now it will be for a greater cause. I will be defending my faith and my home and I will be certain the others are safe. I have made my peace with my fate."

I swallowed hard, my throat constricting with guilt. All Arthur and I had wanted to do was keep her safe, yet it looked as though we'd inadvertently condemned her to a martyr's death. "I pray it does not come to that."

She smiled. "So do I. But until that day, it is my duty to keep my sisters safe and help them grow in faith." She glanced over her shoulder toward the side door. "Speaking of which, we should probably join them in the refectory. No one may begin eating until the abbess is present."

I followed her into the gloom, already missing the brightness of the church. A handful of sisters were standing around the frozen well, chipping at the surface with a rock. When Mayda approached, they backed away respectfully to allow her access. She dipped her hands into the cold water and splashed it on her face, washing away the ashes, before drying her face with the hem of her gown. I did the same, starting at the shock of cold but relieved to remove some of the grime of the road, even if it meant my cheeks went numb in the process.

Inside the refectory, the sisters had removed their veils. The ashes were gone too, having served their ritual purpose. Mayda led me to the head of a long table, where she sat with great ceremony. She whispered to one of the sisters at her side, who promptly offered me her seat. There were no others open, so she sat on the floor.

"Please," I said to the sister, "that is not necessary—"

Mayda silenced me with a look. "They know who you are and welcome the humility of giving up what they can to the queen."

The sisters spoke little during the simple meal of bread, cheese, and thin broth, and when they did, it was in their native language. The mulled wine served to me by Mayda and the elder sisters warmed my heart and spread through my veins, leaving me feeling fuzzy and more loved than I had in months. The younger ones, who I guessed from the color of their habits were still in training, much as we had been in Avalon, had to make do with watered ale. Many of the sisters glanced at me curiously, and I smiled in response. To a one, they dropped their eyes to their plates.

Mayda noticed and whispered to me, "They will protect you in any way needed. Have no fear."

After the meal finished and they recited a Latin prayer,

a small bell chimed. Chairs scraped noisily as the sisters hurried to their various duties.

Mayda took my hand. "Come, I will show you to your room." She gestured to the sister who had given up her seat. "Sister Magdalena will serve you. Do not hesitate to tell her of anything you may need."

I glanced from sister to abbess. "That is not necessary. I can fend for myself."

"Nonsense," Mayda replied, her tone indicating the subject was closed.

Sister Magdalena bowed. "It is my great honor, my queen, Mother Abbess."

I leaned in close to Mayda. "Am I to address you as such? I wish to pay you due respect."

"No, you may call me Mother Mayda. You are under no vows and need not make obeisance to me."

From the refectory, which was attached to the kitchen, we trudged through the increasing sleet, careful not to slip on the ice forming underfoot. Once inside the long building attached to the chapel, Mayda led us down a long main hallway to a room near the main church.

"These are our guest rooms," she said. "They are far enough away we should not disturb you with our routine, but close enough should you wish to join us."

When we entered the room to which I was assigned, Sister Magdalena watched me expectantly, eyeing the small pack of belongings I set on the bed.

I smiled softly at her. "I can see to my own things. I wish to rest a while, so you may go about your normal duties."

Mayda nodded. "Sister Magdalena will fetch you when it is time for our late meal, if that is agreeable."

With my assent, both women turned to leave.

"Mother Mayda?" I called. "Is it safe to correspond from here? I would like to be in touch with those who might give me a better idea of what is taking place in the rest of the kingdom."

Her smile was benevolent. "Of course. I will have my messengers on standby should you need to send communication urgently. Though I would advise not to use your true name. Is there another by which those whom you address would know you?" Before I could answer, she laughed. "Oh, I remember now. Corinna. Is that right?"

I squeezed her hands. "It is. It appears the situation is reversed. I am now in your care."

She returned the gesture. "As it should be. God always gives us the opportunity to repay a kindness. May He, by whatever name you call Him, bless you. Rest now."

∽◌ ♋◌∾

Mayda's way of life was not very different from the one I'd lived for four years in Avalon, which surprised me greatly. It had its own rhythm and rituals but provided the same comfort and stability I'd found so soothing during my formative years.

While exploring my room that first afternoon, I'd come across a tiny door in one wall, no bigger than my hands held side-by-side. When I pulled cautiously on its curled handle, it revealed itself to be the shutter to a small barred window overlooking the church. If I knelt, it was even with my head, affording me a bird's-eye view of all that took place below.

When I asked Mayda about it that evening, she told me it had been installed before she arrived for a holy woman who was often ill but still wished to attend Mass. The height was measured so that she could only view the service if she was in the proper posture for prayer. Mayda said although I could not attend their rituals, I was more than welcome to observe from there. After the saintly sister died, when Mayda was still new to the convent, she spent much time in that room, and it was those hours of quiet contemplation that led her to embrace the Christian faith.

Through that same window, I was able to observe the rites of Lent during the fortnight of Passiontide, a solemn time leading up to Easter, the holiest of days for Christians. All of the sisters arose at dawn and dressed in simple white robes. Even though the air was cold and the ground covered in heavy frost, they processed around the church barefoot, each holding a single yew branch, singing Hosanna, before entering and taking their places around the perimeter of the room.

In many ways, they resembled our Candlemas procession so many years before. Grief tugged at my heart as I recalled that day—Isolde's joyous smile on her favorite feast day and Elaine's humble expression as she took up the role of the bride. They were both gone now, victims of fates too cruel for their few years, too awful for hearts so in need of love.

My eyes stung with tears, but soon it was not the ritual nor the faces of my remembered friends that passed through my mind. Instead, I felt the dizzying sensation that meant the sight was upon me. I tried to fight it, but it would not relent. Long ago, the Lady of the Lake had warned me the sight would be out of my control when one whom I loved was in danger. It was a cruel trick of the Goddess, to show me that which I was powerless to control, but I had long ago made my peace with it.

Arthur was alone on the ramparts of Cadbury, his expression set in grim lines as he watched a shadow wash over the horizon, heading straight for the castle. The wave of soldiers did not slow or part, showing determination to engage their king, and leading the way was Mordred.

"All the while I loved you, I also feared you, cursed as you are with your mother's lust for power," Arthur said to his son, who was barely distinguishable from the nearing horde. "I prayed this day would never come, but God did not heed me. My only prayer now is we can turn you away while your heart still beats." His eyes welled, but he did not allow the tears to fall.

Lancelot approached Arthur from behind, and I gasped, unaware he had returned to Britain.

Arthur must have sensed his approach, for he cleared his throat and turned before Lancelot could speak a word of greeting. "You have no business in this battle. Go to Camelot. Find Guinevere and show her I am a man who keeps his word, no matter what she may believe. I will deal with my traitorous son."

They bickered for some time, Lancelot insisting on offering his sword in repayment for the offences he'd committed against Arthur, but Arthur's insistence prevailed.

"You have more than repaid your debt by your valor on the fields of Brittany. I promised Guinevere a new life with you and that I shall deliver, even if it is my final gift to her. Go now. Send Kay to me."

Reluctantly, Lancelot departed. Kay appeared soon after.

This time, Arthur did not turn. "I have no desire to mar this fort by placing it at the center of a war. We will meet them on the banks of the river, press in before they expect us to engage. In that way, we can hope to throw them off."

"Our troops can be ready within a few hours. Mordred will not have gained the river by then."

"Good. I wish them to know their rightful king was expecting them."

With those words, my eyes grew dim and the sight left me.

ᔬᔊ ᔊᔬ

At dawn, I helped the lower-ranking sisters scrub the floors of the church after morning prayer, our bare feet freezing on the cold, wet stones. While we did this, Mayda and the sisters of higher rank stripped the altar of its beautiful cloths and lovingly washed it, preparing it for the rituals to come.

Later, they gathered in the church for Mass and I watched from my room above. Their priest blessed a vial of healing oil then invited the poor of the area to come forth. The sisters humbly washed their feet in imitation of a gesture performed by their Christ before his death. Mayda followed on her knees, kissing the feet of each man and woman before giving them a loaf of bread, flagon of wine, and bag of coins.

Years earlier, when I was a ward in the house of Corbenic, its lord, Pellinor, had performed similar service to the poor of his lands on Candlemas. Looking back, I missed that time and those people. Though often infuriating and perplexing, in retrospect, my years with him, Lyonesse, Isolde, and Elaine were a blessing, shielding me from the struggles of the outside world. Yes, Lyonesse could be cruel, but that was little enough sacrifice in the face of what we would experience in the years to come.

Bowing my head, I prayed. *Thank you, God and Goddess for everything that family taught me. Please bless those of their line who still live and may those who have died be at peace.*

Eyes closed, the sight came upon me again.

True to his word, Arthur's army stood in wait as Mordred's troops poured out from wooded tracts into the open fields sloping down toward the River Cam. The unexpected sight of the opposing wall of warriors slowed their progress, eventually forcing them to halt.

The curving river, with its steep banks, was the only thing separating father and son. Slowly, as if each trying to each decide their own strategy, Arthur and Mordred picked their way through their men until they were facing one another across the narrow waterway.

Arthur made the first move. "I have offered you my

hand in peace time and again since returning from Brittany, only to find you with an army raised against me. One final time, I do so again. I do not wish to move against you, son, but make no mistake, I will if you press on. Greater men than you have resisted my requests for peace and lost their lives for their folly. I would hate to see the same happen to you."

A puff of warm, disbelieving breath in the frigid air was Mordred's first response, followed by a haughty, "It will not, for I have in my employ forces stronger than you have ever faced, men who believe you have wronged this land, abandoned it in the wake of your own selfish missteps. We will not bow to you when a new king is needed, one who will rule this land for all its inhabitants, not just those of native blood."

Behind him, the Saxons and Picts cheered, taking up a steady tattoo with their cudgels and shields.

Arthur ignored them, unfazed by their attempts at intimidation after so many battles. He walked down river to a place where the water narrowed, banks nearly hugging one another, and Mordred followed like a mirror image. "You may believe you fight for something bigger, but this battle is between you and me. As you will not back down, I will offer you one more opportunity to spare the lives of your men and mine. We fight now in single combat, King Stag and rutting buck. Let the gods and our skills determine the outcome."

Mordred studied his father with cold blue eyes, appearing to turn the option over in his mind. Then he laughed. "Do you truly believe that would solve anything? My death would only mean further incitement of my army, whereas yours would mean the crumbling of a nation, and for what? You cannot stop this, Arthur Pendragon. A new era has begun."

For a moment, Arthur's face betrayed his disappointment, but then he bowed his head, muttering a prayer too quiet for anyone else to hear. When he raised his face again, it bore the hard lines of a seasoned warrior. "May the gods have mercy on us all."

The armies slammed into one another with a series of deafening cracks as shields split and spears found their targets, breaking through bone to lodge in the soft tissue beneath. The carrion birds alighted in treetops and amid the trampled grass as bodies fell, turning the river into a mass grave. Soon, soldiers used the bodies of their fallen comrades to cross the breech and face their attackers in units, rather than one by one.

But when the fighting was at its thickest, Mordred did something unexpected. He turned and ran, leading his troops north toward the Midlands. Arthur was not long in catching on, pulling the greater part of his troops from the fray to give chase.

Suddenly, I was back to myself again, lying on the floor of my small room in the convent, panting and covered in sweat from the exertion of my visions. I lay on my back, staring at the wood support beams overhead, trying to understand what I had seen. The rebellion had begun. But why did Mordred not finish it there? Why run? He was obviously not retreating. His movements were too orderly, too planned. It seemed there had been a prearranged signal, some sign that told certain contingents when it was time to follow him away from the battle. But why?

I sat up, fighting a wave of dizziness. I pulled myself to the ewer of wash water and poured some into the basin, willing it to cleanse me of my fear and anxiety as I removed the layer of sweat from my skin and struggled to regain my senses.

For a while, I watched the convent's ritual, thankful for the distraction from my visions. The sisters' voices floated up as they celebrated the Mass, their songs joyful in the triumph of their Savior, yet tinged with sadness, for the worst was yet to come—for their God and for Arthur.

When Mass ended, all the candles in the church were extinguished, save one many-armed candelabra, plunging the congregation into near total darkness. I pinched out the wick of my candle as well, wishing to experience the ritual as they did. The sisters' songs turned to mournful dirges as the priest recited a story about their Lord being betrayed by his closest friend and handed over to the authorities to be tortured and condemned. One by one, the remaining candles were extinguished, until only a lone flame remained.

The church was silent, the crowd seemingly holding its breath in expectation. I scooted closer to my small window, trying to take in everything with heightened senses.

The clear voice of a young boy rang out from the north, intoning "Kyrie Eleison," a plea to their God for mercy. Then the bell-like voice of a sister responded from the south, "Christe Eleison," which meant much the same. The blending of their voices into a mournful chant raised goose pimples on my arms as they repeated the invocation.

Swept up in the chant, my prayers turned to pleas of mercy. *May the gods of war grant us mercy. Protect our king and his heir from all harm and help them see the senselessness of their battle. May they find a path to peace and spare our people the pain and privations of war.*

With two kings pitting the armies of three nations against each other, we needed any help the heavens were willing to provide. Were I there with Arthur, following Mordred's army north, perhaps I could advise him, but here in this convent, so many miles north and east of them, I could do nothing. Well, not nothing. I could pray, just as I was doing. But it felt like so little. I could not defend Arthur with my sword, or try to make them both see sense. I was powerless, for even my magic could not help them. I could not help Arthur strategize or even read the stones for him. He and Mordred were beyond my reach. All I could do was watch through eyes cursed with the sight as it all played out.

Below, in the chapel, the single flame was extinguished. From the west, the deep rich bass of a man's voice sang, "Christ is dead," three times. I shivered, certain to my core that soon a similar elegy would be sung for either the High King or his son.

›‿•‾‹

The rituals did not end each night, but rather they faded into silence before picking up again at the prescribed time, as they would each day until Easter. In the time between, the sisters communicated only as necessary through a series of hand signals similar to those we used during our period of silence just before being consecrated as priestesses in Avalon.

The familiarity made me long for my days on that blessed isle, for the kinship and sisterhood these nuns clearly felt and that I had once known. Though I was surrounded by women, my heart ached with the hollow void of loneliness. I wished I had someone here in whom I could confide about my visions, who would understand the frustration, the utter helplessness of watching something tragic and pointless you could not change. But if I told them, the sisters would surely think me as demonic as that damn bishop Marius had.

The snow and ice prevented me from worshiping outdoors and I could not face being alone in my tiny cell, so on the night of the new moon, I slipped into the back of the chapel, intent on performing my own rituals while the sisters sang and adored the bare cross placed before their altar. I searched the shadows for a place I would go unnoticed. To my right was a small alcove with a statue of the Lady Mary. Normally serene and welcoming, tonight she was an ominous specter with her black shroud.

I could not believe I was even considering confiding in her, the mother of a god in whom I had no faith. But yet, how different was she from the myriad of goddesses to whom I had prayed before? Wasn't she the same woman, called by a different name? Was she a being like Deichtine, Cú Chulainn's mother, who, while incarnate on this earth, was singled out by her god for a special purpose?

It was not as if goddesses giving birth to heroes was a new idea, or even one confined to the Christians. Taliau was the mother of Lugh; Dôn had given birth to Arianrhod and Gwydion, all of whom I worshiped, so why could I not pray to Mary? I had no interest in the redemption offered by her son, so I was in no danger of abandoning my faith. I was simply adding another goddess to my pantheon, something my forebears had been doing for hundreds of years.

The previous night at dinner, after the sisters had covered the statues with a thick black cloth—a tradition of their faith I found rather odd—I had asked Mayda about the statue and the woman it represented. "How does she relate to your people's faith? Did you have trouble accepting her when you were new here?"

Mayda had answered through a mouthful of hard bread, the only daily sustenance until Easter. "No, not really. She is much like our goddess Ostara, who gives fertility to the land and its people. Her feast day is usually close to Easter." She scooted a little closer to me in her seat. "We would never tell the bishop, but the flowers we lay at her feet on Easter are less to gladden her heart at the resurrection of her son than they are to honor her. We still hold our families' traditions in our own ways."

Mayda's honesty warmed my heart, a comfort I carried with me now as I contemplated Arthur's conversion to Christianity, and then Morgan's. Had she found this goddess and accepted her as one and the same as those we'd worshiped as part of the rites of Avalon? Early during my time in Pellinor's house, I had noted the similarities between his faith—with its Host that so resembled the full moon and its rituals that invoked the elements in incense, water, candles, and bread and wine—and my own. Even some of this Christ's teachings were like those of the Druids. And now there was this Mother goddess. Had Morgan been able to look beyond the names and see enough of Avalon in this new faith?

If so, she was indeed a wiser woman than I, for there were aspects of this Christian world I could not accept. No matter what Mayda and her sisters may believe in secret, their faith still forbade the ancient gods, who were in so many ways our tie to the land and to our ancestors. Pious bastards like Marius made certain women had little place in or influence on the faith—and that they would never be worshiped in any proper way. Plus, I would never be able to believe we needed to be saved, much less that the death of one man could achieve such a monumental task. I believed in right and wrong and had seen both tremendous good and horrific evil, but the idea that one man's sin, brought about by a woman—of course—so long ago could be the reason why we did wrong today was hard enough to believe and then to tell me that the torture of one man, god or not, undid all of that and made it tolerable for me to do wrong, so long as I asked forgiveness for it, was simply too much. Father Dyfadd and I had had many rounds of debate on these points when I sought to understand Arthur's faith, but to no avail.

I gently removed the material that covered the statue,

setting it aside so I could recover it before any of the sisters knew of my transgression. There she stood in blue robes so much like my own as a priestess, beckoning me to know her as another Lady of Avalon. I lit a candle with the flint and fire steel I'd brought from my room. Setting the candle before the statue, I gave the sign of Avalon and looked into the Lady's hollow stone eyes.

"Great Mother, called by many names, hear this priestess who requests your aid. Safeguard our king, he whom my heart holds so dear—" My words stopped as the sight took over.

I was riding with Arthur, Kay, and the Combrogi at a hard pace, still giving chase to Mordred. The land there was flat, grazing pastures and farmland as far as the eye could see. We were about a day or two's ride from Cadbury, in the heart of Salisbury. We rode for what felt like hours and the land subtly changed, sprouting trees at intervals, until we were once again in forested land. Somewhere nearby, a river or brook trickled.

"We need to rest the mounts soon, or they will falter," Kay advised.

"Agreed. I wish I'd known that little cur was going to lead us on a hunting expedition. I could have sent word to Powys to prepare new mounts, extra soldiers, anything." Frustration colored Arthur's voice over the pounding of the hooves.

Where was Mordred leading them and why?

"We'll find him, Arthur, and when we do—" Bedivere never got to finish his thought, because he was slammed sideways off his horse.

"Ambush!"

The cry went up from the head of the line and was quickly echoed to those at the rear, but not before Mordred's army descended, larger and more heavily Saxon this time, if the weaponry was any indication.

Arthur hacked a line through the onslaught, laying low man and woman alike. I didn't need the sight to know he was on a mission to get to his son and end the violence once and for all. But if Mordred was in the fray, he was well hidden. No doubt this attack had been orchestrated to inflict maximum damage on Arthur's army while keeping Mordred at a safe distance. For all anyone on the battlefield knew, Mordred had already retreated to some hideaway and was watching the battle unfold through his mother's second sight, just as I was doing now.

One member of the Combrogi fell, then another. Owain was badly wounded, but fighting on. Gareth and Garheis were not so fortunate, brothers to the bitter end. Gareth perished defending his younger sibling, their limbs tangled in death, eyes glassy and staring, their souls fleeing to the safety of the Otherworld.

As blood spurted from hacked away limbs and the agony of death throes filled the air, I had a moment of lucidity where I was grateful to be only witnessing this horror. Yet my hand involuntarily reached for the sword that slept on the cold floor beneath my pallet in my room above, my warrior's instinct aiming to protect those I held dear.

For several moments, the chanting sisters filled my ears

with the lamentations of their God. *"I led you out of Egypt, from slavery to freedom, but you led your Savior to the cross."*

And then the visions and sorrowful voices mixed.

My attention was drawn not to Arthur but to Aggrivane, who was battling a large Saxon wielding a spear and a sword simultaneously. Aggrivane was on the defensive, backing away as the Saxon poked his spear at Aggrivane's guard, then sought an opening with his sword. Even without a shield, the Saxon evaded all of Aggrivane's attempts to wound him, only snarling in pain when a Combrogi saw the situation and stabbed the Saxon's sword arm from behind, severing the main muscle in his shoulder.

"For forty years, I led you safely through the desert. I fed you with manna from heaven, and brought you to a land of plenty; but you led your Savior to the cross."

Aggrivane took advantage of the Saxon's pain to slash out, tearing the Saxon's leather chest plate, but otherwise inflicting no damage. If he could repeat the move, the Saxon would be dead. Aggrivane circled around, seeking another moment of inattention as he and his ally took on the ox of a man now snorting like a raging bull. Aggrivane lunged, burying his sword in the soft part of the Saxon's side, just above his hip bone.

But he was too late. The Saxon had seen an opening too.

"What more could I have done for you? I planted you as my fairest vine, but you yielded only bitterness: when I was thirsty you gave me vinegar to drink, and you pierced your Savior with a lance."

Aggrivane's eyes went wide and his mouth twisted

into a wicked grimace. The Saxon's spear had caught him low, probably in the belly, and the wound forced him to the muddy ground. Men blocked my view, so I only saw flashes of his face as he grimaced and twitched in pain, hands wrapped around the shaft of the spear as his life-blood poured onto the unforgiving ground. The next time I caught sight of him, his head had lolled to the side and his hands were slack, chest no longer heaving.

"I raised you to the height of majesty, but you have raised me high on a cross. My people, what have I done to you? How have I offended you? Answer me!"

My scream ripped through the worlds, and for a moment, the battle ceased. Each soldier stood frozen, heads and eyes turning to locate the source of the unearthly sound. Some crossed themselves, while others made the sign of Avalon, and a few ran away in terror. For three breaths, everyone was silent and motionless, paying respect to a pain that rattled through the core of each man. Then the battle began again as though nothing untoward had taken place.

Back in the chapel, my body crumpled, reacting to the trauma of what I had seen before my fragile mind caught up. I clawed at the statue's feet as though she could save him, as though by hanging on to her, I could will Aggrivane back to life.

Her serene face was the last thing I saw before my sight shattered into a blinding field of stars, their white heat painful to behold in the blackness that sought to consume me. I grasped my head, unable to see, crippled by the pain turning my blood to ice. I was crying, I had to be, for the neck of my sleeping gown was wet and my chest muscles were spasming in time with my heart. How it still beat, I did not know. I could barely draw breath.

Mayda's strong arms gripped me beneath the shoulders as she and Sister Magdalena lifted me from the floor and carried me past the faces of startled sisters. I gave into the pain, senseless.

I woke in my cell, retching before I was even fully conscious, but Mayda was there, holding a bowl beneath my mouth, supporting my shoulders and holding back my hair. When I was finished, stomach muscles cramping, too weak even to lift my head, she placed a cool cloth on my forehead and squeezed my hand. That small gesture was all that kept me from giving up completely. I wanted to sleep and never wake, to join Aggrivane in the Otherworld. I had been there once; the transition was easy. All I had to do was will it. But the warm reassurance of her hand was like a cord tying me to this world.

Weary, I looked at her. Mayda's lips moved in whispered prayer.

When she noticed I was awake, she smiled. "I will be with you as long as you need me. No matter how long it takes for the pain to stop." She wrapped me in her arms, holding me like a child.

"How did you know I would need you?" I asked weakly.

"Do you think the Britons are the only ones gifted with the sight?"

I had never considered the possibility of Saxon women having it too.

"I do not have the gift, but I have seen it many times, so I knew what to expect. I know you are tired, so I will not trouble you with questions, save one. The rest you can tell me when you are ready." Her gaze met my eyes, which hadn't stopped pouring since the visions ended, making certain I understood her. "Does our king live?"

I nodded weakly.

She breathed a sigh of relief. "Good. Then we will redouble our prayers. Our good Lord cannot fail to hear us in this holy season."

I envied her confidence, her faith. My Goddess had abandoned me, never to return, or so said the impenetrable cloud in my heart. I knew little of Mayda's god, but if he made Arthur's victory possible, I would seriously consider following him.

෴ ෴

Two days later, thanks to Mayda's expert ministrations, I was strong enough to be on my feet, though I did not leave my cell. Mayda had been called away to the visitor's parlor for a meeting with King Cuncar, ruler over York since its capture by the Saxons decades before, and his archbishop. Why were they here? Could they possibly know Elga had sent me here? When I'd voiced my concerns to Mayda, she assured me they simply wished to make certain everything was in place for the town's celebration of the Holy Week, in which the convent played a large role.

With Mayda occupied and the other sisters wrapped

up in preparations for the upcoming solemnity, I had a stretch of much-needed time to myself to think through all that had happened. I sat on the small bed, elbows on my knees, head in my hands. What had happened to Arthur after my visions ended? Surely he could not be dead. If the Goddess had chosen to show me Aggrivane's last moments, she likely would have done the same for Arthur, so he had to be alive. If he had been defeated, Mayda would know by now. Surely word would have come and the Saxons would be rejoicing.

I sighed, flopping back on the bed, eyes on the sloping timber ceiling, willing myself to think through the situation as I had been trained. There had been heavy losses on Arthur's side. That much was certain. Many of his best men had died. I forced the image of Aggrivane lying still amid the carnage out of my mind. Those who had survived would have taken shelter somewhere nearby—wherever that was.

Would Morgan have chosen Arthur or backed her son? How does one make such a choice? I shook my head. I'd been down that line of thought before, and it had no clear answer. Only she could say where her loyalties truly lay. Even without her, chances were good the army had picked up some camp women. Hopefully some of them were priestesses and could help aid the wounded.

And what of Mordred? Surely his army had suffered losses as well. But then how had they gained in number since their attack near Cadbury? Mordred had to have back-up units supplying fresh men and horses. That meant he wasn't fleeing from Arthur; he was leading him on a predefined course, one he knew he could reach before his father and set the next phase of his plan in motion.

Damn Morgan and her influence on her son. She was never one for battle strategy, but that wouldn't have stopped her from teaching Mordred to think through every possibility, to turn every situation to his greatest advantage, just as she had been doing her whole life. Damn Lot for teaching his fosterling battle strategy. He'd thought he was preparing the heir to the kingdom. Little did he know he was arming a tyrant.

My blood went cold. Damn me too. I had taught him to read the Holy Stones, the one weapon of war neither Lot nor Morgan could or would pass on. I had armed him with a conduit to the gods. Damn my ignorance.

I tapped my thumb against my leg, turning a thought over in my mind. Two could play at that game, and I had more experience. No one was likely to have a set of stones in a house of the Christian god, but that never stopped the poor children on the streets who thought it only a game to be played with whatever pebbles littered the ground.

Standing, I touched the wall, fighting a wave of dizziness as my mind leapt ahead of my body. Most of the things I needed would be easy enough to procure. I still had the platter from my dinner; it would do as a board. While the sisters were attending to their prayers tonight, I could read the stones. But where would I get the stones themselves? Several feet of snow on the ground outside made it unlikely I could simply pluck them from the garden. Plus, I needed stones of pure quality to ensure the accuracy of my visions. Thanks to my hasty departure from Camelot, the only stones of any value I had with me were set in the ring Arthur had given me. I was not about to take it apart, but it gave me an idea.

Quietly opening my door, I peered down the hall, finding it deserted. I made my way toward the sisters' work area. They embroidered and affixed jewels to robes for the bishop in one of these rooms, or so Mayda had told me when she gave me a tour. I didn't expect them to leave such valuables out in the open, but I was willing to bet they'd be easy enough to find.

As I neared the end of the hall, a small, clear bell tolled twice, calling the sisters to prayer. I stopped, flattening myself against the wall as they passed. Some of them smiled in greeting, while others ignored me. A few looked at me askance, no doubt wondering why I was in their hallway when no one had seen me since I fainted in the chapel, but no one could question me as they were currently under the commandment of silence.

Once they had all passed out of sight and the soft murmur of their prayers filled the air, I slipped in and out of small workrooms until I found the one I was seeking. Light filtered in from a bank of windows on the west wall, illuminating two spinning wheels, three looms, and a few benches laden with silks and delicate thread in a rainbow of colors. I approached the latter, hoping to find a stole or other garment I could take and rip out the jewels—I could always sew them back in later. But after rummaging through all of them, I found Fortuna was not with me.

Mayda must have kept the jewels in her office. My skin prickled at the thought of invading her private space. That would be wrong. I did not want to betray her trust, but this was something I needed to do. Surely she would understand, and she needn't know if I returned them quickly.

I skittered down the long hall lined with rows of cells until I came to the largest. I tried the handle, but the door was locked. No matter. I had borrowed a long needle and thin metal implement used in affixing jewels to fabric from the workroom. They would work to spring this lock, as well as any that secured the stones. With a snick, I was inside.

Mayda's room was comprised of an outer office and what I guessed was her bedroom beyond a closed door. The office was only slightly bigger than my cell, so it didn't take long to locate a small wooden box with a heavy iron lock inside one of the chests behind her desk. This had to be it.

I carried the box over to the light. Pausing for a heartbeat, I closed my eyes and said a prayer of thanks to Isolde for teaching me this forbidden skill. When the lock popped open, I turned over the box, letting its contents fall into my palm like raindrops. I counted the glittering jewels. Exactly forty waited at my command, enough to represent both armies. But I was still missing the queens.

After running back to my room, box ill-concealed beneath the folds of my robe, I dove under the bed and withdrew my pack. Rummaging through its contents, my fingertips touched brooches, parchment, a bone comb, and an old wooden dog figurine I carried for protection. The stones were not there. Running my hands over the gowns hanging on pegs on the wall, tears pricked at my eyes as I traced one empty skirt after another. Just when I was about to give up, my fingertips met a reassuring lump in the seam of one hem. Reaching in, I retrieved the two red stones Isolde and I had won, lost, and won back again so many times over the years.

After kissing the queens, I arranged the stones in their proper formations, snuffed out all the candles save one, and took up my place before the board. Closing my eyes, I chased away all thoughts and concentrated on my breathing. With the first dizzying tingle of weightlessness, I opened my eyes.

This time was different than those that had come before. It was not a battle the gods were communicating, but something else. I stared past the stones I had so precariously procured until the knots and grain of the wood platter formed pictures, just as the clouds had when I would watch them as a child from the hillsides around Northgallis.

I saw Mordred pacing the halls of Camelot like a caged wolf waiting to be let out. Then I saw him barring the gate and filling the walls to the brim with archers. A rain of arrows fell on Arthur's army, forcing them to choose retreat or die trying to scale the impregnable walls of Camelot.

The visions ended, leaving me with a chilling certainty. Mordred was leading them into a trap they could not possibly escape. He knew it and Arthur soon would too. I had no way of getting word to him, but I could warn those who would help him, and perhaps provide him with some fresh reinforcements too.

Slowly, my hands moved the stones until I had twice played out the likely outcome, once with Arthur's current army, and again if I was able to help him. Both situations were dire, and oddly, each ended in a stalemate where the two queens and their kings remained, but there was no way for either side to claim victory.

The outcome vexed me so much my bowels rumbled, but there was nothing more I could do, at least not with the divination tool before me. I used the glowing taper to relight the others with shaking hands and hid the plate and stones so Mayda would not find anything amiss upon her return and suspect my very unchristian activity. With trembling fingers, I took up the stylus and composed a letter to Owain's wife, who was loyal to Arthur and the only one within range to augment Arthur's army while her husband fought at his side.

Not long after I sealed the letter, a knock broke my concentration and Mayda appeared in my doorway. I looked up, trying to appear as though nothing had changed from when she left me.

"How was your visit?" I asked brightly.

"It went well, thank you." Mayda's face grew solemn. "They brought news of Arthur."

I bit my lip and smoothed my skirt, trying to delay the inevitable news in case what I had seen was wrong, a product of wishful thinking. When I looked at her, my face was passive, though it took all my might to school it so. "And?"

"He lives. What is left of his army continues north, but to where we do not know."

"I may." I glanced at the letter on the desk. "How quickly can your messengers deliver this?"

Mayda picked it up. "Two days, four at most." Her expression betrayed concern and not a little apprehension, but she asked no questions.

"That will have to be fast enough. Please see that it is on its way as soon as possible."

I may not have been able to fight next to Arthur in the clash that was to come, but I could do everything in my power to assure he was as prepared as possible.

◦◦ ◦◦

A week later, the church was dark and silent, black-veiled sisters watching in vigil like wraiths at a tomb. In many ways, the day's rituals were more arcane than our native rites of Samhain. Both feasts mourned the death of a god who would come again, but this Christian tradition focused on the brutality of his death. Long Friday, as they called it, was the most solemn day of the year, with rites beginning in the middle of the night and lasting half the day.

Mayda came forward, crowned in thorns in imitation of her Savior. She and Sister Magdalena, her attendant, veiled the empty altar in black cloth. Mayda then held up a skull, to which all present genuflected. The archbishop said a brief prayer in Latin, and the sisters chanted as Mayda gently placed the skull on the altar. Two sisters set heavy wooden chests on either side of the altar. Mayda had explained earlier that they contained bones of the sisters who had passed away since the convent was founded so that all might be present at this most solemn vigil.

The Latin chant was intoned so low that I could not make out the words, but the haunting melody seemed to transcend time and space, opening the veil between worlds so that the souls of those who witnessed this man-god's crucifixion could rise from their graves to recount the deeds of that terrible day, lest it ever be forgotten.

The sisters swayed as the chant lulled them into a trance, and I found myself slipping into the Otherworld with them. Mayda and the bishop prostrated themselves before the altar, and my vision blurred. For a few frightening moments, blackness engulfed me. Then the clang of metal and grunts of exertion and pain reached my ears.

My sight cleared and I found myself in a mist-filled valley near one of the forts on Emperor Hadrian's wall, a place called Camlann I had been many times with Arthur, looking for any signs that the lowland tribes were stirring. Now the fort was crumbling, a shell of its former greatness.

Around me, battle raged, Briton against Briton, Saxon and Pict allied against them all. Owain's men were among the warriors, so my letter had made it to its destination in time to help Arthur. Thanks to the extra troops, this battle was less of a slaughter than the previous two had been, both sides holding their own in a tiring stalemate.

Mordred stood well back from the main engagement, watching and issuing commands from atop the wall. He didn't seem to notice as Arthur approached him from behind, flanked by Kay and Bedivere.

But before Arthur could attack, Mordred whirled, blade drawn, ready to strike. "I took you for many things, Father, but a coward is not among them. Would you really stab your own son in the back?"

Accolon and Bors stepped out of the mist, holding Arthur's companions at bay several steps behind.

"It is only what you deserve after setting upon me and my army unawares." Arthur raised his own blade. "But this does not concern them. It has always been *our* fight. Our time has come."

Mordred smiled darkly. "Indeed it has. If you are of the mind to die, lay on."

Arthur struck out, and their blades met with a deafening clash.

The force of the strike vibrated through me as though my own weapon had been hit. Dizzy, my sight faltered, pulling me into an in-between world where the keening of the sisters' chant made the hair on the back of my neck stand up, but I was not fully in my body either. Vaguely, I heard the priest intone the words of Jesus, who had descended into hell to condemn the devil and liberate the souls therein, including the first man and woman. To Adam, he commanded, "Repent of your sin and be freed by my blood."

Instead of an answer, Arthur's grunt of pain reached me as Mordred swung his shield, connecting squarely with Arthur's left cheek. Arthur stumbled back on the rocky, wet ground, doubled over, but he managed to block Mordred's stab, swatting away Mordred's sword before spitting a mouthful of blood onto the stones.

When Arthur stood upright again, he was less steady, turning his whole head to locate his opponent, which made me think he'd lost the sight in his left eye. He recovered quickly and lunged at Mordred. Despite the sucking mire underfoot, they parried and thrust with exhausting speed, as though they were in a hurry to kill one another.

Mordred lost his weapon first. He took one of Arthur's blows on the edge rather than the flat of the blade, and it broke, making Mordred lose his grip. The remnants of his sword sank in the mud. Momentarily stunned, Mordred left himself open to Arthur's fury but managed to avoid injury. He grabbed a low-hanging branch from a silver birch, partially broken in a storm, and wrenched it free, wielding it alternately like a club and a staff. Arthur advanced with confidence but never took the killing blow. I suspected he was trying to tire Mordred, to force him to yield the fight, and hence, the kingship.

But his son was too persistent and too clever for that. Fighting with the tough branch, he resembled the Oak King seeking to overthrow the Holly King. Mordred held his own, eventually disarming Arthur with a crack to the wrist of his sword arm that made my teeth twinge, even in the spirit world.

Soon the two were locked in a skirmish that more resembled the brute force contention of horned goats than the engagement of two highly trained warriors. They wrestled one another to the sodden ground, Arthur's bulk easily overpowering his lithe son.

"Call a halt," Arthur demanded as battle raged all around them.

"Never," Mordred declared.

Arthur fumbled at his belt. "I will give you one more chance," he said, holding a dagger to his son's stomach. "If you yield to me, you will live."

Arthur was so busy watching his son's reaction, he couldn't see Mordred's right hand creeping along the ground toward his broken sword.

"And if not?" Mordred's hand closed around the jagged blade, freeing it from the mud.

"Then I am afraid I will have to kill you."

"Please, Father. Don't."

His pleading gave Arthur pause, just long enough for Mordred to raise the sword and smash the hilt into Arthur's head. The force of his blow hammered Arthur's body downward. Mordred yelled, his eyes going wide. He scrabbled backward like a crab. As Arthur's unconscious body fell away from Mordred, it revealed Arthur's dagger protruding from Mordred's stomach.

Time stood still.

Or at least that was how it felt. Realization hit me with the force of a gale sweeping down a canyon face, pulling me inexorably to my own death.

A bloodcurdling scream fell from my lips, echoed by another that held even more pain.

Morgan.

As my spirit body pushed through the thick of battle

toward my husband, she dashed to her son's side, flying across the field like a banshee. Of course. She would have been having visions of her own while nearby with the other camp women.

"Get them out of here! Get them to safety," Kay yelled as he, Bedivere, and some of the others fought through the crushing mass of bodies to shelter their king and his heir from further harm.

They took them into the remains of the fort, its skeletal walls casting odd shadows in the half light and affording us some measure of dryness and privacy.

In this odd place between worlds, I could touch them. I sank to the floor at Arthur's side and cradled his head in my lap, begging him to open his eyes. His pulse was faint and fluttering under my fingertips, so he lived—for now.

I inspected his wound even as Kay tried to bind it to stop the copious bleeding. Mordred's blow had been powerful, smashing Arthur's helmet and rending the side of his head with a deep, angry gash. At the rate his blood coated my hands, I feared a small artery had ruptured on impact. Even if that were not the case, the blow would cause severe swelling that could lead to host of problems, should he survive long enough to experience them. He needed help beyond what battlefield medics could provide.

Morgan gathered her son's body onto her lap, weeping so hard she could find no voice. He stroked her cheek. "Mother."

"Stay strong, my son," she answered as though hope still remained.

But the only outcome for him was death. No other ending could be read in the pool of blood gathering black around him.

His gaze flicked to me. "Guinevere." He smiled. "I am so sorry."

I swallowed hard, trying not to choke on the tears streaming down my face. That he could see my spirit-self meant he was close to passing through the veil. "All is forgiven, Mordred. The Goddess knows. She will have mercy."

His features smoothed as his breathing slowed, the lines of hatred and anger that had marred them over the last year disappearing until he resembled the boy who had welcomed me upon my return to Camelot from captivity, rather than the bitter monster he had recently become.

In my lap, Arthur groaned. His eyelashes fluttered and he opened his good eye, squinting at me. "I knew you'd come."

"I would be nowhere else." I squeezed his hand, ignoring the twinge in my gut that told me his seeing me meant he was near death as well. "Arthur, I love you. If you remember nothing else, let it be those words."

He shifted, turning his head to have a better view of me. "And I you." He caught sight of his son, slumped in Morgan's arms. "Son?" His voice was thick with confusion.

He did not know what he had done. Mordred's blow must have rendered him unconscious before his blade pierced his son's flesh. Now was not the time to tell him.

At least Morgan seemed to feel the same. Still crying, she grasped Arthur's other hand. "He died in battle. Is that not what you have always wished for him?"

Arthur gave a small bark of a laugh. "A hero? Yes. Death? No." He drawled the last word like a drunkard. The darkness was about to claim him.

I patted his cheeks, gently at first then harder when he did not respond. "Arthur, do you not wish to say farewell to your son?"

"My boy," was all Arthur managed before he fell into unconsciousness again.

I shook his shoulders. "Arthur! Arthur, no!"

As his breathing slowed, I sobbed harder, glancing over his shoulder at Morgan. She was weeping so hard her whole body shook as she clasped her son to her breast, his hands flapping limply at his side, the bloody dagger at her feet. Her skin was as pale as moonlight, her red lips twisted into a silent scream of anguish.

Kay stood, shaking his head while tears rolled silently down his cheeks.

Mordred was dead. For all intents and purposes, so was Arthur. That was the news Kay emerged from the fort to tell their men. I lay Arthur gently on the floor and went to the window to watch the armies react. As word spread, men ceased fighting and turned to face the fort. To a one, every Briton fell to one knee in honor of their fallen leaders.

Only the gods knew how things would have been different if everyone on the battlefield had shared their allegiance. While most saw the ceasing of hostility as a sign of respect, others used it to their advantage. The rumbling of horse's hooves shattered the silence as a Pict on horseback raced through the crowd. Swinging his axe like a scythe, he removed the heads of eight kneeling Britons before anyone could react. The Saxons followed suit, stabbing another dozen with their javelins as they mourned their kings.

"Raise your arms, men. Defend your fallen kings with your life. This is your final tribute to them," Kay yelled before disappearing into the fray with Bedivere.

Morgan and I were alone with the bodies of our beloved men. She reluctantly laid Mordred on the floor, passing her hand over his eyes. She crossed his arms over his breast, hands forever laced with the pommel of his damaged sword, before she bent over him.

"Goodbye, my son," she whispered and kissed his forehead.

Arthur's heart beat lightly beneath my hand, the sensation carrying with it a thousand memories—the first time his gaze met mine at the tournament, his expression of adoration when I told him I was pregnant, even his grief when he thought me dead, his joy at my return after my exile with Malegant, the wonder and regret in his eyes as he traced my scarred face when we met again after the fire. All those things and more tumbled over one another in my mind as I contemplated what must come next.

I knelt, pressing his hand to my lips, grateful for this last moment with him, for I knew it for what it was. "For all that we were, all that we dared to dream, I love you. In this life and the next." I turned to Morgan. "He's yours."

She was still staring at the lifeless body of her son. She'd barely heard me. "What?"

I walked over to her and took her shoulders, forcing her

unfocused eyes to me. With exaggerated volume, I repeated myself. "I said, 'He's yours.'"

She blinked at me as though I spoke a foreign language.

"Arthur is not dead, not yet, and I know the only place that can heal him." I shook her lightly to get her attention. "Morgan, listen to me. You are the only one who can help Arthur now. I concede the last of his life to you. Get him to Avalon and summon Helene in case she needs to say good-bye to her father. She will be safer there than with Owain and Accolon in the days to come."

The mention of her daughter's name brought Morgan out of her grief-stricken trance. She blinked at me again, shook her head, then came to life. "You are not really here. But I am. I can save him." A wicked grin spread across her face. She stuck her head out of the back of the fort. "You!" she called to a woman standing nearby. "Find Grainne and Mona and tell them to bring the Grail." She turned to the man guarding Arthur. "Get him to a horse. We must away to Avalon."

"Not a horse, lady. It will be faster to take him by water," one of the women said. "I will take you." She was one of Sobian's girls, one of a handful who'd stayed to fight with Arthur even when their leader refused. She would do everything she could to ensure he made it in time to be healed.

They took him from my arms, and all of my strength bled out as though I were the one with a mortal wound. Arthur was in the hands of the Goddess now, and those of Morgan as her representative and his wife. My vision blurred. Gray tendrils of smoke rolled in from its edges until I could see nothing more. I was vaguely aware of rejoining my body in my cold, small cell. But I did not care. I embraced the darkness with all the passion of a lover.

After twenty-four years, it was over. Camelot was no more.

I woke to the bright light of Easter morning and the joyful song of "Alleluia" wafting in from the open window overlooking the chapel. For a few moments, I floated on this optimism, my spirit buoyant and free, my mind clear of all but the light and song.

But when I sat up, my head throbbed and memories returned in flashes—Aggrivane fallen among his brethren; then Arthur senseless on the ground, a bloody gash to his head; Mordred clutching his abdomen; the grief-stricken face of Morgan. Her voice rang in my head, "We must away to Avalon."

Was I meant to follow her? For the third time in less than two years, I had nowhere to go. Avalon was a logical choice. I would be safe and welcome there. But yet, as comforting as that idea was, it didn't feel quite right. There was something else I was yet meant to do, and Avalon wasn't where it would happen.

I shuffled mindlessly as I gathered my few belongings, rolling robes and cloaks into a pack for my departure. I may not have a destination, but I could not stay here. I had troubled the poor sisters enough. They had shown me more kindness than I could ever ask. I could not turn around and ask them to harbor me in what would likely be dark days ahead.

Now that Arthur was at the very least severely incapacitated and his heir dead, there would be a fight for the throne of High King. Just as in the days following Uther's death, men with any claim and none at all would turn against one another in the quest for power. If my whereabouts were known, I would be a target for everything from assassination attempts—lest I make my own bid for the throne, which I had no intention of doing—to insurrections in my name, or even yet another abduction by one who sought to use my sovereignty to bolster his claim. I would be a danger to everyone I came in contact with.

That didn't even factor in the Saxons and the Picts, who, even if the last of the Combrogi managed to contain them, would likely be making their own bids for expanded land. I had a feeling Elga still lived, and if I was correct, she would come here to seek my blood. I would not let Mayda pay for her sister's twisted sense of vengeance. Plus, even if the Picts chose to turn tail and return to their homelands, they would no doubt wreak havoc on their way, and sooner or later, they would resume their centuries-old war with the tribes of the north. With no strong Briton leadership to stop them, they would press as far south as they could.

No, this was not the time for me to retreat into the mists. Let those who will believe I died in a convent, but I would complete my life as I had started it—as a warrior's daughter. There was only one place for that—my mother's homeland and its capital of Din Eidyn.

I knelt one last time, squinting through the small window to ensure the sisters would be at Mass a while longer. My gaze traveled over the white-robed women, hair covered in light lace veils and crowns of lilies, and alighted on Mayda. She was at the head of the group of older sisters, nearest to the priest, her face suffused with joy at the resurrection of her god. I would miss her terribly. I couldn't predict what her sister would do when she showed up here and found me missing, but at least Elga would have no reason to harm her. That was the best repayment I could give—for now.

I smoothed out the bedspread and turned in a circle one last time, making sure I hadn't left anything. On impulse, I swept a hand under the bed, and it brushed against something hard. I withdrew the box of jewels. I opened it, tempted to take one to safeguard my passage north. But I could not. It would be wrong to use my hosts that way.

I closed the box and set off to return it to Mayda's office. On the way, I passed the kitchens, silent save two young maids, one turning the spit and the other minding a bubbling cauldron, both of which would be served at the feast after Mass. They were so intent on their duties, it was not hard to slip past them and into the small larder. As I would not be around for the morning meal, I did not feel guilty about taking some bread, cheese, a bit of smoked fish, and a skin of wine for my journey.

Provisions packed, I unlocked Mayda's door and placed the box back where I had found it. The light caught on Arthur's ring in its customary place on my right hand, and

I realized I had the means to fund my journey after all. I could easily pawn it in town. No one would recognize me, and it was doubtful any enterprising man would turn down a rare piece of gold and jewels. It was also fitting, I supposed, that I leave my last vestige of Arthur behind, as I was leaving behind my life as queen.

I stepped out into the bright light of the courtyard with a heart weighed down by sorrow. No one was around to witness my leaving, not even the porter. She too was attending Mass. But that also meant there was no one to witness my grief. As I closed the latch of the convent gate, I didn't even bother wiping the tears away or trying to stave off the throbbing of my thrice-broken heart. Facing the open road and an uncertain future, I gave in to my loneliness and misery, praying that at my journey's end, I might find some measure of peace.

PART TWO

People Of The North

Chapter Nine

Summer 520

On my way north, I detoured to Traprain Law to express my condolences to Lot and Anna over the loss of their sons. Not long after I arrived, word reached us from Avalon that Arthur was dead; even the ministrations of nine priestesses hadn't been enough to save our king.

Anna and Lot shared my loss and understood my relationships with Arthur and Aggrivane better than anyone, so they allowed me to fall to pieces in ways few others would have tolerated. I did not sleep and refused to eat, taking only a little bread and water and only after Anna practically forced it down my throat.

I had lost my husband—estranged though we were—and the man I considered a son even though we were not related by blood. Mordred's death brought back the stinging pain of losing my own children in childbed, redoubling the bitterness that lingered in the cockles of my heart. I mourned Mordred's unfulfilled potential, for what could have been had he not been corrupted by the lust for power that poisoned his blood, a curse inherited from his mother. He had been a brilliant man, perfectly suited to carry on Arthur's legacy, but somehow he had gone astray, forming loyalties that may have destroyed our country had he lived to overthrow his father.

I railed at the gods for the loss of Arthur. Despite all we had been through, he was my husband and I still loved him. I grieved the man that only Morgan and I truly knew, the humorous, tender soul behind the gruff, noble exterior. The man who built the labyrinth and garden at the center of Camelot out of concern for my welfare, who laid his new-born children to rest alone when I was too ill to attend their funeral, who accepted a madwoman back into his heart and made room for me beside the woman he truly loved instead of consigning me to the whims of fate, as was his right.

I had been so focused on hating Arthur for his missteps over the last two years that it took his death to make me remember what a truly remarkable man he was. I shed tears over my shortsightedness and mourned the loss of any chance of reconciliation. I would have relished watching him grow old from afar, passing Camelot on to Mordred and enjoying his twilight years in peace. But such is not the fate of a warrior, much less a king, and somewhere deep down, I knew his soul gloried at having died in battle, even if it was against his own son. Perhaps they were even now making peace in the Otherworld.

Then there was Aggrivane. Of all the losses I had faced in my life—my mother, father, Arthur, Octavia, countless friends and warriors dead in war—this pain was the most bitter. Aggrivane was my first love, and with his death, I grieved the end of the hopes I still held from our youth. He had been my first great mistake, but one I would make again if given the chance. A man I betrayed in my efforts to safeguard both our hearts and our reputations; he had betrayed me too, but he had also been there for me in the darkest moments before what, by all rights, should have been my death. To say goodbye to him was to bid farewell to so much of who I had been, to dreams buried deep, to a love that could never be.

In his death and the end to all I held on to from my youth, I had to accept my own aging and mortality. I was no mere girl, nor even the thriving queen who had once over-seen the whole of the country; I was now an old woman, a crone, who had seen forty summers. Tangled with my mourning was a loss of self unlike any I had ever known. Even as a young girl facing my reflection before stepping onto the boat to Avalon, I had been secure in the knowl-edge I was the daughter of the king and queen of Gwyn-edd. I may not have known whether I was fated to become a priestess or rule a kingdom—or both, as the years later revealed—but I was certain of my roots. I had a foundation on which to build my budding personhood.

Now, all I had was a pile of discarded identities—lover, wife, queen, mother—none of which fit anymore. I didn't even know what had become of Lancelot. Had he tried to find me in Camelot? What fears had plagued him when I was not there? Was he still searching for me? Until I was settled and could send a message of inquiry, I had no way of finding out. The only thing that was certain was that I was still a priestess, for that honor was etched into my very soul. That was the only comfort I could wrap around my cold, shaking shoulders.

None of this made any sense. In Avalon, the Lady of the Lake had taught us to trust in the gods and follow their voices, but in my grief and uncertainty, all I could do was question their wisdom. They had taken not only Camelot's future, but its leader as well. Why? What was the purpose? Yes, Arthur had fallen on hard times, but I had to believe that, given time, he could have earned back the trust of the people, especially if he had separated from Morgan and dedicated himself to securing peace once again. Did the Goddess wish us to fall into foreign hands? What a strange and unknowable future that would be.

What was my role in this? Why could Lancelot and I not have lived our intended life in Brittany? What was my purpose in this land? All of the other times I had questioned the will of the Goddess—when I arrived in Avalon, when my mother's death forced me to return to Northgallis, when Father Marius's hatred forced me to live in Dyfedd, when I unwillingly became queen, at the death of my children, during my captivity and its aftermath, and when Arthur and the bishop nearly had me killed—the Goddess had been preparing me for a new role.

What could possibly be her will now?

⊶⊰⊱⊷

While I was struggling to find my place, Anna showed remarkable strength, continuing to direct and protect her kingdom in an increasingly unstable country, with Lot by her side. I stood in awe of her. She had lost three sons in the last two years—only Gawain remained of the four— yet she carried on as though her bones were made of stone and her blood fueled by her private tears. Surely she had the same questions as me, but she never showed her doubts in public, remaining stoic until we were alone, with only the deepened wrinkles around her eyes and on her brow and her chalky complexion betraying her pain. Lot showed his sadness more readily, retreating into himself and conducting a fast borne of grief until he became a hollow shell, more ghost than man. He stood sentinel at his wife's side, but he was not really present.

Together, she and I watched from afar, like nesting eagles looking down upon the forest, as Britain reverted to its native state and warring tribes and ambitious men fought for the throne Arthur had left empty. Some, like an uprising in Powys, were easily quashed, while others, like Constantine, rose with each kingdom that fell to his sword. Constantine's closest competition was the joint forces of the sons of Rheged, Owain and Accolon, who were known to all as loyal members of Arthur's Combrogi and had the support of Morgan, the former royal wife and mother of Arthur's only living child. If I knew her, she was really supporting them to give her daughter a chance at the throne. If they defeated Constantine, she could declare Helene queen and rule as regent until she came of age. Together, they dominated the northern part of the country and protected Camelot, while Constantine ate up the south and central kingdoms. The confrontation of those two forces was inevitable, and when it came, it would change the course of our country utterly.

In many ways, it was like watching a game of Holy Stones play out, only these consequences were immediate and often devastating. Borders were redrawn with such speed that the cartographers gave up trying to accurately reflect the changes. In the cities and towns, workers supplied the armies with weapons, and able-bodied men—and a few women—enlisted to support the noble of their choice, while in the countryside, people moved animals to safer pasture and hid valuables and food against marauders and defeated armies. The Irish, smelling the blood running from the battlefields, attacked our western coast with a vengeance not seen since my childhood. To the north, the Picts rumbled, forcing the tribes between the walls into high alert. Only the Saxons remained silent, watching and biding their time just as we did, which chilled my blood more than if they had shown up on our doorstep demanding vengeance.

Soon, Lot and Anna would have to travel to Din Eidyn to pledge their allegiance to the Votadini, for they had no desire to be involved in Britain's war. Though Lot and Anna had been loyal to Arthur, their kingdom was historically an annex of the Votadini tribe, and now Anna desired once again to bring her people under the protection of the Votad and Votadess, as their leaders were known, trusting them more than any of her former countrymen. I was to accompany them in order to claim my ancestral lands inherited from my mother, the only choice left to me as a throneless, homeless former queen with no living relations.

Our departure was delayed when, near midsummer, Lot was felled by a mysterious ailment that caused his blood to boil and consumed him with fever and sweat. That he succumbed to the illness was of little surprise to those of us who had watched his grief eat away at him, but the speed and ferocity of his decline frightened us all.

Lot lay abed, walking between the worlds in fever dreams that made him cry out to his dead sons, offering them apologies for offenses both real and imagined and declaring his eternal love for them. He even spoke with Arthur in a conversation so seemingly lucid that I could make out what Arthur was saying to him. Not long after, Lot reached out into the open air, eyes focused on something I could not see.

"My ancestors call to me." He turned his head, and a smile like the dawn lit his face. "Ah, Gareth, Garheis, my boys, come to see your father home, have you? I am ready."

After Lot breathed his last, Anna closed his eyes with silent sobs and a gentle kiss. I rested my head on his shoulder. I had few tears left with which to bathe him, but my heart contracted all the same. In its bitter consequences, the Battle of Camlann had taken one final life and one of the last remaining shards of my heart in the man who should have been my father by marriage.

Now it was my duty to help Anna settle into the role of widow. Then I would continue to Din Eidyn as planned. Lot would not see the new kingdoms that would sprout from his body and those of so many others fallen in battle, but I would, and I needed allies if I were to survive. Drying my eyes and calling on the last dregs of my resolve, I faced north. It was time to go home, even if I had to face my new life alone.

Chapter Ten

Autumn 520

Anna chose to cede control of Lothian to Gawain, so after Lot's funerary rites, she and I set off for Din Eidyn, riding through hills and mountains resplendent with autumn color. All around us, fiery oaks competed for attention with rust-colored rowan, while elders offered their juicy purple berries as a final harvest before winter. Birches provided a splash of sunlight even on days of driving rain, especially when set against emerald pine and green alders that refused to give up their summer foliage. On the banks of mountain streams, willows and birch gilt the water's course with showers of golden leaves, and in the mountains, fields of fragrant heather defiantly bloomed pink, even as the mornings took on a slight chill.

Only a few days remained until Samhain when we arrived, and lines of travelers clogged the roads into the fortress both overland and leading up from the harbor.

Anna explained that it was tradition that those who sought employment or married into other lands return to their tribal capital to honor their dead on Samhain.

As Arthur's sister, she would commend him, Lot, and her sons to the Votadini tribal gods during the Samhain rituals. After, she would become part of my household as an advisor and lady's maid. Having given Lothian to Gawain, Anna wanted nothing of power or war, only to live out her days in peace. In that, as in so many things, she and I were a good match.

We pushed through packed streets thundering with the guttural tongues of many tribes. Imprinted on the forearms of men and shoulder blades of women were tribal markings declaring the birth tribe of each person: the Votadini horse, the Selgovae raven, and even a few Novantae stags. Noticeably sparse was the Damnonii wolf. Above the din, blacksmiths' hammers rang as they mended wheels for those transporting goods from the countryside and sharpened swords for the Votad's army, and merchants hawked their wares, tables heavy with apples, nuts, and meat freshly slaughtered for the coming winter. With the boisterous exchange of goods for what currency remained, Din Eidyn was thriving despite the chaos looming to the south.

Compared to Camelot, the castle itself was small, cramped, and dark, but from the outside, it presented a formidable façade, blending the intimidating strength of a fortress and the opulence of a castle into the black mountainside. Inside, men and women jockeyed for position in the great hall, eager to present themselves and their needs to their rulers. Anna had explained that here, they only held pleadings four times a year—for the three days before, during, and after the full moon nearest the major feast days—so their subjects were even more desperate for attention than ours had been. On top of that, there was no orderly system of presentation such as we had had; petitioners were seen in the order they could rush forward and fall to their knees before the throne.

Anna stood to my left, whispering advice and commentary to help me understand the rules and players at this court. On my right and to my back stood strangers covered in woolen tunics and fur coats reeking of sweat, eyes attentive to an opportunity to move forward. My line of sight, however, was blocked by the fur cloak in front of me. Not for the first time, I cursed my short stature. Because Anna could see over most of the crowd, we agreed that if she saw an opening, she would shove me forward so I could plead my case and she would follow immediately after.

Being on the other side of the throne, praying to be noticed instead of being the one to listen and dispense solutions, was humbling, a stark reminder of all I had lost and that I was once again dependent on someone else for my welfare. A choking insecurity bore into my chest at the thought that the Votad and Votadess, Mynyddog Mwynfawr and his wife, Evina, held the power to grant my request and secure my future or cast me out into the mud to fend for myself. With the hindsight of age, I wished I had had this perspective before taking my own throne; it would have made me a more sympathetic and patient ruler.

After several hours, my feet tingled and my muscles were locking in place, but at least the Votad was clearly in my line of sight now. As the crowd shifted, preparing to spit out its next supplicant, I turned my shoulders to the side and stepped forward, determined to push between the human barrel in front of me and the gaunt woman next to him. As I took a breath to wedge myself between them, hands grasped my shoulders and pushed. I fell forward, knocking the couple to either side. My right knee hit the stone floor with an impact that rattled my teeth, and I narrowly missed scraping my chin on the paver in front of me. Gracefully or not, I had made it before the throne.

Cheeks flaming with embarrassment, I dared to look at the Votadess. She so closely resembled my mother that, for a moment, I could not speak. Her hair was a bit lighter, closer to brown than the black I'd inherited, but her glittering green eyes and the pout of her lips were nearly the same. Even now, years after my mother died, it took my breath away.

"Surely this is one of your kin, eh, Evina? She could be your double," the Votad said, his voice holding more than a hint of amazement.

"Indeed," was all she said as her eyes roamed my face, skipping over the scars that marred its left side and taking in every unblemished feature. Her cool tone did not match the openness with which she regarded me. Was it merely surprise that dampened her welcome, or did she not relish having one of her blood appear at her court? Perhaps both.

Unlike his wife, the Votad was delighted by this turn of events. "Tell us your name and purpose here, kinswoman."

As was tradition, I recited my ancestry, which was the best form of identification a man or woman could produce. "My lord and lady, I am Guinevere, born in Northgallis, but Votadini by blood through my mother, Corinna, whose father was Cunedda, who defended Britain against the Irish and established a safe haven for our people in Gwynedd. He then arranged for my mother to marry Leodgrance of Gwynedd, thus securing an alliance of peace for both tribes. You may have known me as High Queen of Britain, but I am now only one of your humble subjects. I have come to ask for the inheritance which is my right by blood, the lands belonging to my mother north of Stirling."

The petitioners murmured sounds of surprise and disbelief. In the front of the room, the small crowd of men surrounding the royal couple stirred, and an older man with a graying blond beard whispered something in the Votad's ear. He nodded and signaled to one of his men, who quickly departed to fulfil his master's command.

"How do we know you are whom you claim to be? Have you anyone to speak for you?" Evina asked, though she didn't sound suspicious, just rightly wary.

As Arthur had discovered when I was taken by Malegant, frauds and pretendants to the throne were many, and some of them were convincing. The Votad and Votadess could not be too careful, especially with lands as strategically important as Stirling at stake.

"I will." Anna stepped out of the crowd before bowing to both rulers. "I am Anna of Lothian, sister to the former High King of Britain, Arthur Pendragon, and wife of the recently deceased King Lot. Surely you remember me and will take my word that what she says is true."

Mynyddog nodded to Anna. "We do. Please allow me to offer my condolences on the deaths of your husband and sons." The regret in his voice was sincere.

Anna bowed her head again. "Thank you, Votad. I wish you to know that it was my husband's intention to accompany me on this journey and pledge his sword in your service. But the gods did not allow it. I pray that you will treat my son, Gawain, with the same esteem as his father, as he is now ruler of Lothian and wishes to be brought under your protection."

"Of course," Mynyddog responded. "I will send one of my sons to Traprain Law within the week to welcome him as a member of the Votadini tribe and confer his blessing. He has been marked, has he not?"

"Yes, sire. My husband marked each of his sons when they came of age. Though he followed Arthur, he always considered himself a Votadini at heart and bore both the horse and dragon—symbols of your tribe and his—on his arm."

Evina had been chewing her lower lip as she listened, as though mulling over thoughts heavy with meaning. She sat forward and addressed me. "If you are whom you claim to be, you will also be marked. If you will, please show us."

I swallowed hard and shook my head. "I do not have a mark, Votadess. I was away in Avalon when my mother died, and there has been no one since to mark me."

Evina threw her husband a suspicious glance. "Is that so?"

"It is. She speaks the truth," came a silky French accent from the back of the room.

All heads turned. Waves of shock and soaring joy threatened to overwhelm me when I recognized Lancelot. I had to grab Anna's arm to steady myself. Lancelot was here. He was safe. Thanks be to the gods. But why? How? What a silly question. Finally, one thing in my life had turned out for the good; the details didn't matter.

The crowd parted to allow Lancelot to approach the throne, and it took all of my willpower not to run to him and throw my arms around him. As he approached, the silver in his black hair caught the light, as did a new scar on his left cheek. Two years and a war had taken their toll on him, but he was handsome as ever.

"I have served Guinevere for the better part of my life," he said when he reached my side. "She is my queen, and I am her champion. She is also my beloved. Please accept my words on pain of honor as they are the truth."

Evina gave him a dazzling smile and raised him from his bow by the hand as though asking him to dance. "Of course, Angus. If you say she is true, then she is true."

The years of war had not dampened Lancelot's natural charisma, for Evina was as taken with him as every other woman. But why had she called him Angus?

Evina's gaze slipped to me, her smile fading a bit. "We will still need to have you marked. You cannot rule in our lands without being fully brought into our tribe." She thought for a moment. "If Corinna was your mother, then I am your cousin, so it falls to me. Three days hence at dawn, you will officially become a Votadini woman.

"As for your claim to the lands north of Stirling, I will have to consult with our records keepers, but I believe it is legitimate. The only complication is that Rohan, cousin to Morcant, leader of the Damnonii and conqueror of Bernicia, currently rules those lands, so to oust him will cause tension between our tribes."

"You mean it will *increase* tension between our tribes," her husband corrected dryly. "There has been tension between us for generations. Rohan will take some convincing."

"With respect, you misunderstand me," I said before Evina could reply. "I have no desire to rule another kingdom. All I ask is to take possession of my lands and be given the freedom to live on them. Nothing more. I have no wish to upset the current way of things."

Evina arched an eyebrow at me as though she could not fathom why anyone would wish for such an arrangement. She and Mynyddog exchanged a look that said they were unsure if I was a fool or simply insane. "If that is what you will, then it will be done."

In the corner of my eye, I saw a shadow detach itself from the wall and slip out. A spy, no doubt, on his or her way to inform Rohan of the new claimant to his lands in Stirling.

Pushing those implications to the back of my mind, I curtsied to Evina. "Many thanks for your generosity, my lady. I do not know what form your court's oath takes, but please know that I honor and respect your position of authority over me and do swear my loyalty to you. In the names of my ancestors, I pray for a long life for both of you and promise to do all in my power to defend you in word and deed."

It was Mynyddog's turn to raise me from my curtsy. "Your oath is hereby acknowledged, and we bestow upon you our blessing."

"Now that the business is concluded, may I see these ladies to a guest room, for I think they have nowhere to stay," Lancelot said, looking from Anna to me for confirmation.

"Of course," Mynyddog said. "You are our most honored guests. Take them to Sorcha. She will know where we have vacant rooms." He motioned for us to depart.

Turning from the throne, I let out a deep breath. That had gone much better than I'd expected. Perhaps too well. The Votad and Votadess may have been agreeable, but there may still be repercussions for interrupting the established order of things. This was only the beginning. The people would spread the news of my return across the four tribes. By morning, everyone from Hadrian's Wall to north of Soloway Firth would know the former queen has returned to her native land.

It did not surprise me to hear cries of "This will not stand!" and "Rohan will tame her before the next full moon," before the doors closed behind us. But the most chilling prediction was not proclaimed across the hall, merely whispered as we passed. "Gods be praised. The rightful Votadess has come home."

That night, Lancelot and I lay together in the moonlight for the first time since before Mordred's lies ruined our lives. I had not seen him in any meaningful way since before the Grail's spell of peace broke and Camelot began to crumble. After that, we were estranged, and once Mordred betrayed us, Arthur's guards kept us apart.

Now, two long years later, his arms felt like a heaven I had finally earned. At last there was no more guilt, no more lies and deception shadowing our love. We were free to give fully of ourselves and receive in return. He was no longer Arthur's knight and I Arthur's wife; we were one another's chosen lovers, belonging to no one else.

I breathed in his scent, so like the heather on the hillside that it made my heart soar. "I haven't had the chance to thank you." I burrowed deeper into his arms and nestled my head against his chest, as if the heat of his body could heal me.

"For what?"

"For saving me—again. For coming back when everyone else had abandoned me. For not believing what the bishop said and leaving me to die"

"Do you not remember?" He angled his body so I had to look up at him. "I am sworn to you until my dying breath. I have been yours since I thought you gave me that flower at the tournament. I chose you over the Grail. Why do you think I would abandon you when you need me the most? I love you and I always will."

Emotion welled up in me and tears pricked at my eyes,

an overwhelming combination of happiness and fear. "Even with this?" I turned my head so he had a clear view of the part of my neck and cheek that would forever be withered.

He stroked the side of my head, where my permanently ravaged hairline met my face. "Beauty fades. Had the fire not damaged your skin, time would have eventually. You are still beautiful to me, even more so for your scars. You are a warrior woman. You earned your scars just as truly as if you had received them in battle. When I look at you, I see a woman who triumphed over the strongest adversity and lives to glory in her victory. Even more than that, you have your sight, your hearing, and your mobility. You still have a bright future ahead of you."

His hand slipped down my neck, tracing my scars to my arm and across my left breast. "Those flames may have marred your skin, but they did no serious damage, and they certainly did not touch your spirit. *That* is why I really love you. I love your ability to come back from every attempt of your enemies stronger and braver for it. That is what will always make you Sovereignty herself, title or no."

I kissed him, letting myself be swept away by the softness of his lips and the warmth of his skin against mine. He followed the line of my scars with his tongue, sending a shiver across my ribs. His hands gripped my hips, and he kissed my navel before continuing downward. As he pleasured me, my hands explored his back and shoulders, finding new ridges and scars where there had previously been only hard muscle and sinew. When his lips next met mine, I wrapped my legs around him, forcing him onto his back and taking my fill of him.

After, we lay in each other's arms, listening to the night orchestra of crickets, cicadas, and other insects.

"Why *do* they call you Angus?" I asked, turning onto my stomach so I could look up at him.

He kissed my forehead. "To answer that, I have to mention a man I know you would like to forget." The concern in his eyes was so deep that it could only be one person.

I shuddered. "Go on."

"Do you recall Malegant mentioning that he had a Votadini wife?"

I murmured my assent, breathing deeply to ward off the tension that turned my muscles to stone every time I remembered those horrible months of captivity in Malegant's hidden island tower. Nearly twenty years had passed, but panic still surged through my veins at his name.

"As you can imagine, he treated her very poorly," Lancelot continued. "Her father hired me to put an end to her suffering by killing Malegant. Obviously I failed, but when Malegant tired of her and tried to take her family's land by force, I was there to defend it. My men and I gave him a beating he nursed for many years."

"No wonder he was so angry when you rescued me. You were taking his prey from him for the second time." A whole new respect for Lancelot blossomed within me. This man who had been a blessing from the gods for me on so many occasions had also been one for many people before I knew him.

"Not only that, but I had replaced him as your personal

guard. He was not going to let me have you again. That was why he was so determined to kill me on that beach. He wanted to end our feud once and for all. But I killed him instead." Lancelot squeezed his eyes tight then opened them wide, as if trying to rid himself of the memory of Malegant's body on the shores of the lake. "In return for my service to the Votadini, Evina's father gave me the land of Angus, a title I still hold. I always thought of it as a failsafe, a place to retreat to if ever I needed a home. As the war in Brittany proved, that was a wise decision. When I could not find you in Camelot, I went there, hoping to hear word of your whereabouts. I did not know you'd come to Din Eidyn. I was only at court today because Evina wished me to evaluate candidates for her weapons master."

"It is fortunate you were. I'm not sure if Anna's endorsement of me would have been enough to sway Evina. I could have spent this night on the dusty floor of an inn had you not arrived when you did."

He smiled, wrapping an arm around my neck and pulling me even closer. "It was not luck; you of all people should recognize the hand of the Goddess when you see it. It is she who reunited us."

"And she who gave us a home. I cannot wait to spend the rest of my life with you."

"And I you. Will you marry me and make me your husband in truth? Now that Arthur is gone and we have secured our future, I see no reason for us not to wed." His eyes lit with hope, reflecting the youthful enthusiasm he would always possess, no matter how many years passed.

I pulled away, unable to give him the answer he desired. How could I explain that marriage had become abhorrent to me, that I had no desire to wed again, without hurting him? He had been nothing but loyal to me for decades. He deserved more than my selfish rejection, but to marry him when I felt this way would be unfair to us both.

I met his eyes and shook my head. "I cannot. Please do not be offended. I love you and wish to spend my remaining days by your side, but I cannot, will not, bind myself to another man ever again. Look where it has gotten me, all it has cost. Surely you of all people can understand." My last words were both a plea and a question.

Though he tried to hide it, his face fell. He cleared his throat, swallowing his disappointment. "Of course. What is marriage anyway but a contract, and you and I need no document or witnesses to prove our love true." He forced a smile. "I believe we did that for all time in the Bloody Lane when you leapt onto my horse's back."

"And will do so again at Stirling. Anyone who sees us will not be able to mistake our fidelity."

⋙ ⋘

Three days later, in the bluish-gray pre-dawn light of Samhain, Evina led me down a sloping path to the base of the rocky hill, then out into the heather and across a broad plain edged by low hills on either side. Soon a lone quiot rose ahead, white and stark against the overcast sky. The ancient tomb was formed by three vertical megaliths, a horizontal capstone lying on top. The last was so wide as to form a roof tall enough for a man to stand under without stooping.

Nearby were three women, all pale, with hair as black as midnight. One of them saw me, and for a moment when her eyes fixed on me, I thought my mother had been raised from the dead. But then she moved, squinting in the bright sunlight, and lines formed around her mouth and eyes and I could see she only resembled my mother. Another relative.

Evina linked hands with the others. "For generations, the women of our tribe have gathered to witness their daughters become women. For you, that transition occurred long ago, but without the rite that is your due. As your mother has passed through the veil, Calliac, our high priestess, will be the one to mark you. Yet you will not be without kinswomen in your time of joy. I have called together our closest living relations through your mother's bloodline. This is my sister, Maracail."

Maracail, the one who so closely resembled my mother, stepped toward me. "Greetings, Guinevere. I am your cousin, and these are my daughters, Gavina and Fia."

The two younger girls raised their hands in greeting.

I embraced each in turn. After so long only having one blood relative, my cousin Bran, who was a relation through my father's line, meeting four in a matter of days was astonishing. "It is an honor to meet all of you."

Calliac was the first to pass beneath the dolmen, followed by Evina and then me, as our relatives brought up the rear. Evina's guards stood sentry at the entrance, ensuring we remained undisturbed. We did not stop in the area beneath the stones but continued into an earthen cave not visible from the surface. Once inside, Calliac struck a flint, and a spark of light glimmered, caught in her torch, and soon was reflected in several lanterns placed around the chamber.

As my eyes adjusted to the light, images appeared, painted on the rock walls and carved into stones that sealed niches. They were ancient and crude, done by inexperienced hands, but their meaning was clear. In one, a woman danced in a field of heather, surrounded by six children, while the one next to it depicted a warrior with a bloody spear on the field of battle.

Calliac spread a blanket on the ground, then removed the stone showing a woman presenting her young daughter with a horse. She withdrew a clay beaker, long ago stoppered with wax or some sort of gummy sap, and placed it on the ground at one end of the blanket.

"This," she said, pointing at the beaker, "is the remains of your grandmother—Corinna's mother—last of your line to die in our lands. It is only fitting she should bear witness to this rite. All around us are the bones of your ancestors. Were it in my power, I would bring your mother to rest here too, but it is best to leave her where she is. Perhaps one day you too will lie in eternal sleep here, once your spirit has moved on. But that is not for me to say."

She built a small peat fire in the center of the room and cast upon it a handful of herbs that perfumed the air with a rich, sweet scent. Then Calliac held out a small offering dish. In it was a tiny white stone, small chunk of bread, a bit of wine, and a thistle blossom.

My mother had set up similar shrines on Samhain in Northgallis. For her, the objects represented the relatives whose bones she could not venerate. Today, they stood in place of her bones, which were buried in Northgallis.

I took the bowl from Calliac and laid it carefully in front of the beaker. Kneeling back on my heels, I made the sign of Avalon and closed my eyes. "Mother, had circumstances been different, I know you would have rejoiced in this rite and in the woman I have become. I wish with everything in me that you could be here today, but I am confident you will watch over this gathering of women of your blood. Receive these my offerings with love. May you be at peace, may you never hunger, may you never thirst, and may you always find beauty, even between the worlds."

I touched the beaker. "Grandmother, though our eyes never met, your blood flows in my veins and I am certain our spirits know one another. I rejoice in finding my family and in finding you. Matriarch of my line, please bless this rite and welcome me as a woman into our family."

At Calliac's gesture, I discarded my tunic and lay flat on my stomach on the blanket. This was the opposite of the ritual that had marked my entrance into womanhood, the day I became a priestess and received the crescent upon my brow. Then, I lay face up on a stone beneath the rising sun, surrounded by priestesses. Today, I lay with my forehead to the ground, deep within the cool earth, among the bones of my ancestors and guarded by women who share my blood.

Calliac struck a small gong, and the others gathered

around us. "Daughter of the Votadini, hear now the tale of your making, the knitting of blood and bone through the generations that resulted in your life," she intoned as her instrument bit into my tender flesh, leaving behind the first mark.

Maracail took up the tale. "In the days of old, we were of two hearts, the people of this land. We came from wanderers, the people of continent who knew no fixed home but followed the land and its seasons, living not off the earth but from their flocks, paying homage to the oldest of gods through blood and stone, living and dying according to their will. They were short and dark, the children of the ancient ones."

"But we were fair and sinewy, a brave, adventurous people who traveled out of the wilds of the mainland to found great cities. By their blades, whole tribes rose and fell. Their fires forged great beauty from bronze and weapons of iron," Gavina continued, her songlike voice dulling the teeth of the needle and lulling me, along with the heat and heady aroma of the incense.

Soon, the story became real and I walked with the shades of my ancestors, traveling through time with them, age after age.

Fia added her voice to the rhythm of the story. "They thought themselves unstoppable until one day, they woke in the shadow of the eagle. Bearing her talons, she chased them into the sea, where the god Lir and his son Manannan took pity on them, setting them down in the verdant lands we now call Britain. Never ones to be content, they explored that land, eventually meeting up with our darker half."

By the time the story came back to Maracail, I was barely conscious of the needle's sting. "When they came together, first it was with fire in the head and the fierceness of battle fury. There was much bloodshed as the old ones sought to protect their lands from the newcomers, each trying to hold sway over the other. But soon, they saw this was only decimating their population, so they drank of the horn of peace. They intermarried, their children a mix of light and dark, just as you are today. Over time, the new-comers' knowledge of the land allowed our people to live in one place, and they formed kingdoms and tribes, which they jealously guarded."

"Just when it seemed peace would prevail, the eagle, their long ago enemy, returned, seeking to destroy their new home," Gavina said. "But this time, the people were ready, having learned from their history. They fought when they must, but they also bartered with the eagle, for the comingling of the two people had produced many tal-ents. They agreed to live under her protection from those who lingered in the north, an insular people who thought their mixing with the light ones from the mainland an abomination."

Fia paced as she spoke. "Trapped as we were between two people, we were always on our guard, training our women as well as our men so we would have as many war-riors as possible should the need ever arise to defend our-selves. In your grandfather's generation, a great hero of our people journeyed south to answer the call of a king and, in so doing, gave our people a place of refuge in the new land.

To secure this alliance, your mother was given as a bride, and the old and the new joined once again, giving birth to you, a great warrior queen like the women of old."

"Though from your loins no living children spring, your influence will forever change this tribe, as does every generation that tells this tale. This is the story of the Votadini, of our people, of which you are now officially one," Evina concluded. As I sat up, she embraced me, careful not to touch my enflamed shoulder blade.

I shook my head to clear it. My mind was fuzzy, as though I was waking from meditation or a powerful dream that still threatened to pull me back into the depths of sleep. The sight danced around the edges of my mind, tempting me with visions that flickered and flamed out before I could grasp their meaning.

They seemed to be coming to an end when one burst to life in violent color. In it, two armies were fighting over an island—not Avalon or Mona, but like them, it radiated a holy air, one of asceticism and peace. Before the conflict was over, the shoreline was tinged pink with blood. A man's image rose before my eyes—light red hair and beard, near my age. He wore the strangest cloak, embroidered with a green wolf on his left side and a blue bird of prey with a particularly large, sharp beak on the right. The same symbols and colors were painted on his shield. On a desolate plain beneath a midnight sky flashing with heat lightning, he met a woman with golden curls. Elga. She smiled wickedly, then the vision splintered apart.

Still blinded by the sight, I turned toward where Evina

had last been standing. "Votadess, you should be wary the red king, for he will turn his loyalties and betray our people. He is in collusion with the Saxons."

Her strong hands gripped my shoulders, shaking me a little, as though she could will me out of the grip of the sight. "Who? Who is this man?"

I shook my head. "I do not know his name, but even now he meets with her, forming an alliance that will affect us all." I closed my eyes and opened them. The visions had stopped. "I am sorry. That is all I know."

Evina turned away, pacing while I recovered myself.

When I indicated that I was ready, she stood before me, holding two feathers, one black as night, the other creamy white. "There is yet one more step to formally welcoming you into our tribe. As the scars on your shoulder attest, you long ago won your sword. This day I invest you with the feathers of your clan, one for being a warrior and the other denoting your family's status." She affixed the feathers to my braid. "Wear them when we gather and no one will dare question if you belong here, for you are now one of us as truly as if you had taken your first breath among the heather."

⁕⁕⁕

Within a week, we were on the road to Stirling, the land growing steeper as we traveled northwest. Here, the trees had shed their autumn colors, surrendering to dormancy in shades of tan and gray. A light kiss of frost each dawn marked the footsteps of the winter hag as she descended from the mountains, trailing winter in her wake.

By mid-morning of our second day on the road, we passed the hillfort of Stirling, where the army was garrisoned and from which Rohan ruled the countryside. Our destination was still several hours off, a castle nestled in the valley between the Ochil Hills and Strathern Mountains.

The sun shone high in the sky when we approached my new home, casting the mountains in the distance into deep purple shadow and making the river below sparkle as though it were made of jewels. The fortress itself was gray stone likely mined from the surrounding hills, which gave it the quality of having sprung straight out of the land like a hardy flower turning its face toward the light.

Inside, the great hall was clean and bright, lit by large windows that let in pine-scented breezes, while two large fireplaces chased away the sharp wind. The full staff—a bevy of cooks, bakers, maids, and pages—was assembled to greet us. As soon as they were dismissed, they scurried away to their duties, all but Kennon, a balding man of average height whose thick arms made him look more captain of the guard than steward of the house. He solemnly handed me the keys and pulled me aside.

"Evina instructed me to give you a gift," he said in a conspiratorial tone, glancing over his shoulder to be sure the others didn't hear.

"She did? She said nothing of it to me."

"I think it was meant to be a surprise. She said you would know what to do with him."

Him? Had she given me a horse or a hound? Or perhaps a bull in the field? What else could Kennon possibly mean?

He whistled, and the main door opened. One of the guards entered, leading by the arm a man shackled at the wrist, a metal slave collar around his neck. He gave the man a nudge in my direction.

"Meet your new mistress," he said without warmth before turning on his heel and slipping back out the door.

The man kept his head down, long black hair obscuring his face. He was shirtless—I supposed so I could assess his physique and worthiness for any task I might desire. I could not fail to notice the angry scars that twisted up his right arm from wrist to elbow, for they were much like my own, the result of skin warring with flame. Yet they were darker somehow, as though the skin beneath had once held a tribal tattoo. Their location was too precise to have been the result of an accident; he had been intentionally burned and the sign of his tribe removed.

A pinprick of recognition tickled my spine, though I could not quite place him. Something about him brought to mind the memory of a white rose, a wooden cross, and a fresh purple thistle. The items were clear in my mind's eye, but I couldn't quite give them context. *It couldn't be—could it?*

I crossed the room to get a closer look at the man who was now my slave, whether I wanted him or not. As I drew closer, my heartbeat sped and the niggling sense of knowing grew stronger until my pulse was pounding in my ears. It *was* him.

"Galen," I whispered as I used my index finger to raise his chin to force him to look at me. I expected to find fear in his eyes, or maybe even anger—we hadn't parted on the best of terms—but all their blue depths reflected was my own surprise.

"Hello, lass. I dinna expect to be seeing you again."

"Nor I you. How, why—"

"How did I become a slave?" Galen hadn't lost his knack for reading my mind. "'Tis a long story."

"One that I wish to hear. Come, sit." I led him to a bench near the window. I fumbled with the chatelaine at my waist, searching for the key to release his bonds. "You may be indentured, but you are no danger to me, that much I know."

None of the keys seemed to fit. I desperately wished I had something to offer him, even a meager cup of broth. I called to Kennon, instructing him to have the kitchens bring a light midday meal. Leading Galen by the forearm, I crossed to the rest of our party, who warmed themselves by the fire, trying to pretend they hadn't noticed the intruder. When I introduced Lancelot and Anna to Galen, the slave shivered despite the warmth.

"Do they allow you no tunic?" I removed my cloak and draped it around his shoulders.

His dimples appeared, along with a wry smile. "Aye, they do, but not on first introduction. I suppose they wish you to see I am indeed enslaved." He lifted his arms, displaying the grotesque scars on his right arm. "They burned my tribal markings away and gave me this." He lifted his chin so I could see the marking on the side of his neck. It was a crude tattoo, handwritten: *daor*—slave. "They put it there, over one of the major veins, so that it cannot be removed without endangering my life. So as you can see, though I live within Votadini lands, I am no longer one of them."

"That's terrible." I picked up the cord around his neck. At the end was a key that must fit his shackles.

He bowed his head, allowing me to remove it. For the briefest of moments, we were close enough to kiss. Butterflies tickled my belly at the thought. After all these years, I still desired his touch. I prayed Lancelot had not seen the slight frisson of attraction.

My cheeks flamed as I pulled away, breaking the spell. "Please, tell us your story."

Galen shrugged, looking at each of us in turn. "There's not so much to tell. Isolde took me with her to Ireland, and I ended up here as part of a bargain she orchestrated. It was my own people who condemned me." The manacles clicked open, and he rubbed his wrists. "Serves me right. I could not expect mercy after bringing shame on so many families." He looked at me. "I owe you a great deal, even more so to Elaine and Isolde. Tell me, how do they fare?"

I turned away, unable to face him when I answered. "They are both dead." I wiped at the tear rolling down my cheek. "So you have no one to apologize to."

He took my hand. "I am afraid I do. I am sorry for leading you on, for getting you involved in my affairs."

I pulled my hand away, not wishing to forge any bond that would be inappropriate in my new home. "It was a long time ago. All is forgiven. We need only look forward, not back." I looked him straight in the eye now.

"Of course," he said quietly. "What will you do now?"

"Right this moment?"

"No, I mean now that you are here."

"I was just asking myself the same question." I shrugged. "I would like some time to simply be. That is why I am allowing Rohan to continue to rule in my stead."

"A generosity you will no doubt regret," he muttered. "You have as much claim to rule this tribe as he does, if not more."

Seeing my puzzled expression, he hastened to explain. "You still do not understand your lineage, do you? Evina is your cousin. She rules because she is doubly royal through her grandfathers of Cunneda's line. But you"—he traced his fingertips gently down the scars on my arm—"are his direct descendant. I doubt Evina has figured that out yet, but when she does, she will rue allowing you to stay, and more so granting you lands that are of such great strategic importance. You'd best be on your guard."

Lancelot scoffed. "That is ridiculous. Why would Guinevere approach her as she did if it was her intention to challenge Evina's authority?"

"People have done stranger things."

"But I have no desire to rule a people I know nothing of." I paced the large room that was closing in on me. I worked my fingers into the folds of my gown, twisting the material. "I cannot even tell you at what hour dinner is served or where, much less what is best for this land and its people."

"But you are well known for your wisdom and diplomacy," Lancelot said, grasping my hands as I passed him. "The ambassadors sang your praises during your reign with Arthur. Once word gets out, there will no doubt be those who will support your cause."

"Even if I do not raise it?"

"Especially then. Those who oppose Rohan or Evina will grasp at anything to bring someone else to power," Galen said.

I ran a hand through my hair. "I do not want this. Let me be clear. I have had more than enough of ruling and intrigue to last a lifetime. I came here to find a home, not a crown."

"'Tis not I you need to convince." Galen looked at me wonderingly. "Have you ever been anyone's subject before? Besides Lyonesse, I mean." He chuckled darkly.

I punched him in the arm good-naturedly. "Of course. I was Arthur's subject long before I was his wife, and I obeyed his father before him, but you have a point. I do have much to learn about this court." Decades earlier, when I was first introduced to the house of Corbenic, Isolde warned me that in order to survive in a new household, one had to understand the players. It was time to heed her advice. "We know Rohan and Evina will mistrust me once they figure out I could be a threat. What else do I need to know about them?"

Galen's face lit up. "That's the woman I remember. I am afraid our affairs are not much more stable than the ones you recently escaped in Britain. It seems the time for peace is at an end across the isle, I'm afraid." He took a deep breath, seemingly trying to decide where to begin. "Evina always knew she would be Votadess. She was raised to marry whomever became Votad after Cunedda's successor. Unfortunately, as these things often go, the line of succession was not so simple in flesh and blood as it was on parchment. The throne changed hands many times and Evina was shuffled around with it. Finally, the tribal leaders gathered and agreed to dispense with all previous plans and go back to the old way of electing the Votad from among their number. Mynyddog, brother of the Cunedda's successor, Clydno Eitin, was chosen. Evina married him, and I believe you know the rest."

"What is her goal?" Lancelot asked. "I have yet to meet a ruler who does not have a motive beyond staying alive and keeping the peace."

Galen grinned. "Wise man. I like the way you think. It seems to be that that she has two main intentions. One is to keep the Picts at bay. They have been harassing this area since Camelot fell. I believe they are testing their boundaries. It is Mynyddog's responsibility to keep them within their ancient bounds. Evina is also focused on overthrowing Alt Clut so she can rule all four tribes. She studied Arthur's reign closely, and I think she aims to emulate it here."

"But the Damnonii of Alt Clut and Votadini she rules are only half of the tribes. What of the others?"

"I am afraid they are weakening by the day. The Selgovae and Novantae haven't produced a capable ruler in nearly fifty years and are slowly being absorbed by the two more powerful tribes. I predict that within a generation, they will cease to exist."

A somber pall fell over the room. For a long while, no one spoke, each envisioning a future in which whole peoples could disappear in a matter of years. In many ways, it seemed far-fetched, but with battalions of men dying every day in the service of power mongers, it wouldn't take long for women to outnumber men and birth rates to plummet. With fewer babies born to each tribe and the possibility of conquest, the Votadini and Damnonii might well be the only ones left.

My thoughts drifted back to my experience at court. Despite her kindness during the ritual of marking, I couldn't shake Evina's initial coldness toward me. "Evina seemed suspicious of me when I presented myself to her. Why should she worry about me?"

"You know as well as anyone that a ruler's crown is never secure." Galen gave me a sardonic look. "The rules governing us and our relationships with the other tribes, even the nature of our boundaries, are much more fluid than you are used to. Though we have a Votad and Votadess, they are not High King and High Queen with absolute authority like you enjoyed with Arthur. Evina is our ruler only so long as she can prove herself worthy—a battle she fights every single day. There are many who would hasten her fall. All they need do is expose a single weakness and raise another candidate in her stead." He looked at me, expression concerned. "But I fear I have overwhelmed you. That was not my intent."

"No, not at all. We need to know this. Thank you." I smiled at him, regretting my suspicions of long ago. "I am sorry for the unkindness I showed you in the past. It's ironic that I used to mistrust you and now you are the only one in my new household I am certain I can trust."

Before Galen could reply, a deep, commanding voice reached us from the back of the room. "I hope I will quickly earn your trust."

All heads turned toward the sound. We had been so absorbed in Galen's tale that none of us had heard the guards admit a guest. I would have to speak to the head of security in the morning about increasing the layers of admittance. From the look of him—thick, fur-lined cloak of royal blue over a well-made burgundy tunic—this man was not an assassin, but then again, I wouldn't have guessed Sobian to be one either.

Lancelot must have been thinking the same thing, for he shot to his feet, blocking my body with his own. "Who are you and what is your purpose here?"

The man bowed, showing a shock of orange-red hair held back by a circlet not dissimilar to the one Mynyddog had worn. "Forgive me. I did not mean to startle you. I am Rohan of Alt Clut, and this is my home. Or it was, until recently." Despite our guarded reception, his tone held no animosity and his green eyes sparkled with capricious mirth. "Consider it well prepared for you." He bowed again with the sweep of an arm.

What type of man thought it appropriate to barge into someone else's home unannounced? He seemed kind enough, but his presumption grated. His former role as master of the house would explain why no one thought to make a fuss or question his presence, as they were likely used to seeing him come and go, but it was still disconcerting. Best to be wary until we learned more.

When no one spoke, Rohan continued, looking from face to face as though trying to ascertain who would be his most likely ally. "Please forgive the breech of protocol, but I could not wait to meet you and see how you were settling in." He stepped toward me, and Lancelot tensed.

I stepped to the side so I could see around him. "I appreciate your enthusiasm, my lord. I too look forward to getting to know you. I have just called for the midday meal. Would you care to join us?"

⁕⁕⁕

By the time the roasted chicken was but a pile of bones, Rohan had charmed us all with his quick wit and even sharper tongue. He was a pleasure to listen to, partly because of his intelligence, but also because his voice was attractive—smoky and rich, yet smooth as ice. It put me in mind of the spirit they drank in these lands, the one with the spicy tail that had gotten Arthur so spectacularly drunk on our wedding night.

Rohan insisted on giving us a tour of our new home, taking special pride in the size of the town—which, unlike Camelot, was not clustered around the castle but spread out for miles in every direction—the fact that the blacksmith produced the strongest swords in the area, and that the far-rier could shoe a horse with a new set in under an hour, something he assured me would prove useful when the next attack came. He was certain it was only a matter of time.

When we reached the tiltyard, talk naturally turned to Lancelot's many victories in the ring, including the one over Aggrivane that had brought him to Arthur's attention when we were all much younger.

"I was there that day," Rohan recalled, a boyish look of wonder spreading across his face. "I was not yet a man, but I'd earned myself a place at court, one I sadly had to give up after a year when my father was wounded defending Alt Clut from the Picts." His gaze became distant as his mind traveled back in time. "You were spectacular. I have always envied your ability to disarm and subdue a man without harming him. I tend to favor a more... direct approach. I wonder if you could help me refine my technique."

"Certainly. I believe mastery of the sword begins with mastery of the mind. Any brute can hack and swing and stab and kill, but a man who can link his brain and his blade has a better chance of escaping a duel unharmed."

Rohan gave me an impish look. "I wonder how Guinevere would have fared against you. I hear my lady is quite the swordswoman. Have the two of you ever sparred?"

"We have, many times." Lancelot put an arm around me. "I daresay she taught me as much I have taught her."

"I had the advantage of my mother's training," I demurred, knowing that would win me points in her homeland.

"Indeed, she was legendary." Rohan looked away,

pressing his hands to his lips as though praying in the Christian manner. "I wonder… would it be impertinent of me to ask you for a demonstration?"

"You want me to duel with you?" That was not a question I ever expected to hear, much less from someone I hardly knew. Was it meant as a compliment, or was he testing me to find out if the rumors were true? Either way, it was yet another large presumption from a stranger. "Or am I to perform like a tamed wolf?"

A predatory grin spread across his features. He bared his right forearm, showing off his mark. "They are my clan's animal, so if anyone should be able to tame a she-wolf, it is I."

Lancelot jumped in, pushing Rohan back with a light touch to the chest. "Mind your tongue, else you do battle with me."

I pressed my lips together to hide the smile that threatened to betray me. Two powerful, handsome men fighting over me was quite a compliment for an aging queen. "Gentlemen, please. There is no need for a real duel today. Lord Rohan, yes, I will spar with you, but only briefly as I am well out of practice and have no desire to make a spectacle of myself so early in my time here."

Once in the ring, Anna picked out two blunted practice swords for us and we faced off across the dusty field.

"No blood. First contact is the winner," I stated.

He nodded. "Lay on."

We didn't circle one another for long. Though he was nearly three hands taller than me, it took only a moment of footwork before I spotted his weakness. He relied on the length of his arm to protect him, so in order to defeat him, I needed to bind up his sword. Instead of advancing on him, I drew him toward me with a series of fake attacks that enabled me to push his sword aside and get past the range of his blade. He, meanwhile, tried to push me back. Finally, I was able to strike his wrist, ending the fight.

He shook out his arm. "I find myself regretting agreeing to allow you to live here but not rule. You would be a boon to our army, even in training if you no longer wish to fight."

I opened my mouth to retort that it was rude to allude to a lady's age, but then I froze. Something in the way he turned his head, the glint of the sunlight off his reddish-blond hair, forced a memory from the depths of my mind. My blood went cold. This was the man in my vision, the one who would betray us all to Elga.

He bent over, palms on his knees, catching his breath, oblivious to my dark thoughts.

I shouldn't let on that I knew, should I? Or would it be best to confront him, try to stop this disaster before it went any further? He was already in league with Elga, so I had to be careful. It could all go south too quickly if he knew what I suspected. Isolde always told me knowledge was power, so for now, I would do nothing but smile and pretend nothing had changed. As far as he was concerned, nothing had. But as soon as he went back to the fortress, I had to investigate him. Luckily, I knew just the person for the job.

Chapter Eleven

The following morning, I woke to find word had spread not only of my presence, but also of my encounter with Rohan. A line of men, women, boys, and girls waited patiently for me in the courtyard, as though I was still queen and it was pleading day.

The low hum of their conversation reached me through the walls and windows as I went about my morning ablutions. Though they waited with uncommon patience and civility, my palms grew damp and my hands shook as I fumbled with the buttons of my gown.

"What do they want?" I asked Galen when he seated me at breakfast. I eyed the offerings warily, my queasy stomach urging me to choose something bland.

"Why, to see you, of course," he answered with a knowing smile.

I rolled my eyes at him, tearing off a hunk of bread and

passing the remainder to him.

"Clearly. But why?" I popped a piece into my mouth, savoring the still-warm sweetness of its honey glaze.

"You'll have to ask them. But if you want my best guess"—he swallowed a mouthful of spicy ale—"they want to see if it is true that Corinna of the Votadini has returned from the dead."

I stopped chewing. "Tell me you jest."

He grinned around a hunk of half-chewed bread. "'Tis the story I heard on my way to the kitchens."

My shoulders sagged and I muttered to myself, "How do these tales get started? Now I must contend with my mother's shade as well." Louder, I said to Galen, "I suppose they will all be disappointed to find me of flesh and blood without a trace of Otherworldly essence."

"You have more than a trace, lass, as you proved to Evina," he said, referring to the prophecy about Rohan, which I'd told him about the night before. "I reckon she'll nae like the attention you're attracting."

"Best to disperse them quickly then." I rose, smoothing my skirt. "Are you going to open the door for me, or must I dismiss you for incompetence, slave?"

Galen chuckled at my lighthearted reminder of his position and rose to do my bidding. "Are you certain you wish to meet them out in the courtyard?"

"Of course. That way everyone can see I have not called them here in rebellion and have nothing to hide. I'm sure there are at least one or two of her spies among them."

The chatter ceased as the door opened. Every eye

turned to me. I smiled self-consciously, at a loss for where to begin, how to address these curious onlookers who were within my new realm but not my subjects. I was saved by a rugged man with dark hair and dark eyes, who detached himself from the crowd and approached me. His face was familiar, yet I could not call up his name or how I knew him.

"Lady Guinevere." He inclined his head to me. "I am Nachton the Huntsman. You may remember me from my visits to your husband's court."

I took his hands and squeezed them fondly. "Of course I do. You were close friends with Lord Tristan. I still maintain we would not have survived Caledon Wood without the two of you."

Nachton's cheeks reddened. "It was my honor to serve you and the Lord of Lothian. Now it is also my honor to welcome you to Stirling. We"—he swept his arm wide, taking in the whole of the crowd—"mean you no disrespect by gathering here and will leave if you wish."

I took in the assembly, counting no more than two dozen souls—far too few to be suspected of a riot. "No, please stay. I know no one in these parts, save for those who traveled with me and my new steward. If I am to live here, I would like to get to know my neighbors."

For the next several hours, as the sun rose higher, I talked with them about all manner of things. Many inquired about my scars and asked if Arthur's death had been confirmed. Still more—some of them relatives both distant and near in relation—wished to hear of my mother and father and why I had returned.

A few of the young women asked me to use my sight to tell them the name of their one true love, which my gifts did not allow, but I was able to confirm to one that her love was planning to ask for her hand, while I assured another that her beloved sought to make his true feelings known.

A gaggle of young men had heard of my tussle with Rohan and wished me to show them the sequence that had brought him down.

"No one has ever seen his face in the mud before," one noted.

"We want to learn how to make it happen again," another said with vehemence unusual for one of his age. What had Rohan done to carve such a groove in a young heart?

I eyed them, taking in skinny limbs and fledgling muscles attempting to make the transition from boy to man. They were clearly used to hard labor and exercise, but it was unwise to instruct them in such an advanced maneuver when I hadn't assessed their skill level. Best to begin by demonstrating the two moves that were the basis of the complex string of footwork and blade skills.

"It is easier if I show you first. Then I will explain it as we go." Picking up two fallen sticks, I handed one to the most inquisitive of the boys. I motioned him toward me. "Come at me with great force."

After a moment's hesitation, he lunged. I sidestepped his branch, pivoting on the balls of my feet and bringing my own fake weapon under his with a crack. To his credit, the boy kept his hold, spinning away from my grip then pushing me back, forcing me into defense position.

"Very good, Cinon," a husky female voice called from over his left shoulder.

I looked up, surprised to see a tall blond woman approaching.

"Well met, Master Kiara," my opponent greeted her with interlaced fingers touched to his bowed forehead in a gesture of deep respect.

One by one, the boys fell into a straight line. Each made the same gesture.

"Master Kiara?" I asked when she reached me.

"I am one of the weapons masters for the Votad and Votadess, recently appointed to Stirling to help Rohan with the new students."

I took her measure, from the soles of her thick hide boots to the deep brown braccae tucked in at the knee, and her gray tunic hung loose and unbelted, as though in readiness for movement. She exuded confidence but not a single trace of malice. "I am sorry if my instruction gave you offense."

She waved away my concern. "On the contrary, I was hoping to see you in action. Please, continue."

Now that I had an audience, especially one who would note every misstep in my teaching, I second-guessed everything I had known for years. My plan for instructing the boys completely fled my mind. "Let's do it again."

As we moved through the familiar—at least to me—motions, I relaxed, losing my concern over Kiara. Who was she to me? My mother had taught me, and there was no way she would have let me persist if my technique was weak.

When we reached the end of the first movement, I showed them the second and then demonstrated the connecting footwork, which I in no way expected them to learn yet. "Now split off into pairs and practice what I have shown you. Your master and I will be here if you have questions."

The boys did as instructed, the sharp cracks of their practice blows punctuating my conversation with Kiara. I twisted to one side then the other, seeking to relieve aching muscles as I watched her. I wasn't as young as I used to be, so fighting was no longer as easy as breathing.

"I must admit that when I first heard Corinna's daughter was in Votadini lands, I did not believe it," she said. "But even if you did not so strongly resemble your mother, your skill proves it, just as Evina says."

Kiara's implied knowledge of my mother was suspicious. She was likely half my age, so she couldn't have known her. "Did you know my mother?"

Kiara shook her head. "I am Selgovae by birth, Votadini only through marriage. But my family knew yours. In fact, we are pledged to your service for the next three generations." She paused, observing the boys' progress. "Kian, you're dropping your right shoulder. Hold it steady and you'll be less vulnerable." Turning back to me, she resumed her line of thought. "But that is not why I came to see you."

"No?"

"No. I wanted to see your skills for myself. I could use some help training our wee ones." She held up a finger, staving off my objection. "Before you plead old age, know you don't fool me. Anyone who can execute a dancing dragon with no preparation is more than capable of taking anything these lads and lasses can toss at you. Besides, I only ask you to help the youngest, those still learning to hold their weapons."

I stared past her at the walls of the fortress, where the guards were changing position, some slinking off to sleep or drown their sorrows in drink, while others steeled themselves for a long afternoon of attentiveness. In my mind's eye, I saw myself with the Votadini and Damnonii children, helping them learn to balance their blunted blades and heft spears. That was one of many things I missed about not raising children of my own. In Camelot, we'd had others to see to the boys' training. At least here I could do it myself and—as Kiara implied—I would be teaching girls as well as boys, so I could pass on my mother's knowledge, even it was to those not of my own blood.

I swallowed a lump in my throat and blinked back unbidden tears. "I accept."

Kiara grinned. "Tonight I will tell Rohan of our agreement. If he does not object—and he won't, I will be sure— you can meet the rest of the youngin's on the morn."

We sat in companionable silence for a while, every so often shouting correction or praise as the boys went over and over their drills. By the end of the hour, Cinon had picked up the whole sequence, including the footwork, and was correcting the technique of the others.

"He is remarkable," I said.

"Cinon? He is. His father was one of our greatest

warriors. I only wish he could have seen his son complete his testing. Would you like to bear witness? It is your right twice over as one of royal blood and a warrior yourself."

My shoulders relaxed and my heart lightened at the prospect. My palm already itched to hold a sword again. This was what I had been trained to do, not sit on a throne. Plus, Kiara's offer would give me the chance to see the trial of a Votadini warrior first-hand. My mother had hinted at the arduous test over the years, but because I was never able witness it or complete my own, it captivated me even now. "I would. Thank you."

"It will take place at the next full moon."

⚜

A few weeks later, in pale hours of a crisp, cool morning, I mounted my horse and took off in the direction of the closest village, Galen at my side. The people who had gathered at the castle had helped me to understand that in spite of Rohan being their ruler, most citizens were in need of someone to be attentive to their needs. That was not to say Rohan was a bad king; he collected taxes, judged disputes, and protected the surrounding countryside with his army, but he didn't seem to understand that was only part of the duties of a ruler. From what they'd told me, despite his charm, he had none of the interpersonal skills that would appeal to the people.

When I suggested to Galen that perhaps this was because Rohan didn't have a wife to tend to them, he burst out laughing. "You have the measure of him already, I see. Watch your back, else he aim to put you in that position." I opened my mouth to protest, but Galen voiced my thoughts first. "Don't go thinking Lancelot is any bit a deterrent to him. I ken he fancies wooing you away from Lancelot as a challenge."

What good would it do Rohan to try to charm me? He was already ruler of the area and had previously lived on my lands. Unless that was it. Perhaps he wanted to formally return my lands into his control through me. But no, that didn't seem likely enough, even if he was genuinely attracted to me, especially with the prospect of having to best Lancelot for my affections. There had to be a greater plan at play that I wasn't seeing.

As we rode through winter-dimmed valleys of moss and dying grasses hugged by rocky, mist-shrouded mountains and forests of deep green pine, I imagined a map of the area, trying to tease out Rohan's strategy. This was a strategic area connecting the Damnonii to the west, Votadini to the south and east, and holding the Picts at bay to the north. If it were an independent kingdom, I could see the Damnonii and Votadini fighting over it, but it was clearly in Votadini control. Perhaps Rohan was scheming to wrest it from Evina. If he held sway over the border with the Picts, he may be able to use the threat of invasion to bring her to heel.

The more I thought about it, the more sense it made. Just as Evina harbored ambitions to rule all of the lands north of Hadrian's Wall, so might Rohan. If that were the case, I was merely a pawn in their scheming—a perilous place to be. I had to learn more—and for that I needed Sobian, wherever she was.

We slowed our mounts as we approached a village that seemed to have sprung up in the shadow of a Christian church, like violets in the shade of an oak. A few curious faces popped out at the sound of hooves, and I greeted them, inquiring after their welfare.

A man of middle years emerged from one house, crossed his arms and scowled at me. "Why are you here? Ain't no one ever cared about us before." He raised his chin in the direction of Stirling. "All them kind want is taxes and men to bleed in war. Most of them battles don't affect us none, 'cept in making widows and orphans. Now you 'spect me to think you don't have no reason for being here other than kindness. What are you—a gruagach?" He chuckled at his joke.

Inwardly, I groaned at the insult. It was not the first time I had been compared to a benevolent household spirit, especially with my short stature and dark coloring. Now, with my scars, I probably resembled one of the wrinkled fae more than ever. I wanted to hit the man upside the head and yell that I was only trying to help him, but his wariness of outsiders was understandable, especially ones that came bearing gifts and asking nothing in return.

Instead, I said, "If you wish to think of me that way, then so be it. Regardless, I am here with your welfare in mind."

While we were talking, a woman who had slipped out of a small house across the street sidled up to us. "Never mind him. John is still sore about his time in Rohan's army." She raised a hand in greeting, as friendly as he was cold. "I'm Gin. I know everything that goes on in this town, so I can probably help you."

For the rest of the morning, we followed Gin from house to hut to hovel. Gin's familiar face eased the introductions. Galen noted needs and made plans to send food and supplies upon our return to the castle, while I offered employment in my household when I could for those willing to relocate, and did my best to heal the sick.

One household, recently quarantined from the pox, wanted nothing to do with me as a priestess. They were proud Christians, the woman of the house told me, faithfully attending the church we had seen on our approach to the village. Covered in ruptured scabs that indicated she was only recently recovered, she would let me no closer than the door, despite my assurances I could not be infected.

"I understand. Shall I arrange a visit from the priest? Surely he will bring you comfort," I asked through the slightly cracked door.

She snorted. "He never sets foot outside the church. Ain't no holy man who's paid us mind since ol' Ringan told us 'bout Christ and then moved on." She gestured over her shoulder to her husband and three children who lay, unable to move, on mats on the floor. "As you can see, we can't go to him."

I balled my fists at my side. Yet another Christian priest shirking his duty to his people. Father Dafydd, whom Marius had exiled to this part of the world in a bid for control over Arthur, was not like that. Why couldn't there be more like him? Combined with Rohan's inattentiveness, it was no wonder John was wary.

"I will speak with him." I glanced at the sickest of the children, whose tiny body was riddled with pustules so close together as to be nearly indistinguishable from one another. He cried, his mouth and tongue so covered that he likely couldn't eat and had little hope of recovery. I did not wish to raise the possibility with his mother, but they had to be prepared. "May I ask, if the worst happens, do you have sufficient funds to see that your loved ones are properly buried?"

Her eyes flared with anger. "Look around. Do we look like we kin afford a shovel, much less to have that priest say his fancy words over our dead bodies?" She threw me a look so full of disgust, I involuntarily stepped back. "Begone! Away with you!"

I hurried back down the lane behind Gin, Galen bringing up the rear. Once we had put three blocks between us and the sick house, I stopped Gin with a hand to her forearm and held out a small purse of coins. "Will you hold these for me? I would like them to be used in the event anyone from that family dies. If they all recover, have a Mass of thanksgiving said in their honor."

Gin looked at the coin purse, then back at me, her eyes full of wonder. "How generous of you, my lady, especially given the way she treated you."

She stowed the purse in a pouch beneath her tunic as we headed back toward the church, where the priest assured me he would visit the house, but only once everyone was recovered. I closed my eyes, fighting to remain calm. His timing would be too late to offer them any comfort, which was what they so desperately needed.

"How were you able to speak with that family?" Gin asked as we departed for the stables. "Even the priest isn't brave enough to go to them, and he has the power of Christ on his side. Most of us would have given the house a wide berth, yet you gave them food and counsel. Are priestesses unaffected by the pox?"

I smiled. "No. But there was an outbreak when I was a young girl."

Snippets of those dark days flashed in my memory—my mother pressing a cold cloth to my forehead, her face dotted with red marks; my father hacking away at half-frozen ground to bury my little brother; Octavia sacrificing mourning doves to her old Roman gods to keep the worst of the pestilence at bay. We eventually recovered, but some, like Arthur's kinsman King Mark, were permanently scarred. Hundreds died.

Gods preserve us from another summer like that one. "From what we were taught in Avalon, a person cannot be afflicted twice. I am blessed that my family only suffered a mild case. Many others were not so fortunate."

We stopped in front of the stable. John, the suspicious man we'd encountered at the start of our venture, blocked the way.

He stood tall and stepped aside as we drew near. "Beg pardon, my lady, but I wanted to say thank you for what you've done fer us today. Many of them people is sayin' you're the rightful queen o' the Gododdin, and I ken they're on ta somethin'. You've been more a queen to us today than anyone in a crow's age. If you ever have need of us, ask an' it's yours."

⁂

The next several weeks passed in a blur of parchment and ink, as I called in every contact I had to try to find Sobian. Lancelot did the same. But the information that made its way to us wasn't usually about our favorite spy; rather, it carried news of the current political climate, which had slipped my mind since arriving in Din Eidyn. Now, between the two of us, we were getting a pretty good idea of how fractured Britain had become.

"Accolon says that Mordred's fellows have disbanded and returned to their own tribes," Lancelot said.

I looked up from the letter I was reading. "The Saxons have not. Elga is still intent on ruling as much of the country as she can. Owain reports that she is allying herself with whoever has the most power at the moment and is considering marriage again—no doubt to increase her own standing."

"Then she should next fix her gaze on Constantine." Lancelot flicked a page toward me. "Read this."

I picked up the letter. It was from Bran. As I read, my stomach twisted. This was a detailed account of kingdoms falling under the boots of Constantine's army. First

Dyfnaint and the parts of the Midlands not already under Saxon control. He skipped the Summer Country because it was already under Elga's rule. Cornwall was resisting, and Gwynedd too. But Powys had surrendered. He was even putting it about that Helene was his top choice for a wife, once she grew to marriageable age, an idea Morgan vehemently opposed.

"He aims to be High King," I said, shocked at how much progress Constantine had made since we left Traprain Law. The lands we had once roamed so freely were now under the control of a man with great ambition. But then again, that was not much different than what Arthur had done to become king.

At least on the surface. The more I read, the more troublesome the clash of thrones became. As they pressed north, Constantine's gigantic army ruined the harvest, descending like a plague of locusts, eating or confiscating bales of wheat, bushels of fruit, and robbing families of livestock they were depending on to see them through the winter. In their footprints lay acres of stubbled fields, naked trees, and bloodied earth from the slaughter of animals— normal sights in autumn to be sure, but now whole towns starved even before the first snowfall and despaired what would become of them in the cold, shadowy days ahead.

Oblivious to my concerns, Lancelot asked, "Would it be so bad if Constantine prevailed? He has a blood claim through his relation to Iggraine, and Arthur always liked him."

"He did. I suppose what is happening is only natural.

Are we really getting so old as to begrudge a new generation their successes? I have lost my taste for the intrigues of courtly life."

"Then what are we doing here?" Lancelot mused.

I put his letter aside and picked up another. "This is what really worries me. Morgan and Accolon have made an alliance aimed at holding the north from Constantine's advances and retaking some of their ancestral lands in Bernicia. For some reason, they are focused on the Isle of Winds. I don't see why they would be interested in a small island north of Catraeth."

"That is a key strategic point for blocking any Pictish attack by water. Whoever holds it controls whether or not the Picts can access Britain via the Firth of Forth."

"How do you know that?"

"My time in Din Eidyn and Angus has taught me a great amount about politics and strategy in this land."

I looked back at the letter. "It says here Morcant hired a group of Saxons to patrol the waters." I shivered. Tragedy had resulted from a similar offer made by Vortigern decades before I was born. The result was the Saxon presence on our eastern shore. "That must be why Owain and Accolon are interested in the area. I would be concerned if I were them."

"It certainly makes taking back their lands that much harder." He shook his head. "One of these days, perhaps your people will learn not to trust those back-stabbing bastards."

We lapsed into silence, each studying the map of Britain before us.

"I wonder if we will ever experience peace again," I whispered, more to myself than to Lancelot.

"There is one way to know for sure," he replied.

I looked up, intrigued. "What's that?"

"Be the one to bring about peace." Lancelot's gaze on me was intense. "I know you said you wanted nothing more of politics, but I also know you are not one to sit idly by and let others suffer. If you were, you wouldn't have ridden through the villages. You would have let them rot under Rohan's neglect." He leaned toward me and grasped my hands. "I think you should consider it—making a bid for the throne, I mean. The time is ripe, and the people would willingly rally behind you."

I cleared my throat, fighting a sudden constriction. "How can you even ask me that? I have seen enough blood-shed, feuds, and petty fighting to fill three lifetimes. While I was queen, I was kidnapped and almost killed twice. You know the dangers I faced better than anyone."

"But the people are crying out for a strong ruler. These letters"—Lancelot tapped his index finger on the pile, as if trying to illustrate his point—"tell us that. They have no love for people who march into their lands with hordes of soldiers and declare themselves rulers, be they Saxon or Briton. You would have no need to do such a thing. You earned their trust long ago."

I fled to the open window with its tranquil view of the river. I breathed in deeply, desperate to be physically away from him and the argument he was spinning. He was appealing to my need to protect Britain's people, the very reason why I'd assented to be queen in the first place. The dutiful part of my mind said I owed them my protection as long as I was strong enough to give it. But I could not, would not take up the mantle of power again. It had cost me too much. Lancelot knew that. Why was he pressing this?

"Some of them may trust me, but not all. You saw how quickly our friends turned against me during my trial. And what of those who supported Morgan as Arthur's rightful wife? He divorced me, took away my title as queen. To them, I am not fit to lead. Then there are those who never liked me in the first place. You were not there in the Bloody Lane. You did not witness the jeers and taunts, how they relished degrading me in the broad light of day. I would still have to win over their fickle hearts, which just as likely now would support a Saxon over a woman whose weaknesses have been on display."

"Surely they are in the minority. Anyone who seeks the throne will have some enemies."

"That may be, but I am no young queen anymore. Plus, all my detractors would have to do is point at my scars. The most ancient laws forbid a maimed person from being king or queen out of fear their imperfection will ruin the land. That's why Bedivere was doomed to live in Kay's shadow. He would never be whole, and neither will I." I sighed then finally looked back at him. "Do you wish to be king? Is that why you are making this argument?"

Lancelot scowled. "You know it is not. I only wish for you to be sure in your heart, so you do not look back on this time and wonder if there was something else you could have done."

"I know my heart, as do you. Do you not remember what we said to one another when we were reunited in Din Eidyn? I wish to live out my days in peace."

"I am afraid peace is not something the gods are willing to grant us for a while."

"I have to agree." My gaze drifted to the ships on the river below.

Was Sobian even now on a ship like those, perhaps somewhere far out at sea? Was that why we couldn't locate her? But surely the current political instability was rife with opportunity for one with her skills. She had to at least be keeping an eye on the situation.

As a crew unloaded their boat, I recalled how quickly rumor spread among the shipyard workers. With people coming and going from a multitude of kingdoms each day, information was, in many ways, more valuable than the cargo contained in the ships. "Lancelot, I think we have been seeking information in the wrong place. If you were Sobian, would you not maintain your illicit connections?"

He followed my gaze to the boats bobbing in the harbor. "I suppose so. Do you think they know where she is?"

I was already headed toward the door. "There is only one way to find out."

◈◈◈

Sobian's laughter reached us before she appeared at the top of the gang plank, a bird perched on one arm and a long rectangular box about the length of my arm in their other. She was followed by two men carrying chests and other luggage. For a woman who had lived on the river when she first came into our lives, Sobian certainly had grown accustomed to the lifestyle of being one of Arthur's highest ranking officials, his head spy. Wherever she had been since before Camlann hadn't damaged her lifestyle any.

She met us at the bottom of the ramp. "You lured me out here by appealing to my basest instincts. You knew I would not be able to resist solving one more mystery with you." She took off her leather gloves and handed the hooded falcon to Lancelot as though he was in charge of keeping hunting birds.

"Do you always travel with such creatures?" he asked, struggling to use one of her gloves to shield his wrist from the bird's talons.

"Only when I feel they might add something to my ability to track the person I seek. You would be surprised what they can be taught. As it does not sound as though I will have time to train one here, I brought one already accustomed to my will." She placed the box vertically on a stack of crates and opened a door set into one side, revealing a perch made of rope. Carefully, with the tenderness of a mother, she guided the bird from Lancelot's arm onto the perch, removed its hood, and shut the door.

She held out the box to me, but I motioned to Galen. "This is Galen. He is my"—I still struggled with calling him my slave—"servant. He will see to your needs as well while you are here."

Sobian looked him up and down in the same appraising manner she had first used on Arthur. A small smile played on her lips as she took in his dark hair, shimmering with silver at his temples and on his chin. His bright blue eyes met hers not with deference, but with equal challenge and equal lust. "I shall enjoy getting to know him." The attraction between them was instantaneous and palpable. I leaned over to Lancelot, voice low so that only he could hear. "This will either be the strongest love affair anyone has ever seen or combust in a matter of days."

"Either way, I think we have just witnessed a meeting of equals."

I held my arm out to her. "Shall we go back to the castle? I am sure you wish to rest after so long a journey."

Sobian fell into step next to me, Lancelot following. "No. I feel suddenly invigorated. I would like to hear how you came here and what happened for you to call on me. I hear the sight was involved?" She tapped her forehead.

"It was. But I would prefer not to discuss it in so public a place."

Sobian entertained us with tales of sailing the Irish Sea until it turned into the North Sea. There she clashed with a fleet of Norse pirates and faced off against the Witch of Orkney, who prophesied she would lose her heart to a man whose father was murdered by a god.

By the time we were settled by the fire and all that remained of the midday meal were crumbs and sticky fingertips, I was beginning to doubt the validity of Sobian's tales—lying *was* part of her job after all. But knowing

Sobian, every word was probably true. Only she could find such fantastic situations, yet live to brag about them. That was exactly why I needed her. If anyone could uncover Rohan's motives in time to preserve the peace, it was her.

As though she could hear my thoughts—and I often suspected she could—Sobian said, "So tell me about this prophecy of yours."

When I had finished recounting the day of my marking, all I knew about Rohan, and that I needed someone to get close to him, Sobian stretched and slowly gave into a languorous grin. "This sounds like your most fun assignment yet. I accept. Do you think he'd take me for training at the fort?"

"No. Our approach can't be so direct." I stirred the fire with a poker until it hissed sparks. "We need him to accept you into his confidence, to trust you. He would never spill his secrets to one of his men—even if she was a woman."

"Sounds like I'll be playing a prostitute again." She considered the idea, watching the newly stoked flames.

"Actually, infiltrating a brothel not far from the barracks wouldn't be difficult," Lancelot said. "One hears all sorts of rumors in a house like that…."

Sobian sighed. "You may work wonders with horses, Lancelot—and please do not be insulted by this—but for a renowned warrior, you know so little about so many things. That is too obvious. Plus, a man like Rohan doesn't need an average whore. I need to be irresistible, someone whose position and beauty are useful to him."

"You already have the beauty part down," Galen observed.

Was it my imagination, or did Sobian blush? I had never seen her flush once the whole time I'd known her.

"Let's step back for a moment," I said. "If we're right and Rohan wishes to overthrow Evina, he first has to best Morcant and me. He needs power, wealth, and position to do that. He can either gain those through war or marriage, and we know he favors the latter because he has been trying to woo me. What if we give him a more attractive option?"

All eyes fell on Sobian.

She raised an eyebrow. "You mean I get to play a noble this time, instead of your lady's maid?" She made a gesture of happiness.

"Not just any noble," Lancelot said, picking up on my line of thinking. "You need to be a relative of Morcant, one who promises to enrich her husband greatly."

"His kingdom is so close to the Pictish border that I have no doubt he has some woad-covered by-blow. Why can't you be one?" I winked at Sobian. "I know Morcant from his visits to Camelot. I think I can get him to agree. After all, if it means unmasking a traitor in his midst and possibly strengthening his alliance with Evina, he has nothing to lose."

Galen cleared his throat and caught my eye. "If I may interject?"

"Galen was not always a servant," I explained, having forgotten Sobian didn't know the sordid tale of how we had known one another. I would have to fill her in soon, but now was not the time. "He was once a noble who was very good at getting others to believe exactly what he wished them to." I narrowed my eyes at him and twisted my lips, remembering how deep his subterfuge had gone. "Then he crossed the wrong person. A life of slavery is his punishment." I turned back to Galen. "Go on."

He cleared his throat again, more anxious at addressing Sobian than I'd ever seen him. "Forgive me, kind lady, but you are not from here and are unfamiliar with our customs. If you are to do as you say, you will need a translator at the very least, and a guard at the most. I hear tell you can defend yourself, but Rohan will not know that. If you will allow me, I can provide a cover for you." He looked up at me, as if just remembering he would need my permission. "That is, if Guinevere will allow it."

I nodded.

Sobian eyed him again, brow wrinkling and lips pursing as she considered her options. "I usually prefer to work alone, but you make a valid point."

"You don't happen to speak the Pictish tongue, do you?"

Sobian proceeded to ask him in their language how he thought she'd faced down the Witch of Orkney if she could neither understand nor speak to her.

"Don't underestimate her skill with languages. She's like one of those rare birds that can imitate any of its kin," I said. "Galen, I suppose you speak it as well?"

"I do, lass. I knew a bit of it when we were young, but when Isolde sold me back to my people, I was forced to learn it while working in a mine in Dalriada. But that's a story for another day."

I looked at Sobian. "Well, then. Now all we have to do is create your new identity and arrange to have you visit your 'father.'"

"And paint her skin with woad," Galen added, a task his prurient grin hinted he would gladly volunteer to take from me.

PART THREE

The False Queen

Chapter Twelve

Spring 521

My name was being whispered in the wind. It tickled my hair, brushed my skin like a feather, and sometimes, it woke me in the night, pressing into my mind like a probing lover. Sobian was still in Morcant's capital of Dùn Breatann, but I didn't need her network of fishermen and sailors to know my name slithered through the waterways too. My name was attached to a word that could condemn as easily as it could seduce—insurrection.

Treason found me on an ordinary spring morning, shortly after Beltane, sparring with Kiara and our students in the Stirling barracks south of my holding. Like a dog whose scent I thought I'd lost back in Camelot, it came bounding through the gates in the person of Nachton the Huntsman. My conflicted heart did not know whether to leap at seeing a friendly face or dread hearing the news he brought from the surrounding countryside. Since my arrival in Stirling, Nachton had become my favorite and most trusted informant.

He bowed low before us, but would not meet my eyes. He kept his gaze on his shoes while fidgeting with his cap. "My lady, I dare to interrupt your instruction only because I bear news of great import."

Kiara and I exchanged a worried glace. Without a word from me, she rounded up the children and led them inside.

Once we were alone, I said, "You look like you ate a bowl of worms. Your news cannot be that dire unless someone is dead. Spit it out."

His words tumbled over one another in a rush as though he could contain them no longer. "A contingent of Selgovae, Votadini, and Venicones have banded together in your name west of Din Eidyn, near Velvniate. They seek to overthrow Rohan and install you as ruler of both Stirling and Alt Clut."

"What?" His image winked in and out of view as I blinked rapidly, trying to make sense of what he said.

Nachton nodded so vigorously, he nearly bowed. "'Tis true, my lady. They took over the fort in your name. My brother in Carriden confirmed the movement has spread to this side of the wall. He predicts that within a fortnight, insurgents will be proclaiming you Votadess from here to Dùn Breatann."

"What?" I said again, still stupefied.

I shook my head, eyeing Nachton closely, certain this was a prank, an elaborate jest I failed to appreciate. It had to be. We'd long known the people favored my rule over Rohan, but short of John's jest that he would join my army any day and occasional prodding from Lancelot, no one had dared openly suggest I raise my station, much less engage in open sedition.

Kiara returned to my side. "Who is calling you Votadess?" Her voice was as light and inconsequential as though she were speaking of the direction of the wind rather than high treason.

I held up a hand, forestalling Nachton's answer. On the tail of a deep breath, I explained. "Nachton is under the delusion that a rebellion is taking place in my name to the south."

Kiara studied him, running a finger across the braids holding back her golden hair. She pursed her lips and cocked her head. "It's possible." Her eyes went distant with thought, then she snapped her fingers. "I know who may be able to tell us."

She disappeared into the fort commander's quarters.

"You can answer this easily, though the only question is in your own mind," Nachton said. At my puzzled expression, he added, "What use is the sight if you don't employ it?"

I narrowed my eyes at him. I never liked using my gifts except under absolute necessity. It wasn't that we were forbidden from using them—Morgan did every chance she got before she converted to Christianity—but it had always felt to me as though I was taking advantage of the gods. However, given that Evina would have my head if what Nachton said was true, perhaps it was wise to make an exception.

Tossing aside the practice sword I still held, I sank onto a hay bale and closed my eyes. At first, the whistling of the wind through the pines was all I perceived, but as I willed my inner vision southward, the whistling became a snapping and I saw a rough blue flag with a crudely drawn crowned white horse at its center flying high above the fort. They were flying my standard.

Willing myself free of the sight, I struggled to breathe, each gasp too fast and too shallow. There was no going back now. I was involved in a war of the people, like it or not. My hands shook. I buried them in my skirts, but it was too late to hide my distress.

Kiara returned. "The commander says he has heard the same. We had a messenger this morning from Caimlan who told him of the unrest."

I sighed, all the strength draining from my limbs. "That means Evina will know soon as well." Her steely glare flashed before my eyes, turning my stomach to lead. Even from several days' distance, I could feel her wrath. I stood and motioned for them to follow me. "Come, come, we must discuss this with Lancelot and Anna. We must devise a solution before this becomes unmanageable."

"If it is not already," Nachton whispered ominously.

❧❦❧

Longing for Avalon and the labyrinth Arthur had built for me at Camelot, I carved out for myself at the center of my new home a sanctuary of another sort, a small room in which I could meet privately with Lancelot and dear advisors of my choosing. The room itself was small, dimly lit by a single window that faced the rushing river below and a dozen or more flickering candles. There was no fire, so as the sun dipped below the purple mountains, turning the river to liquid bronze, we hugged our cloaks about us.

It was there that Galen, Lancelot, Anna, and I discussed what could not be spoken anywhere else in the kingdom, lest we find our heads on pikes outside Din Eidyn. My younger self would have focused on the why, wondering why I was being used this way yet again and wailing at the injustice of it all. In my mind, I snickered at her, knowing now the only question that mattered was what we were going to do about those who sought change in my name.

I took a deep breath, pacing the circumference of the small room. "I will not kill the rebels to silence them, so we can forget that option straight away. I suppose I must choose whether to try to tamp them down and convince them to pledge allegiance where it should be—to Rohan and Evina—or to be the beacon they seek." The weight of such a decision threatened to bow me once and for all. I sank into a chair.

"Here is how I see it," Lancelot said, rubbing his cheek wearily. "After Camlann left a gaping void in the succession, the world as we knew it ended. All the rules were erased, gone with the souls of the wise rulers who died that day. Now we are living in a world where young fools reign, in their hubris thinking themselves wise." He sipped a tankard of ale Kennon had supplied us with before retiring for the night. "I'm not saying we always know best, but at least we have the wisdom and experience to know right from wrong. I asked around today, and most of the people who back you are the sons and daughters of your generation, those who look up to you as their only remaining mother."

I shivered. Not long after my babies died, I'd vowed to be a mother to my people. Now they were asking me to lead them. Who was I to say no simply because I was tired? When did my mother ever ignore a single one of my cries, even when she could barely open her eyes long enough to tend to me? My people needed me, and I had a responsibility to scoop them up, dry their tears, and do what I could to make everything better once again.

"There is good reason they feel that way," Anna added with a small tut of disapproval at those currently ripping the country apart in their quest for power. "And I say this as one of the ruling class. But I am also a Votadini, and I have seen the results of my peers' actions. We nobles have abused our power for too long, and it is the country that suffered. I fear Evina and Mynyddog will be no better. Our country has gone from a patchwork of tribes to cowering under Roman rule, only to be abandoned then split asunder by more rulers in more formations than can be counted. Arthur attempted to stitch us back together. You can continue his work. We need someone who can call upon the power of the elements, upon the earth herself, to make us whole again. Rohan, Evina, and Mynyddog fear you because they know you can lead us and that your collective power is greater than all their commands ever will be."

I had to admire Anna. Logic like that was why Arthur was wise to put his sister in charge of Lothian so many years ago, after her husband had attempted to overthrow him. Anna was a born statesman with a strong knowledge of history and a gift for flattering words. Many times she had advised me over the years like the mother she should have been, had I married Aggrivane. But this time, I could not allow myself to capitulate to her words so easily, not without serious reflection.

"Anna, I don't think—"

"I know you don't want to listen to me, but please at least hear me with an open mind. What you do beyond that is on your soul. Balance needs to be restored. We need someone to be the sutures binding us back together or we may bleed to death. You can do that. You are both them and us, the old and the new, the threshold. The people are scared, but so are the rulers. They fear that one day the people will rise up against them. Well, that day has come. That is why the people are asking you to lead."

I sat back in the chair, rubbing my temples. "I hear you. I understand your argument." I let out a forceful breath. "I simply do not know if I can do this again. I was a younger woman, full of drive and ambition, the first time around. Now… now, I just want peace."

Galen smirked. "No doubt you meant for yourself, but you just admitted you share the same goal as the people who call upon you to lead them. All they want is peace. If they thought the current Votad and Votadess could give them that, they would not have left their fields and their planting." Galen patted my hand. "You may fancy yourself helpless, but you are nae. You nae'ver have been. You have options, more than you realize."

I gave a sarcastic huff. "Like what?"

"This island is at war on at least four fronts, and you could lead any of them, save the Saxons. I dare say they'd slit your throat if you tried. But look here." He stabbed the map on the table in front of me with a narrow finger. "I may only be a slave, but I have eyes and ears and I used to rule a sizable part of this land. I know as much as those at court. As you say, you could join this foolhardy quest to overthrow Mynyddog and Evina. The easiest way to do that is either to ally with Rohan or kill him. Depends if you want Mynyddog as your enemy or your ally."

"I vote for ally," Lancelot put in.

"Or you could take back Camelot's throne." He ticked off a second option on his fingers. "Constantine would bow to you and the people would back you." I opened my mouth to protest, but he cut me off. "I know, I know, you don't want it. You've made yourself abundantly clear on that score. I didna say you had to keep it. You could hold it long enough to end this bloody civil war. Then you can pass the crown on to Constantine or Helene or whomever you wish. My point is that in that role, you could put pressure on our enemies to get anything you will."

I shot him an unconvinced look.

"If that doesn't please you, you could back Owen and Accolon in their fight against the Saxons," Lancelot said, warming to Galen's line of thinking. "But in order to be of value, you'd have to have an army behind you, which necessitates being queen of some kingdom—which puts us back where we began."

Anna and Galen nodded.

"Why does it always come back to power and a throne?" I threw up my hands, wishing I could punch something to relive the growing frustration within me.

Galen smirked. "Have you nae been paying attention? It's your destiny. You were born to rule, to lead this country, this land through times of great uncertainty. That much was plain to me the first time I laid eyes on you as a lass, which is why I knew I could never woo you as I did Isolde, nor break your heart like I did with Elaine. You had too much of a role to play for me to muck it up simply for my own amusement." His eyes were shining with pride.

I dropped my gaze to the floor, no longer able to look at him directly. To think, so many years before, while I was second-guessing his every move and pouting that he chose Isolde over me, Galen had already foreseen the heights to which I would rise. My throat tightened and tears pricked the back of my eyes. I could not speak now even if I wanted to.

Galen gently took my hand. "Let me ask you this. What would you do if you were not in power? Go back to Avalon and spin your magic until you die?"

I shook my head. I had already considered that upon leaving Mayda's convent. As much as I loved Avalon, the life of a resident priestess felt too... contained. Deep down, my spirit told me there was still something I needed to do before I retired to a life of solace on the holy isle.

"Good. We've eliminated that possibility. Despite all your protestations to the contrary, I certainly do nae see you settling down with Lancelot to live a quiet life." He shot Lancelot an apologetic look. "If you had wanted that, your inclination would have been to flee to Brittany after Arthur died, not come here. No. You came here because you wanted to reconnect with your kin, with your blood. And that means accepting your power."

Galen was right, but if I did what he was proposing, what they all were proposing, I would be mirroring the actions for which I'd criticized Mordred so harshly. For was I not moving against my own kin? But then again, my name was being used without my consent, so I was linked to this evil even if I never acted. Would Evina believe me innocent? Not likely. If my reputation was already in tatters, what did I have to lose?

I looked to Lancelot for advice. He had been so quiet, so unusually reserved, I feared he objected to what I was considering.

He breathed out forcefully through his nose, snorting like a bull. "I can't say I relish another war, and I never thought I would challenge my sovereign lords, but what must be done, must be done. I will stand with you against Evina, if that is what you choose." He entwined his fingers in mine across the table. "I am yours in all things, be assured of that."

I nodded, buoyed by his support, and blew out a breath to calm my jangled nerves and jittery stomach. "Then I suppose it is decided. But we must remain silent until we are certain this revolution has teeth. As far as anyone else is concerned, this is nothing but a silly rumor."

Chapter Thirteen

Spring 522

A year passed without a whisper of my role in the ongoing clashes between the people and lords who supported me, and the Votad and Votadess. Thanks to Sobian's network of spies, I had an easy way to funnel money, food, and weapons to those fighting for my cause—all without a single link to my name. The only person who knew I was the source was Sobian, and I was confident she would tell no one.

While I was acting as ghost benefactor, Sobian was playing her part as Eithne, daughter of Morcant. She had done such a good job slithering her way into Rohan's affections that she was now living with him in Dùn Breatann. He expected to marry her at Lughnasa, so we had only a few months to conclude her role and send Eithne back to the Picts.

I invited the two to stay with me for a while in the

hopes I could help move along the ruse. Morcant was supposed to arrive from Bernicia two days before them, ostensibly to discuss how we could deal with the revolutionaries spouting my name at every turn, but so far we had no word from him.

We had been hunting earlier in the day and were now taking a much-needed break from the chase. Sobian and I waited by the riverside for Rohan and Lancelot to return from field dressing our kill and seeing to their horses, which both men insisted on doing personally, though an abundance of capable grooms flocked around them. I suspected Rohan went along with it only because it was Lancelot's way and he didn't wish to be seen as inferior or lazy in comparison.

I had already laid out our cloaks, which were no longer needed as the day grew warmer, along with a small feast of bread, cheese, fruit, and a flagon of ale. Sobian trailed behind me as I plucked leaves, flowers, and roots from the edible or medicinal plants that grew along the bank.

"Rohan's father wasn't killed by a god, was he? Otherwise you may be fated to stay with him beyond Lughnasa," I teased, referring to the Witch of Orkney's prediction.

Her answering laugh was a tinkle that never failed to lighten my heart. She turned to face me, and for a moment, my breath caught. Though I had seen her a few times since she began this ruse, I was still astounded by how thoroughly she had changed her appearance. She looked a decade younger, hair tinted slightly red with a dye given to her by a Greek merchant's wife, and the whorling lines of woad around her eyes and on her cheeks masked the age lines that could have betrayed her deception.

"I think not. But I'm a betting woman, so I'll take that wager. Besides, it's not like much would change if we did marry. Let the deception play out in its own good time."

"How does it not make you nervous living two lives?" I asked quietly, after reassuring myself no one was near enough to hear.

She shrugged. "I've been doing it for so long it comes as second nature." She stopped me with a touch to my wrist. The weight of her fingers said something serious was on her mind. "Do you not find it strange that Morcant is delayed? Should he not send a rider on to let us know of illness or other problems on the journey? It doesn't feel right."

"One would think, but I'm sure there is a very good reason," I said, trying to assuage both of us. But the tingling in my brow had already begun. A few more steps and I sank to my knees, unable to resist it.

Once again, I was flying on the wings of a bird, soaring above a sky tinged with smoke curling from the remains of a badly scarred hillfort atop a double-peaked mountain that stood out from the Cheviot Hills like a woman's breast. We circled the area, borne on warm air currents, moving closer and closer to the smoking walls with each pass. To the north, the white-capped North Sea endured the abuses of men's boots and boat hulls as hulking Saxon ships overtook British curraghs in the narrow waters between the mainland and the Isle of Winds. Below us, tiny and insignificant as ants, men, women, and children scurried over the fragrant heather, panic and fear etched into their faces alongside tear tracks, clutching what few belongings they could hold, seeking sanctuary they would not be granted by the invaders who had destroyed their town. Finally, we lit on a crumbling stone fence that had protected the fort and its occupants for centuries, but today failed miserably. One look inside the central keep revealed Yeavering Bell was now in the hands of our enemies. Ida, king of the Saxons, sat in Morcant's place.

My vision ended before I could tell whether or not Morcant lived, but it was enough. Cold to the bone with shock, I leaned on Sobian as we stumbled back to the castle to assemble an army and depart to support our ally and overlord. While Lancelot and Rohan saw to the muster, Anna prepared for a hasty departure to aid her son, should the Saxons press north into Lothian. I gathered our fastest messengers to send word to Owain and Accolon. They likely already knew of the coup, but more than that, they needed to know we would stand with them in the inevitable clash at their eastern border.

"I told those fools years ago that paying the Saxons to hold the Isle of Winds would come back to haunt them," Sobian raged, pacing my study while I wrote. "Morcant summoned me to help organize their naval defenses, but he would not listen to me in any other capacity. Arrogant dog." She punched the windowsill before stalking back toward me. "Just you wait—he will come crying to me for help. I should refuse him, but we both know I can't resist the call of a sea battle."

"I'm glad you will be there. If Owain and Accolon attempt to retake the isle, which I believe they will, we will need your help. Rohan and I can lead the ground troops across the causeway and onto the island, but the last thing we need is them surrounding us in those sea-serpents they call ships."

"I will put the call out for my girls to meet us in Din Guayrdi."

My eyes widened with a chilling thought. "How will you handle Rohan?"

In all the chaos, I had forgotten he still thought her to be a Pict. She would travel with us, and him, and once we reached Din Guayrdi, she would fight by his side. He may even recognize her. That would ruin everything.

Sobian gave me an impish smile that so reminded me of Isolde, my heart squeezed in pain. "I've already got that planned. Tonight when Rohan returns to our rooms from overseeing the last of the troop details, I will tell him I think it best that I, or rather, Eithne, should return home. The Picts will be anxiously watching the outcome in Bernicia, because the fight over the Isle may give them an opportunity to slip in and take control of the waterway. If they do, Lothian and Bernicia are done for. Eithne will want to be sure her troops are prepared." Her face darkened, and she stuck out her lower lip in mock sorrow. "Of course, it will be a very tearful departure for the lovers, with many promises of fidelity and love." She cackled an evil laugh.

Given that Lord Morcant was nowhere to be seen in my vision, I suspected he was already on the run and would arrive here soon—if he indeed had escaped the Saxon's wrath—but I was not prepared for what greeted us a week later when the guards called out that a large number of visitors were requesting admittance just after nightfall. I had been expecting a small party of Morcant and his guards, perhaps a few attendants, not the remnants of his whole household with horses, furniture, and other trappings in tow. Their bedraggled state indicated they had fled in the same panicked state as their people.

"Lord Morcant. Thank the gods you are alive and hale," I greeted the young, dark-haired man in the courtyard with a curtsy. Behind me, Lancelot, Rohan, and Sobian did the same.

Instead of the slight incline of the head I expected, one of his men stepped forward. "By order of the king of the Damnonii, Morcant Bulc, by whose benevolence you hold these lands, you are hereby ordered to vacate this fortress by daybreak. He invokes his right to seize any assets at will."

Stunned, I could only stare at Morcant, whose impassive face betrayed not a hint of embarrassment or guilt at making such a request. Rather, he was simply doing as needed.

Finally, Morcant stirred atop his stallion. "I am sorry to impose upon you this way, but as you no doubt know, I am in need of a new capital. You and yours may occupy the smaller holding at Dùn Bhlàthain. I have sent word that its keepers are to prepare it for you."

My mind swirled with thoughts and protests, but every time one slipped to the front of my mouth, I had to swallow it down by reminding myself he had every right to do as he wished. I was no longer queen, but his subject, directed by his will in all things.

"Dùn Bhlàthain is not a castle. It's a ruined fort not fit for a pack of wild dogs," Lancelot spat under his breath. When I glanced over my shoulder at him, he stepped forward and squeezed my hand. "Do not worry," he said into my ear. "We can always stay on my lands in Angus if we need to. I will not let you go homeless."

Rohan stepped forward, smirking. He obviously saw the irony in this situation, as I had not long ago run him out of his home, the very same fortress Lord Morcant was now demanding I vacate. I steeled myself for a sarcastic quip, but he showed concern instead. "My lord, will you not give her time to prepare? Or take my holdings in Both an Uillt instead. Surely they are more to your liking."

Lord Morcant turned a stare on Rohan that may as well have pinioned him to the wall. "If I wanted your holdings, Lord Rohan, I would have seized them." His gaze flicked to the castle around us, then south to the fort in the distance. "No. Now that the Saxons hold Bernicia, all of Alt Clut is vulnerable to attack. I wish to direct my forces from the fort of Stirling, not far away in the Vale of Leven." He turned his dark gaze on me, jaw taut with irritation. "Besides, perhaps when they see you humbled, my people won't be so eager to proclaim you their new queen."

Ah, so that was what this was really about. It was no

mere coincidence that Morcant needed a home and chose to take mine. This was a punishment for the insurrection. He was stripping me of what little power and resources I had. Still, his reprimand stung, just as he'd intended.

"Am I to understand that you intend to join Lord Owain in his fight to reclaim his island from the Saxons?" he asked me.

"Indeed. Although since you have taken my lands, it is really your army to command. Shall we lead them under your banner?"

Morcant grunted noncommittally, looking from me to Rohan and back again. "It is a fool's errand, don't you see that? As long as the Saxons hold Din Guarie, even if Owain is victorious, he will have to keep fighting to hold the isle. All the Saxons have to do is send out yet another contingent of men. Eventually they will overwhelm Owain's forces." He flicked his fingers dismissively at me. "Go if you will, but you will go alone. I will not have you move in my name with my army. You no longer speak for the people of this land. Is that clear?"

◈◈◈

"It was generous of you to offer your lands to Lord Morcant," I said to Rohan as our party—down from nearly a hundred to only Lancelot, Rohan, Galen and me—rode southeast the following day.

In the hills around us, gorse bloomed a vibrant yellow and scented our path with its distinctive nutty aroma.

Lapwings and crossbills whirled and dipped overhead, chattering in their tongue as we conversed in ours.

Rohan grimaced. "What he has done to you is deplorable. Those lands are yours by right of blood. After this battle is decided, you must appeal to Evina. He cannot take from you what she has granted."

I gave a small, sarcastic laugh. "I think it is best to stay below Evina's attention at the moment. The last thing I need is to remind her that some people think I should have her title."

"When this is done, we will go north," Lancelot said decisively. "All of us. We do not need any of them."

"What if I wish to come along as well?" Rohan said in mock pout.

"You have a kingdom to lead," I responded.

He took my hand. "But I will miss you so very much."

Lancelot rolled his eyes. "You will get used to it."

I eyed him with a half-smile. He was even more attractive when he was jealous.

In Din Eidyn, we met up with Sobian, the addition of her cadre of girls making us finally look more like an army than a small group of pilgrims. She wore her hair loose, and I noted she had darkened the red with coal ash and maybe some ink; it was slightly darker than her natural dark brown.

"I don't like this lack of wind," she said with a frown. "It will make using our boats under sail nigh impossible in the narrow waters between land and isle. This stillness will make it difficult to maneuver."

"Ah, but a priestess should be able to raise them, should

she not?" Rohan gave me a wide smile.

I glared at his presumption. "I can, but we have to think through if that is the strategy we want to employ. If these winds becalm your ships," I said to Sobian, "they will force the Saxon fleet to stay near land as well. Your girls can fight on land just as well as at sea, but we don't know how well-trained the Saxon navy is for a land battle. It could turn out that they would be easier to defeat at sea. I am of a mind to leave the weather as it is and only challenge nature when we must."

Rohan reined in his horse so he rode alongside mine. "You think of everything, don't you? Are you sure you want to run off to Angus with him if this battle goes against us?" He hooked a thumb in Lancelot's direction. "I think you could make a much bigger impact at my side."

I raised an eyebrow at him. Was he really so presumptuous as to blatantly flirt with me in front of Lancelot? He was either astonishingly arrogant or incredibly foolish.

"Think about how great you and I could be together. No one would deny your right to Stirling if you were my bride."

I looked at him askance. "Aren't you engaged to Eithne?"

"Yes, but that can easily be changed. She is beautiful and valuable, but you…you are so much more. If we were wed, you and I could control the western half of the tribes. Why, Morcant would be a mere figurehead. Then if you really did want to depose Evina, we could make a run at her. Imagine being Votadess." He smirked, suppressing a chuckle. "On the other hand, you could run away with

Lancelot and… do what? Fade into obscurity? We both know you are meant for greater things."

I halted my horse, forcing the rest of our party to a stop as well. In that moment, Rohan reminded me so much of the power-crazed, overly confident version of Mordred I'd left behind that my stomach knotted and I swallowed down bile. I gave him my haughtiest look. "Not. On. Your. Life. Giving you the power of Votad would be signing the death warrant of this land. I would rather die nameless under Evina's rule than be remembered as your wife."

Rohan flinched, his jaw and fists tightening as though he wanted to hit me. Part of me wished he would so that Lancelot and I could wallop him. Perhaps with his pride wounded, he would turn tail and run for home.

"If the only reason you came on this journey was to try to turn my head, you better go back now. I am here to fight for my friends and allies, not to plot another revolution." I spurred my horse on and took up the lead, motioning for Lancelot to join me.

Instead, it was Sobian who rode by my side. "While I admire you for putting him in his place, I don't know that insulting him so badly was wise." She glanced over her shoulder at Rohan. "We still need him in this battle."

"He is driven by power, so it is in his best interest to aid Owain and Accolon. Have no fear. I know him, and I know how dangerous it would be to make him think, even for a moment, that I might really consider treason with him. This way if he chooses to go behind my back and act in my name, I have witnesses who can testify I publicly stated in no uncertain terms that I would not ally with him."

"That is wise. But I still think you should set things to rights with him before we engage the Saxons. I've lived with Rohan for the last year and have seen how volatile he can be, especially when he feels betrayed. You never know what he may do."

⁘

I would much rather our basecamp have been situated in the hillfort of Din Guarie, where we would have had spectacular views of the Isle of Winds, than in a cramped, camouflaged tent on the shore, but the fort was Ida's realm. He was also the reason we had to remain hidden; on this campaign, surprise was of the utmost importance.

I would also much rather not have had Morgan with us. I had not seen her since my mystical journey to Camlann, the site of Arthur and Mordred's deaths. When we met up in Traprain Law with her, Owain, and Accolon, she had been shy and tentative, if not a little embarrassed at me having seen her at her most vulnerable. Though my reflex was still to treat her poorly, I fought it and summoned kindness instead. Camlann had changed us both; we may never be friends, but in our shared pain, we had learned to put aside our youthful pettiness and work together for the greater good.

Inside the tent, Lancelot, Sobian, Rohan, and I collaborated with Owain, Accolon, and Morgan, and their generals to determine our best method of attack. The isle was guarded by a small hillfort at its center, but it was not well maintained. Owain had sent spies disguised as Saxon recruits days before to scout out what we would be facing. Two still remained, charged with opening the gates from the inside when we gave the signal.

Tidal waters controlled access to the island, so we only had a few opportunities each day to transport our troops to the island, otherwise we would be either trapped on the mainland with no way to get to the isle other than by boat, or be swept away by the waters. Despite Sobian and her girls standing by on their ships, attack by boat wasn't really an option since the sight of the boats slowly crossing the channel would likely cause the Saxons on the isle to shoot arrows and rocks at us, not to mention alert those in Din Guarie to our activities.

No, this fight would have to be conducted entirely on foot by infantry. There was no room for horses, and the best our boats could do was defend against reinforcements from Din Guarie and any use of Saxon boats against us by those on the isle.

"We must time this perfectly," I said. "There is a period in the middle of the night when the causeway is clear. We should be ready to move as soon as it is safe. Once across, we need to move quickly to build our siege camp inland so that we can be in place before dawn. By then, we will be trapped on the island until the tide goes down in early morning."

"I think we can help with that," Morgan said. "Together, you and I should be strong enough to hold back the waters in case we need extra time on the exposed causeway."

"Good," Owain said. "That will be valuable, should

our plans go awry. Now, when we charge the fort, my men will help by opening the gates, but we will still have to fight our way in. Some of my men are prepared with ladders and grappling hooks so we won't face a bottleneck at the gate. But no matter how hard we plan, I fear this will be a bloodbath."

✧✧✧

We faced the causeway with only the light of the moon to guide us, glimmering on the water and turning the sandbars into ghostly pathways. Any light we would use, no matter how small, would be seen by the Saxon guards in the towers of the fort. Taking careful steps on the slippery rocks and packed sand that was likely to give way with each step, our progress was slow. Occasionally a cloud blotted out the light of the moon, plunging us into precipitous darkness, and we had to freeze until Morgan or I could force it to move along.

Despite the cool night temperatures, sweat trickled down my back and beaded on my brow as I concentrated on each step. As we neared land, one of the Saxon guards in a watchtower cried out, and we all stopped to put our shields over our heads like the Romans did for protection. A few of our men peeled off at a run to dispatch the guard before she could alert anyone else of whatever had alarmed her. My heart pounded so loudly in my ears, it blocked out the rhythm of the surf and should have acted as a beacon to all in the fort above. Oh, how I longed for the familiarity of two armies facing off across a field at midday.

When we finally gained land, we stayed to the shadows as much as possible, working our way to the northern side of the isle, where it would be safest to make camp. The last few men in our caravan were in charge of sweeping away our footprints so no evidence would alert the enemy or lead them to our camp. The sand hampered our pace, especially through the dunes, though rabbits darted across them, mocking our slow progress, but we eventually reached a small patch of grassland protected by the dunes.

By the time we had quietly erected our tents and prepared for the battle to come, the eastern sky was lightening to a grayish-blue. Our full force needed to be in front of the main gates—which thankfully faced west and so would be in darkness a bit longer—before the first rays of sun lit the sky if we were going to take the Saxons unawares.

Morgan and I thickened the shadows as long as we could. We had just settled into formation when the sun's power broke our hold and the guards on the walls stirred. Rohan whistled like a swallow. Within the fort, someone tweeted a response, followed by raised voices as the guard changed shift.

With the first crack of firelight visible through the gates, we charged with a deafening cry. Shields up over our heads, we ran, swords, spears, and elbows at the ready to push aside or kill all who stood in our way. An arrow lodged in my shield with a jolt that sent me to my knees. I sprang up as fast as I could. To remain in one place for more than a moment was to die.

As soon as we approached the walls, my world narrowed into mad whirl of leather, steel, and blood as I attacked and defended, slowly hacking through all who stood in my path. By now, we had lost the element of surprise and the garrison had emptied. We were trapped without hope of retreat until nightfall. A second wave of support was due to arrive any time on Sobian's boat, but chances were good the Saxons would launch their ships as well, cutting off our reinforcements.

Day turned to night in a haze of blood, until finally we retreated to our camp in the gloaming. There we met the second unit, who were happily staking the heads of a few dozen Saxons onto pikes around the perimeter of our base.

"They tried to bring us down," a flaxen-haired soldier reported, "but as you can see, we held firm."

I sighed wearily. "We cannot thank you enough. You have paid a good service to your tribe and to your Votad this day."

After eating a hasty dinner, Lancelot and I retired to our tent. We took turns cleaning one another's wounds, which thankfully were all minor, as we had so many times before. Then we prepared for the following day's battle.

I looked up from cleaning my sword. "Do you ever wish you had married a docile, meek woman who would stay at home and pray while you went off to war instead of pledging yourself to a troublesome warrior like me?"

Lancelot looked up from mending a tear in his leather chest plate. "You mean like Elaine? I *was* married to her. It was torture." He kissed me on the lips. "I would take your troublesome self over her any day. I am a warrior, and no woman could make me happier. Do you ever wish you had married a lord with no taste for war?"

I let out a small "ha" of incredulity. "Does such a man exist?"

"Fair point." Lancelot put down his armor and pulled me onto the bed, taking my sword from me and setting it aside. "Enough for tonight. Let us rest."

Part of me wanted to kiss him, to wrap my arms around him and show him how much I loved him, but as soon as I lay down, fatigue overwhelmed me. Tonight, falling asleep in his arms would have to be intimacy enough.

◈◈◈

Roaring waves, shouts, and snapping wood heralded the dawn as Sobian's crew clashed with a Saxon vessel trying to stop her from ferrying additional troops to shore. At Rohan's command, scouts ran back and forth across the causeway when it was clear, bringing news of the unexpected naval battles.

Because of this development, Morgan and I stayed behind to offer our aid to those at sea while the rest of our army attempted to gain the fort. We sat concealed in a fold in the cliff face, controlling wind and water as needed, trying desperately to help Sobian while not hampering the efforts of our men on land. It was a delicate balance, one so difficult to achieve I had never dared to try it before. But with Morgan by my side, I felt our combined powers might be worth the risk.

Neither side seemed eager to destroy their own boat by ramming it into the other, but still they harried one another, attempting to board the enemy ship and destroy her crew. When that did not work, they resorted to hurling flaming projectiles at one another until one boat finally sank in a haze of smoke and ash.

But as soon as the cheers from the victor's boat died down, another launched, until our meager fleet was surrounded and hope waned. I prayed that no matter what happened, Sobian and her girls would survive to fight again.

"Why don't we just call a storm and make the waves so choppy, they are forced to cease fighting to keep their boats from capsizing?" Morgan asked, her voice indicating she had no concept of the repercussions of such an action.

"Because if we do, we will turn the sand beneath our soldiers' feet to a clinging, slippery mush and endanger them all. You were there at Mount Badon. Do you recall how both sides waited out the storm I called then? There was a reason."

She glared at me then turned her back on me, sulking.

By nightfall, Owain's army had made headway on land, but Sobian's fleet was destroyed. The last scout reported that she and most of her crew—they had lost two, one to fire and the other when she was swept overboard—lived, though they were in hiding somewhere up the coast until they could procure additional vessels from nearby berths or repair what remained of their own.

"Rohan predicts we will take the fort tomorrow," Lancelot

said as he returned from the cook fire with two plates of dinner. He held one out to me.

A heavy sigh escaped my lips as I took it, sniffing at it warily. Dinner was some type of fish, likely caught today while we fought, and the ubiquitous grain-based mush, a staple at every meal while on campaign. "Good. I don't know that I can take much more of this." I rubbed my eyes. "I hate to admit it, but I am feeling my age. The constant physical and emotional toll of battle was easier borne before my bones ached and my vision dimmed."

Lancelot smirked around a mouthful of fish. "Tell me about it. Earlier today I was fighting a spearman, and when I moved to strike, pain flared in my back so strongly I feared it, not the Saxon's weapon, would bring me down."

I nodded. "This is it. After this battle is won, I will hang up my sword."

"And I mine. I would gladly trade it for my remaining years with you." He wrapped me in a tight embrace.

"Promise me something."

"Anything."

"Whether we win or lose, we will not return to Din Eidyn. Evina has soured my heart for the homeland I once so desperately longed for. If we die, then it is done. If we are victorious, we send the army back without us. We can always use the truth—that some will have to stay behind to secure those taken captive—as our reason for not accompanying them. If we lose and still have our skin, we run— far way, to Brittany, where she cannot touch us without starting a war."

"Her assassins know my homeland. They could always find us."

I smiled. "Ah, but we have the best in our employ. We get a message to Sobian, written in Ogham so others cannot read it. She will take care of the lot of them."

"Brittany it is then. The life we wanted before Arthur threw our plans to the wind." He kissed my hair. "Now we have something worth fighting for."

"We certainly have nothing left to lose. That makes us more dangerous than the Votad could ever dream. Plus, it gives me an idea how to incite the troops even more." I turned over so that I was facing him and let my breasts brush against his naked chest. "This is our last night here, and certainly our last alone until all is said and done."

He didn't need me to say any more. His lips met mine with all the fury he hadn't spent in battle, and I responded in kind, kissing him hard, deep, and rough. My hands sought the most sensitive parts of his flesh, eager to stoke his arousal. His teeth grazed my neck while his fingertips dug into the soft flesh between my thighs. Soon we were joined in a feverish embrace. This was not the pretty love making of Beltane, the languorous celebration of life, but the wild rutting of animals who sensed the approach of winter's deadly chill.

⁕

Just after midday, the Saxon resistance faltered. Their attacks at the wall became halfhearted, and when we breeched the fort, the remaining warriors showed themselves to be either too aggressive and desperate in their tactics or lackluster at best, as if they wished as much as we did for this whole affair to be over.

Our army easily cut through them, allowing us access into the keep, where we found Theodric and Osmere, Ida's two oldest sons and those who were leading the campaign, surrounded by a cadre of guards.

But where was Elga? In her unending quest to rule Britain, she had married Osmere not long after Mordred died. She would not allow her husband to go into battle without her, so she had to be there. I turned and surveyed the room, trying to ascertain possible points of ambush or trickery. I would put nothing past her.

Owain faced the brothers, sword drawn and ready but not posing an immediate threat. "My lords, you can come with us peacefully, or we can fight to the death here. The choice is yours."

Osmere sneered at Owain. "Your High King once did us the honor of allowing single combat to decide the outcome of a war. Will you not offer the same mark of respect?"

Owain replied, "I was there at Mount Badon and I remember quite clearly. Your people immediately betrayed the outcome of that combat because it was not in your favor. How can we be assured you will not do the same now?"

Theodric gave a mirthless laugh and threw his arms wide, as if to encompass the whole room. "Look around. We are the only opponents you have left. Surely you are not threatened by less than a dozen men?"

Owain stood his ground. "I am when those men have thousands of reinforcements waiting across the channel. All you would need to do is give a signal and your ships would set sail, treeing us on this isle like a pack of hunting hounds with their quarry. Plus"—he made a show of looking around—"not all of your troops are in this room. Your wife is missing, is she not? Let me guess, she lies in wait to finish us off while we crow in victory?"

"Enough chatter. Let's be done with this," Rohan broke in.

Osmere stood, ignoring Rohan. "Leave my wife out of this. This battle is down to you and me. The victor takes the fort and the whole of the island. I will even allow you to choose the location of our duel."

"I know the perfect place," Rohan declared.

Owain led the men out of the fort, following Rohan around to the back side of the island to a flat jut of land in the shadow of a thick woodland of alder, hazel, birch, and willow. Beyond the sandy beach, the ground was packed and even enough to ensure a fair fight. It was the perfect location. The duel could take place in full view of our camp and the Saxons we had taken prisoner, but out of sight of those on the mainland who may try to provide assistance.

The half-dozen Saxon ships that bobbed offshore, however, raised my suspicions. From my first view of the isle, I'd recognized it as the place in my vision and had been keeping an eye on Rohan, lest he try anything untoward. Now with these ships placed so conveniently close to our battleground, I had to make sure nothing was amiss.

Most of the boats appeared to have sustained enough

damage in yesterday's skirmishes to keep them from being seaworthy. Climbing aboard one after the other, I checked their hulls and cargo holds for stowaway Saxons. All were empty, save one, where I found Elga ostensibly making repairs but more likely preparing for escape.

She hissed and cursed at me in her native tongue as I dragged her onto shore by the arm.

"Oh, stop it," I spat. "I'm not going to hurt you. But I do wish you to witness the single combat that will bring your reign here to an end." I pushed her onto the sand and she responded with a hand gesture that was likely some sort of curse.

Her husband and Owain faced off, each with his brother as second. Osmere struck first, but Owain parried, stepping into a series of complicated blade and footwork moves that even I had trouble keeping up with. He pushed hard on Osmere, never giving him a chance to recover. Osmere, to his credit, fought hard, always on the defensive, pushing Owain's blade back with little opportunity to strike.

The battle was over before it had really begun. Owain tore his blade across Osmere's chest from right shoulder to left hip bone, and Osmere crumpled like a discarded scrap of parchment, trying to hold in his entrails to little avail.

Back at the fort, cheers erupted from our men as the flag of the house of Rheged was raised. On the beach, Elga screamed, rushing toward her husband and brandishing her sword at anyone foolish enough to get in her way. At the same time, Rohan grabbed Owain by his tunic before he could even register his victory, much less celebrate it, and

Theodric turned on Accolon, his blade at our leader's neck.

For a long moment, the three couples stood in deadly embrace, each contemplating their varied futures that were dependent on their next actions. As a spectator, there was little I could do but watch. Elga held her husband's body, rocking much like I had when Arthur fell at Camlann. Rohan twisted Owain's neck, killing him instantly. Accolon lunged toward his brother, trying to stop Rohan's traitorous act, but Theodric's blade held him immobile.

Suddenly, the beach was red with blood. I ran to Accolon, trying to help him escape, but Theodric slammed his fist into my head, sending me reeling. I fell back upon the sand with a thud that robbed me of breath. While I shook off the sparks of light that littered my vision and struggled to stand, Sobian barreled into Theodric, planting her sword in his thigh and immobilizing him. Like the trained assassin she was, she flipped him over and tied his hands behind his back, her knee digging into his shoulder blades. In the same instant, Lancelot tackled Rohan.

Only Elga remained free, and she used the chaos to her advantage, seizing Accolon as he moved toward Owain's lifeless body. She tackled him, slamming his head into the ground and dragging him backward toward the ship I had pulled her out of.

"Move away, all of you, or he dies!" she commanded, using her sword to punctuate each word as she backed him onto the ship. She motioned for a few of her crew to join her, and soon they were drifting offshore. From the deck, she pointed at Morgan. "You killed my husband, so I will take your lover in exchange."

Morgan responded by raising her arms and summoning a storm that threatened to capsize the boat. But Elga's crew were skilled enough to ride it out, somehow sensing that Morgan's power didn't carry as far out to sea as she would have others believe. Morgan howled as her grip on the waves waned. I ran to her side, mingling my power with hers, but still it lasted only a few moments more. Spent, we both collapsed onto the sand, surveying the wreckage around us.

Owain's body lay abandoned on the earth beyond the beach, rivulets of blood seeping toward the sea as though his essence sought its maker. Not far off, Sobian knelt atop Theodric's prone form, frantically signaling her girls to bring a ship around to this side of the isle. Near the trees, Lancelot held Rohan, whispering what I could only guess were graphic threats in his ear.

When I had recovered, I strode over to Rohan, tears in my eyes for my dead compatriot and friend. "Why, Rohan?" I glanced at the piteous form at my feet. "Why did you turn on him? He trusted you. We all did."

Rohan smirked. "What is trust in time of war? My allegiance is with the victors, so when I saw an opportunity to change the outcome, I did."

"But we took the island. *We* were victorious. Shouldn't your allegiance be with us?"

Rohan gave a short bark of a laugh. "This skirmish was a pittance compared to what is yet to come. I don't think in terms of battles; I think about the whole war. We won this tussle, but as Morcant said, what good will it do in the long run? We will just keep defending an outpost we are destined to lose. If not today, someday, and then the Saxons will have free rein into the north. I want to be their ally when that day comes."

"So why even fight with us then?" Lancelot asked.

"I didn't know which way the outcome would go. If they won, I wanted to be here to celebrate with them. As they did not, I rid them of a powerful enemy. Owain would have died either way. Now that they have Accolon in their possession, the house of Rheged is no longer a threat."

"Meaning Evina is their next target," I said.

He tipped his head noncommittally. "Perhaps. Her or you. Both of you are obstacles to their goal."

"Is that why you wanted to marry me, to rid yourself of an obstacle to greater power?"

"Yes, and I wanted your lands back. Nothing I have said to you has been untrue."

"Yet everything has. You and Elga planned this ahead of time, didn't you?"

Rohan smirked. "Of course we did. Why did you think I was in such a hurry for Owain and Osmere to stop their pointless arguing? How do you think I knew right where to lead them? I knew Elga was on that boat, but I have to admit I thought our plans were lost when you dragged her to shore. But the gods were smiling on us after all."

My palms itched to punch the self-satisfied smirk off his face, but I restrained myself. Out of the corner of my eye, I saw that two of Sobian's ships loomed just off the coast. "Well, it won't be long now until you face justice."

We clumsily loaded Theodric and Rohan onto one boat, and Sobian set it on course for the port of Dunbar, just east of Din Eidyn. Since traveling by sea was much faster than by land, we expected to reach our destination by morning. The rest of our army followed in a second ship with Morgan, who was tending the wounded with the aid of the other camp women.

In the small hours of the night, most of us managed to steal a few hours of rest, but not Sobian. In addition to captaining the boat, she took it upon herself to act as Rohan's guard. Once he was chained in the back of the boat, she approached him, taunting him. Even though I advised her to keep her own council about the subterfuge of the last several months, her resolve broke as we neared Dunbar.

She held her hair back from her face in a rough braid. "Do you recognize this face?" She said something in Pictish I could not understand, but from her tone, it translated roughly to "you piece of shite bastard."

When Rohan failed to respond, she poured a mug of water over her head, washing out the coal dust to reveal the lingering red in her hair. His eyes widened.

"Yes, you sorry sod," she said in the Briton tongue. "I was your 'lover,' Eithne. All these months I pretended to be close to you, to care about you, and all I was really trying to do was prove your treason. Yet now you have demonstrated it before a full party of witnesses, Votadini and foreigner alike." She moved right next to him, her breath stirring the fine hairs on his cheek. "Tell me, was vengeance against

Owain worth what Evina will do to you?" She turned her back to him, leaning her shoulders against his like a lover. "I can't imagine much that would be worth sacrificing my stones for, much less my very life."

"I did what needed doing," he said gravely, turning his face away from her. "I ask mercy from no one."

"Good. I doubt you will find much from them." She pointed toward the port.

My gaze swung in the direction she indicated. At the mouth of the pier, Evina and Mynyddog waited, arrayed in their finery. Sobian must have sent a messenger ahead to make the Votad and Votadess aware of the prisoners we held on board.

As soon as we stepped off the boat, guards met us to take Rohan and Theodric into custody. I started to make my way to the second boat to see if Morgan needed any help transferring the wounded, but after a few steps, my path was blocked by two guards. They motioned for me to turn my back and surrender my wrists to them.

"What? What is this?" I looked to Evina and Mynyddog for an explanation. "Have I not regained the Isle of Winds from our enemies? By what charge do you arrest me?"

As if he had been waiting for such a cue, one of the guards recited, "Guinevere of the Votadini, late of Stirling and the lands surrounding, you are hereby reprimanded into the mercy of the Votad and Votadess on the charge of high treason. You stand accused of inciting rebellion and causing the people to rise up against their rightful rulers in your name."

Chapter Fourteen

Summer 522

Thick, stale air threatened to choke my waking breath before I could even draw it. Bright sunlight blinded me as I sat up in my tiny cell, its touch causing sweat to pool beneath my skirts and in my armpits. Judging from the position of the sun, it was just past midday. I pulled my linen shift away from sticky skin, seeking some relief from the unbearably hot room. Though the air outside was likely warm and refreshing, I had no such hope in here, for the prison was in the path of runoff heat from the kitchen fires. With so little time between the break of fast and the second meal, even in winter the air did not have time to cool. Perhaps that was by design to torture the prisoners, or maybe the gaol was placed there because no one would live in such conditions voluntarily.

I must have fallen asleep, something that happened frightfully often since being taken captive some weeks before—I'd lost count of how much time had passed. Between the heat and boredom, a drowsy stupor was my normal state. Little of what went on outside the walls reached my prison cell, only snatches of conversation when the guards conferred at shift change. Early this morning they had whispered about their strange orders for the summer solstice ritual tonight, so something important was afoot.

The clink of metal on metal at my door interrupted my thoughts. With a grunt, one of Evina's guards heaved open the heavy wooden door far enough to poke his head in, as though I wasn't worthy of moving his entire body. "Lady Guinevere, you have been summoned by the Votadess. You are to wear your best gown and bring any personal possessions with you, as you will not be returning to your cell. I will wait outside to escort you."

For a few dreadful moments after the door boomed shut behind him, I sat in my bed, shivering despite the heat, certain I was being called to my death. What had I done to warrant Evina's wrath after she had looked the other way for so many months? Which of my actions on the isle had tipped the balance? Something had to have. According to the guards, my supporters had been lying low since word spread of my containment, but rumblings still rolled across the countryside like seeds of thistle in the summer wind. Until they were silenced, I remained a threat, so perhaps there had been a riot I was unaware of.

Slowly, as though I was moving underwater, I braided my hair into a rough plat and donned the midnight-blue tunic I had been lent to substitute for my dirt-stained, bloody battle gear. It may not have been a royal gown, but it was a fine enough garment to lose my life in. I tipped water over my hands from an ewer and rubbed my cheeks, invoking the Goddess as though I washed with Beltane dew.

"Mother, guide me. Give me strength. If this is the day I am to meet you, I am ready. All my life I have followed your voice and tried to do your will. When I breathe my last, may your judgment be swift and merciful."

With a deep breath, I rapped on the door, offered my hands to be bound, and followed the guard out to meet my fate.

⚛

I stumbled down the slopes of Din Eidyn into the darkening fields where a great crowd had gathered. They parted like summer barley in the breeze as we approached, revealing a wooden platform on which stood Evina, Mynyddog, and Calliac, the high priestess, surrounded by guards and attendants. Lancelot and Sobian waited nearby, under guard but unfettered, but I didn't see Morgan anywhere. Unlike the rest of us, she seemed to have escaped Evina's wrath unscathed.

To my left, more soldiers ringed a large wooden pen taller than a man, the like of which a farmer might keep cattle or horses in at market, but it was not open to the air. It was covered by a thatched roof like a house. When I tried to peer into the darkness within, the guards crossed their spears to prevent it. On my other side, the crowd laughed and talked, while a few jeered or cheered as I passed. Thankfully, they were much too distracted by the free-flowing ale and the men jumping bonfires or rolling flaming sunwheels down the hill to pay much attention to me.

When we reached the dais, the guard halted me with a hand to my shoulder. He nodded to Evina, and at her signal, the rhythmic pounding of drums began, followed by the jangle of horse tack as mounted men and women ringed us on every side. What was this? No ritual I had ever witnessed required so many armed men, much less a ring of cavalry. Perhaps the purpose of this gathering was much more dire than it appeared. My heart hammered, fear of the unknown replacing my earlier detachment. I swallowed. Perhaps I would indeed die tonight.

Calliac stepped forward, bowing her head so all could see the equine skull she wore as a crown over her long silver hair, then she raised and dipped her arms in gestures of supplication and praise, her voice lost in the din. As Calliac turned, she drew nearer, the rough surface of her horsehair cloak catching the light. The brown strands woven into the cloak were not ribbons, as I had thought, but rather the thick hairs from a horse's mane or tail. She was the embodiment of our tribal goddess, Rhiannon.

Four priestesses adorned with feathers and antlers stepped forward and bowed before her. She placed a hand on the crown of each one's head before entrusting her with a pottery bottle and sending her off into the dark. As we watched, the priestesses went from rider to rider, sprinkling them with the contents of the jars and giving them each a torch. The last rider blessed by each priestess took possession of her jar, and when the benediction was done, the four singled out gathered at the crossroads directly behind the dais. The other riders surrounded them in a circle.

When all had assembled, Calliac raised her staff, topped with the skull of a pony, and cried out in a language I did not know. The Otherworldly sound raised the hairs on my arms and forced a shiver down my spine. Whatever she was doing summoned great power, the like of which I had only seen twice before: in Avalon, and on the night Aine raised the dark spirits in Malegant's tower. With a scream like a banshee, she struck the earth with her staff and the skull burst into flames. She used it to light the torch of the rider nearest to her, and within moments, the circle was alight.

Calliac ceded the dais to Evina, who with her hair pulled back in complex braids and soot staining the skin around her eyes, resembled a wraith raised from the dead. Her eyes gleamed with a feverish intensity as she looked over the crowd, silent now in anticipation, and perhaps a little fear.

"My people," Evina's voice carried across the fields, "as you know, our homes are threatened on three fronts. To the north, our old enemies, the Picts, are stirring."

A few men in the crowd called curses upon on all sons of the Highlands.

Evina moved with feral grace, stretching her limbs like a dancer each time she changed direction. "To the west, we keep vigil against treachery from our own people, which some have recently enacted."

A loud hooting and booing rose from the crowd when a guard forced Rohan up onto the platform. Like me, he was bound at the wrists, but he wore no finery. His chest was bare, exposing the bruises and gashes of torture. Cries of "traitor" and "kill him" burst forth. If they so easily called for his death, was the same spectacle planned for me?

Evina gestured for the crowd to quiet, which they did by slow degrees. "And to our south, the Saxons roam our borders, looking for even the smallest crack through which to pass and harry us all."

The crowd was shouting, working themselves into a frenzy of bloodlust and hate. Outraged faces circled me on all sides, jostling and shoving. A young woman with shorn red hair pushed between my guard and me, and for one disconnected moment, I thought I was back in the court-yard of Cadbury on the night Malegant abducted me. Panic rose in my throat so fast I thought I would retch. I doubled over, breathing rapidly, a cold sweat weighing me down. I coughed and heaved, but my body produced nothing.

When I straightened again, Lancelot was beside me, having broken from his guard. I threw my bound hands over his head and hugged him tightly.

"Praise to the gods that you are here. I don't know how I would have faced this alone." I looked around. "Whatever this is."

Lancelot ducked out of my grasp and held my shoul-ders firmly, staring deep into my eyes. "No matter what may come, I am here. Know that they will have to kill me before they harm a hair on your head. So even if you die, I will precede you and clear the way to glory."

I made to respond, but Evina's powerful voice interrupted, forcing our attention back to her.

"We are not helpless, even in the face of such formidable foes," Evina declared. "Oh no, far from it. That is why tonight, we invoke the goddess Rhiannon, she who is also called Epona and Macha, patroness of our tribe and of our bloodlines. By the strength of her horses and with their speed, she will protect us and bring us peace."

She turned so that her back was toward us as she faced the circle of riders. The sun had dipped below the horizon and was losing its battle against the onslaught of night, bleeding into the sky in vivid streaks of burgundy, burnt umber, and ocher. Against such a backdrop Evina resembled a goddess herself, one who represented retribution and rage.

"You, my beloved ones, have been specially chosen to act in her stead this night. Go now! Go forth and trace the borders of our kingdom, sealing them by Rhiannon's power to keep our enemies at bay and protect our land. May she speed you on your journey."

With a collective whoop, they scattered to the four winds, torches like beacons in the night.

When the riders were no longer visible, Evina turned back to her subjects. "You, my people, have been false." She wagged a finger at the crowd like a remonstrative mother. "You have laid aside your vows to me to raise up a false queen. And why? Have I been so terrible to you? Have I ignored or abused you? Tell me now, why have you turned against me?" She signaled to the guards ringing the pen. "Bring them out."

The four guards nearest to the door of the pen stepped aside. Two disappeared inside, only to emerge holding the arms of two bound captives. I didn't know either face, but I was willing to wager they were Sobian's contacts, the leaders of the insurrection in my name.

The strong hands of my guard shoved me forward and I tripped, the ground rising fast. My hands hit the grass, and searing pain erupted in my knee as it met the hard earth. Before I could catch my breath, I was lifted, face to sky, on the hands of the priestesses, who cooed oddly soothing words in my ears as they raised me to the platform.

Once I was standing next to Rohan, Evina put her hands on her hips. "Well? Tell us why. Why did you back this usurper?"

The two captives stood erect as statues, impassive and empty expressions on their bruised faces. She would have no answer from them. Likewise, I could give no explanation that would satisfy her. I hadn't sought the throne, nor did I believe she had proof that I was in any way involved. But it was my name they proclaimed, and that was crime enough.

"Does it matter?" Rohan asked. "In our eyes, you were unfit to rule. Or at best not the most worthy of the throne. We proclaimed the one who was. So has it been since our ancestors first divided into tribes and so shall it be into our children's children's time. It is the way of things."

"You do not have the right to give testimony before me, traitor," Evina spat. "*You* have committed the worst crime of all. Moving against me is one thing, but to move against your country, your tribe, *and* your people is inexcusable." She looked around, taking in the mass of people. "Those who ally with the enemy have moved beyond the bounds of justice, beyond our codicils of fines and laws. There is but one punishment for traitors." Evina unsheathed her sword and held it up. There was no mistaking her meaning.

My heart sank to my feet, and I struggled to swallow the oversized lump in my throat as my earlier fear was confirmed.

Evina stalked around Rohan at arm's length like a wolf circling prey. "But do not fear," she said with a cold laugh. "You will not die alone."

I expected her manic gaze to fall upon me, but instead, she faced the pen again. One guard whistled, and two lines of people—men, women, and a few boys just barely of marrying age—stepped out, blinking at the torches like moles in the sunlight.

"These are your people, those who rose with you, are they not?" Evina asked the man and woman. Without waiting for an answer, she shoved them off the platform toward the lines of prisoners. "Let this be a lesson to all of you. Those who incite others against their rulers die alongside them." To the soldiers, she added, "Take them away."

While the lines were herded back inside the pen, a few men and young boys shoving against their captors in a futile bid to escape, Evina stood in front of me, staring into my eyes. So much of my mother was there, but this woman lacked her warmth. After tonight, I believed she lacked a heart—and possibly a soul—as well. I swallowed and willed my shaking knees and hands to be still. Keeping the image of my mother before my eyes, I held Evina's gaze, queen to queen, one granddaughter of Cunedda's line to another. This madwoman would not see how much she frightened me.

Finally she turned away from me, swinging her sword in a showy arc, before kneeling at her husband's feet and presenting the blade to him with bowed head. He took it and approached us, the determined, stoic expression of a warrior writ across his features. He raised his blade, and I closed my eyes, steeling myself for pain. Rohan grunted next to me, and a whoosh of cool air rushed over me. I opened my eyes. His headless body had collapsed next to me, a patch of blood already forming at my feet. I exhaled loudly and stumbled backward, shock and relief warring in my veins.

A slow grin spread across Evina's face. "No. Not you. Not now. I have other plans for you."

As Rohan's blood stained the boards and seeped between the cracks to the earth below, Mynyddog squatted and drew his fingers through spreading pool. He rose and painted his wife's face in streaks of crimson so that she appeared ready for battle.

"The traitor is dead. But the scales remain unbalanced. Just as a mother punishes a child who goes beyond the bounds of her law, so as your Votadess am I honor bound to give correction to my people. Unfortunately, the offense committed here goes beyond fines and the making of outlaws. I will not tolerate insubordination." She raised her arms to the sky, face turned toward the starry heavens. "As I am strengthened by the blood of my enemies, may the goddess Epona accept the sacrifice we offer this night. May our land be protected and forever blessed."

Before I could comprehend what was happening, the guards surrounding the pen wound thick lengths of chain around it and secured the door with a padlock before resuming their places. From the inside came a few shouts and whines of protest. Below us, the crowd stirred in response, shifting uneasily from foot to foot, heads turned toward neighbors in question.

"This is the summer solstice, the longest night. We celebrate the power of the sun and beg it not to leave us behind for its winter home, encouraging its potency through fire and flame." Evina nodded toward the pen. "For ages, our people have lit a bonfire representing the spirit of the Votadini people and kept watch over it through the night. Usually the honor of starting the fire belongs to my husband or me." She turned to me. "However, since you so desperately wanted to become Votadess, I will allow you to light the fire."

Shock reverberated through me as though I had been struck by lightning. This was no ordinary ceremony, and she was no ordinary woman. The Votadess was asking me to be responsible for the deaths of dozens of her people, my people, whose only crime had been trusting me. I squeezed my eyes shut. This went against everything I had ever been taught or thought I stood for. I had taken lives before, but those were lives lost to war and the gods understood that. This was far different, the murder of innocents to assuage one insecure woman's overblown sense of justice. I could not, would not comply, come what may.

I opened my eyes. Evina and Mynyddog were staring at me.

"You are a priestess, are you not?" Evina gestured toward the pen. "Light the flame."

I looked for a proffered torch, but none was being held out to me. Everyone around me stood in silent expectation. Then I understood. Evina was asking me to use my skills as a priestess to execute those she had deemed guilty. *No. No. I cannot! This goes against every single precept of Avalon, every rule governing the use of my skills. I cannot. I will not!*

"Unless you wish to join them, you'd better make it look as though you are trying to comply," an authoritative female voice threaded its way into my mind.

I turned my head, trying to find the source of the sound. Most were still waiting for me to do something, but Calliac caught my eye and shook her head almost imperceptibly, silently commanding me not to let my face reflect what was happening.

I narrowed my eyes and focused on the pen. I had to make it look as though I was willing the fire from the guards' torches to fly to the thatched roof.

Calliac glided toward me, stopping at my side. "My lady," she addressed Evina. "Fear blunts our abilities. No doubt you have frightened this woman with your awesome display of justice and authority. Perhaps you will allow me to aid her power?"

Evina considered this. "Do you mean like adding more spark to the kindling?"

Calliac nodded. "Just so."

"Proceed."

Calliac took my hand. Again her voice rang in my head. "You need do nothing. I will start the fire so your conscience may remain clear." She squeezed my hand. Smoke wound skyward from the roof. "My form of magic is different from yours," she silently explained. "Though the taking of a life in ritual is usually frowned upon, it is permitted in certain circumstances, so I am doing nothing against my own faith. You bear no guilt upon your soul for what is about to happen."

With a pop, the roof ignited, followed shortly thereafter by one of the walls. Soon the whole structure was aflame.

Around me, the crowd dispersed, some fleeing the heat and horror, others throwing themselves against the guards, seeking to save the people inside, while a handful ran to the well and tried to organize a bucket line to staunch the flames. But all their efforts were in vain, for no mortal could be faster than the wind that whipped up from the west, spreading the conflagration with elemental speed.

For the rest of my life, the screams and cries of those trapped and dying souls would ring in my ears. I would wake from dreams reliving this night, imagined blood on my hands and very real blame on my soul. With each beat of my heart, I would see their shades in the shadows and hear their accusing voices. But at the moment, all I could do was stand in mute horror, tears pouring down my face as their bodies blackened and charred like so much over-cooked meat, paralyzed, unable to defend or to rescue them. For all my wealth, my powers, and my wisdom, I was helpless in the face of such tragedy.

⚜

With her immediate enemies vanquished and me publicly brought to heel, Evina resumed her duties as though nothing unusual had happened. She even allowed me to take a room in the main castle and for Lancelot and Sobian to be housed nearby. Our accommodations were nothing grand, but anything beat the sweltering gaol. I should have been grateful for her generosity—the fact that all of us still had our lives was nothing short of a miracle—but I couldn't help being suspicious of Evina's motives.

My fear of her revenge made every waking moment torture. There was no way Evina was ready to call my punishment complete, so I expected her vengeance around every corner. Sleep came in short, fitful bursts, just enough to keep me from getting ill or losing my mind, but not nearly enough to allay my constant state of alert anticipation and humming nerves. Each meal was torture, since I suspected each cup or bowl set in front of me was laced with poison. Sobian grudgingly began sampling a spoonful or sip of each part of my meal so that I wouldn't starve to death. Anytime we left the safety of our rooms, I insisted Lancelot walk before me and Sobian guard my back. Evina said nothing but watched me with shrewd eyes that were constantly plotting, calculating, feeding my troubled mind a steady diet of fear and doubt.

A fortnight after the solstice, Evina summoned Lancelot, Sobian, and me to her private chambers, and my stomach dipped in agitated anticipation. This was the moment I had been dreading, the reckoning I had been waiting for.

Evina and Mynyddog sat in throne-like chairs, surrounded by assorted sycophants and friends. Mynyddog slouched in his seat, relaxed, drinking ale and laughing. Slave women weaved between guests, bearing trays of meat and cheeses, fruit and delicacies, as though serving at a feast for close friends. Did they always dine this way? Or had we interrupted something?

As soon as Evina saw us, she snapped her fingers and everyone stopped what they were doing and departed. When we were alone, she did not offer us seats but required us to stand before her.

She toyed with the rim of her leather cup, looking at us through her eyelashes. "I have a proposal for you, one that you may refuse, but know that the other option is death."

I eyed Lancelot. So much for free will.

"You are too valuable for me to kill, which I suppose you have surmised by now. You have skill and experience that cannot be replicated. It pains me to need you, but each of you are necessary to the future of this kingdom. Lancelot, we need your skill with the sword and your ability with horses. Sobian, you are a master of intrigue with a network that rivals my own. Guinevere, your knowledge of strategy and of the hearts of the players on Britain's field of battle are second to none. Plus, you wield the power of Avalon. All of these skills combined will position us to be supreme rulers of the four ancient tribes. So I am asking you…" She cocked an eyebrow and gave us an all-knowing twist of her lips, her eyes gleaming menacingly. "No, I'm telling you, that you will remain by my side as my advisors in the coming war. And it will come to that, have no doubt."

I did not doubt it, even for a moment.

Evina stood, coming to rest before Lancelot. She placed a hand on his shoulder, a gesture that seemed to encircle him far more than her physical connection with him would allow. "To ensure your loyalty, Guinevere, I will take Lancelot's life as my own. Know that if you disobey me, even in one small matter, he will pay the price."

I swallowed hard, understanding the severity of the situation, for it was nearly an identical position to the one Lot had found himself in after his own failed coup against Arthur. Would that I had learned from him; perhaps then we'd all still be living in peace in Stirling. But that was not the case, and I had to deal with the here and now, not what could have been.

I bowed to Evina, so low that my head nearly brushed the floor. "As you say, Votadess. I am yours to command."

"As am I," Lancelot and Sobian echoed.

She smiled. "Good. Now we can get down to business."

Evina finally invited us to sit. When we were settled, she continued. "You likely have noticed that thanks to the

Saxon war, Morcant's relocation to Stirling, and the Pictish threat, my army now has three fronts to patrol, which means fewer and fewer men in each regiment. I can afford to stretch my northern army thin, but I certainly don't wish to underestimate Morcant's ambition—if he senses weakness, he could rebel as well—nor can I afford to skimp on troops guarding the border to Bernicia." She pinched her mouth with her thumb and forefinger and pulled downward, as if doing so would relieve the strain such words placed upon her. "Therefore, I feel that the only way forward is to conscript soldiers from the people, which I know that they will hate, especially since harvest time is nearly upon us and all hands are needed in the fields."

I shook my head before she'd even finished speaking. "No. That is not the strategy you should pursue. Unless further rebellion is what you desire, then by all means, continue."

"What do you recommend as an alternative?" Mynyddog asked, speaking for the first time since we answered his wife's summons.

Lancelot looked at me as well, as though curious as to where I would take this line of thinking.

"After the battle of Badon, when the Saxons were quelled and the Holy Grail had granted us peace, we needed something to do with the soldiers and brigands who usually occupied their time fighting for the king. Several suggestions were put forth by the Combrogi. One man thought we should establish a school to train future members who may not be able to afford to travel to Camelot to serve Arthur directly. Another thought their skills would be best used as a traveling band of soldiers policing the countryside in cooperation with the local kings and lords. I think the best solution for our present situation might be a combination of the two."

I rose, standing directly before them to better impart my point. "I believe we should bring the remaining Combrogi to Din Eidyn to help train the young and encourage people to volunteer so it doesn't come to conscription. They are well-known, and their names alone will attract people to your cause."

Mynyddog leaned forward, interest plain upon his face. "Tell me more."

"Well, we have lost many of our greatest knights, but you have the two best here in this room. Put it about that Lancelot will offer personal lessons in horsemanship and blade work, and you will attract a certain contingent of young men." I turned to Sobian. "This lady here has a storied past that will no doubt attract women to your cause. Add to that Gawain, whom I am sure could be persuaded to lend his skills in exchange for a fortifying army at Traprain Law, and I know I can convince Bedivere and maybe even Kay to travel north." I turned to Sobian. "You can track them down, yes?"

She looked up as though I had interrupted more important thoughts. "Of course."

Evina sat up straighter. "And you? Will you teach your magic to our people?"

"No. That I cannot do. I can only train those who have

a genuine calling to priesthood and even then my skills are limited. But I can work with Kiara to help the others in training."

Evina nodded. "Yes, I like this plan. Let us see how many people volunteer for our army before Lughnasa." She looked at Mynyddog. "Have it put forth that we are reconvening Arthur's Combrogi in order to defend against the Saxon hordes. Let us see who shows up before we resort to conscription." Evina stood, towering over me. "Guinevere, I hereby charge you, Lancelot, and Sobian with building the greatest army the Votadini have ever seen. You will report to us when the tribes are gathered for Lughnasa."

Lughnasa was only six weeks away. To get the word out in that time would require a spectacular feat of communication, the like of which this isle had never seen. I looked at Sobian, who grinned at me, clearly up for the challenge in spite of having lost two of her best informants to Evina's revenge on the summer solstice. Not to mention we needed a place to house the influx of troops and a plan to condense years of study and practice into weeks, even days, to meet Evina's timeline.

"You can count on me," Lancelot said, once again reading my thoughts.

"Right then," I said to Mynyddog and Evina. I would work with Kiara and whoever else she recommended to produce a training plan for the students I prayed would materialize. "Send word to the people of the four tribes that you require their attendance at the Lughnasa festivities."

Chapter Fifteen

Autumn 522

Looking out from Evina's royal tent over the gathered tribes playing at games of sport and betting on the horse races, it was difficult to believe that it was on this day so many years ago I first met Arthur and Lancelot. I still felt like that girl, though my hair was now shot through with gray and my hips thickened with age. Part of me said I should be one of the lasses dancing 'round the hallowed first sheaf of the harvest. Or at the very least I should be one of the young women being handfast today, as Evina's daughter was being bound to one of Morcant's descendants to ensure peace with the Picts and Mynyddog's youngest brother was pledged to a widowed woman with ties to Bernicia.

But there was I, an old woman lost in the folly of nostalgia of bygone days. It was on that same Lughnasa that Galen disappeared with Isolde, abandoning Elaine to her broken heart and the wrath of her indignant mother. Yet we were together again, Galen waiting patiently behind me to attend to my every whim. Years ago I could not earn his attention no matter what I did; now he was duty-bound to give it to me. In so many ways, life had brought us full circle. I sighed.

Lancelot must have heard the note of wistfulness in it, because he came to my side and slipped an arm around me. "What troubles you, my love?"

I looked up at him, my heart warming every bit as much as it did that first time I had met his gaze at the tournament. "Oh, nothing. I'm just feeling my age, I suppose," I answered with forced lightheartedness.

"Why is that a problem?" he asked with a smile. "I personally find you more beautiful and wise with each passing day." He followed my gaze to the festivities. "Shall I accompany you to the fair? It would be my honor and will take your mind off your troubles." He held out his arm.

I smiled and looped my arm through his. Yet again, Lancelot knew what I needed before I did. I could not have chosen a better champion and lover.

As soon as we stepped inside the maze of tents and stalls, all the aches and pains of age, all the wrinkles and age spots disappeared. I allowed the girl within to take over as we passed from vendor to vendor, nibbling on sweet rolls and admiring acrobats and jugglers. We cheered as Sobian bested Galen in a horserace, and we held hands in anticipatory horror as Kiara performed hair-raising tricks with knives and swords for the amusement of the crowd.

At one stall, Lancelot braided a fine red ribbon into my hair and placed a chaplet of poppies, dried wheat, and cowslip onto my head. We wandered over to one of the many bands providing music for the crowd—this one composed of drum, fiddle, flute, and lyre—and listened appreciatively, sipping cups of sweet heather ale and keeping time by tapping our toes and lightly patting our hands on our thighs. Soon, the music was in our blood—or perhaps it was the ale—and we took hold of one another, dancing bravely into the crowd. We turned and whirled, speeding with the tempo of the music, the world around us blurring until the only sight in my focus was Lancelot's beautiful blue eyes.

"Marry me," he said into my ear.

Lost in the trance of the dance, I shook my head. Surely he could not have said what I thought I heard. "Come again?"

He grinned. "You heard me. Let me take you to wife. After all these years, do you not think it is time?"

We stopped our twirling at the edge of the crowd.

"Do you mean it?" I asked incredulously.

"Of course. You know I do not jest about matters of love. We could be handfast before sunset." He tossed his head back, indicating behind him, where couples nervously stood outside a stone circle, waiting for their turn before the Druid who would bind them for a year and a day. "You have previously said you have no desire to wed again, but I thought since we have escaped death together a second time, it might be wise not to tempt fate. What say you?"

He looked at me with such love, gentleness, and caring, my heart melted and pooled at my feet. Seized by a streak of impetuousness, I nodded. "Oh, why not!"

Lancelot took my hand, and we raced downhill to the small circle of stones, stopping behind a tow-headed couple young enough to be our children.

My heart pounded as we inched closer to the entrance of the circle. Several Druids and priestesses were performing the rites, each positioned at one of the cardinal points within the circle. At the center was Calliac. Gone were her skulls and fierce markings, replaced by feathers and flowers and three blue dots in the shape of a triangle on her brow, where the crescent was set into my own. In place of her horse-hair cloak was a simple white gown cinched by three red cords in varying shades.

She beamed at us. "What a happy occasion to see the two of you here. I assume you wish to be wed?"

Lancelot and I looked at one another shyly, grinning like adolescents in the first throes of love.

"We do," he answered.

Calliac nodded to me. "Do you love this man?"

"I do," I answered without hesitation. "He has been for me a balm in some of my darkest moments."

She faced Lancelot. "And you love this woman?"

"More than anything."

"Do you wish to be bound to one another in spirit as well as flesh?"

In this ancient wedding rite, blessed by the Druids long before the days of Rome and their written contracts, when a couple pledged their love and declared themselves spirit-bound, they were tied to one another until death.

Looking into Lancelot's eyes, I said, "I would like nothing more."

"I am hers and she is mine," Lancelot answered.

Calliac took my right hand, joining it to Lancelot's, and wound around our wrists a thick gold and red ribbon embroidered with intricate Ogham symbols for fertility, love, peace, and prosperity. She then presented each of us with an end of the ribbon. "To show your mutual consent and dedication to this union, your hands alone will tie the knot that binds you."

With nerve-slicked palms and shaking fingers, we wound our ribbons together, at first stumbling over how to interlace them to form a knot. But our second attempt succeeded. We pulled and the knot held fast.

"By sun and moon, light and dark, night and day, you are bound. May the gods bless you and bring you long life and peace, along with every grace and blessing." She placed a hand over our intertwined palms.

The priestesses surrounding the circle sent up a cheer then chanted in a language I did not understand.

"They are thanking the gods and asking their blessing on us in their native tongue, far older than the one we use now," Lancelot explained, leaning down to me.

I placed a hand on the back of his neck, drawing him even closer to me. "Then perhaps we should seal our union." Without waiting for a response, I pulled him in and kissed him deeply, the way I had so long wished to do at Camelot, free of fear and secure in our love.

On the fourth day of the festival, our revelry was blighted by word of war. The Saxons had taken Catraeth, a strategic town south of York that controlled the fork of Dere Street where it branched off into the main trade routes to Corbridge and Carlisle. I cringed inwardly at the news. Elga and her ilk now had a direct line to Camelot, should they choose to try to defeat Constantine. Even though he'd taken Cadbury for his capital, the symbolic importance of Camelot remained deeply embedded in the hearts and minds of generations of Britons. Whoever controlled it, ruled them.

Upon hearing the news, Evina withdrew from the festivities, dragging Lancelot and me with her, leaving Sobian and Galen to entertain and serve her husband. Privately, I questioned the wisdom of that decision. Mynyddog had taken quite a shine to Sobian as of late, something the besotted Galen surely would not appreciate. On the other hand, if Sobian's feelings weren't as strong as I believed, she might well break Galen's heart. She had no compunction about trysting with a married man if it benefited her, and being in the Votad's bed certainly would. Either way, this likely would end in disaster.

"I have sent messengers to try to ascertain whether the House of Rheged intends to try to march on Catraeth," Evina announced as soon as the door to her private chambers clicked shut behind us.

Oh, they would. With Owain dead and Accolon

captured, the family, if not the people as well, would want revenge. Catraeth, though not geographically connected to the kingdom of Rheged, was part of Accolon's ancestral holdings, just like the Isle of Winds. If pride did not motivate them, the town's importance would, for it could prove a convenient staging ground for Elga and Theodric to push west into the fertile lands of Rheged.

"Are you thinking of joining them?" I asked.

Evina chewed her lower lip, eyes faraway with thought. "Perhaps." She sighed. "We have to do something. If we don't oppose the Saxons before they march north, they may be too strong to defeat by the time they arrive here. If anything, the loss of the Isle of Winds made them more determined."

"So why don't we use their methods against them?" Lancelot suggested. At my quizzical expression, he explained. "Look what they did at Camlann. They didn't have enough men to come at us alone, so they joined with Mordred and the Picts. We already have Accolon's army, so if we do the same and ally with the Picts, we should outnumber them." He looked to Evina for encouragement. "Do you think that is something your daughter might be able to arrange through Morcant?"

Evina considered the proposition. "Perhaps." She blinked as if rousing herself from a great stupor. "Guinevere, what do you think?"

I shook my head. "I don't like it. What is to stop the Picts from pillaging Bernicia or Rheged once they get there? Or going back on their word and staying here to fight you? There are too many ways they could use this proposed alliance as an excuse to get a foothold in our lands."

"*My* lands. *You* have no lands," Evina reminded me spitefully.

I closed my eyes and swallowed down a retort to her pettiness. "Regardless, they have shown they are not to be trusted."

"Then why did the Votadess bother to marry her daughter into their line?" Lancelot countered. "If we are not going to begin to trust one another, what is the point?" He turned to Evina. "I have fought in many battles with people from many lands. I can tell you this, nothing unites disparate men like a common enemy. If we can show them the Saxons are as big a threat to them as they are to us, we need not fear treachery."

Evina narrowed her eyes at him, probably thinking through how this might play out. "How do we do that? The Saxons would have to eat up all of our lands before they ever reached the Picts. There is nothing to say their ambition stretches so far that they would pass into such inhospitable land."

"I agree," I said. "I understand your way of thinking, Lancelot, but I don't think it will work. However, we could find a compromise, something that still invites the Highlanders who wish to fight to our table, but does not require anything of those who do not."

Evina's eyes brightened at the suggestion. "Yes. When we make the announcement at the closing feast that we are recruiting warriors from all lands, we can be sure to emphasize that those from the north are invited to join. I want to be certain that—"

Before she could finish her sentence, the door burst open. Mynyddog's personal slave knelt low, head to the floor before Evina.

She jumped to her feet. "Speak, man." Her tone said more about her fear for her husband than words ever could.

"Forgive me, Lady Votadess, but you are needed."

We followed him to the main tent, where Mynyddog sat, clutching his nose. His eyes spoke of murder.

"I want that man publicly flogged," he commanded, pointing at Galen. I could barely make out his words through the wad of fabric he held to his bloody nose.

Evina knelt next to him to examine his wounds. "What happened here?" She looked from Mynyddog to Galen and back to me, as though I would know.

Sobian stepped forward from where she'd been hidden in the shadows. "Galen was only defending my honor," she said, looking at him with great admiration.

Galen, in turn, looked as though he would reach out to her from his place kneeling on the ground, but his wrists were bound behind his back.

"Guinevere's slave punched the Votad," Mynyddog's slave explained.

Evina set her steely glare upon me, as though as his mistress, I was responsible for his actions even though I hadn't been present. "He dared lay a hand on his ruler?" Her tone was incredulous.

The slave bowed. "Yes, Lady."

She whirled on Sobian. "What did you do to provoke this?"

Sobian stared her down, never one to bow to authority, real or imagined. "Why are you so certain the guilt lies with me? Your husband is the one with wandering hands. Ask him." She crossed her arms as though the gesture put an end to the matter.

Evina shook her head. "Take him away," she ordered the man keeping Galen in check. "Toss him in the gaol. I will deal with him later." She stalked toward me, finger pointing into my face. "He is your property, and as such, you are responsible for him. Do you wish to take his flogging, or should I add this to the list of offenses for which you are still in my debt? I would levy a massive fine on you, but everything you have is thanks to my mercy."

As she went on about my responsibility, I questioned her sanity. How was I to be held responsible for another person's actions? Galen was a slave, but he still had free will. Surely she did not think I had broken him entirely. It was foolish for Galen to have struck Mynyddog, but it was not worth all of this.

As she raged, the look in her eyes became familiar, for I had once borne it as well. She felt threatened by her husband's interest in Sobian, just as I had by Arthur's interest in Morgan. Nothing I could say or do would change her mind. All I could do was apologize and offer to make amends, as though such a thing were really possible.

"I assure you no one meant any harm. I will speak with Galen and ensure he understands the gravity of his crime."

Even to my own ears, I sounded like a mother making excuses for a recalcitrant child. "I will also ensure he submits himself to the required punishment. After that, if the Votad would like to have use of him until his debt is paid, he has my blessing." I said the words, but it was a lie. I didn't want Galen anywhere near that man, but I had no choice.

"I suppose that is sufficient," she said, sulking. "But know the day is coming when your debts to me will come due. Prepare yourself."

◈◈◈

On the last evening of the Lughnasa festival, Evina and Mynyddog gathered all the young men and women in training at forts across the four tribes for a friendly competition. The overall victors of the nine challenges would be responsible for helping Kiara and me train the volunteers who came to Din Eidyn to join our army over the next ten months. The events they competed in today would be the exact same training they would administer to those who wished to endure the grueling challenge of condensing years of training into three seasons, a remarkable test of endurance, fortitude, and will.

Before the competition began, Kiara explained to me the tradition behind the way the warriors of the four tribes trained. "For centuries we have been caught between two competing peoples who each want our land, so our strength as warriors is our primary asset against our foes. The ancient tribes trained this way to ensure their land would not be taken by another tribe. Now we do so in order that it not be stolen by invaders."

For the young people, this day was deadly serious, comparable to the day they tested to first become warriors. Just as in actual battle, they painted their skin and limed their hair, drinking henbane and winding themselves up into bloodlust with battle cries, chants, and banging on shields.

For the adults, it was a time of fun, sporting bets, and nostalgia for their own youth. As Kiara and I walked the perimeter of the competition field, I heard more than one lord and lady reminiscing about their own testing or telling tales of battles long since won or lost.

Some of the judges—like Mynyddog, who was off in the forest monitoring those completing the evasion test; Evina, who led the hunt; Sobian, who ran the stealth course; and Lancelot, who was evaluating the competitors' handling of horses—were stationed at specific events. Others, like Kiara and me, were general judges. We had a responsibility to view each competitor at least once in each of the five remaining events.

We had already seen all manner of blade dexterity, from showy sword juggling and spear dancing to more basic skills like knife throwing and general sparring. My ears were still ringing from the voice test, in which each warrior demonstrated his or her ability to strike fear in the heart of the enemy with a fearsome battle cry.

Up next was the spear vault, a famous move I had heard of in tales of old but had never witnessed, not even by my mother. It had been the most common way for warriors to mount a horse before the coming of the Romans, but was rarely used anymore. Those who knew it kept its secret, as it was advantageous in quickly evading the enemy in times of war.

Two men led a small, stocky pony into the center of the clearing. Cinon took up a shorter spear and stood facing the pony as though he was staring down the enemy. Lancelot often adopted that look when he was concentrating. Then without warning, the boy took off at a sprint, racing toward the animal, spear held high. For a moment, it seemed he would impale the beast, but at the last second, he rammed the spear into the ground and leapt like a stag, using the handle to vault himself onto the horse's back.

Kiara and I cheered for his spectacular agility and grace.

At the next station, a girl of perhaps fifteen, face still rounded with the fat of youth, prepared to make the salmon leap. She stood before a stack of wood reaching higher than her head, expression stony with concentration. Rocking back and forth on her heels, she flung her arms above her head and leapt straight to the top, a feat doubly impressive given that she was a little slip of a thing.

Jumping down again, she headed for a thick felled tree trunk at least twice her height. Before she could reach it, a little girl of perhaps seven summers, painted with a single horizontal strip of blue across the bridge of her nose, ran onto the field, begging to be allowed to join in. Bending, the competitor scooped the girl in her arms—the resemblance was so strong, they had to be sisters—and whispered something to her. The girl relaxed and allowed her sister to carry her back to their family, who stood watching from the sidelines.

In a flash of memory, I saw myself as a seven-year-old girl. I had just graduated from a wooden training sword to my first sharpened blade. I was so proud, so certain I was the toughest female warrior of my bloodline—save my mother of course—and I strutted around just like that little girl. That was the same summer I began to boss around Elaine and came into my own as a future ruler. It was also the same year I began having visions and talk of Avalon was first mentioned. That was the age that changed everything for a Votadini girl, and here she was facing a war that even her family couldn't shield her from. But I could. No matter what happened, I would keep that girl safe and see her grow to womanhood.

Her sister sorted, the warrior took a deep breath to regain her focus, bent low, and took a firm grip of the tree trunk. She hugged it near the base before lifting it nearly onto her shoulder. Muscles straining, she took a few uneven steps before letting it fly. The log landed several feet in front of her. It was a good toss—sure to be beaten by the men in the competition, but fair enough to keep her in the running. A grin lit up her face, and suddenly she was no longer the hardened warrior I had seen before, but an uncertain adolescent girl seeking approval from the elders and peers that swarmed around her, offering their congratulations.

As the competitors finished their turns, I calculated their scores in my head. Some were clear standouts for me, but it wouldn't be easy to honor only three. The tribes had many great warriors, a sign I hoped heralded good fortune in the war to come.

و‌نه نه‌ه

Mynyddog stood atop a tree stump so he was visible to all the assembled warriors and spectators, his swollen, bruised nose contributing to his image as a fierce warrior, as though he had earned his injury in the competition, rather than at Galen's hand. "The judges have met and determined our winners. I am pleased to announce that the leaders of our new army are Cinon, son of Clydno Eityn, who once held the office of Votad; Corag, son of Fergus called Quickshanks; and Ailith, daughter of Davina the Strong."

Ailith. That was the name of the willowy girl who had charmed me with her tenderness toward her unruly sister. I would have to watch her over the next several months, for I was still seeking a commander of infantry, and with a little training and maturity, she could be a viable candidate.

The winners had one final stop before they could celebrate with friends and family. I followed them to a tent on the outskirts of field, away from the noise and activity of the competition. There they would meet with Calliac, who represented the Death Mother. She was charged with ensuring each warrior understood that for those who make their living by the sword, everything ends in death—for those killed, if not for the warrior personally. She also had the responsibility of determining if they could handle the guilt and pain that sometimes came with taking life, and if not, she was to let the judges know so another could be selected.

Inside, at the far end of the tent, Calliac sat draped in black fabric, swathed in deep shadows broken only by three candles: one on her right, one on her left, and another directly before her. The two boys and girl hesitantly approached her, and I followed suit, though I kept to the shadows so as not to disturb them. At first, Calliac's veil obscured her face from view, but when she raised her head and the candlelight touched it, it faded from opaque to translucent like dissipating smoke. A ring of human skulls circled her brow, and charcoal painted around her eyes and over her nose gave her an uncanny resemblance to them.

"Welcome, chosen brothers and sister," she hissed in a voice like stones grinding under wagon wheels. She raised a hand, palm up, indicating they were to sit.

To a one, they chose to kneel instead, sensing the power of the one who spoke through Calliac.

"Some of you know me, for I have taken your brothers and sisters, your mothers and fathers unto my breast. I have visited your homes in plague and accidents and have stolen life from the childbed." Her eyes roamed over each of them in turn. "None of you has escaped my shadow, nor will you avoid my touch in the end."

The three glanced at one another nervously.

"Know that in training others for war, you do my bidding, for war has no end but death, no purpose but destruction. You may think your aims noble, but in the end, you are but my scythes, harvesting the souls whom I call to reckoning. Guilt and innocence concern me not; I leave those to Cerridwen, for they are her purview. My only desire is to close the eyes of those who have used up their time on earth." She watched them, as though evaluating each.

Then she treated Cinon to a rictus grin devoid of all warmth. "Know now the gift you bestow upon all you kill and all who kill in your name."

She reached out a bony finger and touched Cinon right over his heart. His face went pale as though he was in a faint, and he choked. The moment she removed her finger, he caught a breath.

She turned to Corag, who made to scoot away from her touch, but she grabbed his wrist. He shook as though touched by lightning. Only when she let go did his body calm.

The Death Mother reached out to Ailith. Unlike the boys, she did not cower, so the goddess lowered her hand and pressed her cold, colorless lips to Ailith's brow. She did not shake or spasm but simply closed her eyes and exhaled, as though resigned to her fate. When the goddess pulled back, she drew another breath.

"You have all experienced the agony of my touch and lived. Therefore, you are bearers of my lethal gift. I ask you now to take it and spread among your enemies. Can you do that?"

The three were silent for a moment, eyes closed in contemplation.

Reverence for their culture washed over me. From the outside, they appeared brutish and brutal, but they treated death with great respect. It was a higher calling among their people, a mindset others would do well to share. Years ago,

Aggrivane had told me that Lot had sent him to study the ways of the Druids before he could go to war, in order to help teach him responsibility and respect. Perhaps this was something like what he'd learned. If all were taught the same, maybe, just maybe, we would have less senseless killing.

Ailith answered first. "Yes."

The others echoed her.

"Then so be it. Your names will be immortalized in song for your great deeds done in war, and down through the ages, warriors will toast to your honor."

Her head snapped up, as though I had made a sound that alerted her to my presence. "But you"—she pointed at me, eyes boring into my own—"you will lead these innocents to the grave."

Chapter Sixteen

Winter 523

By the time the snows began, Evina's army had nearly doubled, with nearly three hundred new recruits in training. As their teachers, we—the remaining Combrogi, Lancelot, Kiara, Sobian and I—had a responsibility to see their training continued through the cold winter months. Though there would be no campaigns until spring, they could still spar and learn basic knowledge. We divided them into classes of approximately thirty students—though twenty would have been preferable—and devised a learning schedule similar to the one used in Avalon so they could study multiple skills at once.

On a leaden day about three weeks before midwinter, we took them north, into the mountains above of the Firth of Forth. Though chances were good we would not campaign in winter, we chose to test the students' endurance and fealty to the commitment they had made by exposing them to the elements.

During our three-day excursion, the warriors learned how to walk with heavy packs, maneuver horses in the snow, and fight on a variety of surfaces, from ice and snow to steep mountain passes. They were also required to swim in a freezing lake and practice rescue and healing skills. They learned to find a defensible position, build shelter with and without usable timber, how to light a fire under a variety of conditions, and how to find fresh water, even when all appeared frozen. Their final lesson was one Lancelot and I had learned by nearly losing our lives when fleeing Malegant's mountain fortress—sound carries differently in the cold and snow and forgetting that can be deadly.

By dawn on the fourth day, we were all ready to head back to Din Eidyn, even though it was snowing. We had just left our campsite—Sobian and Kay in the front, recruits in the middle, and Lancelot and I bringing up the rear—when I noticed Lancelot's horse lagging behind.

"What's wrong?"

Lancelot bent over his horse's neck. "He's not stepping correctly on his left foot."

I pulled up next to him and we both dismounted.

Lancelot took the horse's hoof in his hand and turned it over to examine the underside. He cursed. "An ice ball. I just inspected his hooves earlier. How could one have formed so fast?"

I peered at it. "In these conditions, anything is possible." I picked at the ice ball with my fingers, hoping it would dislodge easily, but it didn't budge.

Lancelot dug at the mound of ice with his dagger, but with the same results. He squinted at me. "It is going to take some time to remove this without hurting him. Go on without me. I will catch up with you."

I was loathe to leave him behind, especially knowing the snow would get worse as the day went on; I sensed it.

When I made to follow him back to the remains of our campsite, Lancelot waved me away. "I'm going to have to rebuild the fire and heat the hoof pick to try to get this out. It almost looks like someone jammed ice in his hoof, then melted it so it would cling to the shoe. The wrath of the winter gods never ceases to amaze me."

"Are you sure you will be all right out here alone?"

"Of course. How many winters did I survive alone on the road before I met you?" He flashed a heart-melting grin. "Besides, I have the remains of this morning's kill with me and I know where you are headed. I'll meet you at the next campsite."

I kissed him quickly and mounted my horse. "Be careful."

⚜

Day turned to night and Lancelot still had not joined us. The evening star replaced the morning star a second time, and I panicked. So many things could have befallen my husband—bears, wolves, snowdrifts, thin ice, cold, hunger. If there was even a chance he was injured or in need of help, I couldn't sit idly by and do nothing.

One day out from Din Eidyn, I broke from our party,

leaving the students in the care of the former Combrogi while Sobian and I retraced our route. We found our former campsite, but nothing appeared amiss. However, a short distance away, we found Lancelot's horse, his ears frostbitten and hoof still impacted with ice, but otherwise healthy.

"Where is your master?" I asked, looking deep into his eyes as though I had Lancelot's talent for speaking with horses.

His eyes rolled as though recalling some unspeakable horror.

With a jolt, the sight came upon me and my mind was transported south. Lancelot was bound and gagged, kneeling at the feet of Elga and Ira. The Saxon said something to him and Lancelot shook his head. A guard drew his sword, then the vision vanished.

"No," I shouted. "No!" Violent spasms racked my frame.

Sobian dismounted and put her arms around me. "Guinevere, shush. Shhh," she hissed in my ear. "We must be quiet or risk triggering an avalanche. Remember what we taught the students?" She took my face in her hands as my wails increased in volume and violence. "Remember? Look at me, Guinevere. Look at me."

I complied, blinking away frozen tears.

"Good," she soothed. "Come now, we must be away from here. You can tell me what has you so upset when we are in a safer place."

In the shelter of the pine forest, I poured out my heart to her.

"I will get my girls on it. If anyone can find him, we can," she assured me with a squeeze of my hand.

"But he is with that unholy witch of a woman," I cried. "She swore to me someday she would have her revenge. What if this is it?"

"Then we will have to kill her before she can do any permanent damage. She should have died at Badon and has been living on borrowed time ever since."

When we were finally back in Din Eidyn, Lancelot's horse safely in the stable, I fell asleep in Sobian's arms, exhausted and unable to find comfort anywhere else.

I was just beginning to dream when Sobian gently shook me awake. "Guinevere, you have a visitor."

My sleep-addled mind leapt to Lancelot, expecting to see him when Galen opened the door. But instead, Morgan stood on the threshold.

She rushed toward me and fell at my feet. "Oh, Guinevere, I am so sorry. I never thought… I never intended…"

Morgan apologizing? Surely I was still sleeping. This had to be a dream; she had never once apologized to me in all the years I had known her. But if I was dreaming, why would Sobian have had to wake me? No. As improbable as it was, this was very real.

I raised Morgan to her feet, holding her at arm's length. Her red hair was disheveled under her black hood, eyes bloodshot, cheeks stained with tears. Her lips quivered as though she was about to let loose a fresh torrent of tears.

"What is it Morgan? What have you to apologize for?"

She looked at me in consternation, some of her old defiance returning. "Lancelot's disappearance, you daft cow."

"What?" I could not believe she'd had anything to do

with it. How could she have known where we would be? I hadn't even seen her since we returned from the Isle of Winds. I must have misheard her.

I was about to question her further, when the complaint of a wooden chair groaning under weight drew my attention across the room to Accolon, sunken-cheeked and missing an eye, but very much alive. Maybe I *was* dreaming. The last time I had seen him, Elga was dragging his unconscious body aboard one of their ships at the Isle of Winds. How had he escaped her and when? And if he was here and Morgan was apologizing for Lancelot's disappearance, that meant—

"Elga offered me a trade," Morgan explained as though she could not keep the words inside any longer. "Lancelot's whereabouts for the return of Accolon." She looked at me, eyes pleading. "You must believe that I never expected she would take him. Now… now…" She reached inside her gown and removed a roll of parchment. It shook as she held it out to me.

I handed it to Sobian, not trusting my own eyes to read it.

"She is demanding your life and the allegiance of the Votad and Votadess in exchange for Lancelot."

⋆⋅ ☙ ❧ ⋅⋆

Less than an hour later, a small crowd gathered inside the smoky council room for an emergency meeting in the wake of Morgan's revelation. Evina and Mynyddog poured over correspondence and maps while a handful of counselors whispered advice and suggestions out of our hearing.

They had been silent for so long, I feared they had forgotten my presence. "We must rescue him," I pleaded for what felt like the thousandth time.

Mynyddog raised a hand as though he could shield himself from my panic and outrage with a gesture. "I understand your need for action. I am troubled by this situation as well, but we cannot simply take up arms without thinking through all eventualities."

Mynyddog's words—no, it was more the surprising compassion in his tone—surprised and soothed me. Deep down, I knew he was not reacting out of any fondness for me, but out of concern for Elga's terms. My life was one thing; he would turn me over to the Saxons in a heartbeat. But asking them to bow before foreign rule was another matter altogether.

"It would be tantamount to murder to send our men on campaign in the middle of winter," Evina pointed out.

"Which I'm sure the Saxons took into consideration," Sobian said, more to herself than to anyone else.

Mynyddog nodded, tapping his balled fist against his lips, eyes distant with thought. "They need time for whatever they are planning. That's why they did this in winter. They want to be ready when we come to them."

"But where will we engage with them? We don't even know where they are," I said.

"Let me try to find them," Morgan suggested, tapping her forehead.

I crooked an eyebrow at her. *I* was the one with an

emotional connection to Lancelot. *I* was the one with the ability to see events at a distance. She could only… see the future. She would be able to see where they *would* be when our forces were ready to move, which was much more valuable than knowing where they presently stood. Inwardly, I scoffed at myself. My petty, jealous pride had nearly blinded me to Morgan's wisdom. If I hadn't exorcised my demons where she was concerned by now, would I ever?

Morgan sank down gracefully before the fire, tucking her feet beneath her and smoothing her gown over them. She breathed deeply a few times, but instead of closing her eyes as I would have done, she stared deep into the fire, letting her vision unfocus. To my left, Accolon tapped a steady beat on the wall with his palms to encourage Morgan's trance. Galen soon joined in.

Morgan's eyes moved, darting back and forth like a dreamer's as she beheld a scene invisible to the rest of us.

"Morgan, what do you see?" I coaxed.

"A hillfort. To the south. It's…" Her brow wrinkled. "It's farther inland than the rest of the Saxon holdings. In Accolon's lands." She turned toward her husband, eyes still blank with trance. "They have taken him to Catraeth and are preparing for a siege. They want us to come." She raised a hand to her head, seemed for a moment to regain herself, then collapsed in Accolon's arms. He quickly carried her from the room.

Evina, who had been listening attentively, ran a finger along one of the maps in front of her. "This is dire news indeed. If they have time to enforce the boundaries around

Catraeth, they can cut us off from Rheged and Strathclyde, effectively blocking any reinforcements or aid from the south."

Mynyddog grunted, his brow wrinkled. "We would be penned in like hogs, ripe for slaughter."

Evina leaned over and said something into her husband's ear. Soon, two of the counselors were blocking them from view.

I eyed Sobian, not liking the enthusiasm with which Evina was conversing with the men.

When she turned back to us, Evina's eyes were sparkling. My stomach knotted in response.

"Leave us," Evina commanded the room. I turned to follow the others, but Evina stopped me. "Not you, Guinevere."

Slowly, I faced her, unsure why they would wish to speak to me in private. Evina waved me toward the throne. I dutifully stepped forward and knelt at their feet.

"Do you remember that I once told you the day would come when I would call in your debts to be paid?" Without waiting for an answer, she continued. "That day has come."

I looked at her, confused. "What is it you wish of me?"

Mynyddog glanced at his wife, then addressed me. "You will lead our army to Catraeth in spring."

"Me? But why would you wish me to command in your name? I thought that was the very thing you forbid."

"Lancelot is your husband, is he not?" Evina asked.

"Yes." I still didn't understand. "But surely there are leaders among your sons or within your army whom you trust more."

They did not respond, simply continued to watch me, waiting.

Slowly, understanding dawned. They had others they trusted and valued more, but they didn't wish to waste them on this expedition. I, on the other hand, was expendable.

"You are not confident of victory." It was a statement, not a question. I marveled at Evina's capacity for revenge as the pieces fell into place in my mind. "You wish me to lead them in case we fail."

Evina smiled cruelly, an expression I had only ever seen on Morgan. "I expect you to fail. We cannot let the Saxon bid for Catraeth go unanswered, but knowing they anticipate us and with our army split as it is, we have little chance of defeating them. I must keep my best troops in reserve here for what may come. I already have a contingent in Lothian and another guarding the Picts in the north, so I can only give this cause so many men." She shrugged.

"Then why send me at all? What is to stop me from beginning the journey to placate you and abandoning them and you for another court, say that of Accolon or Constantine?"

Evina laughed. "Do you think I do not know you at all? You are too loyal, too concerned for the fate of the people. You would never abandon an army to certain death, even if your husband's life wasn't at stake." She leaned forward. "Make no mistake, your troops are not welcome back here without you, and you are not welcome back if you fail. Victory or death are your only choices."

So that was it. After so many months of toying with me

and using me, Evina had finally delivered my death sentence. She would not put me to the sword or hang me in front of a crowd, but I was being executed for treason all the same. She would rather a Saxon blade do the work for her.

I looked at them. "And if I refuse?"

"I will send word to Catraeth that we have refused their terms and Lancelot dies."

PART FOUR

Y Goddodin

Chapter Seventeen

Spring 524

At Din Eidyn, war was as much of a ritual as the turning of the year was to those who worked the fields. In the smithy, weapons were prepared and stored. The kitchens stockpiled rations of dried meat, salted fish, cheese, and other non-perishable food items that would sustain us on the long journey to Catraeth and into the siege beyond.

By the time the winter melted into spring, Din Eidyn was home to a motley band of approximately five hundred trained warriors from Evina, Accolon, and Constantine's armies and another three hundred aspiring soldiers. We had lost a small band of less than fifty boys a few weeks prior when they decided to go off alone in pursuit of the Saxons who had taken Lancelot. Their bodies were found a week later, skewered on pikes in the Pentland Hills, but their heads were never recovered.

When I had told my warriors we had been assigned a dual mission to rescue Lancelot and take back Catraeth, some were eager to begin spilling blood, out of revenge for our lost youths, hatred of the Saxons, and loyalty to Accolon. But others were more reticent.

"This is an ambush!" Bors, who had reluctantly joined us at Constantine's bidding, yelled.

"Yes, it is," I answered. "The Saxons are using Lancelot to lure us to our deaths. But you were once a member of the Combrogi. Can you honestly tell me you could leave him to die simply because of a trap?"

Bors looked down, muttering under his breath. It was as close to agreement as I would get from him.

I turned, taking in my other troops. "Many of you came from Stirling and the lands surrounding it. Once you and your neighbors begged me to lead you as your Votadess. I may not bear that title, but I am asking you to trust me now as if I did. Allow me to lead you into battle. Whether we claim victory or shed our blood in vain, we are fighting for our lands and our families, that they may live in peace in the tradition of our ancestors, rather than under the Saxon's boots."

"Aye," Cinon shouted. "We are the warriors of a people fed from the breast on battle. If we did not wish to risk our lives, we should have chosen to be bakers or blacksmiths or tailors. This is our duty to our families and to ourselves. There is no question of fear of death. We are meant to die in battle, so let's do as we are commanded."

"We have no honor if we don't at least try to take back one of our own," Corag added, watching me. "Angus may be from across the sea, but he has helped so many people, my da included, that he *is* one of us, blood or no." He turned on Bors. "So if you think we are going to back down, you're wrong and you'd better start running. This lot"—he made a gesture meant to encircle the barracks—"does not take kindly to cowards or traitors, and if you are against us, you are both."

⋄⋄⋄

In preparation for our journey south, Evina called a great three-day feast, insisting we celebrate like the warriors of old. No expense was spared, no animal left unslaughtered, or cask of heather ale or honey mead untapped. She knew we may not return, and so gave us a feast to either herald our coming victory or guide our souls to the Otherworld.

On the first night, the great hall was full to brimming with warriors from all the tribes. Votadini made up the majority, but there were also Novantae, Selgovae, and Damnonii, plus a handful of Picts and Britons sympathetic to our cause. Among these were Bedivere and Kay, who had not yet apparently seen their fill of battle.

"It is an honor to fight alongside you one last time," Kay said with a small bow when I encountered him among the throng of bodies inside the hall.

"It may be the last time for you, but I intend to live to see another day," Bedivere joked.

There was no missing the tension and fear underlying their words, so I laughed to try to dispel it. "I do not think even the gods could kill the two of you tough old sods unless you were ready. We have seen much. This is just the next in a long line."

"Before we retire, yes?" Bedivere joked.

"Not me. I plan to die in the saddle, as should you lot," I said.

Kay touched his mug to mine in response. "I'll drink to that."

"To victory!"

As the night progressed, we ate, drank, and danced, trying our best to forget the reason for our gathering, even while listening to the tales of past victories and heroes long dead sung by the bards. Even Calliac participated, singing a particularly moving tale of a husband and wife who died together on the battlefield. Their deaths assured their progeny back home could live, resulting in Mynyddog's bloodline.

On the second night, the mood was decidedly more somber, as the reality of what was to come manifested. The bards sang songs of bitter doom and called curses down on our enemies. The seers made a spectacle of reading the entrails of slaughtered animals, holding them aloft for all to see. But because they foresaw nothing but victory for us and death for our enemy, they were hardly to be believed. No battle, in my experience, was so one-sided.

Around the great hall, warriors huddled in groups or pairs, engaging in some kind of pre-battle ritual. They would speak a few words to one another, draw blood from their finger, palm, or forearm, then touch the wounds together, clapping one another on the back proudly before licking their wounds clean.

"Do they have blood bonds where you are from?" Kiara asked when she noticed me watching them.

"No. Many of our men are close and would gladly die to save the other, but we have no formal way to seal our loyalty."

"You do now. Come on."

She dragged me by the hand to the central hearth fire, where Kay and Bedivere were facing one another like a couple about to be wed. The cheer of another group drowned out most of what they said, and when I looked back, they were hand in hand as though ready to arm wrestle one another.

"In the names of all our gods, I do so swear to bind my life with yours. I will defend you with all my power. If you be cut down while I still live—" Kay said.

"I'll hunt the bastard down and feed him his own prick," Bedivere finished for him before pulling him into a tight embrace.

Kiara turned to me. "In our tradition, you cannot bond with your champion or spouse, as you already have ties to those people which might interfere in battle. Only another warrior is deserving of your solemn oath." She held out her hand to me. "Will you do me the honor?"

Without waiting for me to reply, she took out her dagger and made a slash on the inside of her forearm, where it would not pain her in the heat of battle. For a moment, I could only stare, watching the crimson line form on her arm. Then I looked into Kiara's clear blue eyes. This was the woman who had taken me under her wing when I was new to Stirling and knew no one. In asking for my help training her young warriors, she'd given an old woman back her youth and endowed me with a purpose beyond being a prize for anyone seeking the power. Now, she and I were about to lead the mission to rescue Lancelot and save our people from the Saxons. There was no one else I would rather fight to the death for.

Without a word, I took the dagger from her, sucking in air as I made a similar gash on my arm. I took her hand, entwining our arms until our blood mingled. "Kiara, battle maid of both the Votadini and Selgovae, I hereby pledge my life to you. In victory or defeat, may our bodies and souls be bound."

"In life and in death, I will watch over you and see you victorious or revenged. This do I swear in the sight of all my gods," she finished.

We hugged one another tightly.

"We'll destroy those bastards," she promised before licking her arm.

Our blood was bitter on my tongue as I did the same. "Each and every one."

◦◦◦

The last night was for saying farewell. Kiara, Morgan, and Accolon would be coming with us, so I had few people to address, unlike many of the men and women who were saying goodbye to spouses, children, and sometimes many generations of family. But there were remarkably few tears and many expressions of love and encouragement. This was a culture of war, and this was the moment many of them had trained for their whole lives.

There was one last ritual before we could say our farewells in private. We took our place in a long line of men and women, each with the same dazed, introspective expression. Before us on the right was a large pile of flat rocks. As each person passed, he or she took one, then placed it on top of a stack on the left to form a cairn, the final resting place of the dead who would perish in the coming battle. Those who returned would retrieve a stone, leaving the remainder as a memorial.

I shivered as the stack grew higher and higher, reaching toward the heavens. *Bless us in battle, great Morrigan, and protect us, so that many of these stones may be removed, discarded, and forgotten. May they find their way into walls or roads, rather than remain standing as a symbol of slaughter for generations to come.* Feeling strangely hollow, I placed my own stone on top of the one Evina had designated for Lancelot.

To Kiara, I said, "Let's get out of here. I need to remember why we live for as long as I can, rather than dance among those already dead."

We headed back to our quarters, passing scores of couples who defiantly refused to let one another go. It wasn't long before we found Sobian and Galen, heads bent together, whispered endearments becoming tiny puffs of steam in the chill night air. She was prepared for battle, but he would stay behind in the service of Evina and Mynyddog, so these were their last moments together.

The separation of lovers as one turned their face toward battle was never easy, nor was it fair, but these two were especially unfortunate. They had waited so long to find one another and were so well-suited. As a slave, Galen could not fight unless he was conscripted, but Sobian went voluntarily. She was not of our tribes or bound to our loyalties or laws, yet she willingly faced death out of friendship for me. That had to count for something.

It would. I would make it so. *I may not be able to tell my own fate or those of anyone around us, but I can save two lives and ensure some happiness comes out of this.*

I ran over to Galen and Sobian, smiling amid the tears streaming down my cheeks. "Sobian, take back your stone. You are not going with us."

Her face crumpled. "I'm not? I don't understand. Have I done something to offend?"

"No, no, this is something much better." I grinned. "The affection the two of you have for one another is no secret to anyone, try as you may to hide it." I took Galen's hand. "That is why I release you from your bondage. From this day forth, you are a free man, absolved of all your past transgressions. Take this naughty lass and begin a new life with her."

Galen stared at me, obviously mystified. "But is not Evina the one to release me? Her father *was* the one who condemned me, after all."

I shook my head. "She gave you to me. I may not be able

to restore your tribal mark, but I can grant your freedom." I slipped the key from around my neck and opened his collar, and he rubbed his neck in great relief. "Tell Calliac what I have done. She will be able to cover your mark of slavery."

Sobian still looked concerned, her brow wrinkled. "But where are we to go? I have no permanent home, and Galen cannot purchase land."

"But it can be gifted to him for his service. Galen, Lancelot owns land in Angus. He and I were planning to give it to you when your service was over and you had earned your freedom. Tell them you come in his name and give them this." I slipped a bracelet off my arm before holding it out to Galen. "The whole of the town knows the story behind this gift, which was given to Lancelot in exchange for his service. He wanted me to keep it in case something ever happened to him and I needed to flee. Now it is yours. The people of Angus will treat you like the chieftain's son you were born to be. Plus, you will be safe there from any fighting that may result from our march south."

"I—I cannot accept this. What about you? Where will you live when you return?"

I shook my head. "The gods do not promise that I will live. They make that promise to no man. But when this is over, Lancelot and I will return to Brittany. He has ancestral lands there. Have no fear for our welfare." I placed Galen's hand over the bracelet. "Give me one less worry on the battlefield. Say yes and be happy."

Galen looked at Sobian. "I do not wish to force you into anything you are not prepared to accept."

She grabbed him by the shirt collar. "I have been waiting for you the whole of my life. You are my match in all things. I will not let you go." She kissed him, long and deep. When she finally pulled away, she asked, "Your father wasn't murdered by a god, was he?"

Galen looked at her quizzically. "No. He died in battle on Beltane. He was accidently killed in what was supposed to only be a mock dual between the Oak King and the Holly King."

I gasped. "Then he *was* murdered by a god. Each of them is portraying an aspect of the god during that ritual. One is the god of winter and the other the god of summer. It seems your Witch of Orkney was right after all." I clapped Sobian on the shoulder. "Go, pack your things and leave before first light. You will be long gone before anyone notices."

Galen hugged me tightly, his eyes welling with tears. "Truly, you are a good woman. I wish there was some way I could repay you."

I looked away. "Be happy. That is the best repayment there is."

As they retreated into the darkness, my heart fluttered with joy. I may have mistrusted Galen in the beginning, but his years of captivity had changed him for the better. He was worthy of a woman like Sobian now. I may not have been able to save Arthur, but I was sure that wherever his soul was now, he was smiling, grateful to know at least one of his old friends, a pirate-turned-assassin-turned-heroine with more lives than a cat, had emerged from this strife unscathed.

෨෬ ෭෬

After a grueling week-long journey south, our army, some nearly nine hundred strong, including an equal number of horses for the cavalry that made up a third of our army, finally spotted the fortress of Catraeth. It loomed high above us like a mountain grown out of the edge of the peat-covered Cheviot Hills, where they gave way to the fertile plane of the Tweed Valley. Between us and our target lay fields of bracken, sweet heather, and bilberry, all of which would both help and hinder an army on foot.

Just after midday, when we were still a ways off from the fortress but within range of where we should set up our siege camp, they appeared on the horizon—an awaiting army meant either for ambush or simply to whittle down our numbers before we reached the fortress.

I signaled for the long train of men, women, and supply carts to halt. Had the Saxons seen us? If not, it was possible we could double back and come at them from a different route. They had no camp, so they must have been confident they could either finish us off by nightfall or they were close enough to make an easy retreat within the walls of the fort. Their army had nearly double the manpower of ours, and no doubt their scouts were now scampering back to the fort to report our presence.

There was no way around confronting them head-on. This was my least favorite type of battle, but one we could not avoid. I gave the signal for us to continue, sticking to the original plan. At least now we knew the terrain and general configuration of the army we would be fighting. It was little comfort, but we would take what we could get.

We had come prepared to take a hill fort, no easy task, and now we were faced with a pitched battle too. We needed time to change tactics and prepare before engaging. Accolon sighted a location suitable for our camp and set about creating a home base for ourselves. I saw to the large tent that would house our operations and strategy, while Morgan took charge of the camp women and healers who would stay behind to help while the soldiers fought. Accolon took responsibility for the barracks, smithy, and stables, and the captains organized their men. Accolon also assigned groups of men to surround the fort and cut off any food or other supply lines.

By nightfall, we were ready. The siege itself could last for weeks while we waited for the supplies of food and water inside the fort to diminish. We would attack the fort at the same time, attempting to weaken their defenses and kill as many of the enemy as possible. But first we had to defeat the battalion waiting for us.

At dawn, we would charge, and there would be no turning back. How I missed Lancelot and wished I could hold him one last time before the battle that might end my life. Knowing he was so close—just inside that prison of a fortress—yet so far away and with an army between us was torture. As I lay between Morgan and Kiara in my tent, trying desperately to get some sleep, I told myself that the next time I opened my eyes, I would be mere hours from seeing Lancelot again.

The sky was still dark, moon riding low in the sky, stars sparkling, when my eyes popped open. I would sleep no more this night. I sat up, watching Morgan and Kiara slumber on, and recalled a night so many years before in Avalon when I woke to find Mona crying and comforted her with the wooden toy dog Peredur had given me.

Peredur. I hadn't thought of him in years. Nor his half-crazed sister, Nimue, who had ended up murdering Merlin before taking her own life. I shivered, recalling the night we cast her out of the priestesshood of Avalon, leaving her alone on the Tor to decide her own manner of death. Was my remembering them a sign? Worse yet, an omen of ill fate? One would think with the gift of sight, fear of the future and of omens and portents would be pointless. Perhaps that was the case with Morgan's gift, but mine provided no such comfort.

I rummaged in my bag of personal possessions, trying to find both Peredur's toy dog, which I considered a token of good fortune, and my set of Holy Stones. I had to know what my memory of them meant. Plus, it was time to conduct my first divining for the battle to come.

I must have made more noise than I'd intended, because when I looked up again, Morgan was staring at me.

"Why are you awake?" She sat up, rubbing her eyes. "Better question, why are you keeping me awake?"

"I am doing no such thing. Go back to sleep."

"What *are* you doing?" She eyed me curiously.

"I was looking for a few items to help with my pre-battle rituals." I lifted the little wooden toy and pouch of stones so she could see them. "Do you have any rituals of your own?"

Rather than answering my question, she reached for the dog. "I haven't seen him in years. What was his name? Bricriu?" She gazed at the little dog lovingly. "The last time I recall holding him was that winter night when we were in the House of Nine." A soft smile played on her lips.

"Yes. I'm surprised you remember."

She looked at me, hurt in her eyes. "Please don't think me so heartless. Despite what has passed between us, I treasure our time in Avalon, especially that night." Morgan gestured for me to sit on the bed. "We were, what? Ten? Eleven, maybe? Do you remember I asked Mona if she would try to see into my past?"

I looked away, not wanting to meet her eyes on such a sensitive subject. "Yes. You were hoping to learn the identity of your parents. Was she able to tell you?" I found the courage to face her then, wanting to be able to look into her eyes if she claimed to know her parentage. I wanted to see if she told the truth or if there was any hint of falsehood shadowing them.

Morgan toyed with the top of her brown wool blanket. "No. She was never able to see much clearly for me." Her eyes met mine, and they were shining. "But I do know who they are… or should I say were." She leaned forward so that barely a breath of space remained between us, and her voice dropped to confidential tone. "The Grail revealed their identities to me that night we first drank from it. Viviane is my mother. Merlin is my father. I was a child of the Beltane fires. That is why they chose me over you to be the Virgin Queen. It had nothing to do with our childish competition, or who was really the best among us. They thought I would be more likely to conceive the Sacred King's child because I came from the same type of union."

I sat back, stunned. All these years, Morgan and I had hated one another, vied for attention and recognition and pride of place in Argante's eyes and then in Arthur's, and for what? It was never about us, but about who would continue Arthur's line. If we had only known, we could have avoided decades of animosity and bitterness, and avoided so much pain. If only…

"I suppose they were right, just wrong about the timing," she continued. "As it turned out, I did bear his children." Her voice trailed off, and I imagined she was lost in memories of her dead son and the daughter she barely knew.

Morgan had been chosen by the Goddess because of her bloodline, and Arthur fell in love with her that night. If my father hadn't intervened and proposed my hand to Arthur in repayment of his debt, then Morgan would have been queen in my place. And I would have been wed to Aggrivane. *No,* I corrected myself. *That is not right. I would have been wed to Malegant.* I shuddered. What a living hell that would have been. I found myself grateful—for the first time in my life—for Morgan's interference in my plans, however unwitting.

"I owe you a debt of gratitude, it seems."

Morgan startled out of her reverie. "What?"

"I said 'Thank you.'"

She looked at me warily, as though I had transformed into a rabid beast. "For what?"

I shrugged. "For everything." I did not want to try to explain my reasons to her. "I just felt like it was something I should say, especially given we don't know if we will see tomorrow. I suppose I should say I'm sorry as well—for all that I have done over the years. I'm sure you have kept a mental list." I certainly had.

Morgan continued to stare at me, her eyes growing damp.

I glanced at the opening of the tent, where a small crack of light showed dawn was near to breaking. "I should get on with my divination." I shook the bag, lifted the board, and stood.

"Wait." Morgan grabbed my wrist.

I turned.

"You forgot this." She held out Bricriu in her other palm.

"Thanks."

"I'm sorry too." She squeezed my arm.

⚬⚬⚬

The stones predicted a short period of harrying the Saxon army before the siege would begin in earnest, but they would not yet show me the final outcome. It was blurred, playing out one time in our favor, portending mass causalities the next. I had never encountered a battle where the stones were so indecisive; it was as though some factor I had yet to account for could change everything. All I could do was set them aside and hope I would have time to consult them again before we gained the fort.

The camp rose when the eastern sky was just beginning to pale. Instead of breaking our fast with porridge or stale bread, we gathered around the cook fires for a ritual of a different sort. Warriors broke into their fighting ranks and passed around buckets of slaked quicklime, which had been allowed to cool overnight. Each man and woman worked it into his or her hair so that it stood up and out as much as possible. When it dried, our hair would be stiff and paler than usual, giving us a spectral appearance.

Next we passed around pots of woad to paint one another's skin. Many of the men simply slapped on stripes with their fingertips, but Kiara and I were more artistic, drawing spirals and knots and adding a few sigils for protection and courage.

Then we dressed for battle in the garb of our tribal animals—the horse, the wolf, the raven, and the stag—tunics and braccae made of their skins, their fur slung around our shoulders, skulls attached to our heads as helmets, and teeth and bones worn as jewelry.

Finally, we moved single-file past a large cauldron, into which Morgan and some of the other camp women were dipping wooden mugs. Each man took a cup and retreated to a place of his choosing to consume the sacred drink. When I was but three people from the front of the line, the henbane's noxious scent assaulted me, bringing stinging tears to my eyes and forcing bile into my throat. I coughed a few times before my body adjusted to the acrid, smoky, leather-like scent.

Kiara and I sat next to one another and stared at the viscous liquid in our cups.

"I suppose you have consumed this before?"

"Only twice. We don't drink it regularly because too much can be poisonous." She looked at the contents of her cup again and sniffed. "I think they mixed it with goat's milk to make it more palatable." She grimaced, then looked at me. "What you have heard about its effects is true. It will slowly take you over until you have the undeniable urge to kill, a true thirst for blood. Be prepared."

With one last glance into the cup, I touched my mug to hers then brought it to my lips. The thick, clammy liquid slid down my throat with little effort on my part, leaving a bitter trail in its wake.

"Ugh. I feel like I swallowed a slug!" I grimaced, trying to keep from looking like a total fool.

Kiara laughed. "That would have tasted better."

Her chuckle was the last joyful sound our camp would hear. Slowly, our warriors grew subdued, laughter and boastful shouts replaced by a menacing silence, akin to the calm before a storm. Then slowly, one by one, the soldiers began to fidget, to pace, to glare suspiciously at one another through dilated pupils.

I felt it too—the restlessness. My whole body grew warm and my vision narrowed. I could no longer see to either side, but everything in front of me appeared crystal clear, sharper, more focused than ever before. Then my leg twitched, bouncing up and down without my conscious command. All of my muscles grew taut, ready to spring, poised on the edge of action. I could no longer sit still. I had the aggression of a thousand angry bulls charging through my veins. I wanted—no, *needed* to move. I was strong. I was invincible, and I was ready to attack.

I prowled around the camp like a wildcat until somewhere behind me, a group of warriors pounded on their shields with spear shafts and sword pommels. My heartbeat sped up to match.

"Form up!" I yelled.

The command echoed from man to woman to man across the camp until we were arranged by unit, spearmen and swordsmen at the front lines, archers and slingers at the rear, everyone surrounded by our cavalry.

Kiara took her place at my side. At my signal, the pounding ceased, replaced by several heartbeats of deafening silence. Then as one man, we screamed, charging forth.

The war had begun.

Chapter Eighteen

The heads were the first things I saw, rotted away on poles surrounding the base of the fort like discarded fruit in the summer sun. What was left of our lost group of young would-be heroes barely looked human, their decomposition made even more by violent by the henbane flowing through my veins. Worms crawled out of sockets where eyes had once been. Jowls hung, torn and desiccated like badly butchered meat. Ravens pecked at hair, at tongues or skin, leaving deep divots into which flies gratefully buzzed.

Then their jaws shook as though the skulls would speak.

"Save us," one screeched.

I whirled around, seeking the source of the voice.

Just as quickly, another echoed, "Save yourself."

"No, save him!"

"Who?" I turned again and ran smack into Kiara. "Save who?"

She grabbed my shoulders to steady me. "Guinevere." She shook me slightly. "Guinevere!"

"They want me to save him," I said frantically. I blinked hard a few times, trying to focus my eyes. When I opened them, I was staring into Kiara's face.

She smiled. "You're fine. It's only the henbane. Sometimes it can make you see things that aren't really there, especially when you aren't used to it."

"But they said—"

Before I could finish, Accolon called for a halt. He pointed up at the wall, where figures jostled about, followed by unintelligible growling and a few curses. Some kind of struggle ensued above us, and men were knocked down, only to rise once again. Finally, a familiar head of blond curls appeared. All the other figures stepped back, ceding the primary position to her.

"Yield to us or he dies," Elga commanded, nodding at the man she held by the hair, a sharp blade pressed into his throat.

Lancelot. The henbane evaporated from my blood, my stomach cramping and my bowels threatening to turn to water.

He was bound with his hands behind his back, forced to kneel in front of Elga. Given the way she was dragging him around, his feet were lashed together too. Behind Lancelot stood three large men, weapons trained on him, should he attempt to free himself. There was no way he would escape unharmed unless I did as she wished.

I laid down my sword. "You have asked me to yield, and so I do. But I cannot swear for the actions of others, only myself. Now please, return him to us. He has done nothing against you."

Elga smirked. "Perhaps not in this war, but his blade has meant death for many of my countrymen." She twisted Lancelot's head so he could see the scarred area of flesh above her left clavicle. "You gave me this." She clucked her tongue. "So close to ending my life, yet so far away. Perhaps I should show you how it is done." She pressed the blade into his flesh, eliciting a grunt of pain from Lancelot and producing a rivulet of blood that wound slowly down his neck.

"No. Stop!" I cried. "Spare his life and I will do anything you ask." I made sure the men around me could see that my fingers were making a cursing formation behind my back.

She laughed. "Kneel before me."

I did.

"Will you disown your kin and country, forsake your quest to defeat us? Will you finally admit that I've beaten you?"

"Yes, anything. You have won."

She cocked her head at me. "I do not believe you." She glanced at Lancelot. "Pity." In a flash, she ripped the knife across his throat. As blood bubbled from his neck, she leaned down and kissed him, long and deep, taking in his dying breath. When she looked up again, her mouth was covered in his blood. "Now, kill them all," she commanded her troops.

Primal fury propelled a scream from my lips, a sound more terrible than the war cry of the greatest warrior queen, more chilling than a banshee. Perhaps it was the remnants of henbane, but no grief weighed me down in that moment, only pure hatred. The desire for revenge turned my nerves to iron, my blood to fire. I was on my feet in an instant, lunging toward Elga, who had melted into the sea of bodies within the fort. *Even if we fail to take it, I will get inside and kill her, or the Goddess strike me dead.*

A torrent of troops surged past me as the two armies engaged. From some distant place, I was aware of fending off blows and delivering deadly strikes with my sword in one hand and a spear in the other. I was acting on a warrior's instinct, born of years of training. As my body reacted to defend against threats, my mind had but one goal—find Elga.

As I drew closer to the gates, it became harder to distinguish ally from enemy. The world around me was a dizzying sea of colors and whirling bodies. When I heard my name or recognized a face, I gave aid, but otherwise I did not involve myself in others' strife.

Day passed into night that way, with only a brief respite to tend to wounds, bury the dead, and fall into dreamless, exhausted sleep. Soon we were on our blistered, aching feet again, swords in hand, shields at the ready.

The Saxons kept coming. While our numbers dwindled, theirs seemed only to increase. Kiara had ridden out last night and checked on our second unit, the ones preventing supplies from reaching the fort, and they reported no one had crossed their lines. It was impossible they really were multiplying, but that didn't make them any easier to fend off.

As the sun set on the sixth day, our morale was flagging. There simply were not enough soldiers left. We had already recalled the second unit into battle. Tonight we would have to break camp and press into service anyone who could hold a weapon, whether they were trained or not. The following day would be our last push, an offensive that would determine whether we went down in history as heroes who'd saved our tribe or were eulogized as brave warriors who'd perished in defeat.

I called all of our remaining troops together just after Accolon sounded the retreat for the night. Looking over the tired faces and broken bodies, I summoned all the courage I had left. "I was not going to tell you this, but given that tomorrow we will make our last stand, you deserve to know." I made sure all eyes and ears were on me. "There is no home for any of us to return to, should the battle consume us. Before we left Din Eidyn, our Votadess made it clear that should we fail, we were no longer welcome there or anywhere else within Votadini lands."

Grumbling rose and fell like an ocean wave as the troops took in this news.

"I tell you this not to upset you but to light a fire within you. We may be outnumbered, but we are not without hope. We can take the anger and betrayal we feel toward our leaders and use it to propel our javelins and sharpen our swords. We can show the Saxons what offended Britons look like, especially when their homes are threatened."

Before me, heads nodded.

"And once the Saxons are dead, we will overthrow the Votad and Votadess and install you in their place," someone shouted.

"Aye!" The word rang through the crowd like a tolling funeral bell.

Inwardly, I cringed. I would never accept that title, but they didn't need to know that. Let them believe it if the idea of making me Votadess would give them extra courage to fight. "One step at a time. Now, say your prayers and make your peace with whatever gods you believe in. Tomorrow, we fight!"

✥✥✥

The next morning, a deep, pervasive calm filled my body and mind as I took a final walk through what was left of our camp, checking for deserters or anyone left behind and making sure cook fires were properly doused. The last thing we needed was a fire at our backs preventing retreat, should the day come to that. If we had learned nothing else from Boudicca's disastrous final battle, it was make sure our troops always had a way out.

Near the rear of the troops, I found Morgan with a group of women armored in the discards of the dead, reluctance writ large on their faces.

"You can run, you know," I said to them gently. "You do not have to fight."

"Yes, we do," said a stately dark-skinned woman who

towered above me. "The cravens among us ran already under cover of darkness. The rest of us are here to do our part. We're just scared."

I gently pushed my way into their circle and took her hand. "I understand. I was only fifteen the first time I faced down an army in battle, only nine the first time I defended myself against attack. Nothing I can say will make it easier. Please know you are doing the right thing."

"My husband died in this battle three days ago," a young woman clutching a spear told me. "I want to see his soul avenged, even if it means meeting him soon after."

"I promised my little sister I would protect her, and I cannot do that by running," said Ailith, who had come up behind me. "It would be my honor to lead you into battle. Will you follow me?"

The women nodded. Ailith led them to Accolon, who directed them with hand gestures and words I could not hear.

Once they had all moved off, I was left alone with Morgan. She turned her sword over and over as though she had never seen one before, though I knew full well she had had lessons from both Arthur and Accolon on how to use it.

"I never thought my life would come to this," she said, not taking her eyes from the blade in her hands. "I am a priestess vowed to peace, not a soldier. What do I know of war?"

"You have been married to three kings," I reminded her. "You know more than most of the men here."

She snickered and tossed the sword at my feet. "I don't need one of these to be dangerous. If these bastards want to see what happens when they cross a child of Avalon, they better be prepared." She raised her arms, and a brisk southwest wind stirred our hair. "I will fight in my own manner."

I handed her back the sword. "Please take this. Your powers are no good if you get pinned between two Saxon blades. Even the Lady of the Lake carried a dagger for that very reason, and the Grail Maidens are armed as well."

She sheathed the sword with sarcastic smile. "You still always have to be right, don't you?"

Her words took me back to a day on Avalon when we were but children and were both assigned to clean the sanctuary stairs as punishment for our roles in two mishaps the day before. Then, she had been lording her place as favorite acolyte over me. Now, she may have used the same taunting tone, but all the venom was gone from it.

"Only where you are concerned," I shot back with smile.

"May the God and Goddess of Avalon watch over and protect you," she called over her shoulder as she melted into the waiting troops.

"May your god bless you as well," I shouted after her.

ఞ

On the front lines, Kay and Bedivere were forming a schiltron, or pike block, to try to take out the heart of the defending mass. I slipped underneath the shoulders of some of the taller men to take my place in the second rank of spearmen. We would throw our weapons while those in front of us, armed with swords and shields, would defend us from the volley of javelins likely to be launched in return. Flanking us on all sides was a mass of cavalry ready to charge through the enemy and do their own damage.

At a signal from Kay, each spearman raised his or her shield, forming an overhead and side armor for our crew. A steady beat of sword on shield was taken up by one of the cavalrymen. Its sole purpose was to help us keep in time as we progressed, so that no one fell and was trampled, which would make the whole unit dissolve into chaos. On Kay's command, we surged forward, keeping our steps in time with the reverberation echoing in our ribcages. It was hot beneath the veil of shields and my hand grew slick around the shaft of the spear, but when a volley of projectiles thudded into our shields a few moments later, I was grateful for the protection. A few breeched our defenses, and we parted momentarily to avoid stepping on our fallen comrades, but then it was our turn to attack. On the command, we lowered our shields in unison, standing long enough to throw our weapons before ducking behind our shields once again.

The cavalry surged forward, breaking any formation the defenders hoped to keep. The swordsmen plunged into their depths while another volley of spears came from behind. I unleashed my own sword, hacking down as many Picts, Saxons, and attacking Britons as I could.

"Guinevere!" Kiara screamed above the tumult.

I turned, searching for her. In my quest to locate Elga, I had completely forgotten I was supposed to stay by her side. Now she needed me.

I spotted her a good distance away, near the wall. As

I ran toward her, I sized up the situation. She was defending against an oddly matched pair of Saxons wearing full-face masks that made them look like creatures out of a nightmare. One, who was about the size of an ancient yew, wielded a large battle axe, while his much smaller and more spindly companion jabbed at her with a dagger or short sword. The strategy, if there was one, seemed to be keeping her attention divided between the constant small threat of the dagger and the looming slice of the axe.

Kiara was doing a fine job keeping them at bay, only once being stabbed by the gnat with the dagger. But there was no way she could keep up her position for long and they knew it. I launched myself at the little one, colliding with him from the side and knocking us both painfully into the ox with the axe. As we struggled to right ourselves, he stumbled sideways, giving Kiara an opening in which to attack.

By the time I had the smaller one pinioned to the ground, my sword through his chest, she was advancing on her opponent, finally able to get under his guard. He hadn't yet noticed I was free of his friend, so I greeted him with a sharp slice to his weapon arm. As he howled in pain and dropped his axe, Kiara sank her blade into the tender flesh of his belly, giving him a swift kick so that he landed on his back with a thud.

When we were sure he was dead, she took his weapon, sheathed her sword, and clasped my arm. "Thank you, sister."

"You're welcome. Now, let's get inside." I started back toward the remnants of the schiltron, but Kiara grabbed my arm.

"I think I know a quicker way we can get in, but we'll have to be fast." She pointed at a portion of the wooden wall where the majority of our schiltron's spears had stuck in the timbers. "We climb. It's the only way in until they breech the gates."

I looked at her, slack jawed. "Are you mad? We will be completely exposed."

"That is why I said we will have to be fast." She looked at the battle around us while securing the axe to a strap running across her back. "I hate to say it, but I think the war is turning against us."

I followed her gaze to where more and more of our men were falling, their bodies piling up several deep where the fighting was the strongest. She was right. It was now or never. "Will they not attack us from the walls?"

She grinned. "Not if we distract them. I forged a plan with Cinon in case anyone needed a bit of cover." She whistled sharply three times.

A dozen heads whipped around on the battlefield, and several men emerged from the trees with ladders, which they raced to prop against the walls. Cinon handed us each a length of rope with a grappling hook attached.

As soon as we had the ropes secured at our waists, he yelled, "Now!"

We sprinted toward the wall, relatively unnoticed once we had dispatched the few warriors in our way.

"Couldn't we have used one of those?" I asked, pining for the surety of a ladder as I tossed the hook to the top of the wall, where it bit into the stone.

Kiara was already part way up the wall and using the shaft of a spear to help her stretch down to pull me up. "Only if you want to remain on this side. They will never succeed." Kiara contemplated her next handhold. "They are only meant to draw attention away from us."

A spear whizzed by my head, jamming itself with an audible thwack into the wall above me. I tightened my grip on the rope and redoubled my efforts to climb.

Kiara cursed as an arrow narrowly missed her leg and wood exploded into splinters above her head. Startled by the noise, she looked up just in time to get a face full of sawdust. Coughing and half blinded, she groped hand over hand, pulling herself up.

By the grace of the gods, somehow we made it to the top and over the other side of the wall, near an abandoned tower that led down into the courtyard.

In the streets below, nothing moved—no smoke spiraled from the chimneys, no animals snuffed or clucked, not even a rat slunk along the alleyways. The barracks stood empty, doors shut tight, the stables seemingly abandoned. Even the smith was silent. There had to be reserves waiting for the command to bombard our men, but none were visible.

The hairs on the back of my neck stood on end as I scanned the outbuildings for any signs of life. "Why do I feel like we've walked into their trap?"

"Because we have."

We were headed toward the main keep when the

scrabbling of feet on stone reached us. The sound was too deep, too heavy to belong to animals. It had to be people. I signaled to Kiara to follow me, and we headed deeper into the fort. It was darker on this side, the sun not having risen high enough yet to penetrate the shadows cast by the keep. Kiara touched my shoulder and pointed toward the east. Elga and two of her masked guards were scurrying down a narrow alley, heading toward the anterior gate. With our troops closer to infiltrating the fort, they were whisking their leader away to safety. We followed them, careful not to draw their attention until we were ready.

After ensuring none of them were carrying bows or spears that could be directed at us, I called, "You are many things, Elga, but a coward isn't among them."

All three froze. Elga turned first.

I smiled at her, weapon at the ready. "Where are you going? The battle isn't over yet. Please, stay so we can end this."

She regarded me for a moment, her gaze calculating. "Yes. Our time has come."

With a snarl, she pushed aside the guard who stood between us and came at me with frightening speed. I met her attack with vengeance of my own, leaving Kiara to fend off the other two men. Our swords clashed, the bite of metal on metal vibrating down our arms. In the moment it took for Elga to recover, I knocked aside her helmet and slammed her up against the wall. Her head hit with a sickening crack, but instead of disorienting her, it enraged her more. She pushed back with a primal grunt, driving me into the middle of the passageway. While parrying her blows, I turned so that my back was toward the mouth of the passage, not wishing to be trapped as poor Kiara was, should the fight turn against me.

Elga advanced, pushing me into the open courtyard. One of her guards followed, but Kiara was hot on his heels, having already dispatched his friend. Their movement was enough to distract me, giving Elga the opportunity to change the arc of her blade, a move I didn't see coming quite fast enough. I leapt to the side, trying to avoid her swing, but it caught the outside of my wrist, tearing a gash up to my elbow. Pain exploded before my arm went slack, useless. Reliant now on my sword arm, I kept fighting, trying to find a way to get under Elga's guard before I tired. I stabbed at her, but she was quick, so the tip of my blade barely pierced her leather armor. I had to stop her advance. Otherwise I was likely to trip over something or simply falter from fatigue.

A deafening crash sounded behind us, followed by a boom so loud it shook the ground. The main gates of the fort collapsed inward in a cloud of dust and dirt. Our soldiers rushed in—Accolon, Kay, Cinon, and Morgan among the sea of faces—only to be met by Saxons pouring out of every door and window, emerging from barracks and the keep to engulf our much smaller force. From the direction of stables, a chilling howl rang out, followed by a chorus of growls and snarls as a pack of man-sized wolfhounds were set loose. Within moments, they were tearing into flesh and ripping bones from sockets while their Saxon masters stabbed and sliced their way to victory.

Evina's army would not survive this. But they would die with blood on their swords and courage in their hearts. If the gods were kind, that was the memory that would pass down through the song of the bards when this day was recalled.

I could do nothing to aid any of them, so I turned back to Elga, whose attention was still riveted on the battle at the gates. She was smiling, which only inflamed my anger. I took a deep breath, imagined Lancelot's smiling face, and thrust forward, determined to finish this Saxon whore for good.

Elga blocked my thrust, flicking my weapon aside as easily as if it had been made of grass. Before I even realized what was happening, her boot connected with my ankles and I was knocked off my feet, sword clattering to the ground as I dropped it so I wouldn't impale myself in the fall. I hit the stones, trying to brace myself with my uninjured arm, but it crumpled with a snap as the bone broke. My hip was the next to make contact, sending pain radiating in every direction. I struggled to push myself onto my knees, but my arms were too wounded to be of much use. Elga stood over me, her tall form in silhouette against the blazing sun.

So this was how I would end my days, cut down by a woman I'd made the mistake of trying to aid, who had been my sworn enemy for so long. Like a trapped animal, I searched for Kiara, praying she would come to my rescue and deliver me, but then I spotted her body in the alley, her opponent headed in our direction, no doubt to finish me off if Elga could not. *Please, Mother, be with me,* I prayed, refusing to avert my eyes as Elga raised her sword to deliver my death blow.

But it did not come. Instead, the earth rumbled again. Elga stumbled, her swing thrown off course. A flash of copper hair filled my vison as Morgan threw herself between Elga's blade and me. She landed on top of me, blocking Elga from view.

As I scrambled out from beneath Morgan's unconscious and bleeding body, I saw Morgan's sword protruding from Elga's torso. For one long, frightening moment, she remained standing, staring in shock at the hilt sticking out of her gut. Then she collapsed.

Stunned, I could not move, even as the guard advanced on me. When he was close enough to kick, I lashed out, connecting my foot with his shin, knowing he would kill me.

"Be still, woman. I will not harm you," he barked from behind a full-face helmet, hopping in my direction.

I obeyed, my stomach twisting. There was something familiar about his voice.

"Can you stand?"

My heart lost its rhythm and my spine tingled as he grasped my shoulders and hauled me to my feet. My body recognized him even if my mind did not. I took a deep breath to steady myself, but the scent I inhaled nearly made me swoon. Oak and apple wood. But it was not possible. It could not be. I'd seen him die with my own eyes. Perhaps I had hit my head in my fight with Elga and was simply imagining things.

He pulled me away from the carnage, but I dug in my heels. "I will not leave her," I said, nodding toward Morgan.

"If she is still alive, people are coming who can tend to her better than we can. If not, she does not need our aid. We have to get out of here."

"Why are you helping me?" I asked, my voice tremulous.

Ignoring my question and my protests, my rescuer picked me up and dashed toward Kiara, who was beginning to stir. He kicked her weapon to her. "Get up. We must go or face what is left of Theodric's army."

Holding her head with one hand and her side with the other, she obeyed. They took off at run, darting through the postern gate and into the surrounding wood as fast as their legs would carry them. My weight was no doubt slowing them down, but if I were put down, I would collapse on the spot. This was the best we could do.

A series of shouts went up inside the fort. I could only assume the Saxon horde had found their leader dead.

"Elga had horses tethered down by the stream," the guard said between ragged breaths. "We must hope we get there before someone comes searching for us."

A shiver coursed through me as a hound bayed. It was not one of the war hounds. That was a tracking dog, and it had caught our scent. Likely, I had left a trail of blood that would lead them right to us.

I was shaking uncontrollably by the time we reached the horses. Kiara had to hold me upright while my rescuer mounted his steed. Then she passed me up to him like a sack of grain. When he reached for me, the sleeve of his grimy tunic inched back and I saw a pattern of blue swirling up his arm. Suddenly dry-mouthed, I looked again. Covering his right arm was a dragon, the sign of the house of Lothian. But the men of that line were all dead, except for Gawain, and he was back at Traprain Law. Wasn't he?

The baying was getting closer. Before my thoughts could go any further, we were off, galloping as fast as Elga's steeds would carry us. I clung to the horse's mane as well as I could with my better arm, praying my rescuer's grip on my waist would be enough to keep me seated.

We had been riding for quite some time when he yelled for Kiara to slow her horse. We pulled up beside her and she helped me down, keeping one steadying arm around me.

My rescuer removed his helmet, rubbing his face with both hands.

When he dropped them, I stared into brown eyes I thought I'd only see again in the Otherworld. My lips parted in an astounded breath as I struggled to reconcile what I was seeing with what I knew to be possible. Perhaps I *had* died at Elga's hand after all. It was the only explanation for how I found myself staring into Aggrivane's face.

Chapter Nineteen

hen I next opened my eyes, I was facing the peaked roof of a cloth tent. Where was I? How had I gotten here? I breathed deeply, surveying the pains in my body. Nearly every part of me ached, but especially my hips and my arms. Glancing down, I found my left arm was splinted with a tree branch and immobilized in a sling, and my right arm was heavily bandaged. Slowly, carefully, I sat up, putting as little pressure on my bandaged arm as possible.

Fighting off a wave of lightheadedness, I took in my surroundings. Four canvas walls, one of which was split in the middle to make a door that rippled in the soft breeze. A small fire burned not far away. Hesitantly, I swung my left leg off the pile of blankets that served as a bed and tried to stand. My right hip was bound tightly to restrict its range of motion, but I guessed it was not broken. As long as I didn't put my full weight on my right leg, I could remain upright. Walking might prove to be a different matter, however.

I took tiny, halting steps toward the door flap as pain flared in my limbs. Memories of the previous day returned in a rush, as though carried back to me on a gale. In flashes, I remembered scaling the wall, relived Elga's attack and knowing I was going to die. Morgan's intervention still puzzled me. I owed her my life. *Please, Mother Goddess, let her live. She deserves a few years of solace after what she did for me.* In a flash, I remembered Aggrivane, but I pushed that thought out of my mind. It was too much; I would think about him after I learned where I was and how the rest of our troops fared.

By the time I reached the door, I had to grasp onto the material to stay upright. Sweat drenched my brow, yet my teeth chattered. But I willed myself onward. I had to find out where I was and what was happening.

Before I could venture outside, voices caught my attention—a man and a woman, not far away. They weren't exactly arguing, but speaking intensely.

"I must return to finish what I started," Kiara said. "Our warriors deserve better than to remain exposed, food for the carrion birds. We must burn their bodies and take word of our defeat back to Evina."

"If the carnage is as bad as you say, then you will need my help," the man insisted.

My heart stopped. It really was Aggrivane.

"No. You stay here with Guinevere. There are other Votadini who can help. When you can, flee. Do not return to Din Eidyn. Go anywhere else you will be safe. Just keep

Guinevere out of Evina's reach. I will calm her wrath as best I can."

I could not stand to be in the shadows any longer. I limped out of the tent toward their voices. "Was it really so bad? Were we so roundly defeated?"

They looked up, startled by the sound of my voice.

Kiara rushed to my side, allowing me to lean on her. "I am afraid so. I just returned from what is left of our camp. By my count, less than fifty of our men and women remain, though some may have already fled north. We were slaughtered. Corag and Ailith are among the dead."

My shoulders sagged. "It is all my fault. I led us here. Calliac warned us I would bring about their deaths, but I did not listen. I should have died alongside my men."

Aggrivane handed me a stout branch. "Use this to balance your weight. It is not your fault. I was there. I saw what you did to try to save Lancelot. Be assured Elga was going to kill him even if you had taken your own life before her eyes. Both of you were but pawns in her game. For weeks, she talked of nothing but wiping out the Votadini. She may not have succeeded, but she dealt us a fearsome blow."

"May each of the dead be a curse upon her spirit," Kiara spat. "But even though she is dead, her people will try again. I may not have your gift of sight, but I know in my bones this is the first of many battles. Accolon still lives, and the men of Rheged will not stop until they bring the Saxons to their knees. Luckily for us, I am alive and so is Cinon. If I can convince Evina that she needs us to rebuild her army so that we can fight another day, we may yet live to see victory."

We were silent for a while, the sounds of forest animals and birds a calming backdrop to our sobering thoughts. Finally, I broke the quiet. "You said they were going to burn the bodies. Can I not return to see Lancelot is properly attended to?"

Kiara swallowed hard. "I am afraid they have not recovered his body, nor Morgan's. We fear the Saxons took them as prizes to celebrate their victory."

Aggrivane put his arm around me, no doubt intending to comfort me, but I shrugged him off. The fury I hadn't even realized had been building inside me unleashed like a broken dam.

"Will I never get to say goodbye to anyone I love?" I shouted, tears streaming down my face. "Why is that finality always denied to me? My mother, Arthur, you." I looked at Aggrivane. "Now Lancelot. Everyone I love dies, and I never get the chance to bid them farewell." Sobs racked my body, rendering me mute. Kiara reached out to me, but I shrank away, lowering myself painfully into a ball on the ground.

"I will make sure a memorial stone is erected for him in our homeland," Kiara said. "He was much loved by our people and died defending them. They would never let anything less stand. It is not much, I know, but at least he will be remembered."

She was right. So many of our best had gone home to our ancestors with nothing to mark that they'd ever lived.

I wiped my tears. "Thank you. I'm sorry for my outburst."

Aggrivane helped me to stand. "I'm surprised it didn't happen sooner. You have more strength than me. I would have broken down the moment I remembered yesterday's events."

Kiara glanced at the sun. "I am sorry to leave you, but I must be getting back to camp."

I hobbled over to her and embraced her with my one good arm. I knew I would never see her again. "Thank you for everything. You were my first true friend in that land, and I will never forget the kindness you have shown me. Will you do me one last favor?"

"Name it."

"On the night Cinon, Corag, and Ailith were chosen as our battle leaders, I promised myself I would protect Ailith's little sister. Since I cannot return to watch over her, will you take special care of her and do your best to see her grow into a strong woman?"

Kiara nodded solemnly. "Of course. I will make it my goal to foster her whole generation in Ailith's memory."

I hugged her one more time, squeezing tight. "You are truly a blessing. Watch yourself around Evina. She is likely to take out her wrath on you since I will not be there to abuse."

Kiara waved away my concerns. "I can handle her. I thank you as well for your friendship. We are blood bonded, remember? We will always be in one another's hearts." She nodded to Aggrivane. "Take care of her."

"I will."

Kiara mounted and set off toward Catraeth. As she

faded from sight, all the strength left my body, as though she was taking it with her.

Holding on to Aggrivane with my good arm, I staggered toward the tent. "You are limping. Are you injured as well?"

"No. Just the remnant of my brush with death that I will nurse for the rest of my days," he said with a wry smile.

"What happened? I saw you die. How is it that you are here?"

Aggrivane helped me onto the blanket bed. "That is a story for another time. You need to rest. We should be safe here for a few days." He kissed the top of my head. "Sleep now."

∞∞∞

I lay in my bed, staring at the tip of the tent, completely hollow, for several days. I had no concept of the passage of time, only of the pain in my heart and of what I had lost. My mind kept replaying Lancelot's final moments, guilt goading that I could have done more to save him. I cried so hard my abdomen ached and the tears coursing down my cheeks formed chapped lines that stung with every fresh wave of grief. I recreated my encounter with Lancelot from every vantage, even trying to put myself in Elga's place—what would I have done if I could have abducted her husband?— but no matter now I turned it around, the outcome was the same. Aggrivane was right; Elga would have killed Lancelot no matter what I did. Now I had to learn to live with his loss.

For his part, Aggrivane let me be, interrupting my mourning only to change my bandages or to feed me soup. I was nearly as incapacitated as I had been when Malegant broke all ten of my fingers. I wanted to believe Aggrivane's ministrations were genuine, but the part of me that was still deeply wounded by his betrayal of Lancelot and me to Arthur expected him to deliver me to the Saxons at any moment. After all, he *had* been posing as one of Elga's guards. It wasn't so great a stretch of the imagination to think he could still be working for their side.

The rational part of my mind knew that was ridiculous. He had helped me escape capture by the Saxons. That should have put an end to all of my suspicions, but in my grief, I needed someone to take the blame for Lancelot's death. Elga was dead, so I couldn't rail at her; Aggrivane made for a convenient substitute. I was grateful to him, yes. Without his intervention, I would be dead. But that didn't mean I had to trust him.

I startled awake in the gray hours before dawn, unsure of what had woken me. I strained to make out any movement in the pitiful light cast by the embers. Nothing seemed out of place, so I stilled myself and listened. Above the sound of Aggrivane's breathing came the forlorn howl of a dog. I froze, every muscle on tense alert. Could it be one of Theodoric's hounds, finally caught up to us? Or was it merely the vocalization of one owned by a nearby farmer?

I gently shook Aggrivane. "Wake up. Wake up."

He came alert slowly, rubbing his face with the heel of his hand. "What is it?"

"I hear a dog. I think the Saxons may have found us."

Wait. What if that was why Aggrivane had insisted we stay here? What if he was waiting for the Saxons to catch up? We couldn't be too far from Catraeth. I felt the color drain from my face.

Aggrivane sat up, ears perking to pick up the sound. "Are you unwell? You are pale as a bone." He listened for a long time. The dog called twice more, then was silent. "We should pack up and move. You need the services of a true healer."

"What I need is time," I protested. Nothing could be done for my broken arm or my hip except wait for them to heal. As for my other arm and the relatively minor cuts and abrasions on the rest of my body, those were nothing that could not be solved with a mixture of yarrow and other herbs. Even with a sore arm, I could make such a poultice. But more than that, I needed time to trust him again and time for my shattered heart to knit.

Aggrivane dipped a rag into the last of the wash water and cleaned my face. "Time is something we may have none of or all we wish, depending on what we do next. Hold still." He grabbed my chin with his thumb and forefinger to keep me from fidgeting.

"I may not be able to lift a spoon, but I am capable of cleaning myself, in case you hadn't noticed."

"Not without difficulty," he pointed out. "Besides, I miss touching you."

My heart warmed, but I turned away. "Aggrivane…"

He turned my face back toward him and continued

stroking my skin. "I know. This is all very sudden for you. I am not suggesting anything. It was simply a statement."

I glared at him. "It was more than that. Please, be patient. I have not yet grieved my last love, much less come to terms with your return."

He plunged his hands into the bucket before splashing water over his face and hair. "Fair enough. I will treat you only as a friend until you tell me otherwise." He puttered around the small tent, gathering up the few supplies. "So where should we go now?"

It was a good question. The world as we had known it when last we were together had completely changed. As Kiara had said, heading north was not an option. "What about going to Lothian?"

Aggrivane shook his head. "Gawain and my mother do not know I still live, and I fear the shock would kill her. I wish them to live out their days in peace. Besides, Evina knows you came to her from Traprain Law. She would think to look for you there."

He had a point. But how was I to know where she would and would not search for me? Or even if she would make the effort? Was that to be my destiny then, always on the run, always shrinking from shadows, too scared to settle down? I hadn't stopped running since Elga let me leave Camelot, and I was fed up. If all the future held for me was looking over my shoulder, then I would have been better off if Morgan hadn't taken the blow meant for me.

Aggrivane packed up our meager belongings and saw to the horses while I sat, useless and restless, as we discussed our options. We could not journey south, as that would take us into the heart of Saxon territory. Constantine controlled much of the land beyond that, and we were uncertain whether he would consider us friend or foe.

"We could always appeal to his mercy. He may be kind to us if you renounce your role as queen," Aggrivane said.

"The last thing I want to do is take that chance. I am tired of being the prize in the constant quest for power. I do not think he would allow us to live in peace."

There was a small chance we could return to Gwynedd, but neither of us knew who held power in Northgallis now. Since my cousin Bran had died in the last battle with Constantine, I did not even know if Northgallis was an autonomous kingdom or part of Constantine's burgeoning empire. Anywhere farther south was out because that was his base. But there was one place even Evina couldn't find.

The next time Aggrivane came into the tent, I took his hand and gave it a gentle squeeze. "Are you ready to go home?"

He looked at me, confused.

"To Avalon. It is the only safe place left."

"Are you certain they will allow me to enter?"

"They allowed you to cross their borders once. Why not now, after you have spent your life defending one of their own? You are still loyal to the old ways, are you not?"

Aggrivane nodded.

I fought a sudden, unexpected, and perplexing urge to kiss him. "Then they will allow you in." We lapsed into silence until a thought flashed through my mind. "What ever happened to the Grail?"

Morgan had called for it in the chaos after Camlann. Had it been used to try to heal Arthur? No. If it had, he would have lived.

Aggrivane blinked at me, having trouble following my change of topic. "I truly do not know. I think it is still there in its castle. Why?"

"If the last few years have taught me anything, it is that this land and its people are no longer worthy of it. We need to return it to Avalon."

"I don't know if returning to Camelot is wise," he protested.

"Why not? Everyone who wished us harm is dead."

"But it has surely decayed. Are you sure you do not wish to preserve your memories of it?"

I smiled without warmth. "My memories of that place are of my trial and burning. They are nothing a little ruin will harm."

Aggrivane sighed. "Surely there are others, brighter memories." He tied the last bag onto his horse's saddle. "But I have known you long enough to know when to yield. Camelot it is."

❧❧

The journey across Britain was slow. We were careful to avoid the main cities unless Aggrivane knew for certain someone he could trust was living there. Otherwise, we begged charity from farmers and shepherds, often sleeping in their barns, in the tent, or under the stars, as the weather allowed. In many places, we were welcomed warmly by virtue of my priestess mark, but in others, it was best to keep it hidden under the folds of my veil. We told no one our real names. Yet again, I posed as Corinna, and Aggrivane adopted the name of Declan, a tradition in his family as well.

One night, as we were lying in a grassy field, gazing at the stars, our bellies full of stew made from the hare Aggrivane trapped and the vegetables I saved from the last housewife's generosity, I found the courage to ask Aggrivane the question that had been niggling at me since I first saw his face. "I saw you die on the battlefield at Camlann. How is it possible you are here?"

He turned his head to look at me and took my hand. "I will never get used to that sight of yours. I did die, or at least I thought I did. When I closed my eyes on that plain, I thought my next sight would be of my ancestors in the Otherworld. But the next thing I knew, there was a hard boot in my side. The Saxons and their allies were checking to be sure we were all dead. Those who were not were either captured or killed, depending on how useful they assessed us to be."

"You were captured?"

"No." His eyes took on a faraway look as he yielded to his memories. "They passed me by, thinking I was dead. But Morgan was also on the battlefield, administering help and mercy where she could. She saw that I had opened my eyes. Once the Saxons were gone, she dragged me off the battlefield and took me to a safe place to recover.

"I had no memory of who I was or what had happened for months. Yet every morning she was there, encouraging me to try, saying that 'there will come a day when she will need you.' I can only assume she had foreseen your near-death by Elga's blade and that I would rescue you."

That startled me. How long had she known? If she had foreseen before we met on the battlefield of Camlann that I would one day rely on Aggrivane for my life, why had she not told me he was alive? How long had she known she would suffer Elga's blade—and possibly give up her life—for me?

Great Goddess, protector of the priestesses of Avalon, send your protection to Morgan, daughter of the Lady of the Lake and the Archdruid. If she is still in the land of the living, minimize her pain and give her the strength and fortitude to heal. If her soul has passed beyond the veil, please grant her peace and richly reward her for her sacrifice.

I shook my head to clear it and forced my mind back to Aggrivane's story. "Morgan nursed you back to health?"

Aggrivane nodded. "And then some. My injuries were so bad, I had to learn how to eat all over again. How to walk. It was more than a year before I held a sword, much less relearned what to do with it. You've seen my limp. Without Morgan, it would be the least of my worries." He shook his head. "I can honestly say I would be dead without her."

"So can I." I paused, lost in thought again. "How did you come to fight on the side of the Saxons?"

He looked away. "You have always said Morgan was a woman of two faces. I had grown used to regarding her as a kind healer, but after the Isle of Winds, she changed, revealing the cunning woman behind the mask. You see, Accolon's capture nearly broke her. So when she heard Accolon had offered me to the Saxons as potentially of more use than he was, she jumped at the chance to turn me over to them, hoping they would return him.

"In Din Gefron, Accolon took charge of me personally and spent the next several weeks explaining to me why it would be best to go along with what Elga wanted, as he was doing. The day he asked for my support was the most difficult of my life. By then, I knew Arthur and Mordred were dead, but I had heard nothing of you. I longed to know your fate and thought the best way of obtaining information would be to ally with a powerful ruler. As I had no in with Constantine and I knew my mother did not desire to be a power player in this latest struggle, I agreed, at least verbally, to change my alliance."

"But you said your mother did not know you were alive. How, why did Accolon go along with keeping your identity a secret?"

Aggrivane grimaced. "He believed that Lothian would be easier to overthrow if my parents were weakened with grief. If all of their sons were dead—and the future of their kingdom with them—then they would be more likely to cede their lands peacefully."

"But they did not. Gawain lived, and Anna supported our side at Catraeth."

"Indeed. I fear Lothian would have been Elga's next target, had she succeeded in killing you. As it stands, I do not know if they will attack now or simply wait for my mother to die. I pray it is the latter."

"That explains how you infiltrated the Saxons, but how did you get so close to Elga?"

"That was much easier than I expected. Word soon came of your role at Din Eidyn and then in Stirling. Elga knew I had betrayed you to Arthur and decided to use me as a spy to gain information on you. I told her only what would have been common knowledge to anyone watching the Votadini camps prepare, but it was enough. I have a feeling she intended to bait you using me, but when she realized Lancelot was your greater weakness, she changed tack."

My heart thudded, anticipating where his story was headed. I covered my face with my hands. "Please tell me you had nothing to do with his capture."

"I led them to the location of your camp, but I did nothing to aid in the act itself, I swear to you. Elga lured him by making it look as though we were scouts who would help him and his horse. I did not know what they were planning to do."

"Did Lancelot see you?"

"Yes. It was unavoidable. I think he died believing I'd betrayed him." Doubt must have shown on my face, for Aggrivane continued. "You will have to take me at my word. No proof exists that I can offer. I hope you know my heart well enough to understand that no matter what had passed between us before, I was grateful to Lancelot for rescuing you and taking care of you. In my sickbed, I had no way of knowing if you and I would see each other again. Why would I deny you his love when I could not guarantee I would be there to give you my own?"

Crickets sang their soothing lullaby in the silence that followed as we each mulled over his story. This night, with its beautiful weather and secret confessions, was so much like that of our first kiss in Avalon. Remembering that young man with his dreams of glory and peace, I had to believe in Aggrivane's innocence, no matter what misgivings my jaded heart might now possess.

"And Elga? You were helping her escape when Kiara and I found you?"

He looked away. "Yes. She wanted me out on the battlefield but did not trust that I would not turn coat when faced with my former compatriots. So she kept me behind with her. I was grateful, because it would have been hard to avoid killing or being killed when no one else knew I was not who I appeared to be."

Aggrivane was looking at the stars, as if reading his own story in them. "Elga knew she was in danger, regardless of the outcome of the battle. There was no question you would pursue her to your final breath for what she had done to Lancelot. Even if you fell before reaching her, there was a chance your men would still hunt her in your name. All I had to do was drive home that point, and her survival instincts overrode her considerable pride. The plan was to take the horses to a nearby Saxon convent until the skirmish was over."

I gasped. That was Mayda's convent, the one where I

had sought refuge during Mordred's revolt. I explained to him about Mayda's fate after she'd tipped us off about Badon, my time at the convent, and how I came to Din Eidyn. "Elga may well have taken out her anger at me on her sister. It was something Mayda feared, and rightly."

"Well, now I am especially grateful you foiled our plan. You helped us avoid bloodshed no one knew was coming."

"So am I. How did you manage to continue your ruse when Kiara and I appeared?"

Aggrivane shrugged. "It was not that difficult, really. You and Elga were so intent on one another that your attention was not on me. All I had to do was play at taking on Kiara while my partner did all the real work. Once she dispatched him, I could already see the battle turning against you. I had to knock Kiara out, lest she think I was joining in the attack against you. She has a hard head, that one. As it was, I was too slow to stop Morgan. I was barely able to get to you in time…"

It was my turn to squeeze his hand. "But you did. That is what matters." I scooted toward him, allowing him to hold me for the first time since our reunion. "Things may never be as they once were between us, but there is no one else yet living I would rather spend the rest of my days with."

Aggrivane stiffened at the qualification in my statement. "I know I have much to make amends for. I will take whatever measure of affection you are willing to give."

CHAPTER TWENTY

The once gleaming, impregnable fortress of Camelot was a shell of its former glory. Judging from the trickle of people coming and going, it was still occupied, probably by Constantine's men who were keeping it warm for the day he conquered the entire island. I could only imagine the havoc wreaked inside, the toppled statues of the Pendragon dynasty in the council chambers, the burned-out labyrinth dedicated to gods in whom Constantine did not believe.

We avoided the main roads, not wishing to revisit the places that lived on in our memories or chance being recognized. Instead, we trod the winding coastal roads that led to the harbor. Few people were about, and many of the houses we passed were derelict, feral dogs, cats, and vermin coming and going from their open doors and windows in place of the merchants and tradesmen who used to live there. Rotten shutters hung haphazardly from windows. Thatched roofs went unmended, gaping holes letting in all sorts of weather and rendering whole buildings uninhabitable.

Here and there, there were still signs of life. A stubborn baker cooked his fragrant wares, and a steady tink-tink-tink announced the garrison was keeping the smithy busy, but it was more a sight for sore eyes in the abandoned capital than an expected part of daily life.

When we turned down one street, we were greeted by an unexpected view of the sea. A whole swath of buildings, an entire neighborhood it seemed, had burned to ash, the blackened hulls staring at us like the unseeing eyes of the dead.

Aggrivane whistled. "So it is true. Huh. I thought it was just a tale spun by the victors."

I stopped, facing him. "What was?"

He pointed at the remnants of the street in front of us. "It was said that after Camlann, those loyal to Arthur and Mordred joined forces to try to destroy Camelot so that no one else could ever use it as their seat of power. Tales of the city burning circulated for days, telling of an inferno unlike anything that had been seen for generations. Ultimately, the arsonists did not succeed in burning down the city, but the story of their attempt was lauded as nothing short of heroic."

I tried to orient myself and recall what had once stood here. Though I did not know every inch of the city by heart, I prided myself on knowing most of it. "This was a residential area." I recalled the home of a tailor on the corner of one street. I had helped his daughter give birth to twins.

"Over there is where Sobian lived for a while with her girls." I nodded toward a square patch of land that had once held a fine two-story home. "But what I don't understand is if they truly wanted to do damage, why did they not set the castle on fire too?"

Aggrivane pointed. "I think they tried."

I followed his direction to one of the massive square turrets that had not been visible from the main road. It too bore the indelible stain of soot, but that was from the destruction before Camlann. Down further, one entire section of the wall was gone. Judging from the pattern of scattered stones on the hillside below, it had likely exploded from the heat. Those that remained were unmended, as though forgotten and unloved.

Tears filled my eyes as I surveyed the damage done to my beloved home, to the city on which two generations of High Kings had placed their hopes and dreams, their vision for a unified country, the dream I had shared with them through many years and against many dangers, from invaders to corrupt hearts. A dream that was not to be.

"It really is over, isn't it?" I asked.

Aggrivane placed a consoling arm around me as I wept. "I am afraid so. The world around us is changing, giving way to a new power structure, one in which our ideals no longer have meaning."

I looked at him, my heart cleaved by despair. "Then why did we bother? What was it all for?"

"You bothered because you believed you could make our country and our people better, and you did, for many years. You and Arthur allowed generations of Britons to live in peace. You turned away the Saxons and preserved our ways. What you did is so much more than most people ever dare to imagine doing. You acted out of the urgings of your heart, following the will of the gods as you saw it. But all ages come to an end. It is the way of things."

We walked to the water's edge in silence, each wrapped in our own thoughts. Aggrivane was right; returning here had been a mistake. Everywhere I looked, I saw Camelot as it used to be for a split second before my mind registered the change.

The tide was out, and Aggrivane calculated we had about an hour before it would return, so it was safe to cross the causeway leading to the Grail Castle on foot. As we picked our way across the slimy stones, I looked for signs that it too had been looted or suffered abuse at the hands of angry mobs or those eager to get their hands on its precious treasure. But from the outside, it appeared not to have suffered as the town and fortress had. Perhaps the people had been too respectful or too superstitious to harm the castle.

Then again, perhaps I was wrong. I stopped inside the outer gate. Where once there had been a garden and outbuildings for the upkeep of the castle and those who lived within, now there was a graveyard, at least a dozen headstones marking mounded graves.

"What evil has been done here?" I asked, flitting from stone to stone, seeking to know how so many had died in such a holy place in such a short period of time.

"I did not hear of a plague," Aggrivane mused as he

scanned the names memorialized in stone. "Such news usually travels far and wide."

I fell to my knees at the foot of the graves with the two tallest monument stones. "Oh no. No, no, no!"

The names Galahad and Peredur inscribed on them. Both bore an image of the Grail and recounted how the two men had found the Grail, heroically defeated those who rose against them, and brought their sacred charge back to Camelot. Thereafter, they became priests and guarded it with their lives.

"So that is it. They died protecting the Grail. No doubt they are in heaven with their god." Aggrivane's voice came from right behind me, but I paid him no heed.

Just when I thought I had no one, save Aggrivane, left to lose, no more tears to cry, this happened. I looked at him. "I do not know how much more of this I can bear." I felt like a towel long ago wrung threadbare, with only the slightest, thinnest of stitching holding me together.

"Do not grieve for them," came a female voice a few paces away. "Rejoice. They are the martyrs of the Grail, men who shed their blood for the good of the land, just as their Christ gave his life to save others."

I recognized the voice before I looked up. It was Mona.

I stood, embracing her at once. "And you, how do you yet live?" I stepped back, eyes drinking in her silver hair and dancing eyes. Her face was wrinkled in all the usual places, but she maintained the tranquility of a priestess.

"I could ask you the same." Her smile was as radiant as my first day on Avalon. "The Goddess willed it. That is all I can say. It is not for me to question."

I hugged her tightly. "How have you borne it all these years? You spent your childhood dreaming repeatedly of death and destruction on the isle for which you were named, only to witness equal depravity here."

Her smile was tender now. "It was my fate. Long ago, Argante warned me that my dreams had purpose, even though they seemed nothing more than a cruel joke of the gods at the time. Do you remember that winter night by the fire when we were young and I repeated Argante's advice that to know the past was to be able to change the future?"

I nodded, recalling how we'd sat in front of the fire in the House of Nine in the dark of night while snow fell outside the window. She was in my arms, weeping, terrified from yet another nightmare of the pillage of the isle of Mona. She said Argante had recently told her that her dreams marked her as special, as powerful.

"Later, during my initiation, I had an experience that revealed to me my vocation as the Grail Maiden. I have known from that moment that it was connected to my dreams. It was not until the fall of Arthur and destruction of Camelot that I understood why. I cannot tell you the pain it caused me to know that all these good men"—she gestured, indicating the dead around us—"innocent men, would lose their lives just like the Druids and priestesses on the holy isle of Mona, and for the same reason—the desire for power and control. When the time came, I did what I could to defend them, somehow knowing I would escape unharmed, as would the Grail, for I was its sworn protector. I was as helpless to stop the bloodshed here as I was in my dreams, doomed to be a spectator once again. But I tell you this. These men fulfilled the fate laid out for them with more courage and valor than I have seen in any knight. They are truly worthy of the title of heroes."

I gazed around again, seeing not a drab place of mourning but a hall of heroes, a fellowship united in faith and purpose. Tears once again sprang to my eyes, but this time, they were of pride and joy in having known such courageous men. I sat back down, remembering the first time I saw Galahad in Elaine's arms, grateful I had had the opportunity to watch him grow into a virtuous young man, then a fine priest at Camelot.

I recalled Peredur as a young boy at our home in Northgallis, remembering with startling clarity the moment he gave me his favorite toy, a carved wooden dog—the one Mona and I had shared to ward off our personal fears as acolytes on Avalon.

I dug around in the pouch at my waist and removed the toy dog.

"Bricriu!" Mona cried with joy. "Oh, you truly are one of Ellen's own." Her eyes welled with tears as she stroked the wood, worn smooth with time and the attention of many fingertips.

I looked at her, feeling once again like a girl on Avalon. "I think he has done his service, do you agree?"

"I do," she answered in a tremulous voice.

"Then he should rest here with Peredur, who was, after all, his master."

Mona took from her belt the silver scythe that all Grail maidens carried and held it out to Aggrivane, who wiped his eyes and took it. As he hacked a small hole into the ground at the base of Peredur's memorial stone, I realized that Aggrivane was also grieving the loss of two of his fellow soldiers, members of the Combrogi with whom he had fought in battle and with whom he'd celebrated in times of peace. My stomach clenched. I had been so selfish, I had not been able to see his pain.

I took his hand. "Aggrivane, I am so sorry. I was so wrapped up in my own grief that I failed to recognize yours. Please forgive me."

He squeezed my hand. "There is nothing to forgive. I prefer to pay my respects in private anyway."

Mona joined her hand with mine, and together we knelt to bury Bricriu.

"Thank you, Peredur, for such a special gift. At an age far before reason, you followed the prompting of the gods to bestow this gift upon us. Throughout your life, you continued to follow that same divine urging, which ultimately led you to the Grail and to this place. Your life was one of love and service, to your king and to your god. Please know you are loved and your sacrifice does not go unremembered," I said.

After a few moments of silence, Mona stood. "You have come for the Grail, yes? I will accompany it and you back to Avalon." Seeing my astonishment, she tapped the faded crescent between her brows. "I knew you were coming."

༄༅

Inside the Grail Castle, all was quiet and still, seemingly undisturbed by the violence that beat at its walls and had taken so many lives. I had to stop and hold on to one of the stone pillars to catch my balance because the sense of repeating this moment was so strong. Only the last time I was there, I had been in pursuit of Bishop Maris, who intended to steal the Grail and sell it to the highest bidder in Brittany. Now, we were about to return it to its home in Avalon.

Mona approached the pedestal with great reverence. Kneeling, she touched her right thumb to her forehead, lips, and heart. Then she prostrated herself completely before her sacred charge. Feeling the solemnity of the moment, I knelt, bowing my head. Out of the corner of my eye, I saw Aggrivane do the same.

Mona whispered a few words of quiet prayer not meant for my ears. What must it be like for her, knowing her time as Grail Maiden was coming to an end, that she had fulfilled her vocation? It must be mixture of joy at a job well done, grief for mistakes made that could not be undone, fear of the unknown, and excitement at the anticipation of what was yet to come. I understood because it was exactly what I was feeling. Just as we had been scared initiates together, we were facing the culmination of our duties as priestesses together as well. *Thank you, God and Goddess, for giving me a lifelong companion to experience such things alongside.*

When I opened my eyes, Mona was holding the Grail.

In one hand, she held the same shimmering golden cloth in which it had been veiled when I first saw it.

"Just as we were among the first, we are the last three mortals to behold the Grail outside of the sacred isle of Avalon. Though the people of this realm served it well and faithfully for many years, they have proven themselves unworthy to have such a treasure in its midst. Thus, as its guardian, I remove it from the land of men and return it to its hallowed resting place until such time as it is again called forth by the will of the gods."

Having thus spoken, she broke two cruets over it, one of clear liquid—water from the holy springs of Avalon—and one of crimson. "This is the blood of every Grail Maiden who has ever served this holy relic. Blessed and purified, may it be purged of any defilement brought about by the hearts and minds of men, and sanctified for whatever role the gods decree for it next." She drank the contents of the cup and placed its golden veil over it.

After one more bow to the former altar, she joined us. "Let us go from here. There is only one thing remaining to do."

⁎

We stood on the shore, facing the Grail Castle. To anyone watching from above, we were simply three onlookers curious about the strange fortified island, but this moment was so much more.

"Many people attempted to steal the Grail in the dark days after Camlann," Mona said. "I watched from the shadows as man and woman alike—rich, poor, Christian, Druid, Saxon, and Briton—attempted to take the cup. But it refused to budge from its place of veneration. Just as it knew our hearts when we drank from it and assumed the most appropriate shape for us to understand, so too did it know the hearts of those who came to it. That is why only I was able to remove it. I suspect the two of you would have been able as well, in my absence. So that no trace of the Grail remains except in the memories of this generation, there is one last thing we must do."

Mona reverently placed the Grail in Aggrivane's hands. "I ask you, as one who studied with Merlin and has conducted his life with honor, to please guard this while we work."

Aggrivane looked at her with astonishment. Except for during two ceremonies with Arthur, the only people to have the privilege of holding the Grail were Galahad, Peredur, Mona, and Bishop Marius. He fell to one knee and bowed his head. "I would be honored, my lady."

Mona took my hand. "I have the power to do this myself, but I would much like you to join me. In this action, may you find peace and closure for all the many things you have suffered and those you have lost."

We each took a deep breath and closed our eyes. I sent my consciousness downward, searching until I felt the faint thrum of the Tor, a heartbeat I could always hear if I listened, no matter how far my body was from its source.

Mona chanted in the ancient language that predated Avalon, her voice high and clear. When she squeezed my hand, I added my voice to hers, the words bubbling from my lips of their own accord, with no conscious thought on my part. My vision filled with images of angry seas, of waves growing higher and higher until they engulfed a city I did not recognize. This was the predecessor to Mona, to Avalon, the isle that had been lost beneath the waves many ages before. Then my eyes snapped open, and I beheld the sea churning, the tide lapping at the tops of the outer walls of the Grail Castle.

As we continued to chant, the wind howled, whipping up the caps of the waves until they spilled over the walls and into the castle. Rain poured down in sheets, raising the water levels even higher, until the whole castle groaned and collapsed in on itself, swallowed up by the waves in a matter of heartbeats.

Mona squeezed my hand again, and I fell silent. The chant ended on a sharp note, whose finality was unmistakable. As the echo of her voice faded away, the winds calmed, the sky cleared, and the seas settled. Within moments, our clothes were dry, as was the ground around us, as though nothing had ever happened.

I gazed out over the sea at where the Grail Castle had stood on its island. There was no sign it had ever existed. Somehow, I knew that upon the next change of tide, the causeway would be gone as well, to live on only in the astonished memories of those who would recall the strange storm and tell tales to their grandchildren of the fortress that had once guarded the holiest of treasures.

I turned away, another chapter of my life having come to a close. As we walked away from the coastline and the city, my heart lifted and I smiled. The gnawing grief that had held me in its sway was gone, as was the anger I felt toward Evina and Elga, all of the penned-up pain of my life since Mordred had caught Lancelot and I saying our farewells. It was as though years' worth of healing had taken place in the space of an hour. Somehow, in a way I would never be able to explain, the Grail had worked its magic to heal me one last time.

When the mists parted, Ailis, Viviane's daughter and the current Lady of Avalon, was waiting for us, along with Helene, who had stayed in Avalon after Camlann and was now a second-degree acolyte clothed in green. For a moment, she reminded me so much of Morgan when I first came to Avalon that it seemed time had rewound itself.

But then Ailis took my hands and I was brought back to the present. I ran to her, embracing her as though she were my own mother. Aggrivane genuflected, touching his thumb to his forehead, lips, and heart.

"Welcome, beloved daughters," she said to Mona and me. "And to our brother in peace."

Mona bowed to her and removed the Grail from the sack she carried. "Holy Mother, it is done. I return to Avalon the gift the Goddess so graciously gave to us so many years before."

The Lady nodded. "You have served your calling well, my daughter. Return it to the hidden temple from which it came, that it may slumber there until it is again called forth in another age." She brushed Mona's cheek softly, lovingly. "Then take your place among your sisters and live out your days in peace, secure in the knowledge you have done all she asked and more."

With a small curtsy, Mona turned and headed toward the Tor, Helene trailing at her heels, ready to serve.

"Morgan must be so proud," I said wistfully.

Ailis smiled. "Helene will be Lady of the Lake after me. I have seen it."

The Lady took our hands in hers. "I know what you have suffered. There is no recompense I can give, but I can promise you the protection of Avalon for as long as you shall desire it."

"Thank you, Lady."

"You must be tired from your journey. Come, let us take some refreshment. There is much you should know."

She led us to a small patio outside her quarters, overlooking the orchard. As we drank water from the springs and nibbled on fresh bread, I watched the priestesses at their work. Some tended the gardens, others taught at the center of clusters of students, while many of the older women turned spinning wheels or tended looms on patios similar to ours. There was one bright patch of hair I kept expecting to see among them but could not find anywhere.

"You seek your sister, Morgan, do you not?" asked the

Lady, who had been watching me.

"I do. The last I knew, she lay dying within a fort far from here. I hoped someone had saved her, brought her here to be healed. Was my hope in vain?"

"No. She is here. But you look in the wrong place. Morgan was true to her word and stayed with Arthur until the very end. He is buried here, you know."

I choked back a sob. I had not expected to find him buried here, especially since he was a Christian. "I did not know."

"You may visit him, if you like."

I glanced at Aggrivane, unsure how he would feel. He nodded.

"Please."

I took a step to follow her but paused when Aggrivane whispered in my ear, "I would like to pay my respects, unless you would like a private moment."

In answer, I took his arm and led us both in the Lady's wake.

She spoke to us over her shoulder as we walked. "Arthur was unconscious when Morgan arrived here with him. Despite our best ministrations, he never again woke."

We walked on and on, through the plains and over rugged land that led into the mountains. I had never been this close to the edge of the mists before. The Tor was still visible behind us, but it looked much smaller than it did up close. Still imposing in its shocking grandeur against the surrounding lake and plains, it seemed more like a small hill than a mighty monument. When I stepped over the crest of a ridge of rocks, a shiver coursed down my spine.

The Lady noticed. "We have passed beyond the veil of Avalon. This land belongs to the Christian priests, for Morgan desired to honor Arthur's wishes to be buried on Christian soil."

From out of the mists, a small wattle-and-dub building emerged, its roof crudely made of sticks that were hardly adequate to keep out the rain. In the center, where the branches ended at the chimney hole, a carved wooden cross was fastened with twine to the sticks around it. On both sides were flowering hawthorn trees taller than the building.

So it was real. Legends I had heard all my life said that this was the building Joseph of Arimathea had constructed after he brought the Grail to Avalon's shores from Jesus's desert homeland in the east. Christians believed the hawthorn trees grew from where Joseph sank his staff into the ground and that their miraculous bloom in the middle of winter occurred to honor the birth of Christ.

The hide flap covering the doorway fluttered, and from inside emerged a stooped man dressed in a coarse, gray wool tunic, his bald pate and long beard marking him as a follower of Joseph. His smile warmed my heart. "Blessings, my brother and sisters."

The Lady returned his greeting with a small bow. "As to you, Father Edgar." She gestured toward us. "These are friends of our departed High King. They wish to pay their respects."

Father Edgar stepped forward and took Aggrivane's hands, saying something to him I could not hear. Then he was in front of me, taking my hands like a long-lost friend.

I curtsied to show my respect for his faith and his position.

He beamed, revealing naked gums. "I may be old and my eyes rheumy, but I know the face of my queen. It is I who should bow to you. Welcome to the chapel of St. Joseph, my lady. If I may be of assistance, simply call. In the meantime, I will let you conduct your business in peace." He gingerly settled himself into a rickety chair next to the door and turned his eyes to the mountains, muttering Latin prayers to himself.

The Lady pointed at a clearing between two yew trees. Protruding from its base was a black stone cross. Beyond it was a mound of earth, most certainly Arthur's grave.

"When Arthur breathed his last, for a long time, Morgan refused to believe he was dead, insisting he slept still. It was only when he was buried that she accepted the truth. She grieved hard for him, but her grief was not protracted, for she soon felt a longing to return to the world." She watched me carefully, as though anticipating my every reaction. "We never thought we would see her again. Then several weeks ago, she returned to us, suffering from grave complications in the wake of a nasty wound to the abdomen she appeared to have bound up herself. She said she wished to make amends with Avalon so that she could die in the peace of both our faith and that of the Christians."

As we approached the clearing, I found that the cross had markings inscribed upon it. I narrowed my eyes, but it took me a few moments to recognize them as Latin letters inscribed in the tall block Roman style. As I struggled to make them out, Aggrivane chuckled.

"She got the last word after all," he said, admiration clear in his voice.

I furrowed my brow at him, but he pointed back at the cross. Only when I finally translated the words did Aggrivane's reaction make sense.

Here lies the great King Arthur, with his first wife.

"His first wife? Am I reading that correctly?" I turned to the Lady. "There must be some mistake. *I* was his first wife."

She shook her head. "No, not according to the laws of Avalon. Arthur laid with Morgan in the Sacred Marriage. That made her his wife in spirit long before he wed you in law."

I opened my mouth, but no words would come forth, only copious tears. After so long, our battle was over. Morgan had died in the winning and now, thanks to this inscription, everyone would know he had loved her long before I became his queen. She would lie beside Arthur forever, gaining in death what she had so longed for in life.

Aggrivane slipped an arm around me. "Do you know what this means?" He kissed the top of my head.

I shook my head.

He placed his hands on my hips, turning me to face him. "It means by the laws of Avalon, I was your first husband."

I looked into his eyes, my tears slowing then ceasing. He was right. We had been joined all along by a bond more immovable than the mountains.

"The Goddess puts all things to rights in the end," the Lady said, stepping back so we could absorb the meaning of this in private.

"Do you think we might one day be buried together?"

he asked, his deep brown eyes aflame with hope.

I gazed at him, his smile melting my heart and easing my lingering doubt and pain by degrees, just as the dawn chases away the fog. So many events separated us from our first embrace on this isle. In the years between, I had won and lost his love, become queen, taken a lover and been betrayed by him, as well as my husband and the boy I considered a son, won and lost my ancestral tribe, faced down and forgiven the greatest of my enemies, only to find Aggrivane once again. Through it all, one constant remained—the soft voice of the Goddess whispering her will in my heart. Now she was telling me the time for grief and strife was over, that I could finally embrace this man without fear and without guilt and love the one I had known all along belonged to me.

In answer, I slipped my hand into his. "I do."

I rested my head on his shoulder, overwhelmed by a sense of rightness and completion. It would take time to know him anew, to let my broken heart heal and let my love for Lancelot fade enough so that I could give Aggrivane a permanent place in my heart once again. But even now, the chambers of my heart shifted to make room for him as the small, secret place I had kept for only him unlocked like a long-neglected tomb. Someday, when the sunlight and breezes of Avalon had finally chased away the cobwebs of grief, it would swell to embrace him wholly.

For once, time was not a barrier. After all, we had the rest of our lives.

The epigraph at the beginning of this book sets the tone for the whole story, which is one of warriors, war and change in Britain. It is an excerpt from "Y Gododdin," the earliest surviving Welsh poem, which is also called the "Book of Aneirin." There are two different versions of the surviving manuscript (one is shorter than the other, and generally believed to be more reliable). Cardiff MS 2.81, dates to the 13th century, but the poem itself is believed to be much older and may have first been written down in the ninth century from an oral source dating to the seventh century. Written in Old Welsh and Middle Welsh, it tells the story of the historical Battle of Catraeth between the Saxons and a motley crew of post-Roman Celts, Picts and Votadini sometime near the year 600 AD.

It is used by some to justify the historical existence of King Arthur because of the line "although he was not Arthur," as in "he was good, but not as great as Arthur." However, most scholars point out that this line could be referencing any outstanding warrior who bore that name, and also if there was someone like King Arthur whom people lauded, chances are good many babies would have been named after him, just as we do with celebrities and royalty today.

Traditionally, Guinevere is not involved in the Battle of Catraeth, for she and everyone who knew Camelot are long dead by the time of the battle or, if the story takes place in the Middle Ages, many generations yet to come. But I chose to set this battle about fifty years earlier than most scholars date it because of the Votadini heritage I have given Guinevere throughout this series. The Battle of Catraeth was the penultimate defeat of the Votadini, though here I have framed it as only the first in a line of disasters that would then end around the time of the historical Battle of Catraeth, ushering in the age of the Anglo Saxons and the formation of the country of England.

PART ONE: THE BROKEN CROWN

In most Arthurian stories, after Guinevere is rescued from the stake she flees with Lancelot to his castle, Joyous Gard, which has been variously placed throughout England, though one of the most accepted locations is Din Guayrdi, modern Bamburgh. From there Lancelot defends against attacks by King Arthur. Eventually, they part and Guinevere becomes a nun and Lancelot a monk, both living out their days in penance for their sin.

This ending does not suit the strong, active, willful woman that my Guinevere is, so I chose to make her an active participant in the remainder of her life and in trying to save Camelot. Guinevere's wounds are consistent with second and third degree burns. Why did she get them if she was a priestess? She couldn't control the fire and concentrate on successfully jumping onto Lancelot's horse at the same time. The ointment the priestesses make to help heal her is based on an Amish remedy still in use today. Similarly, the method of invisible ink Morgan uses on her herb and poison vials is historical, invented by Pliny the Elder. (Thanks to the American Bookbinder's Museum in San Francisco for that tidbit.)

Traditionally, when Arthur leaves Camelot in Mordred's care, Guinevere is harassed by Mordred, who attempts to marry her (sometimes she is willing, sometimes not) for her power. I have kept the element of the rulers desiring her sovereignty, but I chose not to exploit the relationship between Guinevere and Mordred, as these characters never had any chemistry to me. They are in my mind, much more like mother and son, than lovers. Besides, I planned to have Mordred and Elga get together and had no desire to create yet another love triangle in this already complex story.

The convent that Elga sends Guinevere to is my own invention, although York is historically known for being a Saxon haven and then later, a capital, and was important enough to have had its own bishopric. I chose to include it as a nod to Guinevere's traditional ending as a nun, but also to provide an update on Mayda's fate from *Camelot's Queen*.

Religious orders, especially those comprised of women, were rare at the time, but we know from the famous example of St. Brigid and her mixed monastery in fifth century Ireland that they did exist in Great Britain during the Dark Ages. The rituals the Sisters enact while Guinevere is at the convent are based on actual Anglo Saxon Christian rituals from around the year 900, as described in *The Dramatic Liturgy of Anglo-Saxon England* by M. Bradford Bedingfield. Some of them may seem familiar to Catholic readers, as the Tenebrae ritual is still used today with some revisions after

Vatican II. If you are interested in the sign language used by the nuns, I recommend *Monasteriales Indicia: The Anglo-Saxon Sign Language* by Debby Banham. A few Catholic religious orders still use similar communication today during the period of their day known as the Grand Silence.

The historical veracity and date of the Battle of Camlann is the subject of much debate. It is estimated as taking place anywhere from 515 – 542 AD. Camlann appears first in written record in the tenth-century *Annales Cambriae*, which says it took place twenty-one years after the Battle of Badon, the exact date of which is unknown. Based on that, Camlann can be placed at 515, 520 or 539, depending on the source, although the traditional date has become either 537 or 547. Confusing things even more, the Irish Annals of Tigernach place it in 541, Geoffrey Monmouth uses 542 and the Spanish *Anales Toledanos* dates it much later in 580.

Scholars have been trying to definitively locate the location of the battle for years. That is one of the reasons why I portray it as a series of battles on the run, rather than being in one fixed location. Sites as varied as Somerset, Cornwall, Wales, and even as far north as Hadrian's Wall have been suggested. I chose to locate the final battle in which Mordred and Arthur are mortally wounded on Hadrian's Wall because that is in keeping with my northern Arthur. Like so much else about King Arthur and the legends that surround him, the true location is something we will likely never know for sure.

The People of the North is a name for the tribes that lived between Hadrian's Wall and Antonine Wall in what is today southern Scotland. There were once many tribes in the area, but by the time in which this book is set, the Damnonii, Selgovae, Novantae and Votadini were the main four. Among those, the Damnonii and Votadini were the more powerful. The titles of Votad and Votadess are my own invention, based in the root meaning of the word Votadini, which is wo-tado or wotad, which translates as foundation or support.

Mynyddog Mwynfawr and Morcant are based on historical people, while Evina, Rohan and most of the rest of the Votadini are fictional. According to Welsh tradition, Mynyddog was the ruler of the Gododdin, which was either part of the Votadini lands or another name for them. His capital is generally accepted to be Din Eidyn, which is today called Edinburgh. It is unclear if his name is a personal one or a title. He is thought to have been a brother or son to Clydno Eitin, a historical ruler of Strathclyde, who is mentioned briefly in this book. Clydno's historical son, Cynan, is also a character. Morcant is the historical Morcant Bulc, the last British king of Bernicia before it became a holding of the Angles. Included in his territory was Ynys Metcault, also known as the Isle of Winds, which is today called Lindisfarne (more on that in a bit).

Traditionally in Arthurian legend, after the Battle of Camlann and the deaths of Arthur and Mordred, the country is plunged into civil war. The traditional contender for the throne is Constantine, who was Arthur's heir beginning with Gildas' sixth century writing. Some authors even say Mordred had children who would have been in line for the throne, but that is not relevant to this story. For a good explanation of both Constantine's role in Arthurian legend and Mordred's possible sons, see *King Arthur's Children* by Tyler R. Tichelaar. I chose to make the two main British contenders Constantine because of tradition and the House of Rheged (Owain and Accolon) because of their historical power.

Guinevere's possession of ancestral lands in Stirling and her mother being a Votadini are based on Norma Lorre Goodrich's theory that Guinevere was a Pict born in Stirling. This theory is roundly dismissed by most Arthurian scholars, but because my books are fiction, I decided to play with the idea regardless of its veracity. The marking ceremony is my own invention, as are the marks and which animals belong to each tribe. The symbolism of the feathers is also fiction, but was inspired by the traditions of many ancient cultures.

The plague that has affected the village outside of Stirling that Guinevere visits is based on the plague of 537, also called the Plague of Justinian, which is generally thought of as the first ever recorded outbreak of plague. It is believed to have disproportionately affected the post-Roman Celts because they frequently traded with Mediterranean merchants (which is also where Sobian obtained the henna to dye her hair). It was more of a bubonic plague than the smallpox/typhus-like disease I have described. I changed it because I didn't want people getting it confused with the better-known outbreak of bubonic plague during the Black Death in the fourteenth century.

PART THREE: THE FALSE QUEEN

The revolution in Guinevere's name was based partially off the real-life insurgency that Lady Jane Grey's family led in her name in the sixteenth century. I know that many others have happened throughout history, but that one is my historical touchstone, especially for a revolution that happened without the person's permission, as the one in this book does at first.

I have purposefully conflated the Saxons and the Angles in this and the final section of the book for ease of reading. I thought it would be awkward to try to explain the difference to the reader in the course of a fictional story, so I chose to attribute everything to the Saxons. In reality, what occurred during the Battle of Catraeth took place between the Celts of the Gododdin and the Angles from Denmark, who were a separate invading tribe from the Germanic Saxons.

King Ida and his sons, Theodric and Osmere, were historical personages, though Ida's reign actually began in 547, much later than I have placed it in this book. Ida did really take over the capital of Bernicia and claimed Catraeth as his own. As cited in the *Anglo-Saxon Chronicle*, his son Theodric led a three-day battle against King Uriens for the Isle of Winds, what we now call the Isle of Lindisfarne.

Its strategic importance is just as I have stated in this book. See Brian Taylor Hope's wonderful book *Yeavering: An Anglo-British Centre of Early Northumbria* for more information. The date of the siege is uncertain, but is usually placed somewhere between 547 and 590, depending on the source. During the battle, Morcant is said to have paid a foreign assassin to murder Uriens. Because I had already had Malegant murder Uriens in *Camelot's Queen*, I substituted his eldest son, Owain, instead, and identified the assassin as the fictional character Rohan.

Evina's ritual with the horses is fictional and the part before the executions begin was inspired by a post on the rituals of the Celtic horse goddess Epona. I may have stretched the bounds of Celtic law in that scene, as execution was a last resort for the Celts, who liked to settle things with fines and the creation of outlaws instead. However, I find it difficult to believe that a warrior people who were rumored to practice human sacrifice and had an obsession with the heads of their enemies didn't employ capital punishment for extreme cases.

The Lughnasa testing and training of the warriors is based in the mythical Tests of the Fianna, which Irish warriors had to pass in order to become part of Fionn mac Cumhaill's band of warriors, as well as the practices of the Scandinavian Berserkers. Examples of skills tested include the voice test (although this is not clearly defined), weaponry skill, stealth, hunting, dancing, scouting, swimming, board games, racing, harping, smithing, wrestling, and endurance of extreme temperatures, among others. For an excellent resource on what the training of ancient warriors may have been like, I recommend *Weapons and Warfare in Anglo-Saxon England* by Sonia C. Hawkes. In the same way, Calliac's Death Goddess ritual is not historical, but it is based in images of the Gaelic hag-goddess Cailleach and various incarnations of the Death Mother around the world.

The winter training that Lancelot and Guinevere put their recruits through is based on both historical and modern military training exercises. My equestrian readers will attest that ice balls are a real problem that plague horses in the winter. My main source of information for this was *Equus Magazine*.

Part Four: Y Gododdin

As mentioned in the opening of these notes, the Battle of Catraeth has a long and storied history, thanks to the mysterious poem "Y Gododdin," which is said to memorialize historical warriors of an actual battle between the ascending Angles and the massively outnumbered Britons. The poem gives three hundred as the number of Britons (a number I have slightly increased for the purposes of my story) and scholars estimate the Anglican force at anywhere between fifty thousand and one hundred thousand. It is said that of the three hundred, only three survived to tell the tale. Given the Celtic fascination with the sacred number three, these numbers are more likely symbolic rather than an actual count.

The feasting hosted by Mynyddog is recorded in the poem and is typical of pre-battle rituals of the time, and similar to the feast in the epic story of *Beowulf*. In her article "Warfare and Horses in the Gododdin and the Problem of Catraeth" Jenny Rowland argues that the feasting may also have served as a recruiting drive for the upcoming battle. The blood bond is my own invention, but Rowland notes that "heroic vows [were] made during the feasting." The use of woad and henbane, as well as its effects, are historically accurate, as is the Celtic obsession with the heads of their enemies and the power they hold.

The nationalities of the warriors on the British side are generally accepted to be mostly Votadini from Gododdin, and those from Alt Clut's warriors, but they are also said to have come from Rheged and as far away as Gwynedd and the Pictish lands.

The location of the Battle of Catraeth is uncertain, but many believe it to be the city of Catterick in North Yorkshire. However, this is far from universally accepted, with Scottish locations such as the border of the Gododdin, Roxburghshire, and Din Ediyn (Edinburgh) proposed, as well as towns in Wales, Cumbria and Yorkshhire in England. I have no opinion on the actual location and so have chosen to use Catterick. The date of the battle is generally thought to have taken place between 570-590, but as with most things during the Dark Ages, this, too, is debated, which is why I took the liberty of placing it when it fit in the timeline of my story.

Assuming Catterick is the correct location, one might ask why a group of primarily Votadini warriors would travel so far south for a battle. That is a question that has plagued scholars for ages. Of course, it could have been to lay siege to a hillfort or take back disputed or key strategic land, but that is a long journey for such an effort. Jenny Rowland theorizes that the battle could have begun as a rescue mission to save the author of the poem from prison, which is one of the legendary explanations for the poem's existence. Similarly, John and Caitlin Matthews note in their book *The Complete King Arthur* that it may have started as the rescue of a Votadini hostage. Both of these theories are where the idea of Lancelot being captured came from. It could also have been a raid, the like of which was very common in Celtic culture. This type of military expedition wouldn't have been important enough for the ruler to attend personally, and so it would explain why Mynyddog didn't lead his troops into battle. Other theories say it could have been a pre-emptive strike against the increasingly powerful Angles and that Catterick is just where the two armies happened to meet, rather than the original end goal.

Kiara promises to set up a memorial stone in Lancelot's honor. At one point in my research, I came across a reference to a memorial stone for him in Scotland, possibly in the area of Angus, and I made note that I wanted to include that, but I have since lost the source. That was the reason for both Kiara's comment and Lancelot holding lands in Angus, as well as why I felt he had to die in this book. There is a website called Electric Scotland that refers to Lancelot as "Lancelot the Angus" and positions his lands as being near Stirling, as well, though it does not list its sources and therefore cannot be verified.

The last point that bears exploring is the burial of King

Arthur in Avalon, which is commonly believed to be one in the same with Glastonbury, England. The grave of King Arthur and Guinevere uncovered at Glastonbury in 1191 has long been thought to be a hoax created by the monks to raise money to help repair their abbey which had been badly damaged by a fire in 1184. When they "found" King Arthur's grave, it was marked by an iron cross that bore the words, "Here lies the famous King Arthur on the isle of Avalon." Some versions also add "with his second wife, Guinevere" to the text.

While it is nearly impossible that this find is real, it is so ingrained in Arthurian legend that I felt I could not let it pass unmentioned. So I chose to play off the idea of Guinevere being Arthur's second wife. In the story I have created, the only logical reason that such a thing could be said was if Morgan was Arthur's first wife by way of the Sacred Marriage. Therefore, in this version of the story, regardless of whether or not the grave found in Glastonbury is authentic, the marker is not the original; the first one mentions Arthur's true wife, Morgan.

⁂

If you would like to know more about the sources I consulted in writing this book, please visit my website, **nicoleevelina.com**, and click on the "Research" tab under the section for Mistress of Legend. You may also wish to search my blog, located on the same site, for additional information on many of these topics.

Acknowledgements

Thank you to everyone who has been with me on this journey for the last nineteen years from my first concept of this series to the publication of this book. It all began with Dawn, a college friend who gave me a copy of *The Mists of Avalon* for Christmas 1998 and unknowingly started this journey.

I have to mention Pam Victorio and Jen Karsbaek who championed this series before anyone else and tried to get it sold to a traditional publisher. That wasn't meant to be, but it wasn't for lack of effort on their part (we got *so* close–three times!) I am grateful for all you did and for your ongoing support as I found another way to get it out into the world.

The teamwork that went into making this book a reality was invaluable. Thank you to my beta readers, Mia Silverton, Courtney Marquez, and my mom. Your feedback was invaluable. Thanks as well to my editor, Cassie Cox, for her attention to detail and for catching all my continuity errors, to Jenny Quinlan for the beautiful cover, and to Nada Qamber for the layout. Special thanks to Tyler Tichelaar for the impromptu line edit/proofreading. You saved my bacon!

Special thanks to Brad Cook and David Lucas for their knowledge of swords and battle techniques. A presentation they gave to the local romance writers group I am a member of is what finally triggered the idea for how Mordred kills Arthur, and they were great resources to verify other details. Special thanks to reader Cherie Postill who pointed out a plot point I had dropped between *Camelot's Queen* and this book and was nearly left out of this book, too.

Of course, I have to thank my parents for their support and my editorial assistants (fur babies), Connor and Caitlyn, for their love and patience. You have my heart and all my love.

I would be remiss if I didn't mention what a great debt of gratitude I owe Brian Taylor Hope for his wonderful book *Yeavering: An Anglo-British Centre of Early Northumbria.* I seriously could not have written the second half of this book without it as it was my main source for all of the details related to the Isle of Winds and the Battle of Catraeth.

Finally, thanks to everyone who reads this book. It's been a hell of a ride and I'm thrilled that you stuck in there with me to the end. I hope you like how things turned out for Guinevere.

About the Author

NICOLE EVELINA is an award-winning historical fiction, non-fiction and women's fiction writer whose books have won nearly 30 awards. The first two books in her Guinevere trilogy, *Daughter of Destiny* and *Camelot's Queen*, were named Books of the Year by Chanticleer Reviews and Author's Circle, respectively. Her most recent book, *The Once and Future Queen*, which was named Non-Fiction Book of the Year by Author's Circle, examines popular works of Arthurian fiction by more than twenty authors over the last one thousand years to show how the character of Guinevere changes to reflect attitudes toward women.

Her mission as a writer is to rescue little-known women from being lost in the pages of history. While others may choose to write about the famous, she tells the stories of those who are in danger of being forgotten so that their memories may live on for at least another generation. She also writes from the female point of view since the male perspective has historically been given more attention.

When she's not writing, she can be found reading, playing with her spoiled twin Burmese cats, cooking, researching, dreaming of living in Chicago or the English countryside…and, of course, plotting her next book.